OUT OF THE NIGHT
THAT COVERS ME

ALSO BY PAT CUNNINGHAM DEVOTO

My Last Days as Roy Rogers

PAT CUNNINGHAM DEVOTO

OUT OF THE NIGHT THAT COVERS ME

THAT COVERS ME

WARNER BOOKS

A Time Warner Company

Warner Books, Inc., 1271 Avenue of the Americas, New York, NY 10020
Visit our Web site at www.twbookmark.com

 A Time Warner Company

Printed in the United States of America
First Printing: January 2001
10 9 8 7 6 5 4 3 2 1

Library of Congress Cataloging-in-Publication Data

Devoto, Pat Cunningham.
    Out of the night that covers me / by Pat Cunningham Devoto.
      p.   cm.
    ISBN 0-446-52751-3
    1. Boys—Fiction. 2. Runaway children—Fiction. 3. Afro-Americans—
Fiction. 4. Sharecroppers—Fiction. 5. Rural poor—Fiction. 6. Alabama—
Fiction. 7. Orphans—Fiction. 8. Aunts—Fiction. I. Title.

PS3554.E92835 O98 2001
813'.54—dc21

                                                  00-032492

Book design and text composition by L&G McRee

For Frances Freeman Jalet-Miller

PROLOGUE

I T was a time in the South shortly before the great up-heaval. All the signs were there—as buds on a bush signal a great blossoming or huge rolling thunderclouds signal the storm—but if you have never seen the blossoming or felt the storm, it is impossible to know what announces its arrival.

PART ONE

CHAPTER 1

EARLIER in the day, a bright Alabama sun had called up the dew. By now, its shine gave shade to only one small space directly beneath the eaves of the depot. He stood in this shadow, staring out.

It sat before him as repulsive as anything he had ever seen, steam rising from its bottom as if it were relieving itself on the tracks. Sweat glistening on its gray-black body, then dripping off onto the crossties. Horrible grinding, clanking noises as it readjusted to its coupling harness. He felt nauseated by the sight.

Outwardly, he was desperate to appear unmoved. His eyes pretended calm study of the engine. His mouth was in a straight line of indifference, as if he were viewing the most ordinary of things. Only his fingers betrayed him. They shook as he pushed up the nosepiece on his glasses. He quickly clasped them behind his scrawny eight-year-old back.

Inside was another matter. Inside, his head was on fire with yelling. When she was alive, he had never even thought of raising his voice to her. Now his head constantly echoed with his yelling . . . *idiot, idiot.* It was the harshest word he knew. A classmate had called him that once, at school, in a game of kickball.

Since the newspapers he read never contained anything approaching bad language and since all the books his mother had ever bought him certainly never had any coarse words, and since he had very seldom played with children his own age, other than at school, he was not acquainted with anything more vulgar than *idiot.*

When she was alive, it had been her job to see that he was not tainted with any of that. In the winter, she would make sure that her only son, John Gallatin McMillan III, never left the house without coat, hat, gloves and galoshes, even on the mildest days. In the summer, especially during the summers when polio stalked the town, he had stayed in the basement with all his toys and books. She had converted the cellar to a playroom. It was cool down there and he was out of harm's way. The maid brought down his dinner every day precisely at noon, a midafternoon snack at four, and when his mother came home, he was allowed to join her upstairs for supper. He had liked it down there. Staying inside all summer had not been unusual in his world. It had been ordinary, expected.

He had known other children casually, his next-door neighbor, the boy down the street. They played outside in the summer, and he felt vaguely sorry for them. They seemed not to have his intelligence, or perhaps they were burdened with mothers who didn't care as much as his mother did. He was not saying that was the case, but perhaps it was.

His head turned slowly as he scanned the engine still squatting there before him. He took a deep breath, trying to regain his composure. Then another, holding it in his lungs, hoping it would slow his heartbeat. *Of course, it's bound to be just fine . . . isn't it? After all, Aunt Nelda is . . . you were her sister.*

He tried to stand up straight and add some dignity to the cheap shorts and shirt Aunt Nelda had given him to wear. The baggy pants blossomed out around his spindly white legs. She had bought them for him the day after the funeral—had gone down to Harold's and bought them. Everyone knew that only country people shopped at Harold's. He should be wearing his dark blue suit. That's what you wore on a train.

We rode on one once before, remember? You said it would be good for me to know about such things: how to ride on a train, what to tip the porters, what to do when you spent the night in a hotel. I was dressed properly then.

He felt a little better now. Just keep talking to her. *Let's see. Let's see, it was the Tennesseean, out of Knoxville, bound for Memphis. You saved a whole year for that trip. Remember?*

He gritted his teeth in disgust. She never answered him. No matter how much he talked, she never answered him, but he knew she was still there. He knew it was like the soldiers he had read about. They would have an arm or a leg blown off, and for days, even weeks after it happened, they could still feel the arm itching, the leg aching, the mother calling. He had heard her in his sleep calling to him, but not when he was awake. No matter, he knew she was still there, somewhere around him— watching.

CHAPTER 2

Aunt Nelda grabbed his arm and pulled him on board the train, right into its bowels. Steam from underneath the stairs floated up around him as he was half-dragged up the steel steps. He held his breath so as not to breathe it in, all the while thinking himself into another place—trying to stem the panic. *Oh yes, oh yes, I remember now. It was a lovely trip. We stayed at the Peabody. They had beautiful blue linens on all the tables in the dining room. You remarked on it.* Her grip was so tight on his arm, it was pinching him. *We, we watched the ducks march out of the lobby at four in the afternoon. What a lovely tradition, you said. What a lovely*—Aunt Nelda was pushing him to their seats in the day coach with all the other people. He was so small for his age, it was easy for her to do that. *We had a roomette, private and to ourselves, remember, remember? And the food, it was delicious.* He stumbled over an errant foot in the aisle. She smiled and pointed him to his seat by the window, then began to re-count all the boxes and bags she had brought on board before going back outside to retrieve him.

He sat with his back ridged, his hands clasped in his lap, his legs dangling. He watched his thumbs. They were circling each other, pretending to be two dogs ready to pounce on each other in a fight to the death. The little dog circled the bigger dog slowly, slowly, until the little dog reached out and crushed the big dog to pieces in one quick motion.

Minutes later, the train lurched back and forth, then pulled forward out of the station. His heart was pounding in his chest. He was leaving the only place he had ever known, the only life he had ever known. He tried to concentrate on the inside of the train. He would not look out the window. He watched Aunt Nelda stuffing a shopping bag under her feet. Then she squirmed in between more boxes and bags that shared her place. His heart began to slow in its beat. Keep talking to her. *Look how thrilled she is over all the stuff you left her. She was on the phone with the moving van people for over an hour last night. They said the big things would be shipped down in a week or two. I heard them talking: all of my books, all of my toys, all of your furniture.*

The train whistle drifted past him; the sound of wheels on tracks fell into a cadence. *I will not look out the window. I will not look out the window. I will not look out the window.*

CHAPTER 3

THEY were a half-day into the journey when she had completely forgotten about him. It had been when they arrived in the Montgomery station around noon. She directed him to a bench inside the huge terminal and told him to sit there and not move until she came for him.

He had suggested that maybe they might think about eating dinner before she left him. He always had a proper sit-down meal every day. *Remember our Miss Mama? She always baked hot biscuits for us. You would ask me what I had read in the newspaper that was of interest.*

Aunt Nelda dug in her purse and produced just enough change for a Coke and a Baby Ruth. Then she rushed on off to make sure all her trunks and packages were transferred to the right train, the one headed down to south Alabama, down to Lower Peach Tree, her home.

Now he sat under the huge dome of the Montgomery station waiting room, eating his Baby Ruth one peanut at a time, making it last as long as he could, all the while being careful that bits of chocolate didn't soil his new shirt.

He watched out the big doors that led to the station's platforms, hoping to catch a glimpse of Aunt Nelda. All he saw were throngs of Negroes, boxes and suitcases in hand, laughing and smiling, passing by on their way to the colored waiting room. He brushed away a fly that was trying to have a drink of his Coke.

"You know what they say," a voice said. "Niggers movin' north, cotton movin' west, ain't nothin' movin' south."

John turned, to see a man settling himself down on an upturned RC Cola crate. One of his legs was missing and that trouser leg was folded and pinned up against the back of his pants. He had put his crutches on the floor beside him. The man leaned his back against the station wall, looking at John. He jerked his head in the direction of the station doors. "That's all that hustle and bustle goin' on out there. Time for the two o'clock to Chicago." The man fished down into a bag he carried with him and brought out a tin cup and some pencils. "Every colored worth his salt leavin' to go on up north. Been doin' it since I got back here." He put the pencils in the cup and deposited it on the floor next to him. Then he began to tune his guitar.

John knew who he was. He had seen men like this in Bainbridge, disabled veterans from the war. The pencils would have I AM A VETERAN printed on them.

We always bought our pencils from Old Blind Willie when he sat outside Woolworth's. Remember? You said it was in memory of my father. I wonder if he knows . . .

He called to the man. "Sir, do you know, 'Will the Circle Be Unbroken?'" . . . *Old Willie used to play that—remember?*

"You got money for the cup?" the man said, continuing to tune his guitar.

John shook his head no and looked away, pretending the embarrassment had not caused his face to burn red. *Whenever we traveled, you always gave me pennies to give beggars, remember? You said it was our responsibility.*

It was a gigantic train station, with a ceiling so high, it made him liken all the people to roaches scurrying around on its marble floor. The wall the man leaned against rose high into the air, then arched to form a ceiling of tile and glass. There were porters hauling boxes, men and women walking fast to catch trains, babies crying, and, on top of it all, an announcer's voice came over the loudspeaker system calling out, every few minutes, train tracks and destinations. He told himself that it would have scared any person, no matter how smart, if he was seeing it for the first time. And besides that, this was not his first time. There had been the Memphis station. It was probably just as big, or bigger. He couldn't remember. He looked down at his feet swinging free, not touching the station floor. He was on one of the hundreds of benches that lined the waiting room. She had said for him not to move from that very spot. After a time, he stretched out on the wooden bench, eyes watching the ceiling. Chords from the veteran's guitar swirled around in his head, then floated up, to bounce off the ceiling and return. It sounded like a symphony of guitars. He drifted off to sleep.

CHAPTER 4

WHEN he woke up, it was midafternoon by the station clock that was posted high on the wall. The veteran had taken his guitar and wood crate and left. Long streaks of dusty sunlight were lined from the tall station windows down to the floor. He lay there blowing his breath into the dust that swirled through the sunlight and then back into the shadows. There was that much to do.

Fewer people were in the station now, but still he didn't see Aunt Nelda. The announcer was saying that a train was leaving in a few minutes from track three. He got up and inched over to the door to look out, all the time keeping an eye on his sitting place. Out on the station platform, an old colored man in a rumpled blue uniform was sweeping cigarette butts. A few straggling people were boarding the train as it sat there steaming and hissing, a bull ready to charge.

He thought he could see her down at the end of the platform, talking to a porter. He yelled to her. "Aunt

Nelda, may I come?" She didn't seem to hear him. He tried again. She still didn't look up.

Maybe she doesn't want to hear me. Have you thought of that? Of course you wouldn't, but I did. I thought of it.

She appeared to give the porter money and then got on board. The train bell was clanging. The porter shouted a last call. John took a few steps more toward the cars as they began to move. Then he ran almost to the end of the platform before he jumped on the moving car he thought was Aunt Nelda's.

He stood holding on to the handrails, breathing hard, hoping he had done the right thing. The train was moving faster and faster now out into the late afternoon of Montgomery. Buildings were passing as in a movie, colors blurring, as the cars picked up speed.

"Well, son, looks like you made it just in time." John jumped, not knowing anyone else had seen him. A huge man in a blue uniform was looking down at him. He was so big, John had to hold his head back to see past the blue uniform into the black face.

"My . . . my aunt is on this train . . . maybe."

"You better hope she is, boy, 'cause if she ain't, you headed to Mobile all by yourself."

A lump formed in his throat. "I'm supposed to be going to Lower Peach Tree. I—did I get on the wrong train?" Despite all his efforts to control it, water glazed his eyes.

"Don't worry, you in the right place. This here train stops at Lower Peach Tree by way of Mobile. We'll find your auntie." The train was up to speed now, rattling along, each car holding tight to the other in a line of perhaps twelve. Five or six passenger cars, a club car and a dining car, a mail car filled with letters and packages to be dropped off along the way to Mobile.

The porter pulled on the door of the coach car and stepped inside. "What's she look like?"

John followed. "She's tall and thin and has frizzy blond hair that kind of bongs out," he said, holding his hands out around his head to describe it. "She has a small yellow hat to match her yellow dress." John stretched his neck, trying to see his aunt. "It's linen, and you know how that wrinkles."

The colored man turned his head to take a second look at John. "No, can't say as I do."

John continued without notice. "And, and also, she bites her lower lip when she's nervous. It's quite a noticeable habit."

The colored man laughed out loud. It was a big, unhappy sound. "Don't you go describin' her like that to her face or she'll sure enough leave you at the next stop."

John would not hear that. "The only other thing is, she has lots of trunks and things with her."

"Oh, now I know who you talkin' 'bout. That lady done been messin' with us all afternoon, makin' sure none of her things is left behind or stole. I done told her, 'Don't nobody steal on my train.'" He pulled John around in front of him and put his hand on the boy's shoulder to guide him down the aisle. "You got a hill to climb with that woman, boy. Come on, she's down in that next car, toward the end, so she can be near all them trunks and boxes of hers."

They walked through a coach car full of people putting up suitcases and settling in for the journey. The train had settled in as well, had found its clicking rhythm and was pulling them along, a little town full of people and things, moving through the countryside.

At the end of the next car, they saw Aunt Nelda arranging and rearranging boxes. John walked up to her and tugged on her sleeve. She jumped and jerked around. "John," she shouted. Her cheeks flushed to a bright pink. "I clean forgot about you." She grabbed him by the shoulders. "Oh my, I was so worried about getting everything changed from one train to the other and making sure nothing was stole. I"—she looked out the windows at the passing scenery—"I didn't even know the train had started. What has got into me?" She looked around to see who was witness to her blunder and saw the porter standing there. "I'll take him now, porter. You can go about your business." The porter turned and walked back up the aisle without a word.

"So uppity-acting," she muttered, then tried to smile at him. "Oh now, all's well that ends well. You come and sit right—" She turned, to see two suitcases and a paper shopping bag stacked in the seat he was supposed to have. She was biting her lower lip as she began to move boxes and bags out of the way.

He stood watching her. She had never even been to visit them before the funeral. He had only heard his mother talking to her on the phone once or twice. On these occasions, his mother had done most of the listening and not much talking. When he had asked her later what they had talked about, she had only said, "Family matters," and that someday, perhaps, Aunt Nelda would come and live with them. She had never said Aunt Nelda and Uncle Luther and Aunt Nelda's children, but only Aunt Nelda.

"It's such a responsibility having to do all this without a man around." Aunt Nelda heaved a heavy suitcase onto another suitcase in the empty seat opposite them. "It's all for you, you know." She squared the suitcase to the one below. "All for your dear mother." The thought momentarily caught her off guard and she stared at the seat cover. Just as quickly, she finished rearranging things to make a place for him to sit. He stepped over a shopping bag and sat down, hands in his lap, face staring out the window. They were on the outskirts of Montgomery now. *We aren't even going to leave the state. It couldn't be that different.* He said this to her as his thumbs slowly circled in his clasped hands. Then he closed his hands, fingers inside, like she had taught him. "Here's the church; here's the steeple; open the door and see all the people." He half-heartedly opened his hands to see the finger people inside, then looked out the window.

The countryside passing before him began to change. The land had flattened out. Even the color of the dirt was different; hard red clay, solid underfoot, had softened to a sandy gray-black soil. Small dirt devils kicked up by the passing train sent funnels of dust into the air.

Here, long stretches of open fields lay off in the distance. From time to time, there was, on the horizon, a big house that appeared to be the center of activity for the people and land. Dirt roads wound out from its center like beckoning tentacles.

After more time, they began to pass miles and miles of dark piney woods that crowded in on the railroad tracks.

John wondered where all the colored people headed to Chicago were by now. Probably up around Bainbridge, where he had come from, probably headed to Memphis.

Now they were on a trestle passing over a wide black river that had trees growing to the water's edge. Their big roots stuck straight down in the water like giant straws sucking up whatever lay beneath the surface. It was unlike anything he had ever seen. Not like the Tennessee River in his hometown, big and wide. For miles, the Tennessee had stretched out before him, an open face. Here, water oaks and moss, scrub pines and palmettos never gave a

The Bend

THE old woman watched as the turkey vulture, wings spread full out, slowly circled in the afternoon thermals that radiated off the sun-soaked river and flatlands of the Alabama Black Belt.

High off the land, the vulture scanned a large horse-shoe-shaped piece of black earth far below. Wrapped around this bend, the Alabama River twisted and turned its way south to the Gulf of Mexico. Thousands of years before, in its meanderings, the Alabama had carved out what now lay visible below the white-and-black wings floating on a late-afternoon breeze.

There was no way in or out of this bend except by a broken-down hunting road that passed through the bottom of the horseshoe. An old ferry that had once served the Bend now sat idle and rusting on the opposite shore of the indolent old river. Small houses dotted the landscape. Each was surrounded by several acres of land, freshly harrowed and then planted in rows of corn, cotton—some sorghum. One of the farms had a pigsty that nurtured a newborn litter. The vulture dropped several hundred feet in hopes of an easy meal. Finding all the newborns in good health, he rose once again on the steamy updrafts.

On the west end of the Bend, the land sloped off into thick swamp before it gave way to the river. Situated on the only piece of high ground in the swamp was the log cabin where the old woman sat in her front porch vine rocker, her eyes following the buzzard as he drifted through the haze.

She was the product of three generations of Benders. Her mother, grandmother, and great-grandmother had all lived out their lives in the Bend, had probably watched the forebears of that same vulture circling in the summer sky.

The old woman, and all the people of the Bend, were direct descendants of slaves who had come from North Carolina in the early 1800s. Their slave master, James Randolph Kay, had ordered them on a months-long journey walking into western South Carolina, through Georgia, across Alabama, and into this place they would eventually claim as their own.

They had cleared the fields and cultivated the crops of what became Kay's Bend Plantation. Through generations, isolated from the rest of the world, most stayed on at the Bend as emancipation freed them, as some married into local Indian tribes, as the Great Depression almost starved them out, and as the world wars depleted their ranks.

Now, in the mid-1950s, there were still very few cars or tractors, no paved roads, little indoor plumbing, and no telephones. It didn't matter to the old woman or the other people of Kay's Bend. Home was a place of common experience, of standing together, no matter that their foothold might be in quicksand. That they didn't actually own the land was of little or no concern to them. Years in the fields as slaves, as sharecroppers, and now as tenant farmers had made it impossible for them to think of its belonging to anyone else.

Again the thermals caught the vulture, and he soared higher. Now coming into his view, far off on the horizon, were the tops of two church steeples, the roof of a train depot, the houses and shops of a small town.

Chapter 5

Aunt Nelda was putting on more lipstick. When she finished with her lips, she took a little off the top of the stick and rubbed it on her cheeks. To John, she looked a little like the Lucky Strike Girls on the back of the *Look* magazines he used to read. This was what Aunt Nelda smoked, Lucky Strikes. He watched her light up.

She just forgot about me for the one second the train was pulling out. That's all.

Other passengers were sitting around half-asleep, lulled by the repeating sound of wheels hitting tracks. Some were reading the *Montgomery Advertiser*. The lights were coming on as the sun went down outside. He pulled the window shade to block out what passed. He thought it rather warm and cozy inside now.

Suddenly, Aunt Nelda jerked in her seat, blew out a big puff of smoke, and mashed her cigarette in the ashtray with one hand as she waved the smoke away with the other. Then she hopped up to motion to a lady coming toward her down the aisle.

"Mrs. Vance, why, hello there, Mrs. Vance. What a surprise to see you." Aunt Nelda was pulling down her dress and patting her hair. The woman stopped and seemed to take a moment to recognize Nelda. She was dressed in the same way as Aunt Nelda, but not in the same style. Her hat and shoes were a dyed match. Her dress didn't carry the wrinkles of daylong wear.

"Why, Nelda," she finally said, "I almost didn't recognize you, I was passin' through in such a hurry."

Aunt Nelda grinned broadly and stepped out into the aisle. "My goodness, I was so surprised to see you. I just couldn't hardly believe my eyes," she said. "Are you on your way back to home?" Her hand flipped in the air. "Well, course you are. That's how come you're on this train." Nelda twittered at her own foolishness. "How silly of me."

"The Judge had bankin' business in Montgomery, so we've been stayin' at the Jeff Davis for a few days," the woman said. She sounded more like a colored person than any white the boy had ever heard.

Aunt Nelda began changing her way of talking to match the manner of the woman. "Well, I declare, y'all musta been havin' a high old time in Montgomery. It's such a delightful town," said Aunt Nelda.

"No," said the lady, "I'm worn out with sleepin' in a strange bed and eatin' out. I'll be happy to get home." She looked over to John, who had stood up when the woman approached. "Nelda, as many times as we've made this trip, I don't believe I have ever seen you or your children on here before."

"Oh, no, ma'am, he ain't . . . isn't my child," said Aunt Nelda. She began whispering to the woman. John stood there, feeling foolish. Of course he knew what she was saying all along. His mother had died. He had no father, no other relatives. She was, out of the goodness of her heart, taking him back to live with her. She finally finished her story. They both looked down at him and smiled.

He looked back at them, words bouncing around in his head. *Idiots.*

Mrs. Vance continued smiling and began to say the usual. My but he was a fine-looking boy, but small for his age, wasn't he? He could have passed for six, or maybe even five. She just knew he was going to love Lower Peach Tree. Always conversation designed to facilitate, to accommodate, never to illuminate. He was disgusted by it and made no attempt to respond. He knew it was impolite, but he didn't care. Then there was a pause; no one saying anything.

"Well," Mrs. Vance finally said, "I mustn't keep the Judge waitin'. I just reserved a place for us in the dinin' car. I'm on my way back to get him."

"Oh, how silly of me, blockin' your way and takin' your time when I know the Judge must be starved." Aunt Nelda blushed.

Immediately, the mention of food overtook his disgust. He pounced on the idea of eating. "This is a good time for us to eat, too, Aunt Nelda. If you didn't have any more to eat than a candy bar, you must be starved also," he said.

Aunt Nelda looked startled. Then she glanced back to Mrs. Vance and laughed. "Oh my, that boy. What with all the movin' around we did in the Montgomery station, and, uh, I wasn't able to leave my things unattended in the station." She laughed and bit her lower lip. "Boys are always hungry, even if you feed 'em one hundred and nine times a day."

"Perhaps you and—I didn't get your name, son," Mrs. Vance said.

"It's John, ma'am." Anxious, the boy stuck out his hand and then quickly pulled it back, remembering the code of manners he had been meticulously taught.

"Well, John . . ." She smiled and offered her hand. Only then did he extend his.

She studied him for the first time, still holding his hand. "I understand from Obadiah that the roast beef is just delicious tonight. Would you like to join us for supper?"

Aunt Nelda grabbed his hand and pulled it back. "That's just too lovely for words, Mrs. Vance. I, that is to say we, would love to join you, but"—she looked around at the suitcases and bags—"I'm just afraid we have to stay here and look out after all of our things. I do hate travelin' with such a load. It just inhibits your social life no end. We'll just stay here and order from the sandwich cart when it comes around."

Mrs. Vance looked mystified. "Well, why don't you stay here and guard your things and John can be our guest for dinner. Would you like that, John?" He began stepping forward, trying to get over Aunt Nelda's boxes and out into the aisle.

"Yes, ma'am, I sure would."

Aunt Nelda caught his shoulder. "Now hold on there, boy." She was biting her lower lip again. "You can't eat with the Judge lookin' like that." She looked at Mrs. Vance. "That's just lovely of you to ask, but he doesn't even have a clean shirt on. Let me tidy him up a bit while you go get the Judge."

"Do as you like, Nelda, but of all the people in the world, the Judge would be the last one to care how he looks." She turned to leave. "We'll be back directly."

CHAPTER 6

Aunt Nelda watched Mrs. Vance as she disappeared down the aisle; then she turned and pushed John back in his seat. She grabbed her purse and began fumbling through it.

"Now listen here, young man." She pulled a white handkerchief out and let the purse drop on the seat next to her. "Judge Vance is the president of the Planters and Merchants Bank of Lower Peach Tree, the one and only bank in Lower Peach Tree. The only place you can get crop loans, or money of any kind. Stick out your tongue."

He stuck out his tongue and she wiped her handkerchief on it. Then she began to clean off his face. "You mind your manners, like I know you can. Don't eat too much. Don't seem too hungry. Don't forget to take your napkin down." She smoothed his hair with the wet handkerchief, then dropped it and started rummaging through a shopping bag.

He was insulted that she would question his social graces, but he let it pass. He was too hungry. "Why do you call him 'Judge' if he's a banker?" he asked. She didn't hear him.

"I was sure I had an extra shirt in here for you. It was one I found in the dining room after we packed everything up." She pulled out his old blue-and-white shirt, one he had outgrown a year ago. Immediately, he could see his mother in their dining room, smiling as she unwrapped his old shirt from around her silver tea tray. "*See how much you've grown? This is the only use for it now.*" She had handed him the tray. "*I want you to take this next door. Tab's mother wants to use it for a party she's having.*"

Aunt Nelda jerked the shirt he had on up over his head, messing up the hair she had just smoothed down. Then she started trying to get the undersized shirt on him. When she finally did, it was so tight around his neck, he could hardly breathe.

"That won't do." She jerked it back off, exposing his scrawny white chest. "We'll just have to make do with what you had on." She smoothed the original out with her fingers against her wrinkled dress and handed it back to him. He pulled it on quickly, embarrassed that others might have seen him exposed in this way. On top of that, he had not been able to stop the tears from welling up in his eyes at the remembered sight of his mother standing in the dining room, holding the silver tray.

Just as he had gotten the shirt back over his head, the big porter was standing in the aisle, looking down at him.

Holding on to the porter's arm and positioned slightly behind him in the narrow aisle was an older man, shorter by several inches than the porter. He wore a dark suit and white shirt stiff with starch around the collar and cuffs. John glanced up at thick glasses set above a graying beard. The man appeared to be looking out the window, detached in some way from everyone else. As soon as

Aunt Nelda spoke, the man turned his head in her direction.

Aunt Nelda was beside herself. "Judge, what a pleasure to meet up with y'all. I had no idea y'all were on the train 'til I saw Mrs. Vance, Adell, awhile back." She put her hand to her hair to smooth it down. "Now isn't this somethin', us meetin' like this." John noticed she said this in her new way of talking, the one she had developed since seeing Mrs. Vance.

"Evening to you, Nelda." He said nothing after this, and there was an uncomfortable silence. Then he said, "Mrs. Vance tells me you have a guest who'll be taking dinner with us."

"Oh, yes, I sure do, Judge, and let me tell you how delightful it is of y'all to have him," she said, turning around to take John's shoulder and push him forward. "This is my nephew, who's comin' to live with me. Shake hands with the Judge, John."

The Judge slowly disengaged from the porter's arm and held his hand out. John took it and felt the warmth but said nothing. He couldn't help staring, even though he knew his mother was watching him and must think it rude. The Judge pulled away and reached for the porter's arm.

"You walk on ahead of me and Obadiah, boy. Mrs. Vance will be along directly."

"Nelda, it's good seeing you," he said as he tipped his head in her direction. Then he turned to the porter. "Proceed on, Obadiah."

Obadiah started down the aisle again, with the Judge holding to the back of his left arm and the boy turning to look at them every few steps, mesmerized by something, but he had not quite figured out what.

Aunt Nelda was saying after them, "Now y'all have a

nice time, and John, don't you eat the Judge out of house and home." He could hear her nervous laugh as they walked away.

Two more cars down was dining. As they walked along, people seemed to know the Judge. They would say hello, and, likely as not, the Judge would say hello right back to them and call their names. Some would stand and say a few words to him as he passed, but he never lingered. Each time this happened, John would stop and stare at the Judge and the person he was talking to. Each time, the Judge or Obadiah would have to remind him to move on when they were finished. Just as the same thing was happening for the fourth time, John turned forward, as he was shooed on, and caught his foot on a piece of carpet. He went sprawling. It was at that moment, as the boy sat on the aisle floor, looking up at the Judge, that he realized and blurted it out. "You, you're blind."

Obadiah glared at him as if he might have discovered a worm on the aisle floor.

The Judge looked down in John's direction. "One of us is, but I'm not sure which one at the moment."

John jumped up and ran the rest of the way to the dining car, furious with his mother.

Obadiah led them to a table with a spotless, if worn, white linen tablecloth and four chairs, next to a window with scenery clicking by. He pulled out a chair on the window side. The Judge felt along the top of the table to find his place.

"Sit across from me. It's always best to sit next to a window to watch the scenery go by."

John took his seat opposite the Judge, who now seemed

to be staring out the window, although John knew that was quite out of the question. The boy took down his napkin and slowly unfolded it, trying to control his shaking hands. Then he placed the napkin just so in his lap, making the corners drape over his short pants and tucking in the sides to keep it from slipping off. There was silence as the noise of the other diners filled in around them. Ice-tea glasses clinked in the stirring; dishes clanked as they were lifted off waiters' trays; laughter from another table drifted down the aisle.

Finally, the boy felt obliged to say something. "Do you like being on a train?" Immediately, he wished he had let the silence alone. It had sounded so stupid, so, so childish.

The Judge said nothing and then seemed to refocus his attention on John. "Yes, I like being on a train. Not many surprises on a train." He found his napkin and changed the subject. "Are you in school yet?"

"I'm eight, going to the fourth grade."

"Fourth grade?" The old man cocked his head, surprised like everyone else when John told people his age and grade.

"I must be slipping," the Judge said. "I would have thought you to be five, maybe six, starting the first grade in a year or so."

"I skipped the first grade. I'm little for my age, but I'm smart. It's . . ." he said in a softer voice, "it's my saving grace."

"It's what?" the Judge said.

John straightened his fork, lining it up perfectly with the rest of his table setting. "It's my saving grace." John cleared his throat of the lump that formed every time he thought of her. "That's what my mother tells—used to tell people." He coughed to try to get rid of the lump.

"She would say, 'I know he's small, but he's smart as a whip, and that's his saving grace.'" His voice cracked on the last word. He felt the sting in his nose as tears formed in his eyes. He hated it—to embarrass himself in front of a stranger. He hated her for letting it happen.

"Oh." The Judge fumbled with his fork, turning it over and over on the tablecloth. There was silence again.

After a time, the Judge asked, "And are you smart?"

"Yes, sir," he said. This time, his voice was stronger. Being smart was a matter of fact that he had accepted without question since he was able to remember such things. His mother had told him this. He smoothed the napkin in his lap, feeling more comfortable now.

"Judge, what can I get for you and Mrs. Vance and the boy?" Obadiah had come back and was standing in the aisle.

"Well, Obadiah, what have you got a lot of? I'm starved."

"I think the roast beef is plentiful. I know Mrs. Vance say that's what she want."

"I'll take that, too. What's your pleasure—John, isn't it?"

"May I have a minute to look at the menu?" he said, reaching for the menu that was standing between the little vase of fresh flowers and the silver salt and pepper shakers.

"You want to look at the menu, do you?" The Judge turned his head toward Obadiah and raised his eyebrows above his glasses. "He says he believes he'll peruse your menu, Obadiah. I certainly hope it's up to his expectations."

Obadiah laughed again to accommodate. "When I was that age, I didn't know what a menu was, much less be pretendin' I could read one."

John kept his eyes on the menu and blinked hard to keep the tears away. He knew he must get over letting the least little thing set him off.

There was a long stillness before the Judge said, "Well now, if you want to know what all they have to eat, we can oblige you. How about if Obadiah tells you what's on the menu? Then you can choose something."

"Thank you, no," he said. He fixed on the first item he saw. "The special of the day is meat loaf and potatoes. That's what I'll have, with fried apples and string beans. I'll have ice tea with my meal and—" He stopped, not knowing whether to order dessert, since the Judge hadn't.

"And what?" the Judge asked.

"Well, they have on the menu . . . they have here coconut cream pie. I was just wondering if we were going to order dessert."

"Obadiah, make that three coconut cream pies."

"And coffee with our pie?"

"Coffee? Coffee? Did you hear that, Obadiah? The boy drinks coffee. Didn't your mama tell you that'll stunt your growth?" The Judge's laugh was cut short as he realized what he had said. "Three coffees, Obadiah," and he turned toward Obadiah, "with our dessert, of course."

"Of course." Obadiah walked away.

The Judge rapped his fingers on the table for a moment and then said, "Well now, John, I think I must have underestimated you." He reached down into his coat pocket and pulled out a rolled-up copy of the *Montgomery Advertiser*. "I was going to have Mrs. Vance read this to me, but maybe you would oblige."

He handed the paper to John, who took it and immediately folded it open to the comic strips, as he had always done with his mother. Then he got up on his knees in the chair so he could put the paper down on the table. He glanced up to see the Judge, who had both hands on the table, looking straight ahead.

"You want me to read all the comics or just the ones you like?"

The Judge's hand reached up to consult his beard. "That's not exactly what I had in mind. Turn back to the front page and start there."

"Oh," John said, embarrassed that he had not thought of it and disappointed that he would not get the news of the comic strips. He began to turn back the pages slowly.

The Judge shifted in his chair. "Now come to think of it, maybe you might read me one, just so I'll know what's going on." He raised his head toward the ceiling as if to contemplate. "Now what's the name of the one that I like?"

"'The Phantom'?" the boy said.

"That's it." The Judge pointed his finger straight in front of him. "'The Phantom.' Yes indeed. Now what's the Phantom been up to lately? And remember, son, you'll have to tell me all about the pictures before you read the words."

"Yes, sir." The word *son* had not fallen on deaf ears.

John turned back quickly to the comic page and flattened the creases with his hands. He told the Judge all about how the Phantom was constantly getting into scrapes in the jungle and trying to protect the lovely Diana, who was always falling into the hands of the wrong sort of people. Then he explained the pictures and read the words of the day's strip. The Judge seemed to like it, but he did say he didn't know why the Phantom just didn't go on and marry the lovely Diana to keep her out of harm's way.

"I myself feel the same way most of the time," John said, studying the Phantom's picture.

He turned back to the front page and began to read the headlines. Halfway through an article about the state legislature meeting to consider a bill to regulate state banks, Mrs. Vance appeared. John got up from his seat and rushed to help pull out her chair. He was feeling better all the while.

"Why, John, what lovely manners." She touched the Judge's hand. "Isn't that the sweetest thing you ever saw?"

"The sweetest thing *I* ever saw," the Judge said.

"Thank you, ma'am." John pushed her chair back in too close, jamming her into the table's edge. She eased herself back out as John took his place across from them. "I'm practicing up for when I go to Aunt Nelda's house. I've got to be as good as everyone else."

The Judge felt for his glass of water. "I, uh, I don't think you'll have to worry about losing a manners contest to the Spraig bunch."

"Now Byron, that's unkind." Mrs. Vance patted his arm. "You know Nelda does the best she can, given the circumstances. Remember those children are half kin to Luther."

"Do you know my uncle Luther?" The boy watched their faces. "I never met him, but probably he . . . he'll like me." John immediately pretended to straighten his silverware again. "What I meant was, I can't think of why we wouldn't get along."

"Why, yes," Mrs. Vance said as she opened her purse to put gloves inside. "I'm sure he'll like you. Isn't that right, Byron?" She didn't wait for a reply. "He . . . he's a very nice man, so I hear."

"Does that mean you don't really know him but you have heard people talk about him? Is that what you mean?"

Before she could answer, the Judge broke in. "Adell,

don't go telling the boy things that aren't even close to the truth just so you can put a good face on it."

The Judge turned his head in John's general direction. "These women! Son, if you didn't rein 'm in once in a while, you would stop recognizing altogether the real world we live in." He cleared his throat. "Now, son, I'm the one who knows your uncle Luther. I do banking business with him. He made a crop loan with me this year."

"You do? You know him?" John couldn't contain himself. "Does he keep all his money in your bank? Does he wear a suit like you?"

"Well now, son." The Judge cleared his throat again. "The hard fact of the matter is . . ." Mrs. Vance reached over and put her hand on his arm. He started again. "The hard fact of the matter is that your uncle Luther is—well . . ." He paused. "Well, I would say he is a man of no pretense. Yes, I can safely say that your uncle Luther is a man of no pretense. Do you know what 'no pretense' means?"

"Yes, sir, I think it means—"

"I'll tell you. It means that what you see when you first meet your uncle Luther is exactly what he's like." He leaned back in his chair, smiling. Mrs. Vance let go of his arm.

"Mrs. Vance, does that statement meet with your approval?"

"Why, Judge, everything you say always meets with my approval," she said as she took down her napkin.

The Judge smiled, shaking his head. "You have to keep these women in line, don't you, Obadiah?"

John looked around. Obadiah was standing there holding three dinner plates and a basket of cornbread and rolls.

"How did you know he was here? I didn't even know he was here, and I can—"

"You can see and I can't? Well, that's not strictly true," the Judge said. " I can still see large forms, but without features. However, the doctor in Montgomery said I won't be able to see that much longer."

"The less said about all of that, the better," Mrs. Vance said.

"Adell, you have to face facts, and that's a fact."

"That doctor just doesn't know what he's talkin' about, and you can quote me," she said.

"You haven't always been . . ." John began.

"Blind?" said the Judge. "No, this is something that has come on over the last few years. Thank you, Obadiah," he said as the porter put his plate in front of him. The Judge felt around for his fork. "That's why we've been in Montgomery."

"That doctor hasn't got the sense he was born with." Mrs. Vance reached for the salt and began angrily salting both of their plates. "Probably went to school up north in some no-account—"

"He has a degree from Vanderbilt, Adell. Been practicing for twenty years."

"I don't care." She put down the salt and began attacking their plates with pepper.

The Judge drummed his fingers on the table. "Adell, are you trying to fix it so I'll die of a stomach ulcer before I go blind? Sounds like you're dumping every condiment you can find on my plate."

Adell Vance looked down at the Judge's plate and laughed. "Oh my. I guess I did overdo it a mite, but those doctors make me so mad."

"Well, why don't you take it out on them and not me."

"I'll just fix everything. Don't you worry one bit." She began to scrape the pepper off his roast beef slices.

The Judge waited patiently and turned his attention

back to John. "Life takes some tough turns, son. You have to learn to cope with them. Mrs. Vance told me about the death of your mother and how you're coming to live in our town. I'm sure you'll learn to cope with your uncle Luther and your cousins." He rubbed his hands together, dismissing the subject. "The roast beef smells wonderful."

Mrs. Vance had cleared the pepper and cut up his meat.

John ate meat loaf, mashed potatoes, green beans, fried apples, and three cornbread sticks and drank two glasses of tea.

Mrs. Vance stayed busy eating her own meal and fussing over the Judge. "Now Byron, you be sure and eat your bread." She guided his hand to the bread plate.

"I'll eat my bread, woman," he said, pulling his hand back. "Have you ever known me to lose my appetite?"

After a time, Obadiah arrived with the coconut cream pie and coffee. He placed each dish just so, then moved away.

John watched as Obadiah walked on up the aisle, supervising other waiters who were serving meals. "Judge, do you know the name of every porter on the train?"

"Well, let me see. I do know the names of quite a few of them, since we're back and forth to Montgomery all the time, but no, not all. Obadiah is special because he was born and raised in Lower Peach Tree. I know all of his family, one of the finest colored families in the county; matter of fact, one of his cousins works for me."

"He doesn't say much," John said. He could see Obadiah at the other end of the car, hands folded, watching.

"You don't have to say much when you're in control,

son. This is Obadiah's car and he runs it like a drill sergeant, knows everything that's gone on and is gonna go on in the future. No coloreds and very few whites mess with Obadiah. If they do, they're long gone."

He pointed his fork in his wife's direction and smiled. "Now watch me get a rise out of Mrs. Vance, son.

"Let me tell you about the time a white man disappeared on this very train one night. They said he was from up north and started drinking too much. Came to the dining car and started acting out. The next thing you know, while the train was on the trestle over the Black Warrior, that man up and disappeared. Never has been heard of since."

"Byron." Mrs. Vance jerked to attention. "Will you stop fillin' that boy's head full of Negra stories that everybody knows are not true. My lands above, you'll have him thinkin' we're a bunch of heathens down here. Don't you pay the slightest bit of attention to the Judge, John honey. There is not one ounce of truth to that tale."

The Judge laughed out loud. "I told you that would get a rise out of her. I'll tell you the rest of that story some other time, when it's just us men," he said.

"You'll do no such thing," she said.

They heard a long whistle from the front of the train as it rounded a curve, sending them deeper and deeper into south Alabama.

The Bend

THE lantern glowing through the kitchen window was the only illumination out into the swamp night. Inside the cabin, the old woman had finished washing up supper dishes. Her hands, rough from years in the fields, brushed crumbs off the table and spread a paisley-printed tablecloth across its surface, smoothing out the wrinkles. Next, she went to the same drawer the tablecloth had been stored in and brought out candles of various sizes, which she placed in predetermined locations around the room. They were calculated to give it a warm but mysterious glow. She stepped over to the lantern in the sink window and turned down the wick until the flame went out. When she looked around to see the effect, she was pleased. The candlelight gently shifted as a breeze from the screened door passed through the room.

She was ready for her first client of the night. Actually, they were her only clients for the evening, a young couple pregnant with their first child. They were willing to pay her—in eggs, four dozen—for the privilege of finding out if it was a boy or a girl. That many eggs would feed her household breakfast for four or five days.

She had already seen the pregnant girl at church last Sunday. She already knew it would be a boy, from the way it rode in its mother's womb, from the color of the mother's fingernails, and from all the other signs her mother and grandmother had taught her. Of course, if it wasn't a boy and the parents came back wanting an explanation, she would always say the reason was because the child was so special that God had not let her see into the womb. This meant this baby was predestined for great things.

This would please the parents even more. "This baby so special, Mama Tuway couldn't even tell what she was gonna be."

Her mother had taught her that, too. This way, the parents would give extraordinary love and care to the infant and, more than likely, the child would grow up with some singular talent or ability, probably because of the exceptional pampering the baby received.

Sometimes she thought she should say this to all the mothers and fathers by way of getting them to treat each child with great care, but most of the time the signs were too obvious. She could tell immediately if it was a boy or girl, without going through the pretense of the tea leaves or the cards. Of course, she always did one or both of those things, to help them believe.

It was strange, though; for a long time now, the tea leaves and even the cards had said someone, some colored person, almost holy, was destined to come and lead the people of the Bend. She never mentioned it to her clients. They might get the big head. Besides, her mother and her grandmother had told her not to get too carried away with the cards or the leaves. They were usually more wrong than right.

She decided since this was their first visit, she should add additional candles, out on the porch and down the trail a bit, get them in the mood as they approached the house.

Mama Tuway gathered up more candles out of her fortune-telling drawer and walked out to the front porch, then on out the trail. As she placed the last candle on a low hanging tree branch draped in Spanish moss swaying in the breeze, she heard the long eerie whistle of the night train approaching the river trestle.

CHAPTER 7

THEIR train arrived at Lower Peach Tree in the dead of night. One dim light hanging from a long wire on the station platform was their only welcome. The station itself was locked tight. Other passengers who got off with them had rides waiting in the darkness just beyond the reach of the light. John saw no one. He heard only the sound of a few cars and what he suspected to be a mule-drawn wagon or two leaving as travelers were picked up and carted off.

Aunt Nelda had not noticed any of this, she had been so busy making sure their bags and boxes were unloaded and accounted for.

The train hissed and smoked and clanged, and pulled out of the station, leaving only a few wisps of steam vanishing in the night air. She was still checking boxes and bags, trunks and suitcases. He sat on the edge of a trunk, watching the wedge of light cast by the hanging bulb move back and forth with the slightest breeze. There were no porters, no people left, no one to pick them up.

Finally, Aunt Nelda disengaged from her things

enough to see this. Then she took studied interest in the business of re-counting, mumbling to herself all the while. "That's just like Luther. I wrote him three times we would be comin' today." She kept her eyes on the boxes, never letting them stray to John. She took a small list from her purse.

"Five, the tablecloths; six, the kitchen utensils. He probably never even went to the post office to get the mail. Now what does he think we're supposed to do?

"Seven, the trunk with John's clothes. Eight is the china. We can't leave our valuables." She glanced out into the dark. For the first time, she looked at the boy. "I thought for sure he would borrow a truck and meet us here. I just know he wants to see all the things we have."

Just then, two lights appeared far off down the road, coming on slowly. She crossed her arms and rubbed them in relief. "There he is. I told you."

Every time the car hit a bump, its lights would flash up into the big moss-covered oaks that lined the road up to the station. Tree frogs, which had provided the only sound, were temporarily silenced. As it came closer, they could see that the light belonged to a red Packard. The colored man who was driving cut off the engine and got out.

"The Judge told me to come on back here and see if y'all needed a ride. Mrs. Vance was noticin' y'all standin' here when I come to pick'm up. The Judge say, 'Go back there, Cal, and see if you can give them folks a hand.' So here I am." He stood there smiling, not looking at Aunt Nelda, but staring at all of her things.

Aunt Nelda began to straighten up the boxes stacked in front of her. "Well, I . . . I know Mr. Spraig will be along any minute. I don't think we'll need your help, Cal. We can manage just fine, can't we, John honey?"

"Yes, ma'am," he said, knowing it was not true.

The colored man turned to go. Just as he was opening the car door, Aunt Nelda began to laugh her high, nervous laugh. "Oh now wouldn't it be a joke on Luther if we just up and got a ride with Cal here, and Luther—I mean Mr. Spraig—on his way down here to pick us up. It would just serve him right, don't you think?" She laughed again, bit her lip, and then called to Cal. "Now Cal, we'll just take you up on that offer from the Judge."

She turned to the boy. "John, you start helpin' Cal load our things." She began telling Cal what to do, all the while talking loudly so that he and John would be sure to see her reasoning.

"Luther will be so upset that he missed us. Well, it just serves him right. Women just have to keep their men guessin', you know."

This rationale was completely lost on the boy, having never had a father to remember or a mother who would deign such an attitude. Cal pretended not to take note.

All their belongings were finally pushed and shoved into some part of the car. A rope tied down the trunk. The backseat was loaded with bags and boxes on either side of Aunt Nelda. John was assigned to the front seat with Cal. Cal started the engine and drove slowly out of the train station. As they drove through what seemed to be a small town, the night breeze from the opened windows closed around them like a damp cloth. John could only imagine what lay in the shadowy outlines of the darkened buildings they passed. Out on what appeared to be a main highway, the one stoplight in town glowed a steady yellow. Cal paused at the light.

"Now Mrs. Spraig," he said, "I done forgot which is your house in Mill Town. Seein' as how they all looks alike, you gonna have to tell me where to go when I gets there."

"We no longer reside in Mill Town, Cal," Aunt Nelda said in a testy voice. "My husband has had a business offer that required us to change residence. Turn left right here and keep going until you come to the first left."

"The first left? Ain't nothin' out there but one of them Rawlston houses," Cal said. "My cousin Lowery worked on shares out there 'fore he went on up north year before last. That ain't the house you mean, is it?"

"Certainly we are not stayin' in the house your cousin stayed in. Don't be ridiculous. It's another one on that same road."

Cal shook his head. "Well, that's the only one I knows about. Bound to be the—"

"Never you mind, Cal. Just drive on and keep your mind on what it is you're doing."

They drove on away from town, no one saying a word.

In a mile or so, the car came to a dirt road that had so many ruts, the Packard, with its heavy load, was hard-pressed to make it through. John held tight to the window frame and looked out into the intermittent moonlight, to see an old broken-down fence on either side of the road that led up a rise and into a group of trees. As they approached, he could see, underneath the trees, the outline of a house. There were no lights anywhere. It looked, in the dark, like some black hole. When the lights from the Packard came around to shine on it, the boy caught his breath without knowing. It was like no house he had ever seen white people live in. This was a mistake. They would drive past this place and go on down the road to the main house.

Feeble steps led up to a porch that was in the middle of the house. Old shutters hung lopsided from the two front windows. A truck with peeling red paint sat to one side near a shed. Two cats sleeping on the porch raised their heads to watch them approach.

"It's—it's a dogtrot house." He hadn't even realized he had said it. He was still taking in the sight.

Aunt Nelda took no notice of this reality. Her language, however, seemed to change to adjust to the environment. "Cal, turn them lights 'way from the house. That's all I need, to wake up everybody while I'm tryin' to sort out just what I'm gonna to do with my things." She turned to John. "Our things." She laughed nervously.

"You've never been to the country before, have you?" She raised her hands and hunched her shoulders. "Only temporary, of course, until Mr. Spraig makes a good crop this year, and then we're on our way to . . ." Her voice trailed off into another thought. "Well, get on out. We got work to do." She put her mind to gathering shopping bags. "Yes, only temporary," she said to herself.

"Now get on out here like I said and start helpin' Cal to unload. In the country, you pull your own weight. That's something you got to learn right off the bat. No more coddlin'. I always did tell your momma she went too easy on you."

John got out of the car, trying not to look at the house. He started stacking things on the porch, following Cal's lead. The night was still hot. Mosquitoes buzzed in his ear and bit at his legs. Sweat and dust covered his ankles and shoes. He was wringing-wet and tired. He slapped at a mosquito and smeared the blood it left onto his shirt. He almost threw a box on the porch. He screamed at his mother, his head pounding. *She lives in a dogtrot house. You can see that, can't you?*

Still no one seemed to stir inside the house. Even the cats, on recognizing Aunt Nelda, had ambled off the porch and found sleeping space on the dirt beneath the foundation, which was raised off the ground several feet by stacks of river rocks placed at its corners.

"Good luck, boy," Cal half-whispered as he put the last trunk on the porch. He turned and hurried to the car, afraid she might find more chores for him. Rolls of dust followed his two lights down the road toward the highway.

"What did he say to you?" Aunt Nelda snapped.

"He said, 'Good luck.'"

"Some people can be just too smart for their own good." She made a face and shook her head. "Just because he works for the Judge, he thinks he's in high cotton. The very idea," she muttered. "His cousin Lowery indeed."

Aunt Nelda straightened up and shook herself loose from the notion. "Now let's see. Home at last, with everything intact. We'll just leave things here on the porch and deal with it in the morning, in plenty of daylight.

"Now John," she said, "let's put you on a cot in Little Luther's room for tonight and work out something better for the future."

She went in the door on the left side of the dogtrot and came back with two quilts that were old and faded from use.

"I'm going to sleep on that?"

She didn't hear the ridicule in his voice and patted the quilts lovingly. "Yes, I made them up myself. One is Wedding Rings and this here one is Tulips.

"You follow on behind me. We don't want to disturb Little Luther. He's almost as bad as his daddy when he gets woke up out of a sound sleep."

"Aunt Nelda, I thought I might wash my hands and face before I go to bed," he whispered. "Mother always made me."

"Oh ain't you a lucky boy." She laughed in a whisper, her hand on the door latch. "We don't do that down here. I know how little boys hate to take baths. Besides, at this time of night, you can't hardly see to draw water from the pump nohow. So come on."

He followed her into the room on the right side of the porch. It was dark, but she found a place on the floor, laid out the quilts, and motioned for him to lie down.

Then she quickly backed out of the room and left him alone.

He sat on the quilts, trying to let his eyes adjust to the darkness, but they would not. It was as if he were in the deepest, blackest cave. He felt around for his shoes and untied the laces.

Maybe this was like camping and tomorrow they would move into a real house. Or maybe tomorrow he would wake up and Aunt Nelda's children would be standing around him, smiling down at him. He heard Little Luther's steady breathing.

He was too tired to cry or even call up her name. He fell asleep.

CHAPTER 8

"Hey, you think you can sleep all day?" Little Luther kicked at the quilts. John roused himself from sleep to the sound of Little Luther striking a match. He lifted the glass off a kerosene lamp to light the wick. Then Little Luther stood over John, holding the lamp to get a better look at what lay beneath the covers. "You don't look much like a football player. Ma said you was a football player." He put the lamp on a rough wooden dresser that seemed to be the only piece of furniture in the room other than Little Luther's bed. He began fastening the shoulder strap to his overalls, still watching John, who lay on his back, holding a piece of quilt over his bare chest. John had been so hot in the night that he had taken off his shirt and laid it neatly on the floor beside him. Now he felt a chill as he watched the person standing before him. A big wide head with hair so short, he almost looked bald. Not fat, just short and solid, with thick arms and fingers, feet like roots growing from one of the water oaks he had seen from the train window.

Little Luther turned around to pick up one of his shoes. "Just goes to show you women ain't got a lick of sense when it comes to ordinary things." He sat down on the bed and propped one foot on the bedcovers to lace up his shoe. John could see his eyes now. They were blue and far apart.

"What are you starin' at?" Little Luther looked up from his lacing. "Ain't you ever seen work boots before?"

"You're going to get the bedcovers dirty putting your muddy shoes on them."

Little Luther set the first boot on the floor and raised up the second boot to start lacing it. "Looks to me like what we got here is a shithead pantywaist. Pa, he said he thought you would be soft as a turd. You probably ain't done a good day's work in your life." He finished lacing and stomped both feet on the floor as he got up.

"We're gonna be workin' down in the swamp field, so you better wear shoes. I don't like to wear'm, neither, but if you don't, you'll get worms." He turned to open the door to the outside breezeway. "You better get up and get dressed or Pa'll be on you, and then you can't work, shoes or no." The door slammed behind him.

John began unfolding his shirt. He would put this on temporarily until he had unpacked his other clothes. He had begun sifting through the quilts to find his shoes and socks when he heard Uncle Luther.

His voice was hoarse, like a man who had a bad cold or a bad night.

"Come on out here and get somethin' to eat. We ain't got all day."

John hopped along as he pulled on his shoes. He felt around for the doorknob before he could open it to the dark morning. Faint light shone from the door on the other side of the dogtrot. John stumbled on an uneven floorboard as he edged closer. The rusty screen door gave a blurred picture of what lay ahead. He could see two figures sitting around what he thought was a picnic table.

He eased open the screen door just enough to step inside. The voice he had heard sat at the far end of the table. Light from the coal-oil lantern reflected off Uncle Luther's face, then danced into the shadows where Aunt Nelda stood over a woodstove, frying bacon. The bacon smell mixed with an odor of old wood walls, damp and decaying.

Uncle Luther looked up from eating long enough to nod his head. Only Aunt Nelda's voice came out of the half dark, saying what he was coming to expect of her.

Weren't we all glad to be home and one big happy family and didn't it look like it was going to be a beautiful day and, oh my, what a train ride they'd had coming home and just wait till you saw all her things. She said all this as she was guiding him to a sitting place across the table from Little Luther.

He had practiced in his mind thousands of times the ritual of this introduction, standing, shaking hands, saying, "I'm glad to meet you." Instead, he sat with his head down, studying the grain of the wood boards in the tabletop.

She brought a plate of bacon, eggs, and grits. He decided that now was not the time to tell her he didn't care for grits. He would inform her of this at some more appropriate time. "Thank you, Aunt Nelda. Would you please pass me the salt, Little Luther," he said. He really was not interested in the salt, but he thought it a good way to break the ice.

Little Luther jumped out of his seat. "Who the hell told you you could call me that?"

John looked first at Little Luther, then to Aunt Nelda. "I thought that was—"

Little Luther reached over and grabbed his shirt. "Nobody calls me that 'cept Ma and my pa." The blue eyes were an inch from his nose.

"What'll I call—"

"Now, now boys." Aunt Nelda was at the table to mediate. "Butch is what he likes to be called, but you didn't know that, did you, dear?

"Now Little Luther, I don't want you using profanity at the table. Luther, you really must speak to the boy about his language."

Big Luther gave no sign of hearing her. He spooned in large amounts of grits, alternating that with gulps of coffee.

Butch let go of the shirt and sat down. John raised a shaky spoon and put eggs in a dry mouth.

Aunt Nelda provided the background noise, droning on about how lucky they were to be together again, what a long trip it was, how nice that now the boys each had a brother.

John tried to concentrate on the kerosene lamp in the middle of the table. Its flame flickered from side to side, the nickel plating of the base reflecting contorted pictures of them all. It was the first time he had realized there was no electricity.

He heard it ticking before he could see it on the mantel over the empty fireplace. Every time she stopped talking even for a second, he could hear it. *Your clock.*

Aunt Nelda had packed it in one of the trunks. He kept trying to hear it tick, trying to make it drown out Aunt Nelda's talking, Little Luther scraping his plate. The eggs felt like glue in his mouth. His breath came faster and faster. He couldn't seem to control it.

He excused himself, rushed out the door, and leaned over the porch to throw up.

The Judge and Adell Vance liked to have their breakfast in the garden on mornings when the weather was right, when he wasn't in a hurry to get to work. They would go out under the big oak in the backyard and have coffee and toast while she read the paper aloud. He would sit in the wicker swing that was suspended from one of the oak's branches. She would take her place next to him in the green glider, both of which had matching green-and-white-striped cushions. He liked the smell of the grass with the dew still there, the occasional scent of the roses she had planted in a sunny back corner. The distant sound of an infrequent car passing by on the road that ran in front of the house gave him a sense of being part of the coming day.

Earlier, she had filled the silver pitcher with steaming coffee and placed a morning newspaper and toast between the creamer and sugar. Then Adell Vance had carried the silver service to the wrought-iron table that sat between them. She had poured coffee and offered toast to the Judge. Now she sat, dressed in a neat flowered silk dress and matching low heels, leafing through the *Montgomery Advertiser.*

"There's so much goin' on, it's just hard to know where to begin—with the national news, with the state news? They got a mess up there in Montgomery; says they might think about callin' a special session of the legislature. And up in Washington—"

The Judge was half-listening as he rubbed his fingers along the coarse weave of the old wicker swing he had hung in this spot some ten years ago. "Why don't you start with 'The Phantom'?"

"The what?" She looked up from the front page of the *Advertiser.*

"'The Phantom'—you know, Adell, that comic strip about the masked man who lives in the jungles of Africa."

She laughed out loud. "Byron Vance, where in the world do you come up with these things? I haven't read the comic strips in years."

He raised an imaginary cigar to his lips and flicked the ashes—his secretary at the bank had told him he did a wonderful W. C. Fields imitation. "My dear," he said, smiling, "I am a man of many faces."

CHAPTER 9

UNCLE Luther was leaning against a pine tree in the front yard, biting off a chunk of rope tobacco he had taken out of his overall pocket. John could see him now. The sun was just breaking over a cluster of pine trees off to the east, sending long shadows across the flat fields that surrounded the house. With the exception of the trees and underbrush growing around the house, there were miles of fields, planted in what the boy assumed, from his reading, was cotton. The light cut across the bridge of Uncle Luther's nose, accentuating his gaunt features. He could have been handsome once. The teeth that had been white were stained brown now. The face that must have been smooth in his early years was wrinkled around the eyes and the mouth. Dirty brown hair grew down the back of his neck and receded from his temples. He reminded John of pictures he had seen in one of his geography books—"These people live in the Appalachian Mountains."

Aunt Nelda was bending down to give John a wet washcloth to wipe his face. "Now Luther, I do think the boy is tuckered out from his trip. Maybe it would be best for him to stay round here today and rest."

Uncle Luther spit and looked at her with eyes half-seeing. He spit again, then wiped his mouth on his sleeve. "He's comin' with me, Nelda. From the looks of him, he probably ain't gonna last the day, but he needs to learn from the get-go—everybody pulls they own weight round here."

Aunt Nelda bit her lip and tried to laugh. "Oh, you men, having to be so rugged." She patted John on the head. "I can see you would rather be with the men than sit around here all day with us girls."

"I wouldn't mind, Aunt Nelda. I don't feel so—"

"Now never you mind, John honey. You go right ahead on with your uncle Luther. It'll give y'all a chance to get to know each other." She turned quickly and went back in the room that held the kitchen. John sat there holding the cloth to his face.

"Ain't you got no long pants, boy?"

John shook his head no.

"Little Luther," he yelled, "get your sorry ass out here. We ain't got all day."

Little Luther came hurrying out of the outhouse that was off under a small grove of trees behind the house. He was buttoning up his pants as he came.

"Bring them hoes with you," Luther said as he turned and walked off down the road.

Little Luther ran to the side of the house and gathered up three hoes that were leaning against the weathered gray boarding. He never looked in John's direction.

John slowly folded the wet cloth, laid it on the porch floor, and stepped out into the dirt that was the front yard.

The sun was well up now. Away from the house, the fields stretched out before them, flat green blankets laid down from fence line to fence line, broken only by an occasional gathering of trees in the slight draws formed by the rolling land. John began to lose the nausea he had felt before. It was hot but not smothering, as he knew it would be as the day wore on. Grasshoppers were jumping all around him as he shuffled through the weeds growing in the middle of the dirt road. Eventually, the land sloped down toward a swampy area. They were headed in that direction.

In his mind, he had decided what they were doing. They were out here checking the cotton plants. They would see how they looked and then go back to the house for dinner after awhile. Not a very pleasant house, but he could tolerate it. Surely this was not a permanent arrangement. After all, in a few days all of his things were to arrive, and Aunt Nelda's things, too. They couldn't possibly live here. Butch's room wouldn't even hold half of his toys, let alone his clothes.

All of these rows of plants they were passing must be cotton. Anyone who had this much cotton couldn't be poor. From the looks of it, half the cotton in Alabama must be here on this farm.

He was beginning to feel better now. There was a breeze stirring. He even ventured some bit of conversation. "Are we going to check the crops?" he asked to either one of them.

No one answered. He could hear Little Luther snicker.

"You certainly do have a beautiful farm here, Uncle Luther."

Uncle Luther kept walking and spitting. "This here ain't mine."

They walked on until they came to a barbed-wire gate. Its fencing surrounded a field bordered by a low-lying

swampy area to the east. Uncle Luther stopped to un-
latch the gate to a field that was not as neat as the others.
Weeds grew up between plants that had a yellow cast and
were smaller and weaker than vegetation in some of the
surrounding fields.

Little Luther closed the gate after he had dragged in
the hoes.

"Take one. Give'm one." Uncle Luther turned to Little
Luther, who had dropped all the hoes just inside the gate.
Little Luther picked up one and tossed it in John's direc-
tion.

It landed on the ground in front of him.

"We got to hoe least half this here today. Don't be
lettin' up just 'cause you come to the end of a row. Go on
to the next one."

John felt the coarse wood handle as he picked the hoe
up off the ground. He tried to mimic the way Little
Luther stood nonchalantly holding his hoe.

"Well, get on with it." Uncle Luther stood staring at
him. "Start with this here one."

"Do I chop down all the weeds around the small plants
or do you want me to chop down the plants themselves?"

Little Luther burst out laughing but quickly returned
to a straight face when he caught sight of his father's expression.

The boy tried to smile. "Well, there is a certain contra-
diction here. I have heard the expression, but what exactly does 'chopping cotton' mean?"

In one quick motion, Uncle Luther stepped forward
and grabbed John by his shirt. "Are you sassin' me, boy?"
He pulled him up into his face. John could see the tobacco juice running down his chin.

"No, sir! No, sir! I—I just never—I never have—uh—
have chopped before."

Uncle Luther spit the words out. "We ain't choppin'. We hoein'. Done finished choppin' two months ago. You think you gonna be a smart-ass, do you, boy? Just 'cause my field ain't far along as t'others."

"Oh, no, oh, no, sir." John shook his head violently. He had no idea what he and Uncle Luther were talking about, but he had obviously insulted Uncle Luther in some way.

"I'll tell you what." Uncle Luther pulled John closer. "You can just hoe two rows for every one I hoe. Maybe that'll learn you hoein'. Now get on over there." He let go of John's shirt and pushed him so hard, he fell in the dirt. Little Luther was laughing out loud now that it seemed he could get away with it.

His father turned on him. "You get the hell busy or you'll get the same or worse."

Little Luther grabbed his hoe and began chopping at the ground.

John tried to busy himself and at the same time sneak glances at Little Luther so as to quickly learn the art of hoeing.

The Bend

In the years before she had come to the swamp, Mama Tuway had lived on the high ground in the Bend, on a neat farm she and her husband, James, had worked. It had been around the time of the First World War. They had planted cotton and sugarcane. They had become famous for their cane crop. People used to come from miles around to help with making sorghum molasses in the fall. Sadie, their old mule, would trudge around and around in a circle, crushing the sugarcanes. James would build a hardwood fire to cook the cane juice. Sometimes, even now, on a bright day in the fall, she could still smell the steam that rose off that old cooking tray.

Those were good years, before James lost his health. Despite all she could do, he kept going downhill. Even then, she had a reputation as a healer, like her mother and her Indian grandmother, but in the end she couldn't heal her own.

After he died, she tried to stick it out two or three more years, doing all the work herself. With no children to help out, it was too much to keep up with.

One day, she woke up and realized she was making more money treating people and telling futures than she was farming, and farming was taking all her time and energy. That's when she got the idea about living in the old hunting cabin in the swamp clearing. She had been out gathering sassafras roots when she stumbled on the deserted cabin. After that, the idea wouldn't go away.

When she moved there, she experienced a freedom she had never known before. All the work and worry over farming were gone. A whole new life opened up for her. People liked coming to the swamp, as if they were going someplace real, to a doctor's office, or to someone almost like a preacher, to get advice.

The people of the Bend got so they wouldn't make a move without her. Being away like that, just that little distance, set her apart. Back then, even the preacher started coming down for an occasional visit. Of course he wouldn't admit he was coming for information. "No, just comin' to pass the time, Polly." That's what everyone called her back then, Polly. It had been before Tuway had come along. After Tuway came, people began calling her Mama Tuway. That was so long ago, she couldn't remember exactly when the transition had occurred. Now that name fit like skin. Polly was someone from another life.

Now the preacher, the Reverend James Kay—most of the Benders had kept their slave last name, and the Reverend Kay was one of them—was a regular visitor. He would come and sit on the porch, rocking away and asking her about everything from cough syrup to cotton prices.

She smiled. She knew it all—and they thought she was reading it out of their palms or looking onto the tea leaves, but that wasn't it. She had other sources.

Chapter 10

It wasn't bad at first. The sun was not that hot. There was a breeze from time to time. John actually liked making a neat chopped row. Each time he finished clearing all the weeds from around one cotton plant, he would check to see how nice it looked. Then he would compare it to all the other plants in his row, making sure to create a precise line as he progressed. The cotton plants themselves were leggy with yellowing leaves. He felt each time he cleared weeds away from one that he was giving it a new chance in life.

After an hour, he was hot and thirsty. His soft hands began to develop blisters. He kept finding new ways to grasp his hoe in order to stay away from a particular blister that was forming. After two hours, his arms and legs were covered with sweat and dirt. He swatted at sweat bees that constantly buzzed around his head and he noticed for the first time that Little Luther and his father had on straw hats, while the sun was baking the top of his head, his neck, his arms, his legs. Skin long hidden in the cool quiet of his mother's house—especially during those polio summers when he lived in the basement—stood full face in the sun, completely naïve to its power.

He pushed back slippery glasses, to see that Uncle Luther and Little Luther were farther and farther ahead of him with their rows.

Along about ten o'clock, he began thinking of ways of quitting. He practiced what he would say to Uncle Luther. "I'm going to get a drink of water and I'll be right back." Or "I need to go to the bathroom and I'll be right back."

Off in the distance, he noticed a girl walking down the dirt path in a sunbonnet, and barefoot, carrying a bucket too big for her. She stopped by the barbed-wire fence to open it and come into their field. When she had fastened the fence gate back, she picked up the bucket with both hands and walked over to him. She looked to be about his age, but bigger in size, of course, with stringy blond hair and eyes that said nothing.

"Ain't you got more sense than to be out here without no head cover?" She stood staring at him. "Look at you. You as red as a tomater and the day ain't half-started."

"Shell," Uncle Luther called from his place in the field. "Bring that water on over here to your daddy and stop lollygagging."

"I got to go. Pa wants his mornin' drink."

"But can't I—"

"I'll be back to you. Pa gets his first, then everybody else." She pulled up the bucket handle and started off again.

By the time Shell finished with Uncle Luther and Little Luther, there was precious little left when she got back to John. He took the tin ladle hanging inside the bucket and dipped out all that was reachable. Then he held up the heavy bucket and drank straight out of it to get the rest.

He drank like he had never tasted water before. He was surprised at how delicious it was. He had never remembered it tasting like that. It had always been second choice at the dinner table, side by side with a glass of ice tea. He had never given water its due.

"Pa says I can give you my bonnet to keep the sun off if I want to, since you work slow as a woman anyway. You want it?"

"My face is getting quite sore and the back of my neck is burning."

She took it off and handed it to him. "Are you sure?" she said.

"Sure I'm sure. Why wouldn't I be? It's hot as blue blazes out here."

"You gonna get fierce doggin' wearin' girl clothes like this here," she said, holding the bonnet out.

"Maybe, but what can I do? I'm burning up, and you said yourself the day isn't half over. The top of my head feels like it's on fire." He took the hat.

"You could keep on, not wearin' anything, like a man," she said.

"Oh," he said, looking down at the hat in his hand. "Well, uh, well, I think I'll wear it just for the morning, till we come in for dinner. We do get to stop for eating, don't we?"

"Yeah." She smiled at him like he might not be too bright. "Yeah, but that's likely two hours off."

"Well, nobody will see me but Uncle Luther and Little—Butch."

"Yeah, nobody but Pa and Butch," she said, and smiled again.

"Is that who you are? Are you Butch's sister? Are you part of our, uh, the family?"

"Yeah," she said. "I'm part of 'um." She pushed her

stringy blond hair out of her face and behind one ear. "Wasn't up when you was up this mornin'. I got to lay out 'cause I been keepin' house while Momma was gone." She walked on off, taking care to step only where the dirt was easy on her feet.

He looked around to see if they were looking at him before he put the hat on. Nobody seemed to be paying him any mind, so he continued hoeing.

A while later, Little Luther caught up with him a few rows over, hoeing twice as fast and not half as neat. It was then he started in on John about how he was so pretty in the bonnet and how he was going to tell all the boys John would be going to school with in the fall. This didn't bother him so much as when Uncle Luther began laughing at some of the things Little Luther was saying. At the end of the next row, when no one was looking, he took the hat off and laid it on the ground. The sun fell unhindered.

The songs of the cicadas in the willows at the edge of the field would rise, then slowly drift away like the dust from his hoe. He chopped around plant after plant for what seemed like hours just to reach the end of one row. Then he would look up, to see an ocean of rows full of weeds. The ground began to move before his eyes like giant waves in a green ocean. He stopped sweating and began to feel a chill.

Finally, it came time to eat. He knew this because Uncle Luther walked past him on his way out of the field and said, "Dinner." John dropped his hoe and began to follow.

"Finish that row, boy. You three rows behind as it is," Uncle Luther said when he saw John following. The boy hurried back to finish and then headed in the direction the others had taken.

As he walked, he realized something was wrong. His eyes were beginning to swell shut. He felt hot and cold at the same time. He couldn't seem to walk in a straight line. When he finally reached the house, he heard, but could not make out, Aunt Nelda standing on the porch. "My God, Luther, what have y'all been doin' out there?"

He heard, but could not see, Uncle Luther come out on the porch to stand beside her. "Ain't nothin' but a little sun. He'll learn to live with it." Uncle Luther walked down off the porch and poked him on the arm. "Damn if you ain't almost done, boy."

John looked up but could only see their outlines against the house. His eyes were almost completely shut now. He felt Aunt Nelda take his hand and lead him up the steps to a seat on the wood bench next to the wall. Every part of his body that wasn't covered by clothing was beginning to burn.

"Honey, you look a fright." She stood before him, twisting something in her hands. Maybe it was a dish towel. "I never thought this would happen."

He spoke in a whisper, his breathing uneven. "My mother doesn't—didn't—allow me. I stayed inside a lot," he said through lips that felt like biscuit dough. "Do—do I look bad, Aunt Nelda?"

Little Luther laughed somewhere on the porch. "Do you look bad? Do you look bad? You look like somethin' on the Fourth of July barbecue pit down at Mr. Arlo's."

"My feet feel funny."

Aunt Nelda took off his shoes to let his swelling feet grow to twice their size. Before he could ask the question, she was answering it. "Of course you're gonna be just fine, nothin' at all to worry about. Just a little too much sun." She was fanning him with the dish towel. "Shell. Shell!" She almost yelled the second time when

Shell didn't appear immediately. "Go get some of my burn lotion, right now." Shell came hurrying back with what looked and smelled like a can of grease. Aunt Nelda smeared it over every exposed part of his body. Her fingers ran over his eyelids, under his nose, around his lips. It didn't help the burning.

"Shell, get him water." Shell left and returned with a pail. She scooped out a ladle half-full and raised it to his lips. He swallowed what he could. The rest ran down his face and shirt.

The men soon became bored with watching and went back in the kitchen to finish their interrupted dinner. "Nelda," Luther called through the screened door, "I need more bread in here."

Nelda rose from her knees in front of John and handed the dish towel to Shell. "Keep fannin' him."

After dinner, the men passed by him on their way out to sit in two straight-back chairs under the big tree in the front yard. John could hear the low hum of their voices as Uncle Luther did most of the talking. It seemed to be about all the money he was going to make off his cotton crop. Even if they didn't have an eight-disk harrow like his friend Arlo, they had made out just fine with what they had. They could always borrow Arlo's tractor if they needed it. There was no mention of Aunt Nelda's boxes and bags sitting around the porch. Little Luther sat and whittled a stick with his knife, occasionally saying, "Yes, sir." Presently, everybody left for chores. Shell got tired of fanning him and went into the kitchen to help her mother.

He sat this way for the rest of the afternoon, feet on the floor of the porch, arms out to his sides, holding on to the bench. He was too burned to lie down, too swollen to stand and walk. Aunt Nelda passed by at intervals, taking up the dish towel and fanning it. "It's gonna be fine. It's gonna be just fine," she would say, absentmindedly fanning. She would put the dish towel down and leave, saying, "I'll be right back," then not come back for an hour.

He had never had occasion to cry out in pain. His needs had always been taken care of long before it got to that point, but as the afternoon wore on and the pain and fear increased, tears began to run down his face. He held tight to the bench he sat on and lowered his head to whimper. "Aunt Nelda," he said as she passed by. "Am I gonna die?"

She stopped what she was doing and came to him. "Here now, honey. Big boys don't cry." She sneaked a glance out toward the fields. "You don't want them to see you cry. You'll never hear the end of it." She picked up the dish towel beside him and began fanning. "I tell you what I'm gonna do. I'm gonna make you your own bed, right out here on the porch." She pointed to a spot in the corner toward the back of the porch. "It'll be your very own place. It's always the coolest place in the house, you know. You'll like that, won't you?" He sniffed and tried to nod yes.

She told Shell to wet a washcloth for his eyes—to help with the swelling, she said. He knew it was to hide the tears. He tried to hold the washcloth in place but soon gave up.

Aunt Nelda went inside Little Luther's room and came back out with a load of quilts and blankets in her arms. "It's just a little too much sun. That's all it is, just a little too much sun." She was folding blankets on the floor, never looking at him as she talked. "Just think, you get to sleep out here on the porch for the next few nights. Coolest place in the house." She added a quilt to the top of two folded blankets. "If any breeze stirs, you'll get it right out here. Nothing like a breeze to make a sunburn feel better. Why, in a few days, you'll be up and around like nothing ever happened." She surveyed her bed.

"I don't think I will," he said through swollen lips.

"You just wait and see," she said, still looking at the bed. "Why, in no time at all . . . I'm going right inside and get you a fresh pail of water so you can have water right by your bed. Much better than one little old glass. Why, it'll be just like your own little room." She opened the kitchen door and went inside.

He saw the outline of the bed in the corner but could not bring himself to move to it. He placed the wet wash-cloth Shell had given him on the top of one leg. Then after counting to ten, he would loosen his grip on the bench and place it on the top of the other leg. It would bring him relief only for the few seconds that the wet cloth touched his skin. Then the skin would resume burning. He wondered if he would keep burning and burning and eventually burn up. Perhaps he would end up like the clinkers the maid removed from the furnace in his old house when they had completely given up their energy and become hard and shriveled.

The day divided itself into minutes, then seconds, then half seconds. It would not end.

Late that afternoon, because he kept falling forward when he felt dizzy, he finally got up and inched over to his cot to lie among the quilts. He yelled out when his skin touched the cloth, but no one heard him. The last thing he remembered was seeing a full moon rising up across the darkening fields. Then he, in some way, became unconscious, whether from sleep or pain, he didn't know or care.

Off in the distance he thought he could hear Uncle Luther and Aunt Nelda standing over him, talking. He pretended he was asleep. In fact, he might have been asleep; he wasn't sure.

"We need to call Doc Hays," she would say, and he would say, "We ain't spendin' good money to have the Doc come all the way out here and say he's done got burnt. Hell, we can see that by lookin' at him. Feed him plenty of water and he'll make it." John thought he heard the sound of tobacco juice being spit out onto the dirt. "Hell, he better make it, Nelda. I need him back in the fields soon as he's up, even if he ain't worth shit when it comes to usin' a hoe."

CHAPTER 11

On the third day, or what he believed to be the third day, he woke, to feel blisters all over his arms and legs, face and neck, even on his head, in his hair. The tops of his shoulders were burned where the sun's rays had drilled in under the cloth. At least the pain had subsided somewhat. As the blisters began to break, an oozing liquid ran out and seemed to glue him to his shirt and pants and then to the quilts he lay on.

His only consolation was that no one bothered him. He slept on the porch at night and feigned sleep in the early morning, when the others went to the fields.

Shell came along every hour or so during the day to dip the washcloth in a bucket of water by his cot. She stood looking at him, then wrung out the cloth and put it back on his eyes. He came to find out her real name was Michelle. She said her mother had liked the name but that her pa had shortened it to Shell, and after awhile her mother gave up and started calling her Shell. He would listen to her, not saying anything, just watching her through eyes that were only slits in a round, puffy, swollen mask that did not feel a part of him. From time to time, he would reach up to his face to test the blisters with his fingers. None of it felt like what he remembered his face to be.

Late one afternoon several days later, Shell came up on the porch to change his washcloth. This time, she changed it and kept squatting there beside him, looking into his face.

"How long you think you gonna lie there like that?" she said. "My pa says them blisters is poppin', and that means you can go on back to the fields soon."

He lifted the cloth off of one eye to look at her and see if she was kidding.

"I'm too sick. Can't you see that I'm nearly burned to a cinder? I might die if I go back out there."

She laughed and went from squatting to sitting on the floor of the porch.

"Well, what you think you gonna do, sit round here all day and do nothin'?"

"I don't see you out in the fields, Shell." He glared at her.

Her long stringy hair fell down over her face as she lowered her head to think about it. "Well, I ain't been told to. I will when it gets to be pickin' time. Besides, I sweep the yard, keep clean water in the washstand, make up the garden so everybody has plenty to eat. I'm needed round here."

"Well, I'm not, and I'm not going to be. You can get sick working out there in the sun. Don't you see that?" He took the cloth off of both eyes to make sure she was looking at his pitiful condition.

She stretched her legs out in front of her and leaned up against the wall. "Well, if you ain't needed, what good are you? Why would anybody want you round?"

She stared at him, trying to determine what he might be useful for. "What did you do in the town you come from?"

"I learned to read when I was only five, Shell. I made straight *A*'s." He lifted the cloth off of his eyes and began searching its dingy gray material, trying to think of the life he had had before this. "I talked to my mother and Miss Mama, our housekeeper, about very intelligent things. I kept my toys nice and neat. You'll see when they get here. They're being shipped with all of Aunt Nelda's stuff."

"All that don't mean a hill of beans. What did you do?"

"People liked me, Shell. They thought I had nice manners. Mother said it was important to—"

"Nice manners?" She started getting up to leave. "Nice manners is makin' sure you got your hat on 'fore you scald the fire outta yourself. Nice manners is not steppin' on a cottonmouth when you're playin' in the creek." She stood shaking her head at him, then turned and walked on off the porch.

He pulled the washcloth back down over his eyes and gritted his teeth. For the first time in many days he was screaming at her in his head. *I am not, not, going back out to the fields.*

The Bend

LATE-AFTERNOON shadows painted a stretched picture of the swamp cabin on its dirt-swept front yard. The old woman rose from her rocker to the sound of someone coming up the path in front of the cabin. Her dogs watched but, knowing, did not bark.

Tuway appeared first, walking slowly.

"What you bringin' me this time?" she said, and settled back in her seat.

"They be along directly," he said. He took a seat on the steps of the front porch and reached for a pack of cigarettes in his shirt pocket.

"You ain't bein' very hospitable, leavin'm to find they own way."

"I'm bein' hospitable as I can be. They strange."

"How you mean?" She searched down the path. "Couldn't be no more strange than some of them others. You always pickin' up some stray cat."

"These two strange. She's strange. Ain't never seen

nothin' like her." He looked to the path. "If they don't come on directly, I'll go back lookin'.'"

"Why didn't you just stay with 'em in the first place?"

Tuway took a deep drag off his cigarette and blew the smoke out. " 'Cause she goes to shakin' every time I come in ten feet of her."

"Well, you do scare some peoples."

"No, it ain't that. She scared of all mens. She scared of everybody 'cept the boy. He the only one she let close." He dropped his cigarette and stood up. "Here they come." He backed away to the other end of the porch.

The little boy, perhaps five or six, and the woman had come into the clearing that was the front yard.

"Here it is," Tuway said. "Just like I told you. Nothin' here but us. She"—he pointed to the old woman—"she help you."

The little boy tugged at his mother's arm. "Come on, Mama."

The woman walked slowly forward, being pulled by the boy. "Don't need no help," she said.

She was close enough now for the old woman to get a good look, and she winced at what she saw. A cut on one arm was bleeding through the bandages. A light brown face that had been badly beaten, and her head—her head was shaved bald.

As the girl came closer, she watched the man out of the corner of her eye. Once she stopped and stared at him. He moved a few more feet away. Only then did she begin walking toward the house again. She finally reached the front porch and let the old woman take her hand and lead her inside.

Tuway walked over and took a seat on the porch steps to wait. The smoke from his cigarette rose straight up through damp evening air as the sun dropped slowly behind the ragged line of pines and water oaks that circled the world of his mother's cabin. How many times, he wondered, and for how many years had he sat watching this scene? It was the first thing he remembered of his childhood, sitting here with his mother, later with his friends, watching the night close in around him. The evening call of a screech owl came from somewhere off in the swamp. Screech owls were supposed to be death omens, but he knew that was an old wives' tale. It was actually a very soothing sound, coming at regular intervals, measuring time.

He knew he could have gone to Chicago like the others. He could be there now, watching this same sun disappear behind tall buildings; catching a whiff of the stockyards; getting ready for a night on the town after payday; but he didn't go or he couldn't go—which was it? In his mind he listed the reasons—or were they excuses?—again. She was getting older now and she needed him. He owed it to her. She was the reason he had survived. Besides, who was up there for him? Besides, if he left, who would do, could do, what he did? Somebody had to. More and more people were hard-pressed to find farming work, and when they did find it and had one or two dry years, the debt got so bad, there was no way of keeping up.

Now, he said to himself, say the real reason. Because, up there, everybody would stare at him and make remarks about the way he looked. Down here, everybody knew him. Everybody was used to the way he looked. In the end, he always reminded himself of this when he was listing the reasons. This helped him look at himself square in the face and not back away from the obvious. He might love this old place, but he would never know just how much with the other weighing so heavy in opposition. So what if he didn't look like he did? Then would he love it enough to stay? He always got to this point and gave up. He couldn't imagine what he would be like if he didn't look the way he looked.

Tuway got up, went to the wall, and lifted a lantern off its nail, then pulled the glass globe up to light the wick. He placed it on the railing that was at the other end of the porch from the swing, where he took a seat. Immediately, night creatures began to circle the lantern. He watched as moths as big as his fist and tiny flying insects no larger than grains of sand began their dances around the light. They never seemed satisfied, so drawn to the thing that might kill them if they ventured too close.

He counted the time his mother and the other two had been inside by the six cigarettes he smoked before the screen door opened. The old woman came to sit in her rocker, opposite the swing.

He waited a few minutes to ask so as not to appear too interested.

"She be all right?"

"We'll see." The old woman looked out at the night. "Some white man done messed with her bad."

CHAPTER 12

JOHN thought that a week of nights and days must have passed as he lay there on the porch radiating heat like some glowing furnace coal. After awhile, he found that if he stayed very still, with his arms straight out beside him, his legs slightly bent so as not to touch the backs to anything, he could be fairly comfortable. He eased his glasses back on over his burned ears and lay there, afraid to move, staring up at the porch ceiling for hours.

Nothing up under the tin roof moved without his knowledge. In the morning, after everyone had gone to work, he could hear Aunt Nelda going about her chores, scrubbing out pans, banking the stove fire for later use. He watched dirt daubers as they flew about the business of making mud houses along the crossbeam that ran above the kitchen door. Around eight o'clock every morning, a sparrow came to sit near her abandoned nest situated in the V of crossed boards running to the tin roof. Above him and to the right, an army of ants formed a line, starting over the kitchen door and marching along a beam and down the opposite wall to a point very close to his head, before they disappeared into the porch floor. They seemed to be carrying tiny bits of cornbread.

He began to tell time by the position of the light on the rafters. In early morning, there was a cool breeze and the light hit against the underpinnings of the tin roof. At noon, they were all—ants, birds, dirt daubers—in the shade. This meant that Uncle Luther and Butch would be coming home for dinner soon. He kept the washcloth over his eyes and pretended to be asleep.

Late afternoon and there was a line of sunlight that cut across half the ceiling and porch floor before it inched closer and closer to him. Then it paled and began to blend in with the shadows as night came on.

Of course, there were times when he had to move from his porch bed. At first, he struggled to make it to the outhouse every time he had to go. At first, Shell helped him up and pointed him in the right direction. After a few times of this, he walked far enough away from the house, just out of Shell's sight, to relieve himself. One night, he realized he could stand on the edge of the porch and accomplish his mission without having to negotiate the steps. He wondered if his mother were seeing this. He didn't care. It served her right. He peed in a great arc out into the dark dirt yard, like some stray dog marking his territory.

Every afternoon after the others had eaten and left, Aunt Nelda brought him some kind of soup, chicken or whatever she had, with cornbread crumbled up on the top. She would frown, watching him as he slowly turned on his side to spoon the soup past his swollen lips. Gradually, he got so he could eat leaning up against the clapboards of the old house. Afterward, he would make great show of being exhausted and lie back down in among his quilts.

He began to feel comfortable there with the birds and ants and dirt daubers. So much so that he was irritated the morning Shell came out on the porch and told him he was well enough to go to the creek for a quick swim. "Ma said for me to go with you and make sure there's no snakes round." Shell stood there waiting for him, then turned to go.

He got up slowly to follow her. He didn't even think to ask about a bathing suit or a towel or a change of clothes for when he finished his swim. "Wait, Shell. I can't keep up," he called after her as she jumped off the back porch and he slowly negotiated the wooden steps. His feet were tender on the bottom and still too swollen on top for shoes. Of course Shell always went barefoot.

She waited for him to catch up. "Last summer was when we first went to the pond, me'n Butch," she said. "Now he don't come much anymore, but I still do." They had walked away from the back of the house, past the water pump and the outhouse, to the edge of their island afloat in a sea of cotton fields. She casually stretched the barbed wires to make a place for them to climb through the fence that bordered the back field. "Go on. I got holt of it," she said as she motioned.

He hesitated. "Are we supposed to be going through where there's not a proper opening?"

"We are, 'less you wanta walk a mile round to the gate." She pointed to the opposite side of the field that looked to be half a mile away. He bent and climbed through. They walked in among rows of cotton plants that were stronger and taller than the ones he had hoed. He was careful not to disturb this field, which, he now knew, was hard-won by some past chopper's labor. On this cotton, the blooms had died away and healthy green bolls were taking shape.

"This here, Pa and Little Luther done early on, so it's had plenty of good growin' time," she said.

"They hoed this whole field?" He looked up, trying to calculate the number of rows, but quickly gave up. He needed to concentrate on where he was going and not step on rocks or other sharp things.

"Chopped it, fertilized it, poisoned it. It's the first one he done, so it's the best. Thing is, the whole time Mamma was gone, he didn't hit a lick on them other fields. That's how come they so puny."

They walked toward a line of trees in the middle of the field. The sun shone in a cloudless sky. Morning breezes swept dust up off the ground and deposited it on cotton leaves. "We should have brought hats, Shell." He was feeling the beginning of warmth on the top of his head.

"We ain't gonna be in the sun long enough to matter," she said. Soon their feet felt the change from hot, dry dirt to the cool grass that grew up under the trees. They had come into a small woodland in the middle of the cotton field.

"This is beautiful, Shell, like a picture," he said. A creek ran through the trees, forming a draw that meandered through the landscape, saving the land from erosion when it was empty of cotton plants. At this spot, the water swelled into a pond where beavers had made a dam. The only sound was the wind passing through tulip poplar leaves high above them.

When they reached the edge of the pond, Shell wandered over and sat down, her back to a tree with branches that overhung the water. "This here is it. Help yourself."

John eyed the grass and trees growing up to the water's edge. "Are there any snakes around here, like Aunt Nelda said?"

"Nah, too grassy. Mamma's just overcautious." She took up some small rocks and pitched them in the water. Nothing moved but the circles of water traveling back to shore. "See? Nothin'. That's 'cause they like big rocks to sun on. I ain't seen any here all summer. Go jump on in. It'll feel good to your skin. I'm gonna sit here and make a dandelion army." She began to pick yellow dandelion heads off their stems.

He hesitated, remembering somewhere in the back of his mind that he should have a swimsuit on. Then he dismissed the thought, eased off his shirt, and stepped forward to the edge, letting the mud ooze between his toes. He watched the water close around the broken blisters on his ankles. It was the first time he had had a bath or what might pass for a bath since he came to Lower Peach Tree.

The water felt better than anything he could remember. He thought about this as he waded deeper and deeper out into the pond. Was it better than Sunday dinner at the Reeder Hotel in Bainbridge or the train trip he and his mother had taken to Memphis? She had always said those were the best things. He was up to his waist now and his whole body began to shake with pleasure. This was better. This was better. He had never felt this happy at Sunday dinner at the Reeder Hotel. He had liked the trip to Memphis, but he couldn't remember much about it now. He ducked his face, glasses and all, down into the water and came up only to take a breath. "Shell, I'm going to stay here all afternoon. You may go back to the house if you like, but I am definitely staying here."

Shell didn't look up from her army of dandelion tops she had assembled and was now dropping one by one into the water. "You can't. The grease Mamma put on you'll wash off after awhile and then the mosquitoes will get you, and the no-see'ums, too."

His feet squished through the muddy bottom until only his head was above water. "I don't care. A few mosquito bites couldn't hurt me." He swirled his arms slowly through the water. "My whole body is thanking me for doing this, Shell." She dropped more yellow tops into the water, then picked up a stick to swirl them around.

"Suit yourself."

They stayed this way in the cool of the pond. He, dipping his head in and out of the water, swishing his arms around in figure eights, and walking the mud bottom back and forth the length of the pond. She, playing with her dandelions, began to make a frog house by covering her foot with mud. When she had packed the mud firmly around one foot, she slipped it out to leave living quarters for the frog. She began to cover the house with dandelions, all the while explaining to him how a lady frog would come and live in this house and have her babies there.

"Why did you come here just last summer, Shell? If I were you, I would have been coming to this pond every day since I was a baby."

"We didn't live here 'til last summer. We used to lived in Mill Town, next door to my friend Melba, and we had a hose with a sprinkler to play under." She looked up and watched him swirling his arms. "That was better than this. I know it was, even if Mamma don't say it was. I know it was better."

"Because why?" He began to feel his head. The blisters had broken and left such a gooey mess of his hair, he would have to let the water slowly loosen his crusted scalp. He looked down at his arms. The dead skin was turning white. He could lift large strips of it off, like peeling a grape.

"Because we could go to the bathroom indoors and we had lights in all the rooms, that's why. All my friends was there." She had completely covered her frog house with yellow dandelions. "If Pa hadn't gone and tried to unload them packin' crates, we still would be there."

"What packing crates?" He cupped water in his hands and poured it on his hair.

"You know, packin' crates at the mill. They use'm to haul off twine in." She had begun to make a little trail leading away from the frog house, using small rocks to line the path. "The foreman said to Mamma, 'Three times was a charm and he was sorry, but it was for safety reasons, and no one would hire him, with him drinkin' like he done.'"

John had dipped his head back in the water and was half-listening to Shell. "Drinking what?"

Shell looked up at him in wonder. "Like when he gets drunk from drinkin' too much. Don't you even know that?"

"Oh, yes," he said, considering it before ducking his head in the water again. "I remember in *Treasure Island,* when Long John Silver was—" He felt her staring at him. "Of course I know all about that, Shell." He bent over quickly to hold his head underwater until the subject had passed. When he resurfaced, she had resumed making her frog house's sidewalk. He decided not to try to explain the life cycle of a frog to her. Let her think that the frog would come live in the house and have its babies. He didn't care.

After a time, he came closer to inspect her house. Then he waded back across the pond to a place where maypops grew on vines tangled in the weeds. He picked a maypop flower and brought it to her for a decoration for her frog house.

She took it, but only out of politeness. She knew maypops did not belong on frog houses.

CHAPTER 13

LATE in the afternoon, Shell said she had to go so she could get back to help with supper. "Besides, I 'spect them no-see'ums is 'bout ready to eat you alive when you get out of that water, you bein' moist and all. The later we wait, the worse it's gonna get. Them no-see'ums is worse than them mosquitoes."

He didn't care what she said. He would stay as long as there was daylight. After awhile longer, she said, "Okay, if that's the way you're gonna be. I'm goin'. I gotta get on back."

"Oh, all right, if you're going to be that way, Shell." He dragged himself out of the water. All the grease that Aunt Nelda had put on him was long gone. He could feel the no-see'ums landing on his legs. He grabbed his shirt and tried to fend them off. On the way back, the no-see'ums struck with a vengeance. Shell was right. He grabbed at himself to keep them off, and when he did that, he would slap a part of his body that was still tender from the sun and jerk back in pain. By the time they reached the porch, he was itching on every part of his body, but every time he scratched, there was more pain. John looked down, to see blood coming from the places he had been scratching. He was miserable if he scratched and miserable if he didn't. He found himself dancing around, stomping his feet, waving his arms to try to keep the tiny gnats away, just as Shell said he would.

Aunt Nelda was standing in the kitchen door, wiping her hands. "Didn't you tell him to get on back here before the gnats come out—and look at that. You don't have a speck of lotion left on you, John."

"I done told him to come on back 'fore the grease come off, but he wouldn't pay me no mind." They both stood looking at him as if he were some pitiful dog come up to the porch to beg.

"Come on, Shell." Aunt Nelda turned to go into the kitchen. "We got to get supper on the table. Get on up under them quilts, John, and Shell will bring you out some lotion and dry clothes directly."

He eased himself down in his quilts and tried not to scratch. That evening, to make matters worse, Uncle Luther said he must come to the supper table for the first time since he got burned. "If he can go swimmin', then he sure as hell's well enough not to have nobody waitin' on him. It's the ones that work that get the waitin' on."

They had cornbread and beans, squash, and tomatoes out of Shell's garden. For dessert, blackberries that Shell had picked down on the road to the swamp field.

Uncle Luther pointed his fork at John. "It's back out to the fields tomorrow." The fork went back to his plate and scooped up a mound of beans. Several beans dropped back on the plate as he shoved the rest in his mouth and began to talk. "Too much work in the fields for lolly-gaggin'."

Aunt Nelda said, "The boy ain't hardly recovered from his sunburn. Look at them blisters on his arms. Look at them pieces of skin." She reached over and stripped a large section of dead skin from his upper arm.

John noticed that the more Aunt Nelda talked to Uncle Luther, the more she began to sound like him. Uncle Luther held an empty fork in midair. "But he is re-coverin', ain't he?" He looked at Nelda with satisfaction. "Well, ain't he? And you wantin' to call the Doc out here to look at him. Think of the money we woulda wasted, and me bein' beholden to the Doc to boot."

"His skin ain't even started to peel good. I just don't think it's a good idea—"

"It don't matter what you think, Nelda. I'm the one does the thinkin' round here. He needs to learn to take care of hisself better." He took a gulp of his water. "Besides the fact I got five more days of work in the swamp field that shoulda been finished up three weeks ago." He leaned on the two back legs of his chair and took a tooth-pick out of his shirt pocket. "You want me to make a crop, Nelda. I'm makin' a crop. But it don't get done sittin' around on your butt." He shook his head no as Aunt Nelda tried to give him a bowl of blackberries. All the while, his eyes were looking around the room. Then the front two legs of his chair slammed down on the floor and he got up. "I got business in town," he said to no one, and headed to the door, grabbing his hat off the wooden peg near the door frame.

"How you gonna go?" she asked. "Don't the truck still have that dead battery?"

"I'll walk. It'll do me good."

Immediately, Aunt Nelda said, "Little Luther will go with you."

Little Luther looked up from his blackberries. "Mamma, do I have to?"

"Of course you want to go with your daddy."

Luther glared at her. "Him goin' with me or not goin' with me ain't gonna keep me from doin' what I want to do." The door slammed behind him.

"Go on with your daddy," she said.

Little Luther put his spoon down and upended his bowl to get the last of the berry juice. Then he scraped back his chair and followed his father out the door.

"Oh, those men. They do beat all." She began cleaning off the table as she told Shell to go draw more water from the pump for washing dishes. "And don't dawdle."

Aunt Nelda brightened. "As soon as we make this crop, we'll be out of this place. Have indoor water again," she called after Shell. "It won't be long."

The boy watched as she cleared plates, revolted with her, with this place, with everything. His eyes were swelling up again because of the bites on his face. His fingers could hardly bend to hold his spoon. His knuckles were cracked and bleeding from the sunburn. He held his head down and mumbled into his blackberries.

"What's that?" she said, still clearing dishes.

"I said," he said softly, "why do you do everything he says?"

"What?" She stopped what she was doing and looked at him.

He raised his head out of the bowl. "I said," he began, and then said even louder, "why?" And then louder still: "Why?" And then almost a shout: "Why do you do everything he says? Why don't you tell him to get out?" He stood up out of his chair. "And why don't you at least tell him to use good manners?"

Aunt Nelda stood there staring at him and then broke into laughter. "That's a good one. That's a real good one, just what I need to end my day, a little joke. If you don't have a lot of your mother's sass in you." She looked at him with tired eyes.

"It's not funny," he said, frustrated tears welling up. "Why do you let him rule us like that? I'm not ready to go back to the fields. It's not fair."

She put down dirty dishes, reached her hand in the pocket of her apron, and took out a crumpled pack of Lucky Strikes, then went to the stove to pick up the big box of stove matches. Coming back to the table, she sat down, got out a cigarette, and lit it. She took a deep breath of smoke and blew it on the match, putting out the flame, then let the match drop out of her hand onto the table.

Aunt Nelda looked straight at him and spoke in a voice he had never heard before. It was direct, almost menacing. "What you want me to do, smart boy? Just tell me, what plan you got in mind?" She sounded like Uncle Luther now, completely devoid of any pretense.

She took another drag on her cigarette and looked at the peeling wallpaper that some former tenant had pasted to one wall. There was only the loud ticking of his mother's clock in this room that passed for a living and eating space.

The clock, which in times past had given dignity to other rooms with its ticking and chiming, now only mocked its surroundings. It had originally belonged to Nelda's mother and had been in the living room of the mill house where Nelda and John's mother, Edna, had grown up. Nelda had always wanted it, but it had gone to her sister because she was the eldest. Before that happened, Nelda had made plans for the clock. It would not waste its life away in a tiny mill house. It would sit over the mantel of the foreman's house in Mill Town. She would not spend her life like her mother, living in the cramped quarters of an ordinary mill house. She had other plans.

Nelda was in the ninth grade when she noticed the foreman's house as she passed by it going to and from school. That would be her house. She would marry someone who was strong enough to become foreman at the mill.

She picked out Luther long before Luther even knew she existed. He was two classes ahead of her and the most popular boy in his class. Of course, Luther was no student, but grades didn't matter: Nelda had brains enough for both of them. Luther was big, and nobody pushed him around. He would make a perfect mill foreman. And she was pretty back then, prettier than her sister. It would be no problem to get Luther. It was only a matter of time before that clock would sit on the mantel in the foreman's house. It had been an honorable and respectable ambition for a girl in her position. All the other girls in Mill Town had no idea what their future might be. They just drifted along, but not Nelda and her sister.

Edna, the firstborn, had worked hard at her studies and won a scholarship to the University of Alabama. Nelda had worked on Luther.

The plan had come unraveled when her mother up and died and left the clock to her sister. By that time, Nelda had dropped out of school to marry Luther, and Edna had married John's father just before he left to go fight in Europe.

She took another drag and blew out the smoke in large clouds that hung in air already saturated with the smells of supper. She jerked her head around to John.

"Just tell me, smart boy! What you want me to do?"

"You could tell him to leave and . . . and never come back or, or if he wants to stay he'll have to be nice."

She looked at him and then burst out laughing. "My goodness, but you just have a head full of sense, don't you?" She shook her head in mock agreement. "Let's see now. He should leave his own house. He rented this here house from the Rawlstons, providin' we make a crop and give them a share. It's his house. It's his crop. Had to get furnishin' from the bank. The Rawlstons wouldn't even scotch us for the seed and fertilizer. Now we gotta pay that back. You got any other brilliant ideas, city boy?" Her fingers mashed the dead match, grinding it into the wood of the old table.

He had no idea what she was talking about, but he still persisted. "You and I could leave here. We could leave here and maybe take Shell and . . ." He heard how foolish it sounded.

"Where would we go—to the mill? What would I do? They only hire men. That's where we was 'fore he drunk hisself out of that job. To the okra factory? They only hire niggers. They wouldn't give me the time of day. To another town, with not one speck of money and no kin left in the world since your mother had to up and die on me?"

She pulled so hard on the next drag of the cigarette that the glow seemed to run halfway up the white paper. Leaning her head back, she let out big puffs of smoke, as if she was going to blow smoke rings, but it came out as big clouds that she looked into as they hung in the musty air. "Hell, I didn't even finish high school. I was so antsy to—" She stopped and seemed to conjure up pictures out of the smoke. "Before he started drinkin' heavy, Luther used to be . . ." She reached over to the pile of dishes at the end of the table and jammed the Lucky Strike out in a leftover tomato slice. "Never mind."

Then she got up and started scraping dishes again, silent for a long time. When she finished, her mood seemed to brighten. "Well," she said, pushing her hair out of her eyes and talking in her old voice. "Well, just never you mind. There's gonna be changes round here. I got me a plan. Just you wait till our stuff comes from your mama."

Nelda hadn't wanted her sister to die, but she had, and now, for Nelda, it was like manna from heaven. All those things, things she had never dreamed of having, were on their way to her. The possibilities were endless: She could keep some; she could sell some. She said out loud, without seeming to think of John, "Heck, I might even sell it all and take a trip to Memphis." She smiled. "Or somethin' else you might not even think of.

"Then we'll see," she said. She stacked the last of the dishes in the open sink, waiting for Shell's water. "Then we'll see."

The Bend

HIS real mother had not wanted him. She had said as much when she came to Mama Tuway to have the cards read.

The old woman wanted him from the moment she saw him bundled up in the worn-out blanket his mother had wrapped him in. His face was covered with irregular white patches. At first, she had thought it was a birthmark, but upon further inspection she had seen that his coloring was like this all over. There was a large patch of white around one eye and down the right side of his jaw. The rest of his face was black or a very dark brown, except for his left ear, which was white. Two of the fingers on each hand were white and the rest were dark brown. A large spot in the middle of his stomach and part of one leg were white. Other than that, he was a perfect baby. He had dark, intelligent eyes that followed her when she moved around the room. He was bigger than most babies his age and he looked perfectly healthy. She was fascinated. She loved things that didn't fit into natural patterns: the tree that grew misshapen, the three-legged cat. To her, such things were far from being freaks of nature; she considered them omens, special gifts to be interpreted by the right person, and, in this case, she knew she was the right person.

That night as the kerosene lantern cast shadows on the back wall of the cabin, she had known what she would read in the cards even before she took them up.

She had added reading the cards to all her other skills because people had assumed she could, living alone in the cabin in the swamp with all the herbs growing in pots on her front porch, and the lawn ornaments, whirligigs and such. She had first put them there because she thought they were pretty, and she had been amused when others assumed they were to ward off evil spirits. Some late afternoons, coming back to her cabin from the Bend, she would smile to herself as she walked up the path in the fading light. There was a carved wood statue on an old tree stump and wind chimes hung from branches. Of course she did have a bottle tree to take care of any serious spirits that might be hanging around.

All these things did give the place a certain feel . . . and she did have a way with medicine. It had been another skill passed down to her from her mother. Her mother had practiced because there was no other place to go for medical help. There were still not many other places to go that her people trusted.

The girl with the strange baby had heard about Mama Tuway and had walked all the way into the Bend from another county. Mama Tuway suspected that her parents had thrown her out once they had seen the baby.

She knew from the beginning she would be able to convince the girl. "I see you alone, travelin' north," she had said the first night. She had droned on and on in this manner until she could see that the girl was beginning to catch on.

"I don't know as how I can handle no child with no two ways 'bout him like this here one," the girl said.

After staying with Mama Tuway for three days, she had left the baby with the old woman and headed north to a new life.

Even though she was in her forties when she got Tuway, people had not been surprised when she showed up with him. They had expected as much of her. They would have been disappointed if she had adopted an ordinary child.

That had been over thirty years ago, and divine intervention as far as the baby was concerned. Instead of letting him become the freak some people might have thought he was, she had made him into something, someone, to be respected, maybe even feared.

When he was a small boy, she had begun drumming into him that he was better than everyone else, that he knew more than most, that God had given him special powers. Mama Tuway had never said what these powers were, and she thought he had suspected from the time he was old enough to reason that she was not telling him the truth, but he had tried to live up to her prophecy. She told him that the marks on his face and body meant he was destined to be a leader. He wanted to become what she thought he was.

Through his childhood, he had come to see that people were afraid of him when they saw him for the first time. He was always big for his age and quite handsome, but people seldom saw that, and he was too shy to give himself another dimension in their eyes. He had never used his unusual size and appearance in a cruel way. Behind the steely-eyed stare, which he employed on occasion, there was nothing to be mad about, no reason to take revenge. The old woman loved him so, and he knew it.

She had him saying his letters by the time he was able to toddle around the cabin. She had gathered up what books she could find that had been brought by the federal government when they had come to the Bend during the Depression.

Once there had been a school, a blacksmith shop, a gristmill. All of this had slowly disappeared after the Roosevelt administration ended, but she had taken advantage of everything that was available when they were there. Eventually the government, like James Randolph Kay, had come and gone, leaving the Benders to their own devices, and good riddance all. White people never helped—all the time building things that were not needed or wanted—coming and going at their own pleasure. Now the children played on the ruins of what had been the Kay plantation house and the people held church services in what was once a government-funded community center. She had used the books that were left behind to teach herself and then to teach Tuway. He had been a quick learner, sometimes getting ahead of her.

By the time he started to the one-room schoolhouse in the Bend, he was well ahead of all the other children. This combination of strange looks and quick intelligence had set him even further apart from others. He had made some friends, but, for the most part, he spent his growing years free to roam the swamp and the Bend alone. No one ever thought of him as you might think of an ordinary person. No one ever thought of speaking to him for any reason other than to ask a favor. No one ever really saw him.

His mother was fine with this way of life. She liked to be looked upon as special. She had had an earlier life, been married, had known what it was to be ordinary, and now, he thought, she delighted in being unique.

As he grew older, he spent most of his time working or doing for other people. All of his childhood friends were married and living in the Bend by now or they had moved away. But he, he had not even been with other women except for a few trips to Selma. Except for his mother, he was so alone that he dared not give up any part of himself to thinking about it . . . and had not until the day she came.

That afternoon, the afternoon he first saw her, she had been sitting in Cal's car, waiting for Tuway to help her, like he had helped so many others. She had been beat up by someone, maybe once, maybe hundreds of times. He couldn't tell, and she wasn't talking. He had brought her to the swamp and left her, but he had never really left her. After that first day, after he had seen her sitting there, she had never left his mind.

CHAPTER 14

THE next morning, John made a great show of his aching body as he dressed for work right before first light. It went unnoticed.

He put on an old pair of Little Luther's coveralls that Aunt Nelda had cut down to size, one of his own dress shirts with long sleeves, and a big straw hat Aunt Nelda found for him.

They carried new equipment today, fertilizer that was stored in a small room just behind Little Luther's bedroom. It was used as storage for sacks of poison and fertilizer and any farm materials that should not be exposed to the weather. All other equipment was leaned up against the house or deposited in a lean-to a few yards away.

The corresponding room on the other side of the dogtrot served as Uncle Luther and Aunt Nelda's bedroom. Shell slept in what had been a large closet off the kitchen area. She hung around as Uncle Luther opened the outside door to the fertilizer room. Cloth bags with brightly colored drawings on the outside were stacked against the walls. When the sacks were empty of fertilizer, the drawings could be cut out and sewn up into baby dolls that could be stuffed with cotton right out of the fields. It was an enticement for the Negro farmers, who were mainly employed in making cotton crops. All of the baby dolls had black baby-doll faces.

"Will you bring me back a sack so I can make a dolly when you finish?" Shell asked.

"What's that?" Uncle Luther was hoisting a sack on his shoulder.

"A sack, when it's empty, so I can make a baby doll like that there." She pointed to the drawings on one of the sacks that remained on the floor. "Mama said she would help me." He grunted as he heaved another sack on his shoulder. "Don't forget," she said.

Uncle Luther pointed to a hand spreader sitting in the corner. John took it up to carry to the field. Little Luther carried one sack of fertilizer, resting repeatedly on the way down to the fields.

Uncle Luther hauled his two sacks down the rutted road that led to the same cotton field they had worked the first day John had come. By the time they reached the field, Luther's back was wet with sweat. He dumped the sacks on the ground, motioning for John to bring him the spreader. Then he sat on one of the sacks and began to check the spreader's various straps and hinges. "Come on over here, Little Luther." Little Luther dumped his sack and Uncle Luther began strapping the spreader to the boy's chest.

"This ain't gonna work," Little Luther said, almost to himself.

Uncle Luther's only comment was to jerk the straps tighter to hold the spreader in place. Then he reached into his pocket and produced a pocketknife to slice off the top of a sack. He began dumping the fertilizer into the spreader until it was half-full, a weight almost too heavy for the boy.

"Waste of time," Little Luther mumbled.

"What's that, boy?" Uncle Luther reached down to retrieve the knife he had stuck in the ground.

Given an opening, Little Luther took it. "It's a waste of time, Pa. This here cotton's too little. It'll never make it to pickin'. We're out here in the hot for nothin'."

Uncle Luther wiped the blade on his overall pants. "We ain't out here for nothin'. This field'll make it if it gets a good soakin' or two."

"Besides that, we need a tractor. Everybody uses a tractor." Little Luther stared out over the field.

"I'm the one knows 'bout cotton, not you." He swung Little Luther around and tightened his front shoulder straps. "Now git."

Little Luther began to walk forward among the rows of cotton, turning the hand crank on the spreader. Grains of fertilizer shot out as from a small rain cloud, skipping off the leaves of scraggly cotton plants, landing in dried, hoe-cracked earth. Little Luther walked on down, following the rows, covering everything within a six-foot distance of the spreader. Midway on his trip back toward them, he ran out of fertilizer and walked back empty.

"Can't you do no more than that?" Luther filled the spreader this time until Little Luther staggered under the load.

"That's all I can carry, Pa." He walked awkwardly out in the field, back arched as a counterbalance, but he managed only a small increase in distance on his next pass.

Luther leaned on one of the fence posts, watching. John stood at a distance, seeing the sun hit the top of the fertilizer spreader and reflect back up into Little Luther's apathetic face as he walked, empty of fertilizer, back up to his father.

"Shit." Luther spit tobacco juice on the dry ground. "Take it off. I mighta knowed you wasn't man enough."

Little Luther began loosening the straps of the spreader.

He and John stood watching as Uncle Luther poured fertilizer into the top of the spreader. The first fertilizer sack was empty. Uncle Luther looked down at the sack lying on the ground. There was the outline of the back of a little baby doll on one side of the sack. He flipped the sack over with his foot. The face of the colored baby doll was drawn on the front. Assembly instructions were printed on the side of the sack. Uncle Luther took out his knife and slit through the sack several times, making it useless. "Ain't havin' none of mine playin' with no nigger baby dolls."

Then he heaved the spreader's weight onto his shoulders and began to walk. He made the trip up and back with fertilizer to spare. After three trips, sweat was pouring off his face. "What the hell are you two lookin' at? Go on back up to the house and get hoes and go to hoein' that field." He pointed to the field they were standing in.

"This ain't nothin' but scrub, Pa. This ain't got ten plants a row."

In one motion, Luther let the shoulder straps from the spreader slide off of his arms and took two or three steps toward Little Luther. Practiced at this maneuver, the boy stepped back the same number of steps. "Okay, okay. I'm goin'."

His father reached forward and grabbed at his shirt. "What did you say, boy?"

"Yes, *sir,* yes, *sir,* I'm goin'."

"That's better." His dignity preserved, Luther retrieved his hat, which had fallen in the dust, slapping it on his pants leg to clear the dry Black Belt dirt. He looked up and saw John and hit him hard on the back with his hat. "You, too. Git, and bring me another sack of fertilizer when you come. I'm supposed to use up all the bank brung. Might as well do it in this field."

They walked back toward the house. "Do banks bring fertilizer?" John asked. Little Luther seemed not to hear him.

"I ain't scared of him when he ain't been drinkin'," Little Luther said. John said nothing, still feeling the hot burn of Luther's hat across his back.

CHAPTER 15

THEY hoed all morning and after a quick dinner, brought back more fertilizer sacks. The boys worked all afternoon in a field full of weeds. Sometimes, John was hard put to find the cotton plant he was supposed to be nurturing. They were smaller than the weeds and not as healthy-looking. In the afternoon, when they were at the end of a row on the far side of the field from Uncle Luther, he noticed that Little Luther would sit down and rest. He began to do the same when he saw that Uncle Luther's back was to them. He unbuttoned his shirt-sleeves so that the cuffs would fall down over the top of his hands, saving every possible inch of skin from the sun.

In the late afternoon, they came together at the fencerow to drink cool water Shell had brought out from the house.

"Oh, my baby dolls," Shell said as she stood looking down at what by now was a pile of empty, ripped fertilizer sacks. "Pa, you promised to save me one."

He stopped drinking long enough to look at what she meant. "Shell, you don't want them nigger babies. I'll get you a good baby doll when the cotton comes in."

"Yes I did. I wanted it." She knelt down and began to sift through the pile to see if anything was worth saving.

"No you don't." He stepped over and put his foot on the sacks. "If you do, you ain't none of mine." He took one last drink and threw the remaining water out of the tin ladle onto the cracked dirt. "You'll see. It'll be nigh on twice as big, and it'll have a china face, too. Now get on back to the house and don't you be forgettin' to bring more water directly."

Shell stood up out of the dirt, still looking down at the ripped-up baby dolls. Finally, she turned and walked back toward home. She was some distance away when she turned and came back. "Mamma says don't forget—you promised to get the mail today."

"I ain't got no time to get no mail." He looked around. "John'll go. Go on to town and get the mail, John."

John looked up from watching a ladybug on a cotton leaf. "How do I do that? I don't know where town is." Shell and Little Luther laughed out loud. Uncle Luther smiled and looked at Shell. "If I didn't know he was a city boy, I'd think he didn't have the brains God give a crow. Ain't that right, sister?" Shell tried to smile at her father.

"It's where you come in on the train, boy," he said. "See that road out yonder?" He pointed in the direction of a dirt road off in the distance. "You take that road and walk it 'til you get to a paved road; then you turn right and keep goin' 'til you come to town. Turn right at the Texaco and keep walkin' 'til you see the post office. Now that ain't hard, is it?" He shook his head, grinning at Shell and Little Luther.

"No, sir," John said.

"Well, don't just stand there."

"Now, right now, you want me to go?"

"Course right now. Just go in the post office and say you come for the Spraig mail. That don't take big-road walkin' sense." The three of them looked at him.

He stared back at them, then slowly got up off the dirt and turned to go.

"Get back here 'fore it turns dark or you'll miss supper."

John began walking through the cotton plants in the direction of the road in the distance. "How far—" But he said it in such a small voice, they didn't hear him, and he was too embarrassed to turn and go back to them and ask.

He walked on toward the dirt road that ran between fence lines separating two fields. When he got to the fence, instead of crawling through, he stood on the bottom wire, holding on to a fence post, to look back at what were now the small figures of Uncle Luther and Little Luther still sitting in the field on fertilizer sacks. He climbed over the wire and hopped down to the other side onto the road. This must have been the one they had taken with Judge Vance's driver. There were deeply eroded tread paths that might have been the same ones they had bounced over that first night. Now that night seemed months ago.

John looked down at his hands. The skin was still peeling from around the fingers, but the blisters on the palms were beginning to callus over. He was to go all the way into town and back by himself, a thing he had never imagined his mother letting him do when he lived in Bainbridge. In the space of a few weeks, he had never in his life been so restricted and so set free.

From time to time, he would hop up on one of the low

barbed wires to make sure Uncle Luther was still there and that he, John, was where he was supposed to be.

When he had walked two miles or so, the asphalt road appeared out of nowhere in between rows of cotton on both sides. There was no road sign to start one or end the other. He sat down on the edge of the paved road to empty the dirt out of his shoes, then got up, turned right, and began to walk along the edge of the blacktop highway. He had never actually walked on a highway before. He had ridden over one many times but never actually touched one. He studied the loose pieces of asphalt on the edges of the road baking to the point of melting in the sun, the debris left by other travelers, puffs of cotton fallen off some gin-bound wagon, discarded cigarette packs. He stepped on each of the Lucky Strike packages he saw and repeated the old rhyme his next-door neighbor in Bainbridge had taught him. "One, two, three, luck for me." He hoped it might help in some way.

Queen Anne's lace and yellow daisies grew in intermittent patches. Every so often, he could see, off in the flat distance, a car or truck coming toward him or he could hear one coming up behind. They passed in a swirl of wind, kicking up loose gravel and dust. He kept his head down, the better to go unnoticed.

After what seemed another mile or so, he came over a small rise in the land, and off in the distance were the trees and houses of Lower Peach Tree. The town meandered off to his right, built almost perpendicular to the road he stood on. Like everything else he had seen in this country, it seemed to have been born out of an accommodation to the surrounding land. There was a concentration of businesses and churches on the main road. As he walked closer, he counted four church steeples. Houses were built around connecting roads that thinned themselves out at the edge of town, until they gave way once again to the rolling fields. The Texaco station was right where Uncle Luther had placed it, situated across the highway, facing the main street. He turned right onto the sidewalk that began at this point. A man in a Texaco shirt and khaki trousers watched him as he passed. John got as far as raising the fingers of his left hand to wave, then thought better of it and kept his arms at his side. A few cars were parked in the painted slots that ran out from the sidewalk. He passed Eller's Five and Dime and the Piggly Wiggly. McKinna's Hardware had a new Dumont television displayed in the window. Three people, one white and two colored, stood watching vague figures on a snowy black-and-white screen. John watched for a minute, couldn't make out what the picture was supposed to be, then kept walking in the direction of the post office. The few people, white and black, who were on the street seemed to notice him but didn't speak, and he felt no obligation, either.

In times past, she had always had him speak to everyone he knew. In those days, he would have rushed to open the door for the lady he saw coming out of the Piggly Wiggly, arms loaded with groceries. He heard a faraway train whistle. The station must be somewhere on the other end of town. He crossed the street to gain the post office two blocks away.

On every corner there was a church: first the Baptist, then the Methodist, Presbyterian, Episcopal, even a small Church of Christ. This town was tiny compared with the town he used to live in, but it seemed to have just as many churches.

A square brick building that sat under a large oak tree, the post office gave notice to the outside world that the town of Lower Peach Tree did in fact exist. There was the

The Bend

From the time Tuway was a child, she had prepared him for the day when he would go off to Tuskegee. He had not been old enough to know what the word meant when he first heard it. She had talked about Tuskegee so much that he had always thought of it as something that was inevitable.

It was not until he was fifteen that he began to question her. Why did he have to go? He hated the way people stared at him when they saw him for the first time. This would be a strange place full of strangers. They would all stare.

She would try to placate him. "Peoples might stare at first, but that don't matter. After awhile, they get used to you. You gonna like it. Be just like here at the Bend. Why, look here," she said. "You remember that time last month we went to town, that Saturday—we went in and had us some barbecue at The Store. Nobody paid us no mind."

He noticed she failed to mention that on Saturdays in Lower Peach Tree there were only colored people in town anyway and on that Saturday a good number of them were neighbors from the Bend.

He would try to argue with her, but she always had an answer for all of his objections. After a time, he would give up, until, on some later occasion, the subject would surface again and he could feel his jaw clinching.

"What about clothes?" he had asked. "I ain't gonna have clothes enough to stay there. I probably ain't got the right kinda clothes anyhow."

She looked at him with a sly smile. "You sit down right there." She motioned him to sit down at the kitchen table and then disappeared into her bedroom. She came back minutes later carrying two shirts. "Done made up these here with cloth I got from the rollin' store." She held up the shirts made of dark green cotton cloth, then brought them closer for him to examine. "Look at that sewin'. Nearly 'bout put my eyes out with that stitchin'. Them stitches so small, you can't see'm." She pulled the kerosene light on the table closer so he might get a better look. "And I'm gonna do more once I get some different-colored cloth. By the time I finish, you be better dressed than any man at Tuskegee."

"That's nice, Mama," he said. That was all he could say as he sat there trying to pretend interest in the tiny stitching, trying to make himself appreciate her hard work. Once again, he let the subject drop.

When he was sixteen, he had taken a more belligerent attitude. "Ain't no reason for me to go on off up there. Jimmy and Calvin, they my same age, they ain't thinkin' 'bout goin'. Calvin's daddy say he wouldn't let him go off and get outta all the work needs to get done."

The arguments always seemed to start at the kitchen table. This time, they were eating supper. He took a piece of cornbread and dipped it in his bowl of stew. "Who gonna keep firewood, fix the roof, all them things need to be done?" He took a bite of cornbread. "No, can't go and leave all them things. People be sayin' I'm not doin' my duty. Can't do it."

"Yes you can, and you gonna do it. How you think I got along before you come? I done it then and I can do it now. Besides"—she looked at him and smiled—"you gonna do them things when you come home on vacation. Tuskegee so close," she said, "you ain't gonna be more than a day away."

He ate his stew in silence.

She had made all the inquiries. She had spent hours sitting at the kitchen table at night in the light of the kerosene lantern, writing and rewriting a letter to Tuskegee. The more she did, the more determined he became not to go.

Finally, on the week before he was to leave, she started packing his clothes. She had saved up to buy him a suitcase made of heavy cardboard, and when he came in from working in the fields of a neighbor, she had the suitcase full of his belongings.

He was tired and hot and the sight made him furious. He walked over and slammed down the top. "I never said I was goin' and I ain't goin'." They stared at each other. "I'm a grown man and I ain't goin'," he said, and walked out to the basin on the porch to clean off the day's dirt. When he finished drying his face and hands, he came back to sit at the kitchen table and wait for his supper.

It was a long time before she came out of his room. When she did, she didn't make a move to get his supper, but sat down opposite him at the table. She took the kerosene lantern that was between them, moved it to one side, and rested her hands flat out on the table.

"I wanta tell you somethin'." Her hands felt the wood table, looking for the right words. "Guess I was too shamed to tell you before, thought you might be shamed of me if you knew." She paused again, watching her hands. "You know everybody always sayin' Mama Tuway knows this and Mama Tuway can do that. Everybody always askin' me what to do, how to do it."

He looked down at the table. This wasn't going to be like the other times when they had argued. Her voice was low. She seemed self-conscious and uncomfortable, shifting in her chair from side to side. She cleared her throat.

"It was a long time ago. I was a little older than you right now."

She stopped and waited for him to look up at her.

"Remember how I used to tell you stories about my farmin' days, when I was a girl married to James?"

"Yes'm." He kept his eyes on the table but sat back in his chair and rested his hands inside the top of his bib overalls.

"Told you all 'bout makin' a crop. We had that one mule, Sadie. We would commence plowin' before light and stay out in the fields 'til the sun was settin'." She smiled, remembering. "Me and James would go to church ever Sunday and pray for rain once we got them seeds in the ground, and then we'd go on back and pray for it to stop once them seeds was up and sproutin'."

"Yes'm," he said.

"Then after that, we lived in them fields, choppin' and

hoein' dawn to dark." She kept her hands out on the table, running them over the rough surface. "I ain't sayin' we wasn't happy. We was happy as can be, even if we was workin' hard every day. We knew if the weather treated us right and the weevils didn't come, we had us a chance to make somethin'.'"

"Yes'm, you told me 'bout that."

"One summer—it was the summer before James passed—everything was goin' right. The rain come when it should and the sun come out when it should. The bolls on them cotton plants was so thick, look like decorated Christmas trees with all them white balls poppin' open.

"We picked cotton 'til we could hardly stand up, but we was so excited 'bout the crop, didn't even cross our minds it was hard work. Had to borrow two extra wagons to take it all to the gin; our wagon wasn't enough. Started out at midnight so we could be close to the front of the line when the gin opened in the mornin'.

"I can still see me sittin' there on that gin wagon, goin' down the road in the moonlight, so proud, tears was wellin' up in my eyes.

"Gettin' there, seein' all that white bein' sucked up in the ginnin' house. Made up a whole five-hundred-pound bale. We went around and watched it roll out of the back of the gin onto the loadin' platform.

" 'Bout then, we went on inside the office and ask the man, 'What you givin'?'" She looked up at the ceiling and pressed her lips together. "And he say"—she was shaking her head now—"and he say, 'See it wrote up there on the board. I'm givin' twenty-nine and a quarter, best price in the county.' That's how he had it wrote out on the board, twenty-nine and a quarter, not the numbers, but wrote out. And he say, 'That's what I'm gonna give you, twenty-nine times that fine five-hundred-pound bale you got out there.' He counted out the cash; then he say, 'And here's your quarter,' and he give us a twenty-five-cent piece."

"What?" Tuway looked up at her face.

"I was all of nineteen years old, had maybe three years of schoolin', and I didn't know no better. I could read some but didn't know nothin' 'bout numbers."

She brought her hand up to her mouth as if she could stop the words. "That's the God's own truth; I didn't know no better."

"He cheated you."

"I know that now, but I didn't know no better then." She pointed a finger at him. "And you wouldn't know no better if I hadn't learned you your numbers."

He looked back down at the table.

"In them days, what he cheated us 'mounted to four, maybe five days of pickin' in the fields." She looked down at rough paper-thin skin covered with scars from years of reaching for boll after boll after prickly boll.

"But the cheatin' ain't the worst part, Tuway. That ain't the worst part." Her hands clasped each other for comfort. "After all them years, the worst part is thinkin' of me actin' like some ignorant pickaninny.

"We walked out of there grinnin' like we was on top of the world, and that white man lookin' after us like we was God's own fool."

She swallowed hard and shook her head.

"It was a month after, we come to find out, standin' on the sidewalk in Lower Peach Tree, listenin' to a man talkin' 'bout pricin' to his boy. My whole body started to shakin' right there on the sidewalk. He said, 'Now the first thing the man gonna try to pull on you is to say a quarter same thing as a twenty-five-cent piece.' I was afraid I was gonna be sick right there on the street.

"Me and James didn't say nothin' all the way home, thinkin' 'bout all them hours in the field.

"That night, I made me a vow, wasn't gonna never let that happen again, never. Next time the rollin' store come through, took my money and bought me a book on figurin'." She nodded her head in the direction of her bedroom. "Still in there. Same one I done used to teach you.

"That next spring, James took sick." She looked over to the flickering lantern. "I coulda used that money to bury him decent when he passed."

Tuway couldn't think of anything to say. They sat there in silence. He could hear the early-evening noises coming from outside the cabin and wished he was in the woods someplace far away from here. He couldn't imagine her not knowing all the answers. He couldn't fathom someone getting the best of her. She had told him a story about a person he didn't know.

Mama Tuway slowly reached her hand to pull the lantern back to the center of the table. Light from the top of the lantern reflected onto her face, making her look like someone he was not sure of. Her eyes watched him across the light. "White man's gonna cheat you. I been knowin' that all along, but damned if me and mine gonna be so ignorant we can't look down on him when he goes to doin' it."

She slapped her hand on the table. The light of the lantern flickered. "Look here at me, boy."

His eyes moved to look straight at her, but his hands still rested in his bib overalls; nothing else of his body moved.

"That ain't gonna happen to you. You too much a part of me. Listen to me, boy."

He was listening.

"You ain't gonna let bein' different cheat you for the rest of your life. That's why you goin' to Tuskegee." She let the tears run down her face. "There's no worse feelin' than somebody takin' you for the fool."

He had never seen her cry before. In all their years together, she had never cried in front of him. He put his head down so she couldn't see the tears in his own eyes.

The next week, he took up his new suitcase and walked out of the Bend all the way to the main highway to catch the bus to Tuskegee.

CHAPTER 16

I T became a routine. Every few days, after being in the fields until midafternoon, Uncle Luther and Little Luther would head home and John would be sent to the post office. Uncle Luther seemed to be less and less interested in the cotton fields, or, as time wore on, he was more and more overwhelmed by the task. There had been no rain since John had come to live with them. He could dig down with his hoe as much as a foot and there was no sign of moisture. The cotton plants in these fields were too young to hold their own against the sun.

As they went about their morning chores, Uncle Luther would say, "Don't get behind, boy, or I'll send you to town right now." At first, he puzzled over this; then he came to realize that Uncle Luther must think he hated going to town because he, Uncle Luther, would hate it. In fact, John looked forward to walking the road to town.

One afternoon as he reached the dirt road, he stood on the barbed wire and noticed that Little Luther sat on the ground whittling and Uncle Luther was walking away in the opposite direction from their house.

That day on the highway to town, he saw two little colored boys with sticks walking up either side of the road. They fished around in the grass, looking for soft-drink bottles. When they found one, thrown out by some passing motorist, they would whoop and dance around before placing it in a burlap bag they carried. When he asked, they told him, "Mr. Tex down at the station give three cent a bottle."

He began to look for old bottles on his trips to town. He found three. Mr. Tex mashed the button on the cash register at the filling station and gave him nine cents without comment. It was easy. On his way home that afternoon, he buried the money under a big rock that was near the entrance to the dirt road.

The afternoon trips to town gave him his own routine. He looked for bottles the length of the paved road. When he came into town, after he had stopped by Mr. Tex, he would pause at the hardware store to see what, if anything, was on the television. Usually, it was a test pattern. He would wander into the Piggly Wiggly to look at the food. When he had saved up enough under his money rock, he would treat himself to a candy bar, spending long minutes in front of the candy display, trying to choose the one that most suited his liking that day. Striding out of the Piggly Wiggly, he was amazed at how wonderful his Goo Goo Cluster tasted. He never remembered candy tasting like that before, and his mother had bought sweets for him all the time.

He began to notice the women who sat on their porches as he passed the mostly white wood-frame houses that lined the main street in between the Piggly Wiggly and the post office. Very few, if any, had air conditioning and so families spent their afternoons sitting under porch ceiling fans, cooled by a breeze that swayed large baskets of Boston ferns hung out over the railings. The porches were like outdoor living rooms, with lamps and tables, chairs with brightly colored cushions, and radios tuned to stations in Montgomery or Selma. Sometimes he saw children sitting on the floor playing board games while their mothers snapped beans or peeled potatoes for supper. He didn't wave, but they did, or they would smile as he passed. He would look quickly away. On a few occasions, he saw Mrs. Vance or Mrs. Vance and the Judge walking along the sidewalk. He would duck behind the nearest tree until she, or they, had passed. John would stand, his back up against the bark of an old oak, remembering the night on the train when he had met them, the Judge's handshake, his stumbling clumsiness in the aisle, the delicious food at supper. The memory would bring a knot to his stomach. He would have to walk long distances for it to go away.

When he got to the post office, there never was much mail, usually advertisements or the Baptist church bulletin. Aunt Nelda said she used to attend long ago and that someday she would go back.

Then one afternoon, sliding across the wood counter straight from Mr. Dover's hand, there was a letter addressed to him. It had his name on the front: "John McMillan, Lower Peach Tree, Alabama."

"Well, pick it up, son," Mr. Dover said. "You're the only John McMillan we got round these parts. Looks to me like it's from your hometown, from up in Bainbridge."

"How do you know I come from Bainbridge?" he asked, still staring at the letter.

"I'm the postmaster, boy; I know everything that goes on around here. I know you come from way, way up above the gnat line. I know you 'bout killed yourself out there in them fields awhile back. I even know you ain't too partial to Mrs. Vance, the way you sneak round every time you see her comin'." He smiled when he said this and called back over his shoulder to his assistant. "Ain't that right, Clovis?"

Clovis grinned through a missing front tooth. "He skitters round here like a rabbit. Scared some woman is gonna say boo to him."

"I am not either." He grabbed the mail and walked out slowly, afraid he might be skittering if he moved too fast.

He waited until he got to his money rock at the head of the dirt road to open the letter; he had put it in his pocket and held tight to it all the way there. It was from his next-door neighbor in Bainbridge. He knew that by the handwriting on the outside. All the way to the rock, he imagined what it would say: that they missed him; that he must come back to them; that they would adopt him and he could live with them for as long as he wanted.

Dear John, My mother said for me to write this. How are you? We are doing fine. Are you playing football? Your friend, Tab.

He turned the paper over. There was nothing on the other side. Not even a return address. Of course he knew the return address, but didn't they know about him, about this place, about how miserable he was? He almost tore it up, but instead, he sat there looking at the paper, folding it over and over into a small square. He lifted the money rock and put the letter underneath.

Off in the direction of the house he heard a large truck coming toward him on the dirt road. It bumped and bounced over the ruts, looming larger and larger, until he realized it wasn't a farm truck, but a moving van. DIX-IELAND MOVERS was the faded sign on its side. The driver raised a finger from the steering wheel, stopped, shifted gears, and lumbered up onto the asphalt. John watched as it disappeared down the highway, headed west. It took a minute for him to realize what the truck meant, a moving van way out here. Then he was up off the rock and trotting down the dirt road faster and faster as visions of what lay ahead came clear to him. It would never be the same, he knew that, but to have some of the things that were his, any of the things that were his and his mother's, even if they were just stacked around him on the porch, even if they had to stay in boxes until they made a crop and moved to a regular house, still they would be there. They would be his. He ran on. He could see the slight rise in the land that would give him a view of the house once he reached the top. He could hear the soft, steady plop of his shoes hitting the dusty road as he ran along, sweat building on his face. He wouldn't slow down until he had reached a place where he could see the house. He tripped in the dust right before he gained the crest of the road and crawled on all fours for the last five or six feet.

CHAPTER 17

THERE, spread out before him, were the leavings of the moving van from Bainbridge. Furniture and boxes were in every part of the yard. Half the boxes were open and the contents spilled out on the ground. Uncle Luther was systematically going from box to box with his pocketknife. He jammed the blade in the top of the cardboard, then ripped it open. Once he had looked inside, he would go on to the next one. Little Luther and Shell followed behind, pulling out the contents and quickly tiring of what they found. Comic books were lying in the dust, pages rippling in the breeze. His set of electric trains was spread out in the dirt, the tracks thrown about, the cars and engines stacked in a pile. Books that he had meticulously packed in alphabetical order had been taken out of their boxes and scattered on the ground so Uncle Luther could see if there was anything of value at the bottom. He watched as Uncle Luther came to the bottom of another box of books, throwing them back over his shoulder. Aunt Nelda was carrying armloads of kitchen utensils into the house, some spilling out as she walked along.

Still on all fours, he eased back to sit on his legs and watch. Everything, everything he valued, was being ripped up and thrown about. He tried yelling but something constricted his throat as if he were being strangled. He threw up, heaving only yellow liquid down into the dust, feeling his stomach muscles knot and then let go time and time again, until he was completely exhausted and rolled over onto his back, gulping in air, his eyes closed to the afternoon sky.

It came to him as he lay there, something he had seen before. The scene was like a picture he remembered from a history book he had read. The Indians had massacred everyone in the fort and now they were discovering all the white man's treasures. In the picture, the pioneers and soldiers lay dead off to the side while the Indian braves were trying on the white women's dresses. The Indian children ran about twirling parasols in the air. The Indian squaws were pulling boots off the dead soldiers' feet.

He rolled over on his stomach to look at them again. Now Uncle Luther was pulling the drawers of his mother's secretary in and out, examining them as if the desk were some strange rocket ship bound for the moon. Little Luther had his bicycle and was riding around in circles, running over books and tracks, grinding them into the dust. Shell sat under the oak tree, playing with his Lincoln Logs. Aunt Nelda was dashing from one piece of furniture to another, dusting.

He had regained his breath now. There was a bitter taste in his mouth that he tried to spit out, but it wouldn't go away. He could have called to them, yelled at them, but he didn't. What would he say? What could he say that they would care about?

John turned over on his back and looked into a fading sky and cried, grabbing handfuls of dirt and throwing them up in the air, then watching as they settled back down over him. In the end, he lay unmoving, like some discarded roadkill left along the highway.

It was not because of the comics or the books or the trains. Not because everything resembling order, his sense of order, had been completely disregarded. It was because he finally knew for the first time, knew beyond all doubt, that she was not there like he had hoped she was. Not there for him to rail against. Not there for him to blame. Not there to make sure things didn't get unbearable.

She had never been there watching over him.

CHAPTER 18

THE next morning, Uncle Luther was the man Aunt Nelda must have married long years ago. He sat at the breakfast table with a shy, almost schoolboy countenance.

Why didn't they just take the day off and go into town? Uncle Luther suggested. Only they couldn't because it was Saturday and only coloreds were in town on Saturday. Uncle Luther was undeterred. Well then, why didn't they take a picnic down by the creek and swim? Only they couldn't because Aunt Nelda wanted to make sure all the furniture was protected. She needed to move some of it indoors and the rest on the porch or out in the toolshed. Uncle Luther was the picture of cordiality. All right, if they didn't want to have a good time, he believed he would help her do the moving, and then he had some business to attend to.

John spent the afternoon in his quilts, which were now surrounded by furniture. He had rescued some books from out of the dust and spent the day in faraway India with the British troops. Occasionally, he was brought back to the cabin's porch by the sounds of Little Luther and Shell trying to hand-run his electric trains between the outcropping of roots under the oak tree. He tried not to hear them.

The next day being Sunday, Uncle Luther suggested that John and Aunt Nelda go to church. Maybe Nelda could see Mr. Holland from the antique store over in Uniontown. "Don't he come to Lower Peach Tree to go to church, him being a Baptist?"

"Why, yes, he does," Aunt Nelda said, surprised that Luther had remembered she wanted to get in touch with Mr. Holland. Mr. Holland handled fine antiques and she wanted him to take a look at the secretary. It was a lovely piece, but it was nine feet high, and she would never have room for it. "Maybe I can get a good price for it—and maybe a few other things," she mumbled when she saw John watching her face.

Uncle Luther even walked the three miles over to Arlo Thigpin's house and had Arlo bring him back in his truck with a battery for their truck. "It ain't gonna run long with that oil leak, but enough to get you to town and back."

Aunt Nelda dug around in some of the newly arrived boxes and found clothes for John and a dress for herself. He had not wanted to go, with Aunt Nelda dressed in his mother's old clothes and him wearing a wrinkled shirt and short wool pants that smelled of mothballs, but no one had asked him his opinion. There had never seemed to be a question of Little Luther and Shell coming along.

He was resigned to enduring it as he sat on the truck's bench seat with her, his hands between his legs. It wouldn't be more than a couple of hours.

"Nothin' like a little light at the end of the tunnel to raise your spirits," Aunt Nelda said to him as they drove out of the yard in the truck. She glanced in the rearview mirror at Uncle Luther. "He really ain't all that bad when things ain't pressin' in on him."

When they reached town, Aunt Nelda had to park the truck two blocks away. Cars lined the sidewalk all the way to the door of the church. Across the street, a smaller group of Methodists were congregating. A few people spoke to Nelda; more spoke to John, raising their hands in greeting or smiling at him. He thought he recognized faces from porches, maybe from the Piggly Wiggly, but he pretended not to be aware of them.

"My goodness," Aunt Nelda said. "How do all these people know you?"

"I don't know," he mumbled.

The minister, who recognized immediately that they were members of his flock who had strayed, enthusiastically greeted them at the door. John took a bulletin from him and kept his head down.

The two of them took a seat on the back row. The people sitting next to him scooted over in their seats, ostensibly to give them more room. He knew it was the mothball smell. He stared straight ahead, the muscles in his jaw flexing.

It was the first time he had been in church since his mother's funeral. He was unmoved. These people were disgusting, all dressed up in their fancy Sunday clothes. Probably never did a real day's work in their life.

After it was over, everyone filed back out into the sunlight. Aunt Nelda and John were standing on the front steps when she spied Mr. Holland from the antique store over in Uniontown. She waved her hankie. "Oh, Mr. Holland, just the man I want to see." She left John standing by himself. He walked down the steps, thinking he would go back to the truck and wait for her there. He recognized the voice before he turned to see her.

"Will you look who we have here. Why Judge, it's little John—you know, from the train. Nelda's nephew, you remember." She wore purple, purple everything—hat, shoes, gloves, dress, and made to match the dress was a thin purple duster. Remembered hours of dyeing Easter eggs with his mother came to him.

She took a deep breath when she saw his face. "My, John, you certainly have . . . have changed since we saw you last." She came closer, studying him. "Is that a bad sunburn you're gettin' over?" She raised her hand to touch his face, but he backed away.

"No," he said, touching his face, but not meaning to. "No, ma'am."

"Well, well, Judge, I do believe he's grown a foot. Why, I wouldn't have known him except that I saw him with Nelda. He . . . he's—"

"He's growing into his responsibilities just like we knew he would. Isn't that right, son?" The Judge seemed to smile. He held Mrs. Vance's arm and spoke to the tree branches behind and above John.

John tried to mirror as much disgust as possible over what he now considered the Judge's condescending attitude. "Yes. Sir!"

The Judge seemed not to notice. "See there, Adell. Why, here he is on a Sunday, bringing his aunt to church. He probably even listened to the sermon, didn't you, son?"

The Judge had not heard the disgust in his voice. He would try again. "Yes, sir. If you say so, sir." He spit it out.

"You did?" Mrs. Vance said, seeming to be completely oblivious. "Why, my gracious. I don't recall ever really listening to a sermon when I was your age. What did you think he was talking about, sweetheart?"

John looked at her, his face a mask. "My mother always discussed the sermons with me every Sunday." He let out a sigh. Mrs. Vance's face still did not reflect his loathing. Maybe it was true what Little Luther said about women.

He let out another loud sigh and continued in a sarcastic tone. "He was talking about salvation. He said if we are truly saved, we will go to a beautiful place when we die." He turned away from her and tried his new voice on the Judge. "Of course, that's not logical."

The Judge caught Mrs. Vance's hand before she could say anything. "Oh really. Well, why is that, son?"

"Because if I truly believed heaven was a better place, why would I want to stay around here? I would just as soon go on to heaven right now."

There was silence.

Mrs. Vance tried to laugh. "Well now no, dear, I don't think that's exactly what the minister had in mind."

John's expression never changed. "That's what he said. Heaven is perfect. You're never scared or tired or . . . or sunburned."

He turned back to the Judge for one last try at being vulgar. "That's what he said. And I don't care to have you calling me 'son,' either." He turned and walked away, hurrying to find Aunt Nelda so he wouldn't be left behind.

Chapter 19

She had hummed "Crown Him with Many Crowns" when they started the trip back home. It had been the closing hymn. Now, as they turned into the dirt road, she seemed to get anxious. The humming stopped. She held the steering wheel with both hands and concentrated on the road. She seemed to know it showed.

"I guess it's just silly of me, bein' impatient to get home. It's just that now that I know, now that I've talked to Mr. Holland—" The minute they reached the rise in the road, they could see things had changed.

They hadn't been gone over two hours, yet there was not a stick of furniture, not one box left in the yard. At first, she drove slowly, looking around, saying out loud, "What in the world? I . . . I know it was all here." Her knuckles turned white on the steering wheel. The accelerator churned the old engine until it whined over the ruts. When she stopped the truck, the road dust caught up and rolled over them like a fog. She got out of the truck, taking her gloves and hat off, still searching everywhere for some sign. She raced to the toolshed and flung it open. It was empty. Then she ran around the back of the house. Nothing.

Uncle Luther was on the porch, leaning back against the wall, his feet on the bottom rungs of the cane-back chair he sat in. She ran past him and swung open the kitchen door.

John had gotten out of the truck and come to the front steps. He could hear her inside, opening doors and closing them. She came back out to the porch, letting the screen door slam. "What did you do with it?" She stood over him, breathing hard. He pushed the tobacco in his mouth to one side and grinned at her.

"I," he said, so pleased with himself, "I made us a deal with Jimmy Mann over at the Trash-n-Treasure in Selma." He raised the glass of whiskey he had in one hand. "You're gonna be amazed at what I done." He held up his hand to keep her from interrupting.

"I called him yesterday from over at Arlo's house. He come out here this mornin' and loaded up the whole thing. Even threw in a bottle of Seagram's for me to sip on." He looked appreciatively at the amber moving in his glass. "That there was a neighborly gesture, don't you think?"

"You what?" Her face turned white.

He was still smiling at her ignorance. "Now don't go gettin' your back up. I wasn't gonna sell him the whole thing, but he said it was all or nothin'." He took a sip, still smiling. "So I says to myself, What the hell? She wants to sell it all anyway. Might as well get rid of it all right here and now. Make a deal on the whole thing so you won't have to worry 'bout doin' it in bits and pieces." He smiled up at her, giving her a wink. "Always have been a good horse trader," he said.

"You sold everything? I don't believe it." She turned and jerked open the door to the kitchen and went in again to search. There was silence, and then they could hear her beating her hand on the kitchen table. "I don't believe it. I don't believe it," she screamed. The door slammed as she came back out.

He was still up against the wall, just watching her. "Now don't get on your high horse. Yeah, I sold it, and got a good price, too. I'm a right smart trader, if I do say so."

"How much?"

"A lot better'n you coulda. A woman tryin' to bargain with old Holland at the antique shop?"

"How much?"

"Men was born good traders."

"How much?" she yelled.

"A damn sight more than you coulda got, and it's all right here in my pocket." He patted his pants pocket. "Cash money. None of this check-writin' stuff, cash money."

"How much?" she screamed again, so loudly that Shell, playing in the dirt with a few leftover Lincoln Logs, looked up and stared at her. Even Little Luther came around from the other side of the house to watch.

Luther let the chair drop all four legs to the floor and stood up, still smiling. "Two hundred and fifty dollars. He wanted to give me two hundred, but I said no. For the whole thing, it'll be two hundred and fifty or nothin'." He stuck his hand down in his pants pocket. "Two hundred fifty U.S. cash dollars. He even give me a fifty-dollar bill." He held the money out for her to see. "Lookie here at that. I can't remember when I done seen no fifty-dollar bill."

She let her back slump against the side of the house. "I can't believe it. After . . . after all the trouble, after all that packin', luggin' boxes, payin' the shippin'."

"I know it's a heap of money," he said. He was still holding the cash out for her to see. "I figure we can—"

"A heap of money?" She started to laugh. "*A heap of money?*" she shouted.

"*Yeah,*" he shouted back. "And I was gonna give you some of it to go out and buy a dress or some such, seein' as you got it all the way down here, but I ain't gonna be in the mood to do it with you on your high horse."

"Oh no, no, no." She let her back slide down the wall until she was sitting on the porch floor like a limp rag doll. "This is too much. This is just too much." She buried her face in her hands. "I had plans . . . I had plans." She was crying now.

"What the hell is the matter with you, woman?" He took one last swig out of his glass and then disappeared into the kitchen. They could hear him getting the bottle and pouring another drink. The screen door kicked open. He walked back out, bottle and glass in hand, and took his seat opposite her, staring at her. "All right, you can have most all of it if you want," he said in a low voice. "I just knowed you wouldn't be tradin' good as me."

She said nothing.

He took a long drink. "Hell, half the fun is in the tradin'."

Finally, she slowly pushed back up the wall to stand. Her eyes were on fire now.

"You fool," she began in a low, quiet tone. Then the sound of her voice rose with each additional word. "You no-count turd. You no-good, no-count, stupid bastard." Then she screamed. "Mr. Holland told me this morning, this very morning, that he would give me twice that for the secretary alone. *For the secretary alone,*" she shouted. "How could you be so stupid?" she screamed. "With all that stuff, I coulda made hundreds, hundreds of dollars.

We coulda bought a good car, maybe got in a *decent house*," she yelled.

He sat there in the chair, his face ashen as what she had said began to sink in.

When he got up out of his chair, the glass dropped, but he held on to the bottle. "You watch your mouth." He took two steps and hit her hard across the face. "Don't no-body call me stupid." He hit her again. Her head, accustomed to the blows, snapped back to glare at him. He stood staring at her, then took a drink right out of the bottle. "I . . . I was tryin' to—"

Shell was sitting stark still, not moving a muscle. Her eyes were staring at the Lincoln Logs on the ground. Little Luther stood like a statue up against the side of the house, not looking at them, but studying the cotton fields in front of him. John made the mistake of backing away a step or two. The movement caught Uncle Luther's eye.

"You." He wheeled around toward him. "You. You're the one caused it. If it wasn't for you comin' and messin' in everythin'." He was off the porch, grabbing for John in such a rage that he let go of his Seagram's bottle and it rolled off to the side in the dust. Uncle Luther pulled John up off the ground. The boy came nose-to-nose with tobacco and alcohol spitting into his face through yellow-stained teeth. He closed his eyes and tried not to breathe. "I'll teach you." He hit John in the face, then threw him on the ground and began to fumble with his belt. The boy sat on the ground, not knowing what might come next. He heard somebody say, "Run, get on out of here," but he had no idea the instruction was meant for him.

Now Uncle Luther grabbed John's arm with one hand and raised his black leather belt with the other. The belt lashed down at John's bare legs. The pain was so imme-diate, so amazing, that John caught his breath and could not scream. He tried in vain to move away, but his arm was caught in the vise of Uncle Luther's hand. Finally, his voice came back and he began screaming, "Aunt Nelda, Aunt Nelda!" There was no answer.

He caught sight of her figure silhouetted on the porch, watching as Uncle Luther beat out both their frustrations on him.

"She ain't gonna help you, boy." He smirked. He brought the belt down across John's legs again. "She ain't gonna help nobody."

The boy wriggled like a worm impaled on a hook, trying to get away from the next blow.

"She's all the time tellin' you what to do," Luther said. "'Make a crop, Luther,'" he mimicked. The belt cut into the boy's flesh.

"'Make foreman, Luther.'" The belt crashed down again.

"Get out there in the sun and work your goddamn ass off, Luther." This last thought caused Luther to come down on the boy with all his might. The belt ripped open John's pants and cut across his fanny.

Now the blows came in rapid-fire succession, John swinging from his arm, screaming when he had the breath to. "What? Please. What did I do?" Uncle Luther beat until he was finally exhausted; then he released the boy, to retrieve what was left in his bottle. He took one last drink and stood there reeling.

John, on all fours, scrambled to the nearest shelter he could find, the space under the front porch where the cats slept. He crawled in among the dust and the cobwebs that hung down from the porch flooring. One of the cats moved to the side to make room. A roach scurried past his head. He lay there curled up in a ball in the dust, his hands covering his eyes.

Uncle Luther looked around, found the truck, and headed toward it. He started the engine and roared off, leaving a trail of dust floating up in the motionless air.

Nelda stood watching the road. Shell and Little Luther still had not moved. John lay under the house, trying just to breathe enough to be able to cry. All was silent except for the fading sound of the truck's engine.

Chapter 20

"Stupid, stupid, stupid," Little Luther said, squatting down to look at John, who was still cowering under the porch. "Don't never move, don't you know nothin'." He reached under and grabbed a leg to pull John out. The boy cried out in pain but Little Luther paid no attention.

"I thought Ma said you was smart." He had John all the way out and lifted him to a standing position. "You ain't got the sense God give a chicken." He took two or three swipes at John's shirt as if to brush it off. "Always stand still. Like a tree or a rock, not movin' a muscle." He inspected John's legs. "Put some kerosene on them legs." Then he walked away, disappearing around the side of the house.

Aunt Nelda was sitting on the porch bench, her head in her hands. Shell was standing beside her, touching the sleeve of her mother's dress.

John hobbled over to the front steps and held on to the rotting wooden boards. The pain overwhelmed him now. He breathed in, gulping the air, trying to keep from passing out. After a time, his head began to clear and he tried to look at the backs of his legs. They were streaked with red and seeping thin lines of blood. He couldn't seem to control his body. It began to shake and he heard himself sobbing.

As he stood there, holding onto the stairs, trying to outlast the pain, he realized he wasn't thinking about how much he hated Uncle Luther. What kept coming back to him, what he thought about—the thing he kept hearing over and over in his mind—was what Little Luther had just said. No one, no one, had ever called him stupid.

Luther was gone almost two weeks. To John, it was worth losing all his mother's things just to have him gone. It was worth losing all of his toys just to have him gone. He didn't care that his legs had turned black-and-blue and that it took three or four days before he could walk up straight again. He didn't care that he had to work longer hours in the field alongside Aunt Nelda and Shell. He was beginning to like sleeping on the dogtrot porch. It was wonderful just to have him gone.

During that time, they were almost like a family. They would get up early in the morning and all help out with getting breakfast, because Shell and Aunt Nelda would have to go to the fields with them to make up for Uncle Luther being gone.

It was the first time Aunt Nelda had seen the swamp fields. She had been watching the progress of the cotton planted around the house and had not known what the swamp fields looked like. When she saw, she didn't say anything, but they knew she was crying while she hoed that first morning.

After a few days, she seemed to become her old self again and would laugh when Little Luther would mimic his father. They would be on water break, and when it was time to go back to work, Little Luther would take a big mouthful of water and spit it in a long stream and then take a grandiose swipe at his mouth as if he was wiping off tobacco juice. "Now what I'm a-tellin' you is to get on out there and work your butts off, 'cause we don't want not one of these here puny, almost dead cotton plants to die of weed stranglin' 'fore they all die of no water, which is what they gonna do any day now."

Aunt Nelda and Shell would laugh at Little Luther's imitation. John would roll on the ground with laughter. He thought it was the funniest thing he had ever heard. He had not known Little Luther had any sense of humor.

One morning while they were in the fields, John had slipped and called him Little Luther instead of Butch. He had braced for Little Luther to come over and flatten him, but Little Luther didn't seem to notice it, or he let it pass. John looked at Shell and they both shrugged their shoulders in amazement.

At the end of the first week, they had worked so hard that Aunt Nelda said they would all go over to Arlo Thigpins's barn for the dancing that went on every Saturday night.

"You never let us do that before," Shell said. "You said them wasn't the kinda people for us to be round. You said—"

"I know what I said, but we ain't got a car and he lives close and y'all done such good work this week."

"If there gets to be too much drinkin', I'll bring y'all on home," Little Luther said.

Aunt Nelda raised her eyebrows at Little Luther but said nothing.

And there wasn't too much drinking, not that night anyway. They had walked over from their house, about three miles. As they approached, they could see cars and trucks lined up along the road. In the dusk, warm yellow light was streaming from all the windows and doors of Arlo's barn. Fiddle and guitar music floated out on the cooling air.

Arlo had a barn dance every Saturday night in the late summer, when the cotton was mostly laid by. He didn't charge admission, but he did cook up a big iron pot of Brunswick stew out in the open air, and that was ten cents a bowl. Some of the other women had brought cakes, and that was five cents a slice. The men could go around back of the barn and, for considerably more, have a sampling of Arlo's whiskey—the real moneymaker.

Aunt Nelda had managed to scrape together ninety-five cents and they all ate themselves silly, running back to her for another dime or five more pennies. Inside the barn, they sat on hay bales and listened to the music and ate their Brunswick stew, which was full of rabbit and squirrel that Arlo had managed to kill during the week. This was accompanied by white loaf bread and Ball jars full of ice tea.

During a break in the music, one of the guitar players spotted Little Luther and insisted he come up and play the spoons on the next song. John and Shell and Aunt Nelda sat there with mouths open as Little Luther performed for everyone else, all of whom seemed to know already that he was an accomplished spoon player. He finished two or three songs and then came back over and sat down by them, trying mightily to convey an air of indifference. "Well, what you think I done when I come over here with Pa? He won't let me drink no whiskey."

They finally used up their ninety-five cents and started

for home in the moonlight, the sounds of "Your Cheatin'
Heart" floating out after them on the night air.

The day he came back, he never said a word. Nobody
said anything. They were all eating supper and tired out
after working all day. Aunt Nelda had tried to keep up
all the chores as best she could. "We can't have the bank
comin' round and seein' us not keep up our end of the
bargain. We'll be out in the road."

They heard his truck drive up in the yard, the door
slam. Shell ran to the window to see who it was. "Pa." She
hurried back to take her seat. His footsteps were on the
porch. No one looked up when he came in.

He put down the box of Whitman's on the kitchen
table and went back outside, letting the screen slam. Aunt
Nelda drank her water and stared at the box. She said
nothing, finishing up her plate. Finally, she flipped the
top off. It landed on the floor. Then she reached in and
took all the wrapped cherry pieces. After that, Little
Luther and Shell, then John.

The Bend

H E had spent the first year at Tuskegee letting them get used to him. He had gone to classes, all the classes he could take at one time, and he had applied for work at the school. They had given him the choice of a job in the cafeteria or stoking the furnace in the administration building. He had taken the stoking job. It required that he get up at four every morning, but he didn't mind. It was warm and quiet down in the furnace room. He would stay for hours after he had finished shoveling coal into the big furnace. There was a sink in one corner of the room. A cracked mirror and a dirty bar of soap rested on a board nailed above it. He would wash the coal dust off and then sit studying and reading at a little table he had set up. Mama Tuway was especially anxious that he do well in math, and he had gotten so he could calculate large numbers in his head.

He had to get used to electricity and running water, things that he knew about but had not used before. He soon found out that he was not the only one. Many of the other boys from farms around the state were in his same shoes. When he went home at the end of the first year, she delighted in having him demonstrate his skills in math. She would call on him to calculate complicated sums as they were standing with other members outside the church after Sunday services. At the end of the summer, he hated to go back, but he knew he didn't have a good-enough reason to stay, since he had survived the first year.

Now, years later, when he looked back on that second year, he realized that if he had been more outgoing or if he had been less shy, it might have turned out differently, but he wasn't and it hadn't.

He took more classes in agriculture and math. The work was easy for him and he was beginning to feel more comfortable.

He had known, in the spring of that year, when Leroy and Raymond, boys in his math class, had approached him and asked if he would like to come to a party that it sounded suspicious, but he had accepted anyway because he was lonely and because he had never been to a party or met any girls since he had been there.

That night, he dressed in one of his green shirts. When Leroy and Raymond suggested going to visit a girl they knew at the far edge of town, instead of going to the party, he had gone along with it, because by that time it was too late to back out, but, by the way they smiled at each other, he suspected it was a joke that he had not been let in on.

It was an old house with a red light in the window. He had not known what that meant and had commented, by way of making conversation, that it looked like Christmas.

They had laughed. "And you the Christmas present," they said as they walked up the steps to the front door.

They began to pound on the door and yell. "Hey, Geraldine." They gave one last knock and stepped back. "Hey, girl, 'member how you always sayin' you want one of them spotted dogs like rides on the fire trucks?

"Come on out here, girl. Me and Leroy done got you one, and this'un wants to wag his tail for you." They were bent over laughing.

Tuway had backed away from the door and they had pushed him forward again. "Go on up there, cousin. You liable to get somethin' free outta this."

Leroy yelled, "Well, come on out here, girl."

Tuway remembered standing there with a stupid grin on his face, not understanding what was going on but trying to be part of it.

When she opened the door, Geraldine burst out laughing. "Leroy, what you doin' markin' up this big boy like that?"

When it dawned on him what they were talking about, he began to shake his head, to back away off the porch, out of the yard.

He could hear the three of them laughing and yelling to him as he walked off down the road.

"Come on back here, son. You don't know what you missin'."

That night as he brought shovelfuls of coal from the coal bin to the furnace, he kept passing by the mirror on the wall above the sink. He had never had a mirror constantly looking at him before. Mama Tuway had never had one in the house.

A short time later, when he had found himself standing in front of the mirror, staring at his image and holding a handful of soot from the furnace, he had thrown the black powder down the drain, run all the way back to his room, packed his clothes, and left Tuskegee for good.

CHAPTER 21

IT was the week after Uncle Luther got back home that Miss Belva came out. They were eating dinner in the middle of the day, when they heard a car coming up the road. John, Shell, and Little Luther came out on the porch to see who it was. Miss Belva stepped out in a dress and hat to match, a stack of papers in her arms.

"Hello, Luther, Michelle." She stood there with a gloved hand shielding her eyes. "And you must be the one I've come to see. John, isn't it?" She took a few steps forward and stuck her hand out. He only looked at it. "I teach fifth grade over at the school," she said, dropping the hand to her side. "The Judge—that is, we—decided that since you're going to be a new member of school this fall, well, we decided that you could use some preschool testing. You know, to see what grade you might be in next year?"

"Howdy, Miss Belva." Aunt Nelda came out on the porch, wiping her hands on a towel. "What is it you say you need to do with him?" Those were the first words anyone had heard Aunt Nelda say, besides *yes* and *no*, since Uncle Luther had come home.

Miss Belva smiled. "You see, what we decided—that is, I—or that is, the school decided, we need to test all new students who are coming in for the first time. So if you'll just let me borrow John for this afternoon, I'll have him back in time for supper."

Uncle Luther pushed the screen door open. He had been standing behind it, listening. "All new students? He's probably the only new student in the whole county 'cept for the first graders."

Miss Belva smiled. "Well, that could be, I don't know, but still he . . . well, he needs to be looked at—that is, he needs testing."

"He can't go to no school testin'; he's gotta work." He let the door slam behind him and walked down the front steps past her and into the yard.

"But the Judge said—" She turned to walk behind him. Uncle Luther turned around so quickly that Miss Belva nearly ran into him. They were almost face-to-face as Miss Belva stepped back quickly, but not before she could see his eye twitching. John jumped off the corner of the porch and grabbed her hand.

Luther spit out juice. "What the hell does the Judge have to do with it? I thought you said it was the school's doin'."

"It most certainly is the school's doing," Miss Belva said. "It's just that, well, it's just that I happened to see the Judge, just by chance on the street the other day, and he said to me . . ." She began to fumble with the papers in her hand. "Well, he said to me, 'Belva, I was just thinking about Luther Spraig the other day because he probably will be coming in to pay off his crop loan one of these days . . . and I remembered that he has a new boy out there I think you should see about . . . see about school next year.'" She studied her papers.

"I don't care who he is. Ain't nobody gonna tell a man what he can or can't do with his kids." He glared at her.

"Oh, I certainly agree with that. That is an inviolate rule, Mr. Spraig. I'm sure the Judge would agree." She cleared her throat. "If anything, the onus is on me. I am the one who would be remiss in my duty if . . . if the Judge didn't think I had attended to these matters. So you see, as the head of the household, you would be doing me a great favor if you would let me take John in for . . . for pre-school testing."

Uncle Luther's mood changed. "Well, I ain't never said I wouldn't do nobody no favors." He smiled and spit out into the yard. "We all got to tiptoe round the Judge, don't we?" He looked down at John holding her hand. "He ain't much count in the fields anyway. You can have him for this afternoon."

"That's very gracious of you, Mr. Spraig."

John dropped his hand from Miss Belva's and walked back to Aunt Nelda, who was watching everything. "Do I have to go wherever she wants to take me?"

"Go get in the car before Luther changes his mind," she said.

He walked slowly over to the car and got in the front seat.

Miss Belva had started the engine and the car was bumping over the roads before she said, "I thought you came to hold my hand because you wanted to go with me."

He looked straight ahead, embarrassed for her that she was so stupid. "I was holding your hand so you wouldn't move. Didn't you see he was getting mad?"

Chapter 22

"WELL now, John," the Judge had said, "how would you like to have a job?" They hadn't gone to the school. They had driven straight to the bank and waited until the Judge could see them. John and Miss Belva sat in chairs out in the lobby, and the people who worked there looked at them but did not comment as they walked by. Miss Belva gave him some papers to fill out. Eventually, Miss Maroon, the Judge's secretary, came to get them. She addressed Miss Belva and gave no notice of John. "I don't know why, with everything else that's going on around here, he wants to get involved in this." She tilted her head John's way.

"Come on, John honey," Miss Belva said.

It was not the best room he had ever seen, but it made him feel like it should be. The Judge's desk was in the center. Big legal-size bookcases lined the walls. There were doors leading off to other rooms, and chairs that sat opposite the Judge's desk. They sat in the two wing-back chairs, facing the Judge. He turned in Miss Belva's direction. "Any problems?"

"No more than we anticipated." She cleared her throat and glanced toward John. "You know, he looks—"

"I know, I know. I heard every detail after church the other day. Now maybe Adell will let me get some peace and quiet," he said.

Miss Belva laughed. "That's not what she tells me. She says this was all your idea."

"You women, we can't live with you and—"

"Never mind. I know who the softy is. I've got an errand to run. Why don't I leave you two and I'll be back in awhile to get him." She got up and walked toward the door. "John, give the Judge all the papers you filled out."

John gave him the papers and the Judge, putting them aside, said, "How would you like a job?"

"Me?"

"Yes, you."

"What kind of a job?" He sat up very straight, trying to look mean like Little Luther. "I ain't got time for no job, what with the hoeing I do all day long."

"You ain't got time for no job? What kind of language is that?"

Tears came, but he didn't care because he knew the Judge couldn't see. The room was quiet while he wiped his eyes and cleared his throat so as not to sound scared. Then he stood up and walked over to grab the edge of the desk. He said with all the meanness he could muster, "I don't have time to do another job. I get up in the morning and I hoe all day. When I finish, I walk into town to get the mail. By the time I get back, it's time to eat and go to bed." Then he shouted, "I don't have time to do another stinking job."

Just then one of the side doors opened. John caught

his breath. A huge man stepped in to scowl at him. He was like no one the boy had ever laid eyes on before. His face was half white and half dark brown. The skin was brown on some parts and white on others. Not shades of brown, but brown *and* white. Where it was white, it was like John's skin color. He looked like a black man, but he was not a black man, or maybe he was. John didn't know. The boy started to back away. He thought this man could probably beat the livin' shit out of him if he wanted.

"You need me, Judge?" the half-and-half man said, still looking straight at John.

John backed up toward the wall, looking for the nearest place to hide.

The Judge smiled. "Tuway, may I introduce Mr. John McMillan."

"What's you yellin' like that, boy?" The man's voice was as thundering and low as he had meant it to be. "The Judge is gonna skin you alive, makin' so much noise, and if he don't"—the man stepped closer to John—"I will."

"He's"—the Judge nodded toward John—"beginning to remind me more of one of my board of directors than a future employee. Thank you for your concern, Tuway, but I believe I can handle him."

"You probably could handle him with one hand tied behind your back." Tuway glared and moved out, slowly closing the door.

"Who . . . who was that?"

"That was Tuway, one of your bosses if you elect to take this job, son. Oh, sorry, I forgot you don't like to be called that. Come back over here and sit down, John."

The Judge sat back in his chair and smiled. Tuway's appearance always had that effect on people when they first met him. It happened so seldom now because everyone in the county knew Tuway or knew of him. His size and his skin color had been one of the reasons he had hired Tuway in the first place, when Tuway had appeared almost out of the blue that day so many years ago.

The Judge's attention turned back to John. "I didn't mean that you had to work another job in addition to the one you have now. I meant that I would like to employ you to work here instead of in the fields, if you and your uncle are amenable. However, we won't for one minute put up with that kind of language and that temper around here."

"My . . . my uncle won't be amenable," he said, easing back over into his chair but still looking at the door Tuway had closed. "He needs me in the fields even if I'm not worth shi—worth anything hoein'."

"Your job would include working at the house, helping out in the yard, doing odd jobs. Maybe even reading to me from time to time, if you can handle it. What do you think?"

"Uncle Luther—"

"Never mind about your uncle. I'll take care of that. I'm asking you if you would like to do it?"

"What about the mail? I have to pick up the mail."

"You can pick up the mail on your way home every day."

"Do I get to come seven days or just five?"

The Judge smiled and stood up. "Only five. You can have the weekends off."

"I don't need the weekends off. I can come seven."

"No, five will be fine. Let's shake on it." He held out his hand. "School will be starting soon; then it will let out again after a few weeks for cotton picking. When that happens, we will have to adjust your hours accordingly."

John grabbed the hand that was sticking out in the air and held it as long as he could before the Judge pulled away. "I have other business to attend to right now, John.

Why don't you just sit right here and wait for Miss Belva to come get you." He pushed a button on his desk. Tuway came through the door. "Is everything set up for the board meeting?"

"Jus' like you like it."

"Good. Why don't you stay here. I'll call if I need you. Miss Belva will be coming to pick up John." He left his chair and walked to a side door with such familiarity, one would never suspect he was blind. Tuway held the door for him and closed it almost all the way, leaving only a crack, then sat down in a chair just beside it. Tuway paid John no mind. The boy sat all the way back in the big leather wing-back chair. His feet were so far off the floor, he crossed them Indian-style and seemed almost swallowed up by the chair's dark leather covering. Now and then, he peered out from behind its wings to steal a glance at Tuway.

He could hear people gathering in what must be a conference room behind the door. The Judge could be heard calling the meeting to order.

Tuway sat with his elbows on his knees, his head bent forward, close to the crack in the door.

"This is not a regularly scheduled board meeting, so let's keep it informal. Miss Maroon will take notes, but only to refresh my memory." There was a shuffle as people began to settle comfortably in their seats.

"L.B.," said the Judge, "you're the one who wanted to have this gathering, so why don't you take the floor."

A rather young, sarcastic voice spoke up. "I don't need to 'take the floor,' Judge, for everybody to know what's goin' on. Hell, Debo here's got the same problem." There was a pause. "Don't go shakin' your head, Debo," the voice said. "Your niggers are leavin', same as mine."

"I'd leave, too, if I was your niggers, L.B."

"Anybody with half a brain ain't gonna farm on no sixty-forty split, L.B.," another voice said. "Since that great little innovation of yours, you've scared off half the coloreds and most of the whites on shares in the county. They all think we're gonna do the same thing."

"Debo's right, L.B. What in the hell did you do that for? Pretty soon we won't have anybody left farmin' on shares, and I don't know about y'all, but I ain't got the money to fork over for one of them fifty-thousand-dollar cotton pickers." There was silence again as chairs shuffled about.

"Now they're heading up north by the carload, whereas before it was just a few at a time," somebody else said.

"They're going, but I don't think by car. That's a long trip, and you gotta have gas money. I don't think that's how they leave or how they come back," the Debo voice said.

"How, then?" someone else said.

"Gentlemen, that's neither here nor there." It was the Judge's voice. "How they get the money to go up north or how they stay there is none of our business. Why are we here today? What does all this have to do with the Planters and Merchants Bank of Lower Peach Tree?"

"You know damn good and well what it has to do with the bank, Judge. I say let's put the economic squeeze on 'em," the young voice said.

"What do you want us to do, L.B., foreclose on their land? It's not their land, remember?"

John sneaked a peek and saw the Tuway man smiling and shaking his head. When Tuway looked up and saw him, John grabbed a magazine from off the side table and pretended to read it. The conversation continued in the next room.

"Smile if you want to, Red," the young voice said, "but you're gonna be smilin' out of the other side of your damn mouth come the end of summer and you ain't ginnin' no cotton."

"If it happens, it happens," the man named Red said. "What do you want me to do about it, chain'm to the porch? I don't think the feds would go for that." He laughed, and so did some of the others.

"You're sittin' around here like you always have, not realizin' what's happenin' 'til it's too late," the young voice said. "They're disappearin' in droves. I went by Lester and Lucy's place this mornin'. Been workin' for my family for forty years. Their place was empty, cleaned out. Now they may be back in the fall and pay me rent, which don't amount to a hill of beans, and God knows where they get the money, or they may stay up north for good, and I'm still out the cotton cash."

"Things change, L.B.," the Judge said. "That's why I keep telling you gentlemen we need to start talking about attracting some kind of industry in here, like maybe a—"

"To hell with some Damn Yankee company comin' in here and rapin' the land. As long as I'm a major stock-holder in this bank, I say no damn money-grabbin' Yan-kees are gonna come in here and—"

"How 'bout some damn money-grabbin' southerners?" somebody interrupted. "I hear over in Atlanta they—"

Just then, John jumped. Miss Belva had come in the room and tapped him on the shoulder.

"John, I need to be getting you back home. Your uncle will wonder what's happened."

Miss Belva stood, shading her eyes from the late-afternoon sun, which was making its way down the sky back of the house. Aunt Nelda was on the porch, impatient that she had been interrupted from preparing supper.

Miss Belva told her that John had done very well on his tests and that the Judge would like to give him work doing odd jobs, if that was all right with Mr. Spraig. She also said that naturally the Judge realized John was too young to handle the small amount of money that he would make, so that Mr. Spraig had better come by the bank every Friday and pick up John's pay and save it for him. He hoped that arrangement would be satisfactory.

The Bend

Now he came to the Bend at every opportunity, usually in the evening, when the light had dimmed, when appearances had softened.

Mama Tuway did not let this go unnoticed. "Tuway, I used to think the best thing 'bout you was how you look at everything right side up. But maybe that ain't the truth." She waited for him to deny it, but he said nothing. "You know that girl messed up in the head. She might be good-lookin', but she don't know it. She don't feel it."

He tried not to think of her as good-looking. If he did, it meant others thought the same thing. He hoped she looked like a freak to others.

"Good-lookin'? What's you say good-lookin'? With that skinned head?"

"You can grow back a head of hair. You know that ain't it. It's what's inside."

A coldness would run through him when she said things like that. "I ain't worried." He would smile at her the way he had when asking a favor as a child. "You fix her.

Get some of them herbs out the swamp. You fix every-body."

She shook her head. "I don't know 'bout that, Tuway."

She had never taken pity on him before and so he didn't recognize it in her.

"Ah, go on. You can fix it."

The old woman looked away. "I do know we ain't gonna let her go on off to Chicago with little Willie—and her bein' like that."

Once her hair began to grow and her face lost most of its bruising and swelling, it was like flies to the honey. Men, upon first seeing her, were mesmerized. They stood together in groups, watching the long legs moving back and forth from the house to the side yard as she helped with supper chores. Eyes followed the arms raised to wipe sweat off her forehead, the profile etched against the fading light. It would have been unnatural if she had gone ignored.

This was before they knew her, before they had heard her.

The first time it happened, everyone had gathered in the yard for supper. One of the younger men from the Bend had started teasing her. It was harmless enough, but when he tried to put his arm around her, Ella went rigid. Her eyes glazed over. She began spewing withering fire, words so repulsive, everyone within hearing distance cringed. Her face contorted, so that she seemed to become someone else. The beauty they had thought was there had disappeared, drained from her body. Like a chameleon, she had changed before their eyes. It was disgusting to look at, embarrassing for them to realize they had been all wrong about her.

On these occasions, little Willie would sit with his hands over his ears, his eyes shut tight. The night it first happened, Tuway had stepped in to shoo away the transgressor. It had not taken much effort. No one would think of crossing Tuway, and besides, Ella had lost all her appeal by then. Tuway stood up from his place around the fire and looked at the man.

The man immediately held up his hands. "Just funnin' with her, Tuway. Didn't mean nothin' by it." This, Tuway now realized, had been great good fortune for him, because after that night, Ella came to see him as a guardian of sorts.

At supper, Tuway would choose a picnic table off to himself. He would sit there carefully studying his piece of fried chicken, turning it in his hands as he ate, pretending not to notice her. More often than not, Ella and Willie would come sit at the opposite end to eat their dinner, never talking to him, never even glancing up at him, but knowing they were in his protected sphere.

Once he had offered her a piece of fried chicken. She accepted it but gave it to Willie. It was trifling, he knew, yet it lasted him for days.

CHAPTER 23

TUWAY was John's new boss. His appearance fascinated John, but he had to be careful. If Tuway caught him staring, he would stare back, and then John couldn't seem to pull away once their eyes were locked. Tuway held him—and even John knew this was ridiculous—in almost a trance.

He had never read about anyone like Tuway, and now there was no one to ask, nowhere to go to find out about such a person. The boy decided that what must have happened was that Tuway had a black daddy and a white mother who didn't mix when they made Tuway. They must have both been very big, because Tuway was bigger than the Judge, bigger than Uncle Luther. He was not frightened of Tuway like he was frightened of Uncle Luther. He was scared of Tuway as one might be afraid of a ghost.

Uncle Luther had taken to the idea of John's job immediately. Aunt Nelda wasn't so sure. "Why, hell yes, Nelda," he had said that night at supper. "He ain't no help in the fields, and this way, at least we get money for him workin'." He glanced up from his plate. "Course I'll save it up for him." No one thought it worth the trouble of taking exception to that. In fact, no one ever even asked what happened to the money Uncle Luther got for selling all John's mother's things. Maybe Aunt Nelda and Uncle Luther had discussed it, but not at the dinner table. John did notice that the truck had new tires and seemed to run better.

The boy would wake with the others, eat breakfast, and walk to town as the morning dew was drying on the fields. If he found any bottles, he would hide them in a nearby cotton field to sell at a later time.

John would sit on the back steps of the Judge's house, waiting, as he had been told, until Tuway came to give him instructions. Tuway would seem to come from out of nowhere, walking past the cemetery that lay just across the street. When John had asked, Mrs. Vance said Tuway lived in a house just outside of town.

Tuway always seemed to have other things on his mind, so the boy would go unnoticed until Tuway got halfway up the back steps, adjusting his tie, buttoning the sleeves of his frayed white shirt. Then he would notice the boy and quickly survey the backyard to give John his assignment for the morning.

"See them rose beds right yonder, the ones with the white roses?" he would say, pointing.

"Yes, sir."

"Weed 'em. Then plump up the ground all round with a hand trowel. By the time I get back here for dinner, I don't wanna see no sign of no weeds. You understand?"

"Yes, sir."

"Well, don't just stand there lookin' at me. Put the hurt to them weeds, boy."

John would jump to his task, hurry to the toolshed directly behind the grape arbor at the end of the backyard, find a trowel, and begin his assignment, all the while keeping an eye on the comings and goings in the house.

At a quarter to nine each morning, Tuway walked the Judge to work. The bank was just three blocks from the house, so every noon they came home for dinner and every noon Tuway came out back to see after John and tell him what to do for the rest of the day.

They took their dinner together on the screened-in back porch, sitting at an old discarded kitchen table. John thought the food alone was worth the job. Real ice tea, fried chicken, cornbread, string beans, and potatoes. Mrs. Vance seemed to prefer to do all the cooking herself. She would bring John an extra-large portion that he would immediately devour and then sit watching to see if Tuway was going to finish his plate. Tuway didn't eat much, and if he looked up and saw John watching, he would push it in his direction. "Don't they feed you nothin' out there, boy?" Having seen no other indications, the boy took the sharing of food as a sure sign Tuway was beginning to like him.

After dinner, Tuway would take his coat off, turn on the overhead fan, and move to a wicker rocker that had seen better days. He would sit studying a small black notebook he had taken from his coat pocket. It seemed to be filled with all the happenings of the day. Sometimes the Judge would come to the back door and ask Tuway if such-and-such was on the schedule for the day. Tuway would consult the book and say when and where.

John lounged in an old green glider discarded from the sunporch on the side of the house. He would read from old newspapers that were stacked in the corner. Tuway smoked a cigarette and stared out into the backyard or at his note-book.

At times, other Negroes came by the back door and called to Tuway in a very respectful manner. "Mr. Tuway, I'd count it a favor to have a word with you." He would look up and study them for a minute before he moved. More times than not, he eased out of his chair to talk to them out in the yard. He always had plenty of time. The Judge, and, in fact, all of Lower Peach Tree, took a nap after dinner. Business got started again around two o'clock.

One afternoon, Mrs. Vance brought out a pitcher of ice tea and cookies. John brushed the dirt off his hands and drank down two glasses before he stopped to thank her. She smiled and took a seat on the glider, holding the big glass pitcher in her lap.

"How are things at home? I mean, how is your aunt Nelda these days, John?"

"She's fine."

"And your uncle Luther?"

"He's fine."

She looked down into the pitcher of tea as if she were seeing something bobbing around in there with the mint and lemons. "The Judge was telling me you had a black eye when you came to interview with him. Is that right?"

"No."

"No?" she said.

"I mean, no, ma'am."

"I didn't mean that; I meant, you didn't have a black eye?"

"I don't have a mirror. I don't know if I had a black eye or not."

"How did you . . ." She looked down in the tea pitcher again. "I just wondered how you came by that eye."

He held his glass out and she poured more tea, which he drank straight down without answering. He wiped his mouth with the back of his hand, still trying to decide what to tell her. He couldn't take the chance of jeopardizing this new job. "I didn't do anything bad, if that's what you were thinkin'. I got it because I didn't stand still, that's all."

"What?"

"I didn't stand still when he got mad, and if you don't stand still, then you're liable to get hit. Did you think I didn't know how to act? I know how to act."

"Oh, no, I didn't think that at all." She got up quickly and went over to the wrought-iron table, where she had left the cookies. "Here, come have some of these cookies. Don't all children like Oreos?"

He didn't say anything but took a cookie and pulled it apart, eating the side without icing and saving the other side. He eyed her suspiciously and took another cookie. "Everybody knows if you stand still, you won't get hit. Most of the time now, I am so still, nobody even sees me."

"Well I never . . ." She grabbed a cookie off the plate and began nervously turning it over and over in her hands.

He watched her as he ate the second side without icing and then put together the two sides with icing. "I won't be missing any days working here 'cause my legs are hurting or anything like that."

Her face had turned pale. She grabbed the arm of the glider and sat down quickly.

John smiled at his homemade cookie before he took a bite. "You can count on me," he reassured her. "Little Luther told me what to do, and Shell. They learned me," he said, and popped the rest of the double-icing cookie in his mouth.

"They taught you." Adell Vance corrected him without realizing she had done it. She was staring at the ground.

He took the last four cookies off the plate and put them in his pocket. "Learned me, taught me. What difference does it make? Now I know what to do." He corrected himself in deference to her. "Now I know what to do, ma'am," he said. "They even taught me how to hold my breath if it gets too bad. I can even hold it to a faint. Want to see me do it?"

She raised her hand and shook her head. "No, no. I believe you. That won't be necessary."

He drank down the last of his ice tea and stood there watching her. "I was just wondering, ma'am."

"Yes, what is it?" She had taken a handkerchief out of her pocket and was fanning herself.

"Are you gonna eat that last cookie you got there in your hand?"

She gave it to him. He thanked her, put it in his pocket, picked up his hoe, and went back to the weeds. He would save a cookie or two for Shell and Little Luther. The rest were for him.

CHAPTER 24

THAT afternoon, while he was weeding under the kitchen window, John heard her talking on the phone.

"It just made my blood run cold. He needs—I am gonna say it. He needs a man's influence—Tuway is not enough. Byron, I know you don't want to get involved. . . . I appreciate that you have other problems. . . . I know the Spraigs will take advantage of the—"

There was a long silence while he talked on the other end of the line. She tried to interrupt him several times but couldn't. Finally, when he was finished, she said, "You know, Byron, if I didn't know better, I might think you were afraid of feeling too much for the boy rather than too little. . . . I didn't mean to imply he was one bit like Mary Beth. There's no comparison. I know that. . . . You're right—we'll talk about it tonight."

A few days later, she called John into the house early in the morning.

"Well now, John. The Judge has decided that he needs you to work for him in the afternoons." She was sitting at the kitchen table and fishing through her sewing box. "Of course, if you're going to work at the bank, you'll need some proper clothes."

"Like a tie and a suit?"

"No." She smiled. "Just some clean—I mean, some new short pants and shirts. We'll keep them here at the house so . . . well, so your aunt Nelda won't be bothered with having to wash them."

"That's okay. I can wash'm. I know how to do it. You take them to the pond and go swimming in them."

"Well, yes, that would be very nice, but why don't we just keep them here at the house. I'll wash them. Now let me measure your waist. I don't want to buy the wrong size."

She even bought him new shoes and socks. All to keep there at the house. "Go on upstairs, honey, and use the bedroom at the top of the steps on the right. The bathroom is at the end of the hall. You take a quick bath and change and come on back down here before the Judge gets home for dinner."

He ran up the stairs, stepping on the first carpet he had felt underfoot since he had left Bainbridge. In the bedroom, he went around touching everything—the bedcovers, the cedar chest at the end of the bed, the books in a small bookcase under the windows that overlooked the front yard. He touched the lace curtains that framed the window, then let his finger trace the flower designs on the wallpaper. From the open window, he could see across the street to the Lower Peach Tree Cemetery that was in among the cedars surrounding it. He had forgotten the smell of a regular house, the quiet, the feel.

He turned and went into the bathroom down the hall and jerked off his clothes. Suddenly, he saw himself in the mirror on the door. He didn't recognize the person standing there. He reached his hand up to touch a face grown dark and angular. While his arms and legs were very dark brown and scratched in places, the rest of his body was the color of a china plate. He stared at himself, turning slowly around to inspect every part of his body. He seemed to be half of what he used to be and half of what he was becoming.

"Is everything all right up there?" she called.

"Yes, ma'am. I'll be down in a minute." He turned on the bath water quickly and sat down in the first real bath he had had since coming to Lower Peach Tree. At Uncle Luther's, they used a tin bathtub or the creek.

The clothes he found in the bedroom fit him perfectly. He ran back to the bathroom to look in the mirror. The Judge would think he looked good, good enough to sit at the same table.

Down the steps two at a time and into the dining room just as they were sitting down. "My goodness me, John, you look like a new man," she said, "and the clothes fit."

He stood, smiling, waiting to be asked.

"Now why don't you run on and eat your dinner. I put it on the porch," she said.

"But I—"

"What is it?" She smiled.

"Oh . . . oh, nothing."

The Judge spoke. "Undoubtedly, John wants to thank

you for going to all the time and effort it took to get him those new clothes."

John could feel his face glowing. "Uh, yes, sir, I do. That—that's what I wanted. Thanks for the new clothes, Mrs. Vance." He turned around and walked through the kitchen to the back porch, hearing her saying it was no trouble at all.

When Tuway saw him, he almost smiled, but not quite.

They started off to the bank around two o'clock. The Judge walked with a cane, but it seemed only incidental to his progress. He would poke his stick around for the curbs, but he was aware of where they were before he reached them. If somebody was coming, Tuway would say in a low voice, "Mrs. Marlie comin' up," so that just about the time Mrs. Marlie would be on them, the Judge would raise his cane, more like a scepter than an aid. "Afternoon, Cora."

And Mrs. Marlie would say, "Afternoon, Judge" as if he were an ordinary sighted person walking by and noticing her.

The Judge kept up a conversation with Tuway the whole time he wasn't greeting people.

"This afternoon, you need to make sure the Pratts and the Willises get poison delivered out to their places. Take the key and open up the basement for Cal."

"What about R.C.? You gonna give him any? You already done give him the seed and the fertilizer."

The Judge slowed down and took a deep breath. "No, I'm tired of throwing good money after bad. Cal delivered his seed out there. He messed around and didn't plant it till it was too late. Then he stayed drunk the whole time he should have been chopping. What's the use? I made a mistake furnishing him in the first place. I'm not going to compound it any more. This has been going on for years. It's not like it's the first time."

"You forgettin' about his children and his wife?"

"No, I have not, Tuway, but what good does it do them? Every time he gets any cash, he drinks it up. They never benefit. You told me yourself the last time you were out there that the children looked like ragamuffins and half the cotton wasn't out of the ground." He paused crossing the street. "Well, didn't you?"

"Yes, sir, Judge, I did."

"Well, what do you expect me to do? I have to answer to the board. I can't just go around throwing away money."

They walked on in silence, John, Tuway, and the Judge.

"Maybe you can try and get his wife a job at the okra plant," the Judge said.

"Done already tried out at the okra plant, Judge. They ain't hirin'."

"Anybody else on our list?" the Judge asked. They all stopped so that Tuway could take out his black book and consult it.

"Only them people out at the Bend, but they done got they full loans at the first of the season. Cal need to go out there to check on'm?" Tuway watched the Judge's face.

"No, too far. It takes half a day to go and come in good weather. Besides, they grow the best cotton in the county."

"I'm just remindin' you—they didn't make back they loan last year."

"Did you feel those staple samples they brought in last year? I thought L.B. was gonna turn green right on the spot when he saw them. No, leave them be. They're some of the best farmers in the county."

Tuway nodded his head and put his little book back in his pocket.

They reached the bank and John ran around them quickly to open the door so they would remember he was still there.

"All right, John, here we are, your first day on the job." The Judge smiled, but not much. "First thing I want you to do is tell Miss Maroon that you're here; then go around and empty all the trash baskets. That's one job she'll be glad to have done on a regular basis. Then go on down to the basement and find Cal. He's the man who drives the truck."

"What truck?"

"The bank truck. He delivers supplies to farmers who have loans with the bank. Tell him you're supposed to go with him to help out. I know you're not big enough to haul sacks, but you can open gates for him to make his trip faster. Tuway, will you—"

"I'll see to him," Tuway said.

There was a loading dock around in the back of the bank that led into the basement. Stacks of fertilizer and poison were on the concrete floor. Cal was loading bags into the truck as John and Tuway walked down the dark steps that led from the lobby to the basement.

"I thought banks had money inside, not sacks of fertilizer." John was looking at what seemed more like a seed and feed store than a bank.

"The money's upstairs. This here is what makes the money."

"Cal, this here is John." Cal turned from what he was doing and brushed off his hand, sending puffs of white dust up into the air. He immediately recognized John.

"I remember you. You the one I took home from the train station awhile back. How you gettin' on with them Spraigs?"

"Fine." John looked out at the fertilizer truck.

"The Judge say for you to take him on rounds this afternoon. He can help with the gates."

Cal laughed as he wiped his head with a red handkerchief out of his back pocket. "Well, that ain't much help, but I'll take all I can get." He was short and chubby, with a round black face and a gold front tooth when he smiled. "The Judge startin'm mighty young these days, ain't he?"

"It more like the Mrs. Judge startin' him than the Mr. Judge, if you make out my meanin'."

Cal turned to grab another sack and heave it into the truck bed, the muscles inside his rolled-up shirtsleeves bulging. "I know you gotta keep them women happy or it's hell to pay." He brushed off his hands again. "Okay, that's it, 'less you want me to take the Spraigs they poison today. I know where they stayin' now, and it's near where I'm goin'."

"No. Remember, this here is a Spraig," he said, pointing to John. "The Judge say stay away from the Spraigs when you got him with you, and that means all the way away. You got that?"

Cal opened the door of the truck and stepped up to the driver's seat. "Yes, sir, Mr. Tuway," Cal said, smiling. "I'd just as soon stay away from old man Luther altogether, if it was up to me." He started the engine. "Well, go on and get on in here." He motioned to John. "We ain't got all day." He reached over to the other side of the cab and opened the door. John ran around and climbed up the muddy running board into the seat beside Cal.

Cal took out a pack of cigarettes. "You know," he said out the window to Tuway, "I got me two extra cigarettes to give to you if you was of a mind to take'm."

Tuway looked down at the cigarettes. Then, without moving his head, his eyes shifted to look at Cal's face. "I ain't of a mind. I done stopped smokin' for the time bein'."

Cal looked surprised. "You done stopped smokin'? What you mean you done stopped smokin'? I heard you took four last week and three last month."

Tuway looked straight at Cal. "I told ya. I done stopped."

Cal held up his hands. "All right, all right, cousin. I didn't mean nothin' by it. You the one got the habit in the first place. I done told you all along it was bad for you. Liable to land you trouble."

He said this as he took a cigarette out of the pack and lit it with one of the big kitchen matches he had stuck over the sun visor. He blew the smoke out into the cab. "We'll be back directly."

Cal's hand jammed the big stick-shift knob into gear and the truck moved slowly out of the drive. John looked out of the rearview mirror on his side of the truck to see Tuway take a cigarette from his coat pocket and light up as he watched them leave.

Chapter 25

They bumped along in the old truck, Cal talking half to himself as he shifted gears. "Don't smoke no more. What the hell he talkin', don't smoke no more. Ain't nobody gonna believe that. He the one started it in the first place."

They came to a dirt road that had potholes the size of the sacks they were carrying. John had to hold on to the open window frame to keep from bumping his head on the ceiling. "Is he . . . is he really your cousin?" he asked between flying up in the air and banging back down on the seat.

"Is who really my cousin?"

"Tuway, is Tuway really your cousin, like you said?"

Cal laughed. "Tuway everybody's cousin."

They bumped along a minute more, not saying anything. Then John had to ask. "Do you have any other cousins that, you know, that look like Tuway?"

"Look like Tuway?" Cal roared with laughter. "Ain't nobody else like Tuway, boy. Don't you know 'bout Tuway?"

John shook his head.

Cal smiled, mischief in his eyes. The gold tooth sparkled in the sunlight. "They say"—he raised his eyebrows—"Tuway had an Indian daddy and a colored mama. His mama done handed him off to a swamp woman right after he got born. Ain't nobody seed Tuway round these parts 'til he was full grown. Then one day, he just 'peared out of the swamps where he been livin' since he was a baby." Cal looked over at John to see if he believed him. He flicked his cigarette out the window. "Why, some peoples say he got the mark on him."

John said nothing and sat in the cab, staring straight ahead.

Cal laughed. "Well, ain't you gonna ask what the mark is?"

"What, what's the mark?" John said.

Cal leaned over real close and said in John's ear, "They say if you cross Tuway, that'll be the end of you. They say he got magic powers give to him by his swamp mama. Peoples don't mess with Tuway."

The truck came to a stop, dust swirling up all around. Cal sat up straight and laughed. "Okay, first gate."

"What?"

"First gate, boy. Remember, it's your job."

John looked out to see a barbed-wire gate across the road. Beyond that was a dogtrot house like the one he lived in, except this one was neat, with painted shutters and flowers growing in old coffee cans that lined the porch railing. Two old tires painted white and half-buried in the ground marked the path up to the steps. He got out and unhitched the gateposts from the wire to let Cal through. Then he hitched it back and walked up behind the truck into the yard, where two little colored children were playing on a tire swing.

CHAPTER 26

SCHOOL began the next week. It would last for four weeks and then close up again for cotton picking. John was placed in the fifth grade, in Miss Belva's class. Little Luther was in the fourth, Shell in the second.

"If we don't let out after four weeks, some parents will take the children out anyway, so might as well let y'all go," Miss Belva said. She was standing in front of the class, looking over her new crop of fifth graders. These were the same group of faces that had been in the fourth, the third, the second, just as hers was the same face all children passing through the fifth grade had seen for the last ten years. This year, the exception was the new boy, John. She had seated him in the front row. She had asked to have him in her class, more to break the monotony than as a favor to Mrs. Vance, although she knew Adell Vance would be pleased. She continued to talk as she began erasing the blackboard. The students sat with their feet on the floor and their hands on desktops, as they had been taught. Conformity was still novel after a long summer.

She had been to Montgomery to visit this summer, she said. She knew that most of the state didn't do this kind of thing anymore—splitting up the school year—and for the life of her, she couldn't see why they kept doing it here in Perry County.

"Not that many people are raisin' cotton anymore, and you don't need to stop school to tend cows." She turned from erasing the blackboard, chalk dust on her dress. "Now raise your hands. How many of you are actually gonna be pickin' this year?" Ten of the twenty raised their hands. She studied the number and dismissed it. "Well, this class is unusual."

A hand went up in the back of the room. "Yes, Horace," Miss Belva said, pointing a chalky finger.

"What's he doin' here?" Horace nodded in the direction of John.

Miss Belva brushed off her hands and walked over to John. "I'm glad you asked that. This is our new student. His name is John McMillan. He is livin' with the Spraigs now."

"Is he just visitin'?" Horace said.

"Oh, no, no, he is a regular student now."

"He's too little to be in with us," a girl in the back of the room said.

"Oh, no, Darlene, he skipped a grade in his old school and another one here. This is where he belongs and this is where he'll stay if he can do the work." She dismissed the subject and went on to the annual first question of the school year. "Now who all wants to tell me what they did during their summer vacation?" Nineteen of the twenty hands went up.

It was not a bad school, an old brick building with two floors. The first through the fourth grades were on the ground floor, the fifth through the seventh on the second. He felt very superior each morning when he walked up the stairs to the second floor, but when he got there, he felt miserable. No one talked to him. He was so small, he wasn't even afforded recognition by the school bullies.

It was so hot, all he wanted to do was wait for the time to pass so he could go to the Judge's house in the afternoons. All the windows were open and there was only one big fan. It blew mostly on Miss Belva, but after awhile, its motor would get hot and start making a screeching noise. Then Miss Belva would turn it off. Flies buzzed in and out of the open windows. He made slow circling motions with his feet, shifting the small particles of sawdust left on the floor after it was cleaned. He could listen to Miss Belva while he looked out the window. Everything she talked about, he already knew.

He never saw Little Luther or Shell, since they were on the first floor and ate and had playground at different times. Sometimes he would see them at school assembly in between the rows of heads in front of him. This year, ringworm was going around the school. Shaved heads painted with purple medicine were lined up in front of him, but when everybody stood for the flag, he could see between the heads and shoulders to where Shell stood. He always recognized the back of her stringy blond hair.

John and Shell and Little Luther brought their lunches in paper sacks. It was usually biscuits with bacon or strawberry jam, but sometimes nothing in the middle. He didn't care. He knew he could get something good to eat in the afternoons at the Judge's house. He would run all the way there when school let out. Mrs. Vance would

have a sandwich and drink for him, cookies and sometimes cake. He would eat and then hurry to change
clothes for the bank. He had never felt at ease with people
his own age anyway.

He was getting to know everybody at the bank. Sometimes he helped the Judge's secretary, Miss Maroon. She
would keep him busy emptying trash cans and ashtrays.
Sometimes the tellers would say, "Would you please take
these pencils and sharpen them for me, John?" And he
would say, "I'll be happy to, ma'am." He loved saying the
words. He loved doing the deeds. The brass on the tellers'
cages needed polishing. The marble on the customer de-
posit tables needed cleaning. He used Windex to polish
up his glasses, and he could see clearly for the first time in
what he thought must be many years.

Sometimes he thought that Shell and Aunt Nelda and
maybe even Little Luther would like to do his job, but
they couldn't, because it was his, all his.

Sometimes he rode with Cal and opened gates. The
more he rode, the more Cal talked. He talked all the time
to himself and to John, answering questions John had
asked him, though John never knew whether to believe
him or not.

"Why do they call him that?" He settled in beside Cal,
comfortable with their rides now. The truck bumped out
over the curb onto the road out of town.

"The Judge? Why do they call him Judge?" Cal waved at
a young girl going into the Piggly Wiggly. "Well, I'll tell you,
but you ain't gonna understand it. See, bankers is judges if
they like the Judge. He the one says if you gets a crop loan
or not. Round here, if you gets a crop loan, you can make

it, and if you don't, you might just as well go on off down the road."

Cal yelled to two colored men at the Texaco as he turned right onto Highway 80. "Jesseeee. I done seen you down there Saturday night at The Store. You bound to get you some, wasn't he, Earl?" Earl swallowed a mouthful of Coke and peanuts before he burst out laughing. Jesse threw up a hand to push Cal on his way.

Cal laughed and shifted into third gear. "Long time ago, the only ones that give you a crop loan was the man that own the land you stay on. Then the Judge come along, and he say if the man don't do you right and you need a crop loan, then you can come to him and he give you a loan. That's how come all the peoples start sayin' if the man don't do right by'm, they goin' to the Judge. Only now, some of the white peoples that got the land, they don't like the Judge 'cause he's takin' way they business, and the Judge say if they was honest in the first place, he wouldn't be gettin' all the business, and the coloreds, they ain't happy with nobody 'cause they ain't gettin' no fair share, but goin' with the Judge is better than goin' with the man. Ain't nobody happy, but everybody got to get along if they wants to eat. And that's what that's all about."

He looked over to John. "I told you you wouldn't understand. Hell, I don't understand. So ask me a question that's easy."

"Okay, this is easy. How much money do you think we have in our bank?"

"Ah, well now." Cal shifted into fourth and the truck rattled and clanked up to its top speed of forty miles an hour. "Some folks say it's near 'bout one million dollars, but I say it's more like round two hundred million dollars. They say they is a secret vault where gold is stored by the stacks, left over from Worlds War Two."

"Is that really true, Cal?"

"I ain't funnin' ya." Cal winked. "It's down there behind them poison and fertilizer sacks, and if we ever get'm all delivered, we gonna find it one of these years. Yessir, I could use me some of that money." They both sat quietly for a time, pondering the many uses of millions of dollars. Presently, Cal broke the silence.

"You see this here highway, the one we on right this minute?" John nodded. "Well, you get on this here road goin' the way we goin' right now and you can go all the way to Savannah, Georgia. You get on it goin' the other way and you can go all the way to California. Someday I'm gonna get on here and just keep goin', and never come back. I could sure use me some of that money then."

"When you go, will you—" But he thought better of it and said, "I bet you don't know how many zeros in a trillion dollars, Cal."

"Let's see here now. You take your finger and you start writin' zeros in the dust up there on the dash. I'll tell you when to stop."

CHAPTER 27

SOMETIMES on slow afternoons, the Judge would call John into his office to read the *Montgomery Advertiser* to him. Soon it became habit for the boy to complete his work and then sit on the bench outside the Judge's office, hoping to be called. He would pretend to read a magazine as he watched Miss Maroon conduct business at her desk in front of the Judge's door. She took all of his calls and would grimace every time L.B. came on the line. The boy watched as her eyebrows rose far up into her brown bangs and her eyes searched the ceiling. Miss Maroon would hold the receiver away from her ear, letting out long sighs.

John had not paid too much attention to who L.B. was until one day at closing time. The boy was in the habit of walking back to the house with the Judge and Tuway before he went home. This afternoon, the three of them were leaving the bank, when a woman, about the Judge's age, saw them from across the street and raised her hand to get their attention.

Her light blue shirtwaist dress, limp in the afternoon heat, rode up a disappearing waistline and pulled at bosoms too large. She smiled and waved to them as she picked her way across the street made lumpy by years of unfettered oak tree roots. The residents of Lower Peach Tree had grown to love the corridors of shade provided by the top half of the trees that lined the sidewalks of their town. They had learned to live with what was bubbling up from beneath the surface.

"Mrs. Yandell comin' up," Tuway said. "And she look like she wants to pass the time."

"Just the man I want to see," she called to the Judge.

The Judge slowed. "Afternoon, Kitty Lou. How you doing?" They all came to a standstill under the shade of a big oak. Kitty Lou Yandell carried a handkerchief that sent sweet smells wafting through the air each time she raised it to dab her face and neck.

"I could do with a little less heat." She smiled at the three of them. "I swear, y'all are beginnin' to look like the Three Musketeers, I see you together so much."

"Well, you know"—the Judge smiled—"us big high-powered business types need lots of assistants." The Judge reached out and put his hand on John's shoulder. The boy jumped at the touch. He was always surprised that the Judge knew exactly where he was standing.

"Tuway, I hope you're keepin' these two on the straight and narrow," Kitty Lou Yandell said.

"Yes, ma'am, Mrs. Yandell. Hope this heat ain't gettin' you down."

"'Bout like it always does. I'm just out from under the porch fan long enough to walk to the post office and see to the mail—but then I saw y'all. I just said to myself, Byron is the one I need to talk to about this. It's been on my mind all day long."

The Judge began immediately. "I know what you're gonna say, Kitty Lou. Every woman in town has been complaining to me about that new furniture in the lobby. I didn't have a thing in the world to do with that. Miss Maroon—"

"No, no, Byron. That's not it at all, honey. It's something else entirely . . . although I will admit I told Red the other day that furniture is a bit—well, never mind about that now. What I want to talk about is what everybody in town is talkin' about."

The Judge cocked his head and turned toward Tuway. "Everybody in town, and I haven't heard about it? Tuway, you told me everybody in town was talking about the tacky new bank furniture." The Judge shook his head. "See there, Tuway. I'm always the last to know."

"Yes, sir, Judge." Tuway couldn't suppress a grin. "You always the last to know."

"Y'all may think this is funny, but it's not funny. It's serious. I wouldn't waste my time comin' over here if I didn't think it was serious." She paused to let the gravity of the situation sink in. Then she took a step closer. "I think you need to do somethin' about that incident over at the Cotton Patch the other night."

The Judge tried to look knowledgeable. "Ah, that incident at the Cotton Patch." His head moved slowly up and down, as if contemplating.

"I know you're gonna say it's none of your business. That's what Red said. But the boy is on your bank board, isn't he? And his daddy was a friend of yours, and his mama does stay in Montgomery all the time, doesn't she? She's no help."

Now the Judge stepped closer to Kitty Lou and said in a loud whisper, "Who is this we're talking about here,

Kitty Lou? I got a feeling it's either Jack the Ripper or L.B. has been getting himself in trouble again."

"You know good and well it's L.B. That boy is gettin' to be a disgrace to the whole town."

"In either case, Kitty Lou, there's not a lot I can do. L.B. is free, white, and twenty-one. Actually, he's more like thirty-five. He's a grown man."

"Grown man? Grown men don't go around gettin' drunk as Cooter Brown at the drop of a hat and tryin' to—" She looked down at John and stopped, then looked back at the Judge and cleared her throat. "Well, don't you think it's a disgrace? Right out there under the street-light. I just think it's appallin'. I wish he'd go on back over to Selma and do his cattin' around. They say over there he's got a"—she lowered her voice—"a Negra girl . . . had her for years."

"Why, Kitty Lou," the Judge said in mock surprise. "What do you think the Baptists are going to say about you gossiping like that?"

"It's not gossip. It's a fact. And the other night, I saw him with my very own eyes, right out there under the streetlamp after Sissy Reed's engagement party. . . . And don't you go and try beatin' me over the head with the church, Byron Vance."

The Judge smiled. "Well, sometimes that works, Kitty Lou."

Kitty Lou was undeterred. "He's just gotten all out of hand, Byron. What in the world do you think they think of us over in Selma . . . or Tuscaloosa, for that matter?"

"He's not the first Black Belt boy with too much land and too much time on his hands, Kitty Lou. Selma has its share." He held up his hand. "All right, all right, I'll see what I can do, but I'm not promising you anything. L.B. doesn't think he needs advice from anybody—especially me."

Kitty Lou was immediately mollified. She patted the Judge's lapels with her handkerchiefed hand, sending lilac smells swirling about them. "I know you'll think of something, Byron. I just knew if I talked to you, you would fix it. I'm gonna tell Bible study you're gonna be workin' on it. We'll put you on our prayer list." She backed off and again started toward the post office. "Y'all have a good evenin', and say hello to Adell."

"I'll do that," he said. The sound of her heels clicked down the sidewalk and the Judge turned toward home again. "What in the world was that all about? What party? What lamppost?"

"You the Judge. You suppose to know 'bout them lamp-post doin's."

"I wasn't going to ask her what happened under the lamppost. If I had, we'd have been there all night, but—"

Just then, Cal honked as he passed by in the bank truck, headed home. They all waved back at the sound of the horn.

"But what did happen"—the Judge leaned in Tuway's direction—"*under the lamppost*?"

"Well now, I tell you, Judge." Tuway was taking great pleasure in the telling. "I ain't one to spread rumors, but the way I hear it was, seems like L.B. come to the party with some loose girl from over in Canton nobody knowed and he commenced drinkin' too much, like usual. Long about midnight, when everybody was leavin', he got her outside as far as the lamppost and—" Tuway stopped and turned around to see where John was. The boy was so intent on every word, he bumped into Tuway's back.

"And what?" the Judge asked, walking on.

"And . . ." Tuway hurried to catch up.

"And what?" John asked, more interested now that the

story seemed to have a surprise ending. "What happened under the lamppost to the drunk man?" Then he remembered something Little Luther had told him. "I know, I know, he humped the daylights out of her."

The Judge and Tuway stopped abruptly in their tracks and turned to look at him. He stared up at them. "Well . . . well . . . that's what Little Luther says Uncle Luther does when he gets drunk. He goes to town and . . ." His voice trailed off as they both frowned at him. "Well, that's what Little Lu—"

"Boy, I'm gonna wash your mouth out with soap," Tuway growled.

"Well, that's just what he—"

"Do you repeat everything Little Luther says?" the Judge snapped, and began to walk on.

"No, sir, I just thought that when you got drunk and you weren't at home, you—"

"*You what?*" they both yelled at him.

The boy was still trying to know. He asked in a small voice, "Well, what exactly does it mean to hump the daylights out of—"

"Don't say it again," the Judge yelled, and held his cane up in the air, signaling them all to stop again. "Eight years old and talking like a Mobile dockworker," he mumbled.

The three of them began to walk on again in silence.

Kitty Lou looked up from her mail and waved to them from across the street. Tuway returned the greeting with a nod of his head. The Judge stumbled over a crack in the sidewalk and cursed under his breath. The boy walked along, watching them both intently, waiting for some explanation.

They were a block away from home before the Judge said anything. "Tuway will explain that to you when the

CHAPTER 28

JOHN sat on his bench outside Miss Maroon's office, watching the comings and goings that were part of board-meeting day.

L.B. always arrived early, then usually Red Yandell or Jason Debo. This day, Debo and L.B. were the first to arrive. L.B. came in, running a comb through wavy blond hair. He put it back in his coat pocket and walked over to shake hands with Debo. "How's it hangin', Debo buddy?"

"This to a man thirty years his senior," Miss Maroon muttered as she gathered up papers and prepared to go through the boardroom door, which was still open, as the others had not arrived yet.

"Can't complain," Debo said. "Too much dry weather, but I'm survivin'." John knew from talk around the bank that Debo owned a large farm to the south of Lower Peach Tree. Lately, Debo had been turning more and more of his land into pasture, the better to build a herd of dairy cattle and get out of the cotton business altogether.

Debo sat down in one of the conference chairs. "Hear you lost more people. Heard R.C. and his family up and moved out on you."

"Yeah, in the middle of the night, with half a crop planted." L.B. straightened his tie. L.B., the Judge, and state senator Comer were the only ones who always wore a suit and tie to the board meeting. The others came in their workplace clothes. "Only good thing about it was, I didn't furnish him. The Judge made that one."

"That ain't like the Judge," Debo said. "He usually calls'm better than that."

John saw L.B. lean closer to Debo, pretending to spare Miss Maroon his comments—she was in the room, putting pencil and paper at each of the places—but John could hear L.B., and so, of course, could Miss Maroon. "Well, you know what with his health problems and all," L.B. said.

"What health problems? I didn't know the Judge had a problem," Debo said.

"Well hell, Debo, I call goin' blind a health problem."

Miss Maroon slammed pencil and paper down on the conference room table. No one seemed to notice but John.

"Oh, that," said Debo, "well, we all know about that. That's been going on for a long time now. I think he's learned to deal with it pretty good."

"Well, course he has. Just the same. You can't ever tell when something like that will—" There was a loud bang. Miss Maroon was in such a huff, she had walked out of the conference room and pushed the door so hard, it hit her desk and knocked over the framed picture of her nephew.

"Oh, I hate days like this," she said, standing with both arms straight down, hands squeezed into fists. She spotted John watching her. "Pick it up. I mean, pick it up, please."

Just then, Red Yandell came in. L.B. jumped up to greet him. "Red, buddy. How's it hangin'?"

Miss Maroon began mumbling to herself, or maybe she was speaking to John, who had come over to pick up the broken glass. "How's it hanging indeed. I'd like to tell him where to—" She turned and walked back into the conference room.

"Why, it couldn't be better, L.B.," Red Yandell said.

"You gettin' the gin all oiled up, ready to do business?" L.B. asked.

Finally, everyone drifted in, and the meeting started after the Judge came in the room from his office door and was seated.

John was on his hands and knees, picking shards of glass out of the carpeting around the conference room door. After a few minutes, he finished and crawled away, unnoticed, to put the glass in the trash and get a Coke from the refrigerator. Miss Maroon had told him that since he was an employee now, he could have one Coke a day. By the time he came back to his place, on the bench, they were arguing, as usual.

"I will readily admit it. I missed on that one," the Judge said. "I took a chance on R.C. and it didn't work out. I knew he was a risk. It's not a total loss, though. He got seed and fertilizer. That's all."

"And that's another thing," L.B. said. "You're treatin'm like children, dolin' out the feed and fertilizer one by one. Hell, that ain't what a bank is supposed to do. You're supposed to give them the money up front."

The Judge took a deep breath. "They wouldn't be coming here in the first place if they could get a fair deal." He turned in L.B.'s direction. "To charge somebody three dollars for a sack of fertilizer that costs fifty cents is out-and-out robbery."

"He's right, L.B.," Red said. "You can't expect anybody to grow cotton like that."

"Are you accusin' me of cheatin'?" L.B. said. "Hell, Comer over here has been doin' it for years, and he's in the state senate, for Christ sake." L.B. gestured to the man sitting at the table opposite him.

Senator Comer shifted in his seat. "I think it's inappropriate to take the Lord's name in vain, L.B."

"Sorry, Comer . . . but"—he looked back at Red—"I don't like to be accused of cheatin'."

"I ain't accusin' you of cheatin'," Red said. "I'm just agreein' with the Judge. This is the fairest thing we can do. The ones that aren't a credit risk get the whole loan to begin with. The others, we dole it out. We've been over this a thousand times. I say let's call it quits for today. Kitty Lou and me are meetin' the Webbs at the Cotton Patch at seven, and if I'm late, she'll have my fanny in a sling. Excuse me, Miss Maroon."

The Judge adjourned the meeting and everyone got up to leave.

John sat on his bench, waiting until the Judge and Tuway came out of the Judge's office. Tuway was walking along beside the Judge, helping him on with his suit coat. "I'm sorry to rush you, Judge, but my cousin Elva, that stays over at Canton, I told her I'd help her out with a leak in the roof and—"

"No need to explain, Tuway. I can walk home by myself."

"No, sir, Judge, I wouldn't let that happen. I just need to get on as soon as I get you—"

"I am not an invalid, Tuway."

"I know you ain't no invalid." Tuway looked down at the bench. "Why, look who we got here. John, he be glad to walk you home, and that'll make everybody happy. Ain't that right, John?"

"Yes, sir." John jumped up off the bench. "I can walk you home by myself."

"John, what in the world are you doing still here?" the Judge said. "I thought you were long gone, it's so late. Don't you have to get the mail and get home?"

"I already checked the mail. There wasn't any, so I just came on back over."

"I don't need—"

"Why can't we let John here—"

"I can do it, I can do it," John begged.

The Judge held up his hands. "All right, all right. I give up. John, you can walk me home, but Tuway, you need to stop by the Spraigs' on your way to Canton and tell Mrs. Spraig that he'll be late. . . . In fact, just tell her we'll keep him for tonight and he'll be home tomorrow, since it's Saturday. That way, we won't have to worry about getting him home after dark. He's at the back door for breakfast every morning anyway."

"Really? I can stay overnight?" Embarrassed by his outburst, John lowered his head before saying, in what he thought a more dignified way, "I won't put you out. I'll stay on the back porch; I'm used to sleeping outside."

The Judge smiled as he felt for John's shoulder. "You are, are you? Well, I'm sure Mrs. Vance will have you sleeping in the lap of luxury tonight.

"Does that suit you, Tuway? This way, if you have to stay

over at your cousin's, you won't have to worry about getting back tomorrow."

"That'll be just fine, Judge." Tuway turned to stare at John with his Tuway eyes. "You know I ain't gonna be happy if you don't do right, boy."

"Yes, sir, Tuway," he said.

It was his first time to escort the Judge home by himself. He was disappointed that no one was on the sidewalks. He wanted to be the one who whispered the names as they approached. He wanted to be the one to tell what cars were passing, if Miss Etta was sitting on her front porch, if the Reverend Riley had gone from the church yet. It was too late for all of this. Everyone was inside, getting ready for supper.

When they were within seeing distance of the house, John saw Mrs. Vance waiting for them on the front porch and told the Judge.

"Son, Mrs. Vance has been waiting for me on that porch every day for the last thirty-five years. I can tell you exactly what she'll say." He began to talk in Mrs. Vance's accent. "'Byron, honey, I was gettin' worried sick about you. It's quarter to six. Where in the world have you been?' Then she'll see you and she'll say, 'Why John honey, what are you doin' here? Your aunt is gonna be worried sick about you.'"

She said exactly those things as they walked up the steps to the front porch. The Judge smiled.

He and the boy sat on the side sunporch in white wicker waiting for supper. The Judge rocked and listened as John read the *Montgomery Advertiser* to him from cover to cover. All the news, the comics, even what was playing at the movies in Montgomery and about the sales in the department stores.

"You have to keep up with what the women are wearing, John. It tells a lot about what the men are earning."

When they went into supper that night, he ate at the dining room table with them. He had thought so many times of what it would be like. He piled his plate high with food. Then he began eating without looking up. It was pork chops with mashed potatoes and gravy, carrots in butter, hot biscuits, and, of course, ice tea. Suddenly, he felt their eyes on him. He looked around, to see them staring at him, then stopped eating and put his fork down slowly. "I . . . I forgot." He took his napkin out of the ring and placed it in his lap, head down, waiting.

When she finished blessing them, Mrs. Vance acted as if nothing had happened.

"Well, John honey, how do you like your job at the bank? Are you learnin' a lot down there?" she asked.

"I like it," he said, trying to eat and talk at the same time, vaguely remembering that it was impolite.

"Do you like ridin' around with Cal? You know everybody likes Cal. He is one of the most popular Negras in Lower Peach Tree."

"Yes, ma'am. Would you please pass me the biscuits?"

"I think the boy is trying to eat, Adell."

"I know he is, but I'm just dyin' to know how he likes it."

"I'm sure he likes it fine."

"What's the mark?" John asked, his mouth too full of mashed potatoes.

"The what?"

He swallowed. "The mark. Cal says Tuway has the mark."

"Oh, honey, don't you pay any attention to Cal," Mrs. Vance said. "He's just talkin'. All the Negras have all sorts of hexes and superstitions. It's not Christian, if you ask me."

"You just told him you wanted to know about his work, Adell.

"What did Cal say, John?" the Judge asked.

"He said Tuway had the mark and that the bank had a hundred million dollars and soon as we delivered all of the fertilizer and poison we would be able to see it because it's in a vault in the basement. Of course I don't believe that part."

The Judge laughed. "I wish to heaven we did have millions in a vault in the basement. That would solve a lot of my problems. I think Cal was pulling your leg."

He glanced at the Judge and Mrs. Vance without raising his head. "Well, I knew that about the million dollars, but what about the mark? He said Tuway could give anybody the mark if he wanted to. He said Tuway lived in the swamp when he was a baby."

"Tuway has an unfortunate skin condition," Mrs. Vance said. "That's just tacky of Cal to say that."

"I don't know," the Judge said. "I believe if I were in Tuway's shoes, I would rather people think I had magical powers than 'an unfortunate skin condition.'"

The Judge began rubbing his beard and speaking in his best Dr. Frankenstein voice. "You know, my good woman, I never knew quite where he came from. He just appeared on the sidewalk in front of the bank one day, probably came up out of the swamps one night when the moon was full."

"Byron, what is the boy gonna think of you? You do beat all. John, don't you pay the slightest bit of attention to him." She got up and headed to the kitchen. "Now who wants dessert?"

"Where did Tuway truly come from?" John asked when she had left the room.

"He and his family did come from this neck of the woods. I'm not quite sure where, but he had a couple of years at Tuskegee some time back. He has a damn lot more sense than a lot of the peckerwoods around here, black or white—sorry, colored or white. The fact that he has an 'unfortunate skin condition,' as Adell puts it, is lucky for me. It seems to give him some sort of exemption in both communities." He drank the last of his ice tea. "Also, I'm sure you have noticed, Tuway is rather large."

John liked it when she was out of the room. He sat back in his chair and tried to affect a casual air. "I noticed you don't talk like Mrs. Vance does. Did you come from around here?"

"Very astute of you, John. No, I don't talk like she does. I hail from up around Winston County, north of Birmingham. That's where I get my twang."

John wiped his mouth with his napkin and tried to imitate the Judge. "And then you had a couple of years at Tuskegee?"

The Judge grimaced. "Your mother sure did keep you under wraps, didn't she? Tuskegee is a colored school. I went to Auburn, over in Lee County."

"Oh."

Mrs. Vance came back into the room carrying a pie thick with meringue and perched on top of a glass pedestal server. She set the server down next to John and began to cut. "Do I hear the Judge haranguin' you with all that nonsense about different counties, John honey? We're all the same. All over the South, we're all the same. I know because

I went to Judson College. Girls from all over Alabama came to Judson."

She cut a big piece of pie and put it down in front of the Judge, who was already amused by what he knew she was going to say next.

"'And the girls over there were all just lovely and they were all the same,'" he mimicked.

"It's the truth, and you know it's the truth," she said. She looked at John and smiled. "It's coconut cream, your favorite."

CHAPTER 29

THAT night, he slept in a real bed. She took him to an upstairs bedroom and tried to give him a kiss good night, but he backed away, pretending to inspect the room. Mrs. Vance told him to undress and gave him an old pajama top that was the Judge's. She said she would be back later.

It felt strange being there, even though he had been in this room once before. He walked around touching the bed, the chair in the corner next to the windows that overlooked the front yard. He used to feel so comfortable in a room like this. Now, somehow, he felt ill at ease and closed in. He tried to think of how it used to be but could not.

She came back later to hear him say his prayers. He had almost forgotten what to say, but mumbled a few things he thought she might consider appropriate. As soon as she turned out the light and closed the door, he scrambled out of the stiff white sheets, which felt smothering to his skin now. He went to the window and pulled the shades up to give moonlight to the room, then sat down on the floor to inspect the contents of the book-case. The names of the books were titles he might like if he were a girl: *The Hidden Staircase, Little Women,* an old *Uncle Remus.* John took the books out one at a time, trying to read in the dim light. The words were hard to see and he thought that must have made him fall asleep and dream the rest.

He dreamed that he woke and was still on the floor, with the moon streaming through the two windows. As he got up to get back in the bed, he glanced out the front window. Through the branches of the big oak tree in the front yard, there was a light off in the distance on the other side of the graveyard. He rubbed his eyes to look again, but this time he saw nothing and was about to get in bed, when, moving through the darkness, three people came walking up out of the other side of the cemetery. When they passed under the streetlight, he could see they were all black except for the one who was black and white at the same time. The dream ended as he heard the whistle of Obadiah's train passing through town.

Chapter 30

THEN next morning, Tuway had not returned, and so it fell to John to take the Judge over to the cotton gin for coffee. Saturday was the day that colored people went to town and white people were supposed to stay off the streets. The white men met at the cotton gin to "shoot the bull," the Judge said. He told John to drop him off at the gin and then go on home. He could find his way back.

"No, sir," he said in a matter-of-fact way. "Tuway said I better stay or—"

"Ah yes, I forgot Tuway's admonition."

They were standing on the front porch, next to large white wooden columns that had seen better days. A small pile of wood dust left by carpenter ants lay at the bottom of the column the Judge held to. "Probably if he doesn't get back, I'll have to stay over till Sunday," John said. He glanced sideways to see the Judge's reaction. Seeing none, he ventured further. "I probably need to so I can go to church with y'all." He glanced again . . .

and nothing. "It's because my religious education is not what it should be."

"Is that right?" the Judge said as he negotiated the front steps, using the black iron railing Tuway had built for him.

"Yes, sir," John said, standing close beside the Judge. They left the steps and front yard to navigate the sidewalk, skirting around cracks in the cement caused by the oak tree roots. The Judge felt with his cane for cracks he had memorized.

"And did you and Mrs. Vance come to that conclusion this morning?"

"Yes, sir, we did."

"The part about how your religious education was suffering?"

"Yes, sir. She said the Baptists would have none of that." He tried to gauge the Judge's face to see just how far he might go.

"None of what? Dare I ask?"

"None of having a little person like myself left to the vicissitudes of life."

"I think you're pushing it there. The *vicissitudes* of life?"

"I'm just saying what she said." He tried, and failed, to look innocent. "She said it right after I told her it had been so long, I couldn't even remember how to say my prayers, only I forgot to tell her that last night, so I told her about it this morning. Probably Sunday school would do me a world of good."

He told the Judge a curb was coming up. They walked across the street in silence. John kept watching the sidewalk but continued selling. "Did you realize she's been the organist at the First Baptist Church of Lower Peach Tree for ten years? Did you know that, ten years? I was just amazed."

"I'll bet you were," the Judge said.

They were entering the cotton gin grounds. Empty wagons with tufts of cotton caught in wire-mesh sides sat idle on a dusty dirt field that served, when cotton was in season, as the assembly line for wagons from all over the county. An aging tin roof covered the building that held the bailing mechanisms. Jutting out from its side was another roof, which held a giant vacuum tube ready to suck raw cotton from the wagons that pulled beneath it. Hours later, it would disgorge onto the back loading dock a giant white brick wrapped in burlap and steel bands—proof of a whole year's labor.

The Judge and John walked toward the side of the gin building where the office was located. "I must remember not to let you two get together too often. You'll devise a plan to conquer the world." He felt for the latch and opened the big wood door.

"All right, sit down out here on the bench and try to stay out of trouble." He walked through the door.

John could hear the other men greeting the Judge. Just before the Judge shut the door, he had turned to John. "Perhaps you might try praying a little while you wait—you know, to keep yourself from a life of sin and degradation."

John jumped back up off the bench. "Yes, sir."

"Good, good." The Judge put his tongue in his cheek and closed the door.

John sat down on an old wooden bench directly beneath a sign advertising Garret snuff. It was shady under the tin roof that covered the small porch area. A bee buzzed around his head and then darted off into the sunny gin yard to search around the clumps of wild daisies that had survived the comings and goings of wagon wheels and trucks by growing in out-of-the-way places next to a fence post or underneath the fringes of the loading dock.

He didn't stay seated long, because it was his duty to see what they were talking about—just like Tuway would do. He stepped off the porch and went around to the side of the building where the office windows were open.

"You take it black, don't you, Judge?"

"Thanks, Red."

"Debo, what the hell kind of cigar is that you're smoking? Smells like blackstrap molasses," the Judge said.

"I'll have you know it's the finest Cuban blend. Got it while I was in New Orleans last week at the Federal Land Bank meetin'."

"Probably out cattin' around with some of them honeys in the Quarter. Thought the fancy cigar would give him more charm." It was L.B., by the sound of his voice.

"With Lee Ann along? All we did was eat at every high-priced restaurant she could find. I musta gained ten pounds. I'm happy to get back here to God's country. Too much farmin' goin' on right now to stay away long."

"Did I hear you got yourself a new hauling truck, Red?" the Judge asked.

"Bought it off a fellow over in Demopolis that went broke. Couldn't resist takin' the chance that maybe the cotton will be good this year."

"Hell, the crops can be as good as gold. If you ain't got nobody on shares, what good does it do you?" L.B. said.

"You know more and more people are giving up farmin' on shares, L.B. You ought to think about it," Debo said, "especially with all that stuff goin' on in Montgomery right now. Did you read the paper the other day?

That colored wouldn't get out of her seat on the bus and—"

"Oh hell. They don't know what they're doin' up in Montgomery. Listen, one politician is just as bad as the next one."

"Did you ever find out what happened to R.C. and his family?" the Judge said, changing the subject.

"Nope. Can't figure it," L.B. said. "I asked Ed down at the station if he had seen them get on a train. He said if they went by train, he would know about it 'cause either he's there or George. Said they hadn't seen any coloreds leavin' by train. And R.C. and Willa hadn't had a car since he wrecked that last one back five years ago."

"You know I don't mind so much about R.C. He's on the road to drinking himself to death anyway. I just hope nothing bad came of Willa and the children," the Judge said.

"Hell, you know nothin' came of'm. They're on their way up north to Chicago, but I'll be damn if I can figure out how," L.B. said. "They didn't have a nickel."

"What matter does it make, L.B.?" said Debo. "If they're gone, they're gone."

"The hell they are. I'd stop'm. I'd repossess their car or whatever they have to make'm repay their debts."

"You can't squeeze blood out of a turnip, L.B.," Red said.

"It's none of your damn business what split I take, Red."

"The hell it ain't. Every time another family leaves, it means less cotton for me to gin. Sure as hell it's my business. You want some more coffee, Debo?"

Red poured Debo more coffee and then got back on L.B. "You need to stop cheatin' the men and screwin' the women, L.B."

There was a noise like the raking back of a chair. John stood on tiptoes to look through the window. L.B. had jumped up out of his chair and was facing Red.

"Listen, you son of a bitch, just because no woman ever gave you a second look." L.B. grabbed a Coke bottle off the table and took a step toward Red.

The Judge stood up, putting himself between the two of them. "All right now, boys, I have a feeling things are about to get out of hand here. You wouldn't hit a blind man, would you?" He laughed. "If you do, I won't know which one did it. So now just sit down and cool off."

"That's right, L.B. Back off, man. The Judge is right. It's too early in the mornin' to be drawin' blood," Debo said. He let his chair, which he was leaning against the wall in, come forward, ready to get up and help out the Judge if need be.

"I keep telling y'all, coloreds or the lack thereof ain't our problem; it's change. The times are changing and we need to change with them. Ain't that right, Debo?" the Judge said, still standing between Red and L.B.

L.B. gripped the Coke bottle tighter, watching Red and talking to the Judge. "You beginnin' to sound like your judge friend, the one they just appointed up there in Montgomery. Weren't you two brought up in the same county? Didn't you tell me you knew Judge Johnson when he was a boy?"

"Now you're really reaching, L.B." The Judge tried to laugh. "Times ain't changing that much, but they are changing; ain't that right, Debo?"

"You might have a point," Debo said, still eyeing L.B. "I ain't sayin' you do, but you might." He put his coffee cup down on a nearby table and stood up.

With that, L.B. knew he was outnumbered. He threw the Coke bottle on the floor and turned toward the door.

"You bastards just can't see the forest for the trees." He walked to the door, jerked it open, and was gone.

Red walked over and picked up the Coke bottle to put it back on the desk. He looked over at Debo. "What are you shakin' your head for?"

"You didn't have to bait him like that, Red. He's a lot younger than we are."

"Hell," Red said, "he is cheatin' the coloreds, and he does have the worst zipper problem in the county. We all know it. He's got to grow up. He's got too much acreage to be so irresponsible. He's laid every colored girl that'll come within ten miles of him and couldn't even get his wife pregnant." Red walked over to the cold-drink box and lifted the top up to get a bottle of Coke. "Why do you think she left him? And where do you think he got his name? It may be Lamar Braxton on the birth certificate, but the coloreds changed that years ago. 'Who's Love Boy humpin' this week?'" He opened the Coke and took a long drink that half-emptied the bottle.

Debo picked up a pack of peanuts off the display rack on the counter. "Yeah, I've heard Cal talkin'. They know what he's like. They say he's had one honey or another over in Selma since he was old enough to get in a car and get over there." Debo poured the peanuts into his Coke bottle. "Boys will be boys," he said, "but I think he has a point about the niggers disappearin'. Seems strange to me."

"I know boys will be boys, Debo," Red said, "but they say he's rough with the women. I've heard rumors."

"Besides, he's not a boy anymore," the Judge said as he moved back to his chair and sat down.

Debo took a swallow of Coke and peanuts. "You gotta have some sympathy for him, sittin' in that big house night after night all by himself. No wonder he drinks so much," Debo said.

The Judge sighed. "I sure do wish old man Dawson had taught him a little about banking before he up and died on us." Then he turned to Red. "Say, Red, how about another cup? That last one got turned over in the fray." He rubbed his beard. "Do you remember when we used to come out here on Saturday morning and enjoy it?"

Just then, Tom Dover, the postmaster, walked in. "Mornin', everybody. How's it goin' there, Judge? Debo? Nothin' like a quiet Saturday morning just to sit back and relax."

They all smiled at him and shook their heads.

"What? What did I say?"

CHAPTER 31

SUNDAY after church—John had talked his way into staying another night—Mrs. Vance was bustling around in the kitchen. "John honey," she called into the living room. "I'm out of mint for the tea. Will you run across to the cemetery and get some from Jesse Clee?" She came in the living room, wiping her hands on her apron.

"Ma'am?"

"It's the big one with the prayin' angel on the top."

He still sat there looking at her.

"Three or four sprigs will do, just the new growth, the little leaves." She turned and left the room.

The Judge lowered the volume on the radio. "She's talking about Jesse Clee, John. He was a farmer around here for a good many years. His family had all that land just south of Brown's Crossing. Anyway, the man was a fool for mint juleps. He loved them so much, his wife planted mint on his grave. Seems all the ladies of the town use it when their supply runs low. His grave is in the back row of the cemetery, the one with the big angel carving on top of it. I think it says, 'Beloved husband, loving father,' something like that." The Judge turned the radio back up and began listening to the news again. When he didn't hear John get up and leave, he turned it back down again. "What is it?"

"She wants me to go in the cemetery and get mint off a dead person's grave?"

"I used to do it." The Judge smiled. There was silence. "It's broad daylight, son. It can't hurt you."

"I know that." He eased himself off the chair. "Yes, sir, I know that."

He walked slowly out of the house, crossed the side yard and street to get to the town cemetery. The gate on the wrought-iron fence that surrounded the cemetery made an ominous squeaking noise. Sticking out of the ground, row after row, like tabs in some mammoth filing system, was the history of Lower Peach Tree.

Off at a distance he could see the marble angel standing on marble tree branches, wings outstretched, ready for flight. Toward the front of the cemetery, on the street side, were tiny markers of children who hadn't made it past a few months. They lay at the feet of the larger crude markers of their pioneering parents. Headstones of later years were carved with Confederate flags and words of defiance and grief. Toward the back, the history became more immediate and top-heavy with men and their more modern wars. Lower Peach Tree had contributed four souls to the Spanish-American War, ten to World War I, and too many to count in World War II. He saw only one headstone from Korea. It was over in the Debo family's plot. Their son Thomas, John calculated, had been nineteen.

Beyond the mint grave were tall weeds, where other

graves were barely visible through the undergrowth. After he picked the mint, he edged over beyond the regular cemetery. There, almost hidden by the weeds, were large slabs lying flat on the ground. The words that had been on these stones had faded away long ago, but one of them had a large *X* across the front, newly drawn in white chalk. He turned to see if his bedroom window was visible from where he stood.

At dinner, he told the Judge he would be glad to stay over another night so he could be there early the next morning and not worry about being late.

Mrs. Vance started to say something, but the Judge interrupted her and said that it was mighty considerate of him but that he had better get on home after he ate.

After dinner, he stretched out the day as long as it would go, reading the Sunday paper to the Judge cover to cover, filling the Judge's pipe with stale tobacco and insisting he smoke it, suggesting they do the Sunday crossword puzzle.

Finally, the Judge put his pipe down and let the strong odor of stale smoke smolder in the bowl. "John, come over and sit down on the ottoman."

John eyed the Judge suspiciously but came and took a tentative seat.

"Do you remember the first time we met?"

"Yes, sir, on the train. We had coconut cream pie. I read the papers to you. We had meatloaf and—"

"That's right. You asked about my blindness. I told you I was learning to cope, remember?"

"Yes, sir."

"Well, I just want to tell you that I think you are doing an admirable job learning to cope with what life has handed you." He waited a moment before saying anything else.

"Do you know what I'm talking about?" He waited again, but John didn't answer.

"You can't change the fact that they are your aunt and uncle. You just have to cope with it."

"I hate'm."

The Judge was silent for a long time after that. Then he said, "That's probably part of what coping is, knowing how you feel and dealing with it anyway. Do you understand what I'm saying?"

"You're saying I gotta go home now."

The Judge raised his hand up to his chin and rubbed his beard. The boy couldn't see his eyes. "Yes, you have to go home now."

John climbed the stairs and changed back into his home clothes, then left by the back door, without telling either one of them good-bye.

Aunt Nelda stood watching him at the supper table. She was smoking her supper as she stood over a pot of spaghetti sauce bubbling on the stove. Spaghetti was a real treat, and the others had already received large plates and were eating by the time he got there.

"Course I know it ain't dinner with the Judge." She let the plate drop to the table in front of him.

Uncle Luther glanced up at Nelda, then took up the cudgel. "We thought you had gone and got yourself adopted." He tore a piece of bread off the loaf in the middle of the table.

John sat staring at the spaghetti. "They don't want me."

Uncle Luther let out a coarse laugh. "Hear that, Nelda? Them people's got more sense than I give'm credit for."

CHAPTER 32

MONDAY, Tuway was back. He walked in, telling the Judge and Mrs. Vance how his cousin Elva was much obliged to him for coming over there and fixing her roof. It was a hot job but he got it done and how were things while he was gone? The Judge said everything was just dandy and that John had done a good job. Between Mrs. Vance and John, he was more than taken care of. "In fact," he said, "they have devised a plan that will free you up most Saturdays."

Tuway said that was fine with him. He said that, as the Judge knew, he was a part-time preacher anyway and that he was going to have to do some preaching over near Burnt Corn later in the year and, this way, he would have more time to get over there.

As always, John and Tuway sat on the back porch at dinnertime. John kept looking at Tuway, wanting to ask him if he was the one he had seen on Saturday night, or had he been dreaming? But the idea of possibly making a fool of himself in front of Tuway, talking about things that might or might not have been, was too silly even in his mind. Every time Tuway looked up at him, his resolve melted. Finally, Tuway said, "What is it you want, boy? The rest of my cornbread?" He pushed his plate toward John and went back to looking at his little leather book.

On their way to work that afternoon, John asked the Judge, "Why is it that you live next to a cemetery?"

"What's the matter? Don't you like being so close to dead people?" The Judge laughed. "Still thinking about your trip to get the mint yesterday?"

"Where I used to live, the cemetery was out on the edge of town."

"The house we live in now was once a plantation house. That was before Lower Peach Tree became a town. That graveyard started out as a family burial plot and developed into one for the whole community as the town grew. Have you ever noticed the graves at the far end over there?" He pointed with his cane in the exact direction of the *X*.

John looked at Tuway. He was walking straight ahead, as if he wasn't listening.

"No, sir," he said.

"Well, back in the weeds are some old slave graves that have been there longer than any of the others. Some are marked with stones. Most aren't. You should take a look sometime. Tuway will show you."

CHAPTER 33

JoHN and Cal were stacking poison sacks for storage a few days later when Tuway came out back to have a smoke.

"Well," Cal said, "I hear you done gone and took up smokin' again, and you told old Cal you done give it up." Cal threw a sack from the back of the truck and went to get another without looking at Tuway. "What's you 'spect? I wasn't good enough to know your business?"

Tuway didn't say anything, staring out into the parking lot, hunched over, his elbows on his knees. He blew out long trails of smoke that hung in the air.

Cal went to get another sack. "All my friends sayin', 'You cousins with Tuway. You talk to him. He listen to you.' And here I am actin' the fool, sayin', 'Old Tuway say he done give it up. I can't help you, brother.'"

"I done give it up. That just was somethin' had to be done." Tuway dropped his cigarette and stepped on it as he stood up. He turned and walked back inside.

John looked to Cal. "Did he give it up just then when he put out that cigarette, or did he give it up the other day when I saw him smoking when he already said he had done give it up?"

Cal looked disgusted. "Who the hell knows 'bout Tuway. Go on, jump in the cab."

They drove out the main highway and had turned onto a side road, when there was a big popping sound and the truck lurched to the right. Cal took his foot off the gas and coasted to a stop. "I know what it is. That right rear been ball for a month now. Get on out. We'll have to change it." Cal got out of his side and rummaged through what little equipment there was behind the backseat of the truck. He pulled out a lug wrench but couldn't find a jack. "Somebody always messin' with my tools. What I'm supposed to do without no jack? Sam done took this truck to Demopolis last week, and that's what happens." He threw a heavy chain back in the space behind the seat and slammed the door shut, disgusted.

"Go on up there." Cal pointed to a drive that curved off the main road. "That's the Dawson place. Find George, he be there, and get him to give you a jack to bring me. I'll be gettin' the lugs off while you go."

John hesitated. There was no house in sight, only a wide drive that disappeared behind a grove of tall cedar trees. "How far is it?"

"It ain't far, maybe half a mile. It's where old L.B. stay."

"Mr. L.B. lives up there?" John still didn't move.

Cal looked up from crouching over the blown tire. "Go on. He ain't gonna bother you. He probably half-drunk by now anyway. George say he do that on days he ain't got to go into town or Montgomery."

Cal turned back to the business of loosening the lug nuts. "Shake a leg," he said. "We ain't got all day. Got to get this here fertilizer delivered. And tell George we don't need no candy-ass jack—this here is a big truck."

John began his walk up the drive. On either side of the entrance, there were large stone columns. Up the road a short distance he noticed plantings on both sides of the driveway that needed weeding. From his hours in Mrs. Vance's garden, he was tempted to stop and pull out the larger weeds.

As he walked on, the cedar trees gave way to the view of a grand three-story house, white, with turrets and porches running across the front, more Victorian in style than the usual larger plantation houses he had passed on his trips out into the countryside with Cal. This one looked as if it had grown up and old along with the towering cedars that surrounded it, not easy grown and not soon washed away.

His shoes made a crunching sound on the gravel of the circular drive, which was outlined with very old mis-shapen boxwood. Moss grew between the crosshatched bricks that formed the path to the porch steps.

He had noticed from a distance that the large oak carved front door was standing open, so when he climbed the porch steps, he didn't think of knocking but walked up to the threshold and peered inside.

There was a wide hall that ran the length of the house, with a staircase that circled the walls up and up until it reached the entrance to the cupola that crowned the roof. A breeze blew past him, down the hall and out the open doors at the opposite end. Threadbare Oriental carpet covered the floor, and four large oil portraits of men and women lined the walls. He turned back around at the door. From this view, he could see that the house sat on top of a soft rise in the land, affording a view of all the surrounding countryside. He could even see the top of Cal's truck off in the distance. The cedars that he had thought were randomly placed were actually laid out in a pattern surrounding the house and edging the drive.

He stepped inside, feeling that he was entering a sanctuary of some kind and that there was something here he should be afraid to disturb. "George? Is anybody home?" He said it in a whisper. Still his voice echoed up through the stairwell and then fell silent. A breeze ruffled the lace doily that centered the cloisonné bowl, which sat atop the mahogany hunt board that anchored the hall, which served as the hub, of this house that cotton built.

He called again, this time a little bolder. "Hello, is anybody here?" He felt silly saying it. Of course somebody must be here with the doors open. He stomped his feet a few more steps into the hall and called again. "Cal sent me to get a jack." He stood very still to listen and thought he heard a faint sound from the back end of the house, so he walked up to where the stairs began and looked down the hall. There was a noise out on the back porch. An older colored man appeared in the doorway, carrying a coat he was hurriedly putting on.

"Didn't hear you comin', Miss Eugenia. I was out back waterin' the—" He stopped short when he saw it was a child. "Oh, I thought you was somebody else." The colored man slowly took off his coat and draped it neatly back over his arm. "What's you doin' here? Ain't you the boy at the bank?" He squinted. "Ain't you the Judge's helper?"

"Yes, sir."

"I thought I recognized you. What you doin' out here? You got a message for Mr. L.B. from the Judge?"

"No, sir. Our truck broke down and Cal sent me to borrow a jack, if you got one to spare, a big one for a truck."

"Where he broke down at?"

"Just outside your driveway." John gestured. "You can see our truck from here."

George glanced out the door. "Think I seen a jack out in the garage, up on the wall. Let me go see what I can find." He turned to leave, and John followed. "No, you stay here. Go wait in there." He pointed to a room off the hall. "I might have to do some searchin'. Don't know as how I seen no big jack in some time now." He disappeared down the hall.

John turned around and looked at the portraits hanging there. One was of a beautiful woman in a bright blue dress. Another was of a man in a hunting outfit. He wandered into the living room. There were Victorian chairs and a sofa around a marble fireplace. Fresh-cut branches of magnolia leaves stuffed in a large brass container filled the fire well. A big gold-framed portrait of a lady in a skirted riding habit hung over the mantel. Photographs sat in frames on the side tables. He picked up a small one and was studying it when he heard a noise from the floor above and then steps on the staircase.

"Mama? I'm sorry. I was just upstairs," a voice called.

John walked out to the hall, to see L.B. knotting his tie and hurrying down the steps.

"I didn't think you would come." He was busy pulling the knot tight and didn't notice John or the stairs. Eight or ten steps from the bottom, he tripped and fell the rest of the way down, sliding on his rear until he reached the hall floor. L.B. sat there half-dazed, not seeming to know where he was.

"You all right?" John stepped closer and was immediately enveloped in the smell of hard liquor.

L.B. took a moment to look around. "I thought you were my mother." He brushed back his hair with one hand. "She comes to visit once in awhile. Said she might come today." He began to try to stand up. "Course I knew she wouldn't. She never comes except to . . ." He held on to John's shoulder and the stair banister to steady himself.

"What are you doin' here anyway?" His eyes focused on John for the first time. "You're the Judge's kid, aren't you?"

"Yes, sir."

"You got a message from the Judge? Is that why you came?" He loosened his tie with one hand while he still held to the banister with the other. "Sure as hell didn't come to visit, did you?"

"No, sir. Me and Cal had a flat tire out on the main road. I came to borrow a jack."

"Oh, well, I guess we can oblige you. George," he yelled. "George'll get it for you. George," he yelled again, "get your sorry ass down here."

"I talked to him already. He's gone to get it for me."

"Oh." L.B. blinked his eyes, trying to focus on the thought. "Well, good. Good man, George."

He let go of the stair rail and stood still, testing his ability to stand alone. "Well now, as long as you're here, might as well come in and visit. Not that I would ordinarily entertain a kid"—he rubbed his back where it had hit the stairs—"but you know the dictates of southern hospitality." His hand moved to his rear end to check for damage. "That's why I'm doin' it, invitin' you in." He swayed toward the door to the living room and motioned John to follow him. "Come on. Come on in here to the parlor."

L.B. walked over to a sideboard that held a silver tray with several glass decanters. "Only touch this stuff when guests come." He struggled to get the top off of the decanter containing bourbon. "That way, it keeps me from drinkin' too much." He turned to John and smiled. "Good plan, huh?"

"Yes, sir."

"You want a drink?"

"I'm too little."

L.B. broke into gales of laughter as he spilled portions of bourbon in the glass and on the tray. "I didn't mean this. This is a man's drink. Didn't start drinkin' this 'til I was a freshman at Alabama." He turned to John and put his fingers to his lips. "Well, maybe a little before that, but don't tell." He began laughing again.

"I meant a Coke, doofus. You want a Coca-Cola?"

"Yes, sir. That would be nice," John said. He was watching very carefully now. This was and wasn't reminiscent of Uncle Luther. He was not sure what would happen next, but he wanted to be ready to run.

L.B. took a hot Coke out of the cabinet directly beneath the bourbon tray, popped the top, and handed it to John as the fizz bubbled over onto his hand.

"Come on over here and sit down." L.B. stumbled to the sitting area in front of the fireplace and sat down heavy into one of the overstuffed chairs. The drink in his hand spilled out onto his shirtsleeve. He took a white handkerchief out of his coat pocket to dab at the spill. Then he stuffed it back in his pocket and sipped his drink while he studied John. "What's that you got in your hand?"

John looked down to the picture he still held in his hand, the one he had been looking at when he heard L.B. on the stairs. "Oh, I'm sorry. It goes over . . ." He moved toward the table to replace it, but L.B. gestured for him to bring it to him.

"Let's see. All these pictures, they got a story behind them, you know. I can tell you a million stories."

John walked over and gave the picture to L.B., who held it at arm's length, trying to focus on it.

"Now this is a picture of a party Mama used to give in the spring. People came from all over the Black Belt. See right over there"—he pointed to the side of the group of people standing in the snapshot—"that's Scottie and Zelda. That's what Mama used to call'm, Scottie and Zelda. Came down from Montgomery just to come to our parties. That's how famous they were." He studied the picture closely. "That's how famous we were.

"You know where this picture was taken?" John shook his head no. L.B. pointed the picture skyward. "Up there." He brought the picture down again to look at it. "Looks like a ballroom out of the goddamn Waldorf-Astoria, but it's right upstairs. Biggest damn ballroom you ever saw. Mama had it built. Most people have bed-rooms on the second floor. We got a goddamn ball-room." He laughed and looked at John. "Is that funny or what?" John tried to smile.

"People used to come in and go up those steps"—he gestured to the hall—"and dance the night away. Hell, you could hear the orchestra all over the house." He stared out into space, his head moving slightly back and forth, keeping time with some long-ago melody. He turned to look at John. "I was a little kid then, but I saw it all. Hell, I saw it all."

He looked down at the picture. "She used to dress me up in black velvet." He pointed to a woman in a long dress. "See this. That's Mama." He looked at his mother for a long time, then leaned his head back on the crocheted antimacassar that covered the top of the chair. John thought he might be going to sleep, but L.B. roused himself. "Here, take this back and go get me another picture. I can tell you a million stories."

John was replacing the picture and about to pick up another, when George appeared at the door carrying a heavy jack handle in one hand. "I think we got us what we need here. Come on, boy. I got the rest outside. I'll help you carry it down to Cal."

John set his Coke bottle down and began to walk toward the door.

"Oh, hell no, George," L.B. whimpered, "I got a million stories to tell him."

"You just sit right there, Mr. L.B., and finish your drink. I'll help the boy and be back directly."

A few days later—it was on a Wednesday; John remembered the day because all the stores had closed at noon—he and Tuway were on the back porch, John reading a Nancy Drew mystery he had found in the room upstairs, Tuway dozing in his rocker. Suddenly, they heard a rustle and Cal came rushing through the wooden gate into the Vances' backyard. He started talking without any kind of greeting.

"Now I know you said you done stopped, cousin, but this one last time I needs your help." He was breathing hard, as if he had been running. "I ain't askin' for myself. It's my cousin Darrell. He been kicked outta where he stay. The law's comin' after him. He gotta have a way up to Chicago."

"Your cousin Darrell?" Tuway was half-awake and had forgotten John was there. "I ain't never heard of your cousin." He sat in his rocking chair, rubbing his eyes.

"That's 'cause he stay over in Selma. Don't visit here much."

"Selma," Tuway almost shouted. "Selma. What the hell you bringin' somebody all the way from Selma? I ain't runnin' no travel bureau here. What's got into you, Cal?"

Cal came closer to the screen and whispered, "He's in bad trouble, Tuway, and it ain't his fault. The man after him for somethin' wasn't none of his doin'. You got to help him." He turned toward the gate and said, "Come on out here, Darrell. Let Tuway see you."

Tuway jumped up out of his chair. "What the— You bringin' him here? Are you crazy, nigger?" He was through the screen door, pushing Cal out of the back-yard. They disappeared around the side of the house.

John sat there for the longest time holding the Nancy Drew book and staring at Tuway's little leather book, which had fallen on the floor as he ran out.

When he reached down to pick it up, his hand was shaking.

It was divided into two sections. The first one said "bank" on the separation tab. In the back was a smaller section. That tab was marked with an *X*.

He looked around the yard and into the kitchen. There was not a sound except for some birds playing in the birdbath in the garden. He turned to the X tab. There were lists of names and then dates beside them. He turned through all the pages till he got to the last one with writing on it. There they were, R.C., Willa.

PART TWO

CHAPTER 34

JOHN had known what he wanted to do from the minute he looked into Tuway's little book, but knowing and doing were different things. All through the fall and into the winter, he kept thinking about it, making plans. Each time Uncle Luther had another "flare-up," as Aunt Nelda called it, John would vow to leave.

School had started again after cotton picking was over. The weather turned cool, never really cold. John had moved his bed into the feed-sack room behind Little Luther's bedroom. This had been just fine with him. It was dusty and, on some mornings, cold, but there weren't as many sacks left by then and he had it all to himself. He had taken Aunt Nelda's broom and swept the floor clean of spiders and other debris. Webs that were too high for the broom to reach, he left.

At night, he lay awake, watching the ceiling spiders spinning their webs by the light of his kerosene lantern and thinking of how he might escape to Chicago. He would follow Tuway the next time he put somebody on the train to Chicago. Tuway, he would say, you have to send me to Chicago, too, or I'll tell, or words to that effect. He constantly worked on that part in his mind, altering the words, thinking of new ways to threaten Tuway.

John knew that was what was happening. He hadn't dreamed it. Tuway was somehow sending people, who had no money to get there, up to Chicago, probably on the train. He would be one of those people just any day now, maybe this next Saturday.

But as each Saturday arrived, he would think of some excuse not to go. The Judge needed him to work in the garden that day or Uncle Luther might whip him again if he caught him trying to leave. He had to make a foolproof plan. The Saturdays came and went.

Uncle Luther sold his cotton and made just enough to pay back the bank and pay rent on the land, with precious little left over. It had not been a good year for cotton. In addition, most of his crop had been planted so late and was so poorly tended that the yield was less than half of what everyone else got. He made great show of telling the supper table that next year they would make twice as much as this year.

Aunt Nelda seemed to know better. At night, she sat at the kitchen table after supper, smoking her Lucky Strikes, looking into the clouds of smoke for answers.

By and by, the merchants of Lower Peach Tree brought out their tensile candy canes that hung on lampposts all up and down the main street. Storefronts were festooned with colored lights. There was a new television set with a big red bow tied around it in McKinna's Hardware window. Someone in town would get a television for Christmas, probably one of the first in a private home in Lower Peach Tree. The houses along the walk to the post office had wreaths in their windows. Plastic bells and Santa Claus faces decorated front doors. In the late afternoons, the light of living room Christmas trees shone through moisture-laden windows. John squinted as he passed by, trying to see the hazy figures moving around the trees.

He got a Slinky, some books, and new clothes from the Vances for Christmas.

At home, Santa Claus gave each one of them an orange, an apple, and raisins with the seeds still in them in a stocking that had a comic book sticking out of the top.

Aunt Nelda stood at the stove on Christmas morning, watching them take down their stockings. Uncle Luther slept late.

Christmas dinner was chicken with dressing and sweet-potato pie for dessert. Uncle Luther had dinner with the family and then decided to pay a Christmas visit to his neighbor Arlo. This had been fine with everyone else. They had all stayed gathered around the stove after he left. It was a cold rainy day outside and so it seemed especially cozy inside with the lingering smell of chicken hanging in the air and the steady tapping of rain on the tin roof.

Shell had begged him, and John had finally come to the kitchen table to read her Santa Claus comic book out loud. She sat next to him, looking at the pictures as he read. When he finished, Little Luther, who had been sitting at the far end of the table whittling, pushed his comic book over to John and continued whittling without saying anything. John took up the comic book and began to read. As he was about to turn the first page, Little Luther came to stand behind him. "Wait a minute. Let me look at them pictures 'fore you turn." John waited patiently and then turned the pages slowly while Little Luther stood behind him, whittling and watching.

After he finished Little Luther's book, John picked up his own comic book. Little Luther sat down on the other side of John for *The Adventures of Captain Marvel.*

Aunt Nelda listened as she washed dishes. The clock on the mantel, which had been decorated with sprigs of pine and pinecones, ticked off the hours of the afternoon. Outside, the rain gathered in furrows, then twisted and turned its way through the open fields, soaking long-dead cotton plants that no longer had a need.

In the late afternoon, they had gone to the porch and, for want of a dry place to play, had drawn a hopscotch game on the wood floor. They spent the rest of the day playing there. Even Aunt Nelda had come out at one point and taken a turn, hopping up and down the squares and laughing when she missed. After awhile, she went back inside to start supper.

As the light was fading, the children noticed on a far-off hill a silhouette walking toward them through the rain. No one mentioned this, but everyone saw it as they glanced up from their play. What had been an easy game with Little Luther teasing Shell and John every time they missed suddenly became serious and quiet. Rocks were thrown and squares were hopped as intermittently all three glanced out into the rain-soaked fields that faded into lighter and lighter shades of gray before disappearing altogether in the fog.

He had been at Arlo's for hours and now he appeared out of the mist. His steps were erratic. He left a path in the mud that zigzagged down the sloping landscape. Once, he stumbled and almost fell in a puddle. They had continued their game but kept an eye on his coming. He was at such a distance, it would take some time for him to get to them.

They could pretend courage awhile longer. Little Luther seemed especially determined to finish what he had started. He threw his rock at a faster pace, then pushed them to hurry with their turns.

As he got closer, Uncle Luther began to walk straighter, sobered perhaps by the rain. This was not a good sign. The drunker he was, the less threatening he seemed to be. The danger was when he was halfway between the two worlds.

It was so dark now that the next time they looked up, he was nowhere to be seen. Without a word, the children gathered their comic books, threw their hopscotch rocks out in the yard, and headed toward their separate rooms. Shell had hesitated on the way into her room. She turned to look at John. "Could I come with you?"

He pretended not to hear her and jumped off the porch to go to his room, which had to be entered from the back of the house.

Aunt Nelda had gone inside earlier and turned up the wick on the kerosene lamp. In the dark, light streamed through the open door onto the porch floor.

John sat in his room and heard boots stomping off mud on the porch steps. Uncle Luther was mumbling words that could not be deciphered. John strained to hear every sound. Uncle Luther had thrown his rain-soaked coat off and was standing in the doorway. "Nelda," they all heard him yell through the thin walls. "What the hell is all this markin' on the floor? You think we live in a pigsty?"

She must have come to the door to see what he was talking about and misjudged his condition, because she talked back to him. "Luther, that ain't nothin' but some game the kids was playin'." The screen door slammed as she walked back inside.

"Don't you turn your back on me, woman, when I'm talkin'." They heard the door jerk open. There followed shouts from each of them and then the low, unmistakable thudding sound of his fist hitting soft skin. Then there was silence.

John lay down on his bed, trying to put the sound out of his mind, trying to remember the one Christmas gift he had given. No one knew about it but Shell. He had taken one of the fertilizer sacks still in his room, one with the cutout colored baby doll on the outside, and had furtively poured the fertilizer out when no one was watching. He knew this would make Uncle Luther furious, because he planned to use this fertilizer next year on a new cotton crop. It was extra the bank thought he had already used.

It had taken several weeks. John had dipped a small amount out of the sack each day and put it in his pocket. On his way to school, he had emptied it out. At last, he had a sack ready to be cut out and assembled into a colored baby doll. Mrs. Vance had given him a needle and thread. He had told her he needed it to mend some things at home.

John had given the baby doll to Shell on Christmas Eve and told her never to let Uncle Luther see it. She was so pleased, she cried, and he felt terrible, because his motive had not been to make her happy but to get back at Uncle Luther.

Someday, after John was gone, Uncle Luther would find out about it. John loved thinking of the moment when Uncle Luther would come to realize that Shell had had the colored baby all along. Before, when he was sewing up the doll, he would chuckle when he imagined Uncle Luther's face. Now, as he lay there remembering the tears in Shell's eyes when she took the doll, he felt like crying himself.

CHAPTER 35

JANUARY had been too cold to go to Chicago. He didn't have a warm coat. February was the same. The days drifted into spring. He woke up one morning and the weather was turning hot. Soon they would be out for summer vacation again. Then he would decide what to do.

It was another Saturday dinner at the Vance house, but a special one. Candles were lit in silver candelabra placed in the middle of the table. Mrs. Vance had set it with a white linen tablecloth, napkins, the good china, and crystal glasses that usually stayed in the china cabinet in the corner of the dining room. There was a silence about the room when they came in to sit down. He felt strange, as if it were in the wrong house. They sat down, and after the blessing, Mrs. Vance went to get the roast.

"Why are we so . . . so serious at this meal?" he almost whispered to the Judge.

The Judge was taking down his napkin and feeling around for his silverware. "Ah, I see we have the good silver out, and I suspect the silver candelabra are on the table. Am I right?" It did not escape John's notice that a few months earlier, the Judge would have been able to see the light from the candles.

"Yes, sir, two in the middle of the table."

"This is the birthday of our child, who died several years ago. Adell—Mrs. Vance—always marks the occasion with a special dinner." The Judge sighed. "You know women."

"Nobody told me you had a baby. Was it a boy?"

"No, a little girl. She only lived three and a half weeks. She was born with a heart condition. Not time enough to know her really, but Adell had already decorated a room and planned her whole future by the time she was born. Now she remembers Mary Beth—that was her name, Mary Beth. She likes to remember her just as if her life had played out as she planned it."

Mrs. Vance came in with a pork roast sitting on a big silver platter surrounded by potatoes and carrots. Then she went back in the kitchen for gravy and hot biscuits and a relish tray. When she came back, she poured a glass of wine for herself and one for the Judge.

"John," she said, taking her napkin down, "this would have been the twenty-fifth birthday of our little girl, Mary Beth. The Judge and I always remember her once a year with a special little dinner. We're glad you could join us." She raised her glass. The Judge did the same, seeming to know what she was doing.

"Mary Beth would have graduated from the university

over in Tuscaloosa by now, and with honors, I'm sure." She took a drink of her wine.

"I'm sure." The Judge smiled and took a sip. "Probably gone on up to Atlanta to become a famous lawyer by now," he added.

"Oh, no, she would have met someone and be planning to get married by now, maybe even be married and pregnant with our first grandchild." Another swallow of wine as she considered this.

"Why did we send her to law school all that time if all she was going to do was get married right out of school?" The Judge smiled. "I thought you told me she was going to law school, she was so smart."

Mrs. Vance took exception. "We gave her the best education we could, so she could be the best wife and mother possible, but practice law? For heaven sakes, Byron honey, who in the world do you know who would do a thing like that?" Mrs. Vance took a drink of wine and contemplated. "No, she met a nice young man at the university, while she was in one of her law classes. Probably from Mobile or Selma, someplace close by. They fell in love and now they're gettin' married." Mrs. Vance was pouring herself another glass of wine and seriously considering all the possibilities.

The Judge was still pretending. "No. What happened is that she fell madly in love with a Yankee down here on scholarship. Now they're getting married and going to New York City to live."

Mrs. Vance and the wine were appalled. "That's ridiculous, Mary Beth would never do that, not in a million years. Don't you know your own daughter? Why, why, we should be clearin' the rose garden out back to make room for a swing set when the grandchildren come to visit."

"Yeah." The Judge laughed. "Probably terrible little monsters who look just like their Yankee daddy."

Mrs. Vance stood from the table, insulted. "Byron, that's a terrible, terrible thing to say."

"But I was only . . ."

She put her napkin on the table and walked away to the kitchen. John watched her leave and then turned to the Judge. "She had tears in her eyes," he whispered.

The Judge took a deep breath, rolled the stem of the wineglass in his hand, and sighed. "I forget, from time to time, that twenty-five years is only yesterday." They sat in silence, the Judge sipping his wine.

Finally, he said, "Pass me some of those hot biscuits. They smell wonderful."

Presently, Mrs. Vance came back in the room, carrying a knife. "I forgot the carvin' knife," she said, face perfectly placid. She began to carve the roast.

The Judge cleared his throat. "I didn't mean to imply that Mary Beth—"

She interrupted him, gushing, "Oh, Byron, I know I can act the fool about her sometimes, it was so long ago." Her eyes were downcast, pretending concentration on the roast. "It seems so silly really." She carved the roast into thick slices.

John and the Judge waited in silence, John looking from one to the other. Finally, the Judge spoke as his fingers felt along the sharp edge of the knife at his place setting. "Caring is never silly, just sometimes . . . hurtful." He sat still, trying to sense any clue to her mood. "It's what keeps us going, isn't it?"

She smiled back at a face that could only imagine what she looked like now. "You always know what to say to me, don't you? You knew it from the first time we met . . . in our Bailey days."

Now he laughed. "Bailey. It's been a long time since you called up that name."

"It's been a long time since you deserved it." She laughed back, stopped her carving, and came around the table to take his head in her hands and kiss his forehead. "I'll be right back. I know how you like watermelon-rind pickle with your meat, and I have a new jar from Jenny Morgan. She put it up just last week." She left the room, humming.

John cleared his throat so they would remember he was still there. After all the time he had been coming to this house, to these people, at that moment, he felt like a stranger.

The Judge cleared his throat also. "It's my middle name, Bailey. When Mrs. Vance and I first met, she thought it was the name I went by. All night long, she called me Bailey, and I was so smitten, I didn't want to take the chance of embarrassing her, or upsetting our beginning . . . so I let it stand." He reached for his dinner plate and began to straighten it on the table. "It's crazy what we do when we first meet someone we know we . . . we care about."

The man and boy both sat in silence. The Judge felt the air of disdain from across the table. "She only calls me that when she wants to tell me she . . ." He paused and began to fumble with his silverware. "Well . . ." He took his knife from the table and began to wipe it off with his napkin.

John had never seen him at a loss for words. He thought it revolting. "That's stupid."

"It is?"

"Either somebody is special to you or they're not. If she thinks that, she should call you that . . . that"—he spit it out—"that Bailey all the time."

The Judge sat back in his chair and thought a moment. "No, I wouldn't want her to do that. That one word conjures up a whole period of our life together. It was a very special time. I wouldn't want it to become so ordinary that it lost its meaning." He hesitated. It was obvious that what he had said had fallen on deaf ears, but he forged ahead. "Words, especially to a blind man, are like pieces of gold."

John squirmed in his chair.

"And speaking of that," the Judge said, "I have a few words I'd like to pass on to you. I've been wanting to tell you how much your coming here has—"

John hurried to interrupt. "I don't know what you're talking about and . . . and I don't care anyway. I'm gonna go help Mrs. Vance find the pickles."

He fled the room.

CHAPTER 36

IT was on a Thursday in the late afternoon. School had been out for just over a week. John had finished all of his work in the yard and Mrs. Vance had left to attend the ladies' missionary society, so he decided to change clothes and go on down to the bank. Usually, he didn't go to the bank on a Thursday—Mrs. Vance said she had yard work for him to do all day on Thursdays—but he wanted to be helpful, maybe see if he could read the paper to somebody.

Miss Maroon said yes, he could help empty the ashtrays in the lobby, since they were about to close for the day. That way, they would be all ready for Friday. He was replacing empty ashtrays when Uncle Luther came in the front door.

"Well, if you won't lookie here at this," he said. "All dressed up like a city boy."

Uncle Luther was standing in the lobby, his fingers hooked in his overalls, rocking back on his heels. "Looks like the Judge gettin' mighty partial to you, dressin' you up in them fancy clothes."

"Hi, Uncle Luther."

He came over and touched the boy's shirt. "Ooh wee, if you ain't slick as a snake." He walked over and took a seat in one of the lobby chairs. "Go on, don't let me stop ya. You just keep right on doin' what you was doin'." He took off his John Deere cap and ran fingers through hair wet with perspiration.

"I'll just sit right here and rest my tired bones. I'm tuckered out. I ain't got no sissy job."

John kept cleaning ashtrays but intermittently glanced up at Uncle Luther. He couldn't remember seeing Uncle Luther in the bank before. Maybe he was coming to take him away, back to the fields.

"I thought you might be getting things ready for planting, Uncle Luther."

"I got business with the Judge." Uncle Luther's eyes landed on a magazine on the table beside him. He picked up a copy of *Life* and began to turn the pages.

Just then, Tuway and the Judge came out of his office. The Judge stopped short when Tuway whispered something to him.

Judge Vance's head snapped to attention, like a dog on point. He turned in the direction of Miss Maroon's desk and said in a low voice, "Miss Maroon, what . . . Why on earth is he here?"

John thought it wrong to be mad at Miss Maroon. She couldn't help it if Uncle Luther had come to see the Judge.

Miss Maroon was immediately flustered. "Oh my, I just didn't think, Judge. He came in and asked to help out and . . . I just didn't think. I'll take care of it right now." She walked over and grabbed John by the shoulders and walked him into the conference room.

"Why is he mad at me?" he asked as she was shutting the door.

"Thursday is the day your uncle Luther comes to collect. The Judge doesn't want to give him any reason to think . . . Oh, never mind. You're too young to understand. Just stay right here and don't move from this room until I come and get you. Do you hear me, young man?"

"Yes, ma'am."

She closed the door.

John immediately got off the chair and went over to the door that led to the Judge's office and turned the handle just enough to crack it. Sure enough, they were coming back into the Judge's room. He always liked to talk in his office, the better to know where everyone and everything was located.

Tuway held the door for them and then went out and closed it. John knew Tuway was probably listening on the other side. He wondered what door Miss Maroon was using. The Judge put his hat on the desk and went around to take a seat.

"Have a chair, Luther. I had about given up on you. I was on my way home."

John's face was so close to the tiny crack in the door, his glasses pushed up against the wood frame.

"Had some extra work to do this afternoon, Judge." He settled into one of the wing-back chairs. "You know a farmer's work ain't never done, and what with me being short a hand, it ain't easy."

"Short a hand?" the Judge said. He had opened his middle desk drawer and was feeling around for something.

"Well, yes, sir, Judge. I know John looks little, but he can put in a day's work right along with the rest of my kids. Yes, sir, sure do miss him in the fields."

"Is that right?"

"Sure enough, Judge, but I can see he's makin' hisself real useful round here. No, sir, I wouldn't want to take him away from y'all." He sat back in the chair and took out his tobacco and some rolling paper.

"You mind if I smoke, Judge?"

"Go right ahead."

"I roll my own. Saves me money, you know." He poured a little tobacco on the paper and rolled it up, licking the edges to seal it, twisting the ends to keep the tobacco in.

"I try to be real thrifty, what with so many mouths to feed." He took paperback matches out of his pocket and lit up, blowing out smoke and looking through it to the Judge. "Course some would say, 'Luther, you're just a fool to let the Judge have a hard worker like John for money that don't amount to no hill of beans.'"

"That's money you're saving for John," the Judge said.

"Oh, right, right." He blew out more smoke in the Judge's direction. "But I say, 'Lookie here, as long as the Judge and his wife is so attached to the boy, buyin' him new clothes and lettin' him work round the bank like he was somebody, well,' I say, 'when it comes time for the Judge to give him a raise, I know he'll do the right thing.'" He crossed his leg and knocked a piece of dirt off his shoe onto the carpet. Then he said almost under his breath, "This learnin' he's gettin' here, be a damn shame if he had to go back out to the fields again."

The Judge had been listening to Uncle Luther and at

the same time taking an envelope out of his middle drawer, turning it over and over on the desktop.

"It would be a shame if he had to go back out to the fields, as little as he is," the Judge said. "Women do tend to get attached to youngsters, but you and I both know men aren't like that. To my way of thinking, John has been doing a less-than-adequate job lately—in fact, downright sloppy in some areas. Maybe field work would be just the ticket for him."

Uncle Luther uncrossed his legs and sat up in his chair. "Well now, Judge, if he ain't been doin' his work, I'll . . ."

John strained to see more of the room without pushing the door open any more than it was.

"Well, you saw for yourself this afternoon." The Judge turned the envelope over and over.

"It looked to me like he was doin' his work." Luther looked at the Judge, his eyes narrowing.

The Judge shook his head. "Here he was down at the bank when he was supposed to be home weeding the garden, and not even informing me he was here. Just out playing around in the lobby."

"If he ain't been doin' his work, you say the word. I give him a whippin', he won't be sittin' down for a week." Uncle Luther put his cigarette out in the desk ashtray and stared at the envelope in the Judge's hand. There was a long silence.

"You sayin' you want to fire him?" Luther said.

The Judge sat back in his chair, still holding the envelope. Finally, he leaned forward and said, "I'm saying I'll keep a very close eye on him and evaluate him at the end of next week." He slowly slid the envelope across the desk.

Uncle Luther took it and stood up. "That's a good idea, Judge. You evaluate him." He turned to leave.

"And Luther, if I feel any disciplinary action is warranted, I'll be the one to take it."

Luther was opening the envelope as he walked toward the door. "That's a good idea, Judge. You do that." He was gone.

A few seconds after the door shut on Luther, Miss Maroon came in from a side door that led out into the hall.

"Judge, you are a past master." She smiled.

"Why Miss Maroon, you listened."

"Every word, but I don't know why I even bothered. He's not a worthy opponent."

The Judge smiled and reverted to his imitation of W. C. Fields, which Miss Maroon had told him he did to perfection. He picked up a pencil and flicked it as if it were a cigar. "Ah yes, my dear, it comes from years of dealing with my esteemed board of directors." Miss Maroon smiled as she brushed Luther's ashes off the Judge's desk.

"Judge," she lied once again, "you do that just perfect."

John relaxed his grip on the doorknob he had been holding and leaned back away from the crack to take a few deep breaths.

Just then, Tuway walked in the door Luther had left by. "I tell you what, Judge, ain't nobody better at ridin'm and ropin'm than you. Old Luther left here countin' his money and happy to have it."

"*Et tu*, Tuway?" The Judge was still W. C. Fields. "Were you behind the door or under the rug, my good man?"

"You didn't think I was gonna miss that, did ya, Judge? I just knew we was in big trouble when we walks out to the lobby and the boy is there all spruced up in his new clothes, with his hair all combed. I could see them dollar marks in old Luther's eyes."

Miss Maroon laughed. "That part where you said you would send him out to the fields again if he didn't shape up—that was inspired. You really sounded like you meant that. It was the perfect touch."

The Judge put down the cigar pencil and leaned back in his chair. His mood had changed abruptly. "Perfect touch or no, Miss Maroon, I did mean it. There are worse things than working in the fields."

John peered through the crack again to see if he could see the Judge's expression.

"Oh, Judge, aren't you just the least bit attached to him?" The smile was fading from Miss Maroon's face as she watched his. "Now come on, admit it." She turned to Tuway. "Tuway, he's kidding, isn't he?"

Tuway was eyeing the Judge. "Everybody got they load to carry. I know that."

"Yes"—she turned back to the Judge—"but you've done so much, and he's so devoted to you, sittin' outside of your office every day, waitin' for the slightest opportunity to—"

The Judge held out his hand. "Miss Maroon. You seem to forget you're looking at a man who'll be completely blind in another two years." He leaned forward and checked with his hands to see that everything on his desk was in order. "On top of that, I may be unemployed to boot if things keep going like they are." He tapped his fingers on the desk, becoming more agitated. "Why in hell's name—sorry, Miss Maroon—would I, could I, think about getting attached to a little scrub-faced kid who doesn't even belong to me in the first place? That's absurd. I have enough to worry about." His fingers drummed the ink blotter. "Don't you see what Luther would do if he had the slightest idea that I might care about the boy?"

There was silence as Miss Maroon looked down to straighten up some papers in her lap. "You're right, Judge. I just didn't think." She cleared her throat. "Well, well now, I think I better be gettin' home. Daddy'll be wantin' his supper. I'll see y'all tomorrow mornin'." She got up and turned to walk out. "You'll get the lights, Tuway?"

"Yes'm."

"Besides, I'm old enough to be his grandfather. Don't you see that?" the Judge called after her. She didn't answer.

He took a deep breath and stood up. "Now where did I put that hat, Tuway?" Tuway handed the Judge his hat and they walked toward the door.

"What was he wearing, Tuway?"

"Who wearin'?"

"You know. When Luther came on him in the lobby. What was he wearing?"

"Well now, he had on a little yellow shirt with a collar. His hair was all slicked back and he had on them—"

They walked out and shut the door.

John eased his door shut. He had been upset when he heard the Judge talk about how sloppy and lazy he was, but he thought it must be for Uncle Luther's benefit. Then when he heard the Judge tell Miss Maroon he might send him back to the fields, a great wave of heat had seemed to pass through John's body. The thought of losing his connection to everything in Lower Peach Tree—the Judge, the bank, Cal, Mrs. Vance—had never entered his mind. For a moment, he had felt faint and struggled to hold on to the wall and not move. Now he stood with his head down, trying to breathe normally.

He was sitting rigid in the chair where Miss Maroon had put him when she opened the door. "I almost forgot about you, John sugar. Come on, it's time we were all home."

He rose from the chair, jerked his shoulder away from her waiting hand, and walked out.

He had been such a child, pretending, like children do, that people were growing to care about him, when they never were; pretending that he might even fit in enough to be . . . to be adopted, a word he had never dared to form in his mind before, but now he could think it, knowing it was not a possibility.

It was so childish to pretend that he would never have to go back to the fields, would never get another beating from Uncle Luther, when, of course, he would if he stayed on.

In the late afternoon, he turned left onto Highway 80 to begin the long walk home and to make preparations.

CHAPTER 37

WHEN John got home, Uncle Luther had bought a bottle. He was sitting on the porch, leaning back in his chair, watching John walk toward him. "Where them fancy clothes you was wearin'?" He took a drink. "We ain't good enough to see you in'm?" The bottle dangled down between sweat-soaked jeans. "Been stayin' with the Judge more than you stayin' here. Too bad you ain't got no home to go to. We'd send you back where you come from for sure."

He had gotten used to the words. Words didn't bother him anymore. John handed the mail to Uncle Luther. A bill from the hardware store, a notice of a cattle auction over in Selma. Uncle Luther took it and let it hang loose in the fingers of his free hand.

John looked carefully at Uncle Luther before he spoke. Like the others in the family, he had become expert in gauging the stages of Uncle Luther's drunkenness. All the signs were there—the half-closed eyes, the slack jaw. Uncle Luther was past the rage he felt when he first started drinking. By this time, he was fast approaching a stupor. John could speak without fear of anything physical happening. "My friend up in Bainbridge, where I came from, is going to ask me to visit soon." He said this with his head down. He meant this not as confrontation but just as information for Uncle Luther to absorb. "She sent me a postcard saying so."

Uncle Luther said nothing, so he ventured further. "Her mother, she'll probably write Aunt Nelda soon, to invite me formally."

"Invite you formal," Uncle Luther mimicked. He took a swig.

"She said she would send me a train ticket, too."

He snickered. "Hear that, Little Luther? John here is gonna ride on the train." He turned to Little Luther, who was standing perfectly still, leery of his father's mood. "Ain't that dandy?"

Little Luther came to and gave a halfhearted laugh. "Yeah, Pa, dandy." Then he stood still again, looking out at the fields.

Just then, Aunt Nelda came to the porch and said supper was ready.

The next week at the bank, he stole some blank pieces of stationery and a pen from Miss Maroon's desk. All afternoon, as he emptied wastebaskets and ashtrays and polished the brass tellers' bars, words were whirling around in his head. When the bank closed, he didn't wait around to see if the Judge needed him. He went straight to the house, changed his clothes, and left for home.

That night, he sat in his room and flipped through a

history book he had stolen from the school library the day school closed. He was looking for what might be appropriate wording.

> *Dear Mrs. Spraig,*
> *I hope you will remember that we lived next door to your dearly departed sister in the town of Bainbridge. I also hope it will be agreeable with you to let your nephew, John, come visit us this summer.*
> *We will be sending him a ticket. I hope it's okay. He will be leaving on the Saturday-night train out of Lower Peach Tree.*
> *Sincerely yours, Mrs. Mary Rutland.*
> *P.S. I will be giving him some extra silverware of his mother's that I had borrowed and forgotten to return. He can bring it back with him when he returns. It is a beautiful silver tea set that is worth so much, I couldn't take the chance of sending it through the mail.*

He folded the letter and put it in the history book. He would wait a week to give it to Uncle Luther, but every night he got it out right before he went to bed and read it, changing a word here, a sentence there. After several revisions, it was ready.

The day he decided to show Uncle Luther the letter, he waited until right after supper. He was sitting alone on the porch, smoking and drinking a small glass of whiskey. It had to be him, not Aunt Nelda. She might want to read the letter. John knew Uncle Luther couldn't read well enough to know what it said. He waited until she was washing dishes.

"I got my letter from my friend's mother today. The one who's inviting me to come for a visit."

Uncle Luther said nothing, just looked at the boy.

"It's right here." John took the letter out of his pocket. "Want me to read it?"

Still Uncle Luther said nothing, looking out at the fields. This was good so far. Uncle Luther seemed only mildly interested. John held up the envelope and hoped Uncle Luther would not notice his fingers shaking. He had glued a used stamp onto the outside to give it as much authenticity as possible, just in case Uncle Luther examined it closely. "Here it is." He slipped the letter out of its envelope and began to read, trying not to give particular emphasis to the P.S.

Uncle Luther took a drink of whiskey and watched a red-tailed hawk circling in the orange of the sunset as John read. If John had figured it right, Uncle Luther wasn't drunk enough to forget what he was hearing, but too drunk to pay close attention. When he finished, the boy slowly folded the letter and put it back into the envelope. His heart was pounding so hard, he was certain Uncle Luther could see it. Maybe he would call Aunt Nelda out and have her read the letter. If that happened, he was in for a whipping. Maybe Uncle Luther would see right through the whole thing and laugh at him. There was a silence that seemed to last minutes.

As if in slow motion, John began to put the letter in his pocket, head down, afraid of what Uncle Luther would see if he looked into his face.

Uncle Luther turned to look at him. "Come here," he said.

John took one step closer. "Gimme that." John held out the letter and Uncle Luther grabbed it and stuffed it in his pocket.

That night, John looked around his room, thinking about what he would take with him to his new life in Chicago.

Three days later, he decided to test Aunt Nelda right after supper was over and Little Luther had left the table. Shell was helping clear dishes. "I guess I'll be going for my visit up to Bainbridge in a few weeks, soon as they send me the ticket," he said. It was getting easier. He felt a surge of excitement, but nothing he couldn't control. His hands rested casually on the table. He sat there waiting for her reaction.

"What's that you're talkin' about, John honey?" She was half-listening, scraping dishes clean.

"What visit is he gettin' to go on, Mama?" Shell asked.

"Didn't Uncle Luther tell you?" He tried to act surprised. "My friend Tab, her mother wrote me and wants me to come visit her in Bainbridge this summer. She's sending me a ticket. Didn't Uncle Luther show you the letter?"

Everyone looked at Luther, who sat picking his teeth with a sassafras twig.

"No, he didn't tell us." Aunt Nelda looked at him suspiciously. "You didn't show me no letter."

"Done throwed it away," he said without looking at her. "Didn't say nothin' 'cept they was gonna send him a ticket." John could hardly keep from smiling. All this time, he had been so afraid of him. Now his fear was turning to something else.

"Ain't gonna let him go anyhow," Uncle Luther said, and John froze. "He's got to keep up his job with the

Judge. Wouldn't seem fittin'"—he eyed John—"not to keep faith with the Judge."

"This will be while the Judge is visiting down in Biloxi," John said too quickly. It was the first thing that came to his mind. "Well, I think it will be anyhow." He tried to sound matter-of-fact. "You know, Mrs. Vance has that cousin who lives down there," he lied, counting on Aunt Nelda's wish to seem a social equal to Mrs. Vance.

"Oh, yes, a cousin. Seems like I do recall that," Aunt Nelda lied in return.

"Well, if Adell doesn't need him, I guess we can spare him," she said.

Luther said nothing.

John left the table feeling like he should shout out loud or do a dance, but he opened and closed the screen door in an offhanded way and slipped out of their sight before he looked up and grinned at the stars that were just coming out overhead.

He knew that when the time was right, he could disappear and everyone would think he was on a trip. The Judge would probably see through the whole thing, if he cared to think about it, but he knew the Judge didn't care to think about it.

As he stood in the night air watching the moon rise up over the fields, he could hear her questioning Uncle Luther, trying to find out more about the letter, but he knew that was a lost cause for Aunt Nelda. He knew Uncle Luther wouldn't let her see the letter, for fear she might read the part about the silver tea set. He would want that for himself.

Now all he had to do was wait for Tuway to send somebody else up to Chicago. Then he, too, would be headed to Chicago on the first train north, or however it was they got there.

He heard the screen door close and turned, to see Shell standing there. She looked at him and then looked back out at the darkened fields. "You're gonna leave us here and you ain't comin' back, are you?" she said.

"Course not, Shell. I'll always be back." He sat down on the porch steps, broke off a piece of weed that was growing up between the steps, and stuck it in his mouth. Shell came to sit beside him. He looked at her and smiled. He was beginning to be amazed at how easily and sincerely he could lie.

Chapter 38

THE weekend had arrived and he was spending another Saturday night at the Vance house. The full moon sent streams of light into his upstairs bedroom as he eased up the window shade, then lifted the window. He had done this many times before in preparation. The old paring knife he had borrowed from the kitchen when Mrs. Vance wasn't looking had been used to cut away the layers of house paint that glued the screen to the windowsill. Now all he had to do was swing it out on its top hinges, and directly below was the roof to the front porch. From there, it was a quick climb down the rose trellis on the far end of the porch to the ground. For the last two weekends, he had watched out the window every Saturday night, trying to stay awake, hoping for a light in the cemetery. He had packed everything in a Piggly Wiggly sack, a book of matches from the bank, stationery, and pencils. He would take along the paring knife, too. And he was right in the middle of a Nancy Drew, *The Secret of the Old Clock*. If it happened tonight, he would take that. They would never miss it.

He had left a note on his bed at home saying that the ticket had come and he was leaving. He had left it on many Fridays and retrieved it on many Sunday evenings. They never had occasion to look in his room.

Here on his bed at the Vances' house, he had left a very terse note saying that Uncle Luther wanted him for some work at home and he couldn't stay for Sunday school and Sunday dinner.

The moon rose and set before he saw the first flicker. He had looked so long, hoping for the light, that when it appeared, he thought it might be his imagination. He must leave now, because as soon as the second light came along, it would be only minutes before the two were put out and Tuway would be on his way.

This was it, what he had been waiting for. Maybe he would wait, he said to himself as he eased open the screen. Maybe the time was not right. There would always be another night. He stood suspended, and then the second light flickered, and then the memory of the Judge telling Miss Maroon he would send John to the fields again.

He eased open the screen just enough to get through. Standing on the roof of the porch, he pushed the screen frame back into place. They would think he had left early in the morning, by the back door, which they never kept locked.

He was standing in the deep shadows of the porch as they passed, talking in low whispers to each other. He let them get across the yard a good distance before he followed. Tuway might not take him along if he let him know he was following so close to home.

Even now, he could go back. Even now, he could turn around and get back in his bed and go to sleep. No one would ever know. They walked downtown past the bank, past the post office. John followed them at a distance. All was quiet. Not one person on the streets, since it was around two in the morning. The other man with Tuway was smaller than Tuway and, he thought, black, but he couldn't tell.

The two men didn't stop at the train station like John had thought they would. They walked past the depot, on down the tracks a good quarter of a mile. There, Tuway and the man hunched down in the bushes to wait. He could see them in the distance. He left the train station and followed the road that paralleled the train tracks for about the distance that he thought they had traveled, and then he began to edge his way through the underbrush very slowly. Presently, he could hear their voices. He inched forward.

"That's what they all say. Now listen here. When the train start to pull out of the station, you got to hop on the car I get on. I know which one is open, so let me go first; then it'll be you."

"How you know which one to get on? They all locked."

"Not the one I get on. Never mind how I know. I just know. Don't you go questionin' me, son. I know what I'm doin'. Done it a million times."

After a time, the whistle of the train coming into the station sounded out into the night. It didn't stop long. Just time enough to load the mail and off-load some freight. John rose up in the tall grass and saw that it was a freight train. No passenger cars on this one.

Now it was coming toward them very slowly. John's

heart was in his throat, beating so hard, he could barely breathe. He could still turn back, leave this place and climb back up the rose trellis to his bedroom. Get back in his bed. The train was getting closer. The big engines, two of them, passed by, then a long series of freight cars.

"Get ready," he heard Tuway tell the man. John took a deep breath and ran forward, through the tall grass, to stand right in front of Tuway.

"I'm going," he said, looking him straight in the eye. "I'm going with you to Chicago," he shouted.

"What the hell . . ." Tuway looked down at the boy uncomprehendingly. "What in the hell are you doin', boy? What are you doin' here?" The sound of the train was getting louder as it picked up speed.

"I'm going with you to Chicago. I'm not stayin' in this town," he yelled.

"You crazy, boy." Tuway looked down at him and then up at the train passing, car by car. "Get out of here and go home, right now. Ain't nobody goin' to Chicago."

"What's *he* doin' here?" The other man looked at John and then at Tuway. "I thought you said this here was top secret?"

"It is." Tuway looked desperate. "Here comes the car."

"I'm not going back, and if I do, I'll tell," John yelled above the roar, and stood directly in Tuway's path. Tuway was trying to move forward, trying to get to the train.

"What's goin' on here, Tuway? You told me—"

Tuway grabbed John like a sack of potatoes under his arm and began running for the train.

"Come on," he called back over his shoulder. John dropped his bag of clothes, trying to hold on, as Tuway ran alongside and pulled back the car door with his free hand. He threw John in like he was pitching hay bales, then grabbed on and jumped in himself. "Come on," he yelled to the man running alongside. The man threw in his suitcase and jumped in.

They all lay there on the floor, breathing hard, watching the night rush by outside the boxcar. The smell of cow manure mixed in with the swirling bits of straw.

When he caught his breath, Tuway turned on John. "What the hell you mean interferin' in my business, boy?" Tuway was half-crawling, half-walking toward the boy as the moving car jerked along, gaining speed.

John began to back up into the corner of the car. Even if he got beat up, he didn't care. That had happened before and he had survived. Now, fear was second to the elation he felt. He was leaving. He could hear the sound of the wheels on the tracks clicking faster and faster. He was out of Lower Peach Tree. He was headed away. He had not gone back at the last minute, as he had feared he might do the whole time he pried up the screen, slipped out of the house, and followed them to the station. He had done it like he had imagined so many times, but this . . . this was real. He could feel the train, smell the manure. The hot night air in his face was thrilling. He screamed out his freedom. "I don't care what you say, Tuway," he yelled. "I don't care what you say."

Tuway grabbed John's shirt with one hand and pulled him up to spit the words in his face. "You smart-ass white boy, meddlin' in my business. I'm gonna teach you a lesson you ain't gonna forget." He raised his free hand. John closed his eyes, waiting for the first of Uncle Luther's blows, but they didn't come. Instead, Tuway lurched over to the open car door and held John out over the passing ground, one hand holding on to the door, the other on to John. John grabbed his big muscled arm, too scared to do anything but stare into Tuway's eyes. His legs dangled down into darkness, his hair whipped around his glasses. Tuway held the boy suspended there, swaying back and forth as the night air rushed past, the clicking of the rails sounding faster and faster. Then Tuway squeezed his eyes shut and pulled John back in, heaving him across the car, close to where the other man was sitting, watching. He landed in cow manure and wet straw.

"You ain't worth killin', boy," Tuway snarled.

"I don't care what you say," John yelled back again, digging wet straw out of his mouth. "I'm never going back. Never. He hates me."

Even there, as the wind swirled around his face and the straw blew past him and out the open door, even with only two other people and the night to hear him, he felt the agony of having said out loud what had been knotted in his stomach since he had closed the conference room door that day in the bank.

Tuway knew. Tuway had known all along. "So you gonna go messin' up everybody else just 'cause your feelin's hurt." He slid down the wall of the car to a sitting position. "How in hell did I get myself in this mess?" he mumbled. "Some stupid know-nothin' kid. That's all I need. I knowed I shoulda stopped doin' this long time ago."

Covering chagrin with defiance, the boy yelled again. "I don't care what you say, Tuway, I'm going to Chicago. You think I care about him?" His hands clutched the wet straw. "No!" he yelled.

Tuway sneered. "You goin' to Chicago, are you?" He looked at John and shook his head. "You and half the

CHAPTER 39

ONLY the outlines of Tuway and the other man were visible to him from time to time as they passed through deep stands of pine trees, then out into the open fields again. He was too embarrassed to ask why they were headed south, so he just sat there wondering why or what or how.

After a time, the train began to slow. He knew they must be heading up to a river trestle, because there were no big hills in this country and no signs of lights or a town. As the front cars eased onto the trestle, Tuway roused himself. "Gettin'-off time," he said almost casually, as if they were coming into a station, but of course they weren't. They were in the middle of the swamps that led up to the river. Tuway stood up by the door. "Get over here, boy." He grabbed John's shirt and pulled him over to the open door again. "When I tell you to jump, you jump, or I'll push you. Whichever—you goin' off this train."

"But . . . but . . ." He tried to back away. "I want to go with y'all."

"You goin' with us, only you gonna be the first one off." He pulled John to the very edge of the open door. The train was slowing even more now, climbing up the grade.

"Roll when you land and then don't move. I don't want you wanderin' off in the swamp."

He stared out into the black night, holding John's arm in a firm grip, waiting for the right moment.

Just as Tuway said, "Jump," he gave John a shove, and the boy was launched out into the night air that rushed by, his hands outstretched, grasping at black space. He hit the ground first with his hands, feeling the gravel along the side of the tracks jam into his palms and scrape at his legs before he rolled over and over down a dirt bank. The cars rumbled past him, the deafening, disjointed noise of steel on steel pulling cattle and cotton, iron ore and coal south to the docks in Mobile. He lay with his head down as the line of boxcars blew past him and small rocks pinged off his shirt and pants.

As quickly as the noise of the train was on him, it had gone on without him, as if he had never existed. He raised his head to watch the red light of the caboose disappearing into the night.

The sound of the train trailed off in the distance and was replaced by the noise of swamp creatures welling up around him. Their chatter was deafening as they called back and forth to one another in the night. He sat very still, slowly rubbing his hands to rid them of the small pieces of gravel that had wedged in his palms as he had tried to break his fall. As his eyes adjusted to the darkness, he saw glimpses of water, right in front of him, at the bottom of the grade that held the train tracks. A stabbing fear ran through him. He had been pushed off the train in the middle of the swamp and left to die among the snakes and whatever else was out there. They had just waited for the right place to get rid of him, a place he could never get out of, could never escape. Tuway and the other man were sitting in the boxcar this very minute, laughing about how stupid he was. Now he longed for the safe haven of the smelly boxcar full of wet straw and cow droppings.

"Hey." He heard it coming from above his head. "Hey, get yourself on up here." He looked up, to see a light dancing along in the dark. He caught his breath in relief. It was Tuway with a flashlight and he was walking the tracks.

"I'm here." He turned, still too afraid to move, remembering all the stories Shell had told him about the size of water moccasins that lived in the swamps. Tuway got directly over him and pointed the beam down the slope making a path up to him.

"Get on up here, boy. I ain't got all night."

John stood and scrambled up on all fours, following the flashlight.

Tuway stood there with the other man by his side. "You gotta hit them banks when they have a good slope in'm. Then it's just like rollin' off a log," he said to the other man, not giving John any notice. "You jump while it flat and you end up breakin' a leg."

They started walking on down the track as soon as John was up the hill. Not a word to him. He hurried to keep up and make conversation to let them know he was not afraid. "I guess we decided it was too dangerous to stay on that train, especially since it was going in the wrong direction." He tried to laugh. No one said anything. They kept walking back up the track. He hurried to share the light.

"I waited almost too late to start jumpin'," Tuway said to the other man. "Nearly 'bout run into the bridge 'fore I could get off." The flashlight began to flicker on and off. "Oh shit. I think I done busted it when I picked up the boy at the train station," he said, hitting it into the palm of his other hand. They stopped to wait on him to fix it. It was impossible to go on with no light. It was that dark. The flashlight flickered on and they walked, but not too far before it went out again. "The path that leads in is right up ahead, but this here light ain't gonna last us. Y'all gonna have to wait here for me to go get some lanterns."

"What path?" They didn't answer him. "Why do we need a lantern? We can just follow the tracks out when it gets light."

For the first time, Tuway addressed John. "You wanta go in the swamp at night, with no moon and no light, and try to find the way?" He turned to the other man. "Not only do I got me a white boy—look how his face stand out in the night—but I got me a dumb-ass white boy."

"I ain't dumb," the other man said. "I'm stayin' right here till you get us some light, Tuway, and much obliged."

"Me, too," John whispered.

"Here's the path," Tuway said. Just then, the light went out for good. He hit it several times but nothing happened. "At least we to the path. Come on down here."

They followed him down the steep slope of the track bed to the edge of the swamp, holding on to each other's shirts and feeling their way. That's what the boy assumed was out there in the darkness, a swamp. "I'll have to go on down to the river and around by myself. You sit tight till I get back. It's gonna take me probably an hour or so. The four o'clock northbound comin' by after awhile. Don't you move a muscle when it comes, you hear? Stay down here, hid out of sight."

He was gone, out into the night.

They stood listening to the sounds of the swamp, tree frogs calling to one another, interspersed with a screech owl or the rustle of leaves as something moved about in the dark. John stepped closer to the man. "Do you think we should sit down?"

"With us not seein' what's on the ground?"

"Oh, yeah."

There was a long silence.

They looked off in the direction Tuway had disappeared.

After a time, they grew used to the sounds and weary of standing. "Suppose we go on up to the tracks and sit on them till the train comes. We can still get back down in plenty of time so it won't see us," the man said.

"I guess that would be okay," the boy said, and followed him back up the hill.

"What's your name?" John asked as they took uneasy seats on the tracks.

The man hesitated for a minute. "Berl. It's Berl."

"I'm John." He would have put out his hand, but there was no way to see.

Berl put his satchel down and sat in silence on the tracks. Finally, John had to ask, "You are going to Chicago, aren't you?"

He heard Berl take a pack of cigarettes from his shirt pocket and fumble for a match. "Reckon Tuway'll mind if I smoke?"

He didn't wait for the answer and struck the match. "You want one?"

"Me?" John tried not to seem surprised. "Uh, no. No thank you."

"Hell yes, I'm goin'. Ain't nobody gonna stop me." The fire from the match gave light to their space for one moment before they disappeared into darkness again. The anonymity of the night, and the longing to talk, even to this little boy, seemed too much for Berl. "Been behind for five years. Then this year when my hogs come down with the cholera"—he took another drag—"and I didn't have no money for vaccine, and Lou Ann run off . . ." He pulled hard on his cigarette and they both watched as its glow ran up the white paper cover. "Didn't have no money, no nothin'. Cal come by deliverin' fertilizer." He laughed, remembering. "I was sittin' there watchin' my hogs tryin' to bed up, knowin' it was the cholera. I musta been a sorry sight."

The boy didn't know what to say. He had never been talked to this way and certainly not by a complete stranger. He was glad for the dark.

"Course I knowed 'bout Tuway," Berl said.

"You did?"

"Everybody know 'bout Tuway." Berl held the cigarette between his fingers and studied it. "Well now, all colored know 'bout Tuway. Everybody know Tuway can get you on a train to Chicago without payin'. Nobody know how he do it; they just know he do it, 'cept somehow he done stopped doin' it lately. Cal done some fast talkin' to get him to take me."

"What talkin' did he do?"

"When he told Tuway the law would be after me for not payin' the man, that's what did it."

"Will the right train come along tonight?"

"No, man." There was disdain in Berl's voice. "It don't work like that. First you gotta come out here and wait for the right train to come along. We was headed south before. Now we have to wait for the right one goin' north. Simple as that."

"So do we just wait right here and then jump onto the next train?"

"Not less you wanta end up in Mississippi or some such. Not less you got money. Me, I either ride the rails or I ain't gonna go."

"How do I—uh, you—know which train to take?"

"You have to wait for Tuway to tell you the right train. I don't know how he know, but he do—which car be open and all. Then you hop on and go. In the meantime, you have to stay put down in the swamp till Tuway say it's okay for you to go."

"How long will that be, do you suppose? I . . . well, I have to meet somebody in Chicago. I think it's a week from today."

"You do, do you? Got yourself some business to attend to, do you?" Berl laughed. "Well, I don't know. I hear tell Tuway have a shack down on the swamp where you can stay till the time to go. Suppose to be not far from here. I reckon that's where he's gone to now."

Off in the distance, a light appeared. They saw it before they heard the engine noise, which got louder and louder as the light got bigger. They both slid down the track embankment to wait as the huge engine came closer, and closer, then rumbled overhead, light cutting into the dark, churning wheels throwing gravel down on them as it passed. They watched as the caboose light swayed in the distance and the noise faded.

"Now that there is a northbound, just like what I'm gonna be on, headed for the Promised Land, away from all this here dirt and sweat. In a year's time, I'm gonna be drivin' a Caddy, gonna have me a suit, gonna have two suits. The women love them suits."

"I'm gonna get one of them, too," the boy said, trying to enter another world, but with no idea how it was done. "And I'm gonna get a Monopoly set and . . . and have lots of friends to play with."

"A what? A what set?"

"Oh, oh nothing. I just meant I was gonna get rich up there, too. That's where everybody gets rich, isn't it?"

"Why, hell yeah. That there is the place every nigger worth talkin' 'bout is goin'. That's where you can make it big. I got this cousin Willie J. Old Willie J. went up there. In one summer, he made enough to buy a car just from working in the slaughter—" Berl froze in midsentence. John looked up. Off in the swamp, a small light hung out over the water like a suspended star. It seemed to be swaying back and forth, in among the trees.

"Looks like a train light," John whispered.

"A train light in the middle of the swamp?"

"Maybe it's Tuway."

"Tuway or the law." They crouched down, both straining to see. The light was hanging above the water, slowly growing larger. They could see, reflected around its glow, the shadow of trees and the glint of water as it moved. Soon the reflection of moss off the low-lying branches gave off an eerie light as what now appeared to be a lantern swayed back and forth, suspended over the water. It came closer and closer. John moved to Berl's side. He hunched down to try to get a better look. "Is that person, whoever he is, is he in a boat?" John whispered to Berl.

"No, too many trees over there to get a boat through." Berl kept moving his head. "Damned if whatever it is ain't walkin' on water, if it's a person t'all," he half-whispered.

John swallowed hard. "Of course it's got to be a person."

"Do you see how a boat could get in amongst them trees? And if they ain't no boat, then what you 'spect they doin' jumpin' from tree to tree? That ain't likely." They watched as the light paused and then continued its journey toward them. "I heard 'bout things in the swamp, but I never paid'm no mind." He stood and began to take a step back. When he did, he ran into John and they fell in the dirt.

Berl jumped up without a word and began to back up the hill. "Where are we going?" John whispered as they backed up together.

"I don't know, but I ain't stayin' here."

Now the outline of a figure appeared walking on the water, not in the water, but on it, holding a lantern above his head. John and Berl slowly backed up the hill to the railroad track and at the same time seemed mesmerized with watching whatever it was.

Tuway appeared in the swinging glow of the lantern, making little swirling pools in the still swamp water as he walked closer. "Come on back down here. Didn't I tell y'all to stay 'way from them tracks?"

They let out a sigh of relief. Even though he still looked like a levitating ghost, there was no mistaking the sound of Tuway's voice.

Berl began to laugh. "Goddamn, Tuway, if you didn't

scare the shit out of us." He began walking back down the incline toward Tuway. "Walkin' up like you some kind of ghost or somethin'." He let out a yell of relief. "Ohweeee. That near 'bout took ten years off my life."

The figure stopped right in the middle of the water and stood silent, the glow of the lantern casting out long shadows all around him. Moss swayed in the trees just above him. He was close, but still offshore, and not saying a word, just standing there, once again a menacing presence. In a split second, their sense of relief had vanished.

Berl stepped closer to the water's edge. "How do you do that, standing on the water like that?" Berl tried to laugh.

Tuway stood there, off at a distance of maybe ten yards, not speaking. There were only the sounds of the swamp until Tuway decided to talk. His voice was as ominous and low coming out of the shadows as he had meant it to be. "I told you not to go up to them tracks and I done told you not to talk." They could see his eyes in the glow of the lantern, staring at them. "Nobody comes into the swamp without I say so, and I don't say so to people don't mind my rules."

"Now Mr. Tuway, you wouldn't leave us out here in the middle of nowhere, would you? Me and the boy here?"

Tuway said nothing, just stood there with the lantern lighting him up like some swamp statue.

"Now Tuway," Berl began to plead. "I know I wasn't suppose to talk or . . . or go near them tracks, but you done give me such a start. I swear, I ain't gonna do it again. Brother, you just get me on a train goin' north and you never have to see the likes of me again."

Slowly, very slowly, Tuway let the lantern down in front of him and began to walk on the water toward them. They watched, fascinated. He came right up to a water oak near shore, hung the lantern on a low-hanging branch, and then jumped the three or four feet from there to solid ground.

"Ain't gonna be no train north until a week from today, and that one already got people goin' on it. You have to wait till after that."

"That's all right, Tuway. Whatever you say. Long as I got me someplace to stay in won't nobody find me."

Tuway said, "You sure you ain't got no peoples can lend you some money 'til you can get a job?"

"We done been through that, Tuway. I told you. I ain't got nobody. Besides, even if I could, I wouldn't want to be on no bus, where the law could find me. No, this is the only way, Tuway. I'll do anything you say." He held up his hand in pledge.

"There ain't no way in or out of here 'cept if I say so. If you go, ain't no comin' back less I say so."

"That's okay by me, Tuway." He held his hand up again for emphasis. "Whatever you say, brother."

Then Tuway glared at John. "You goin' in whether you want to or not."

He turned back toward the swamp. "It'll be light soon. We got to get goin'. Work crews come along the tracks ever so often and the five o'clock pass by before you know it. Now this here is what I want you to do. My boat off in the swamp a ways, but first we got to get to it.

"Right beneath the water is outside planks from the sawmill. They throwed'm away as scrap. I take them pieces and nail'm just below the waterline between the trees to make a path through the swamp that goes from tree to tree and can't nobody see in the daylight. Course you have to be careful where you step and you have to know just what you doin'. Most times, I would take you down to the river and we would row up and into the swamp, but it's too late and the white boy shows out too much. I only use this path when I'm puttin' peoples on the train." He walked up to the edge of the water and jumped back out to the tree.

"Now you come on, boy, and then you, Berl. I'll lead the way and you follow close."

"What if I can't jump that far? What if they're snakes?" John eyed the distance from the shore to the place Tuway was standing.

"I don't wanta hear nothin' out of you, boy. You the one wanted to come. Get to jumpin'."

John took one or two big steps to get a running start and jumped far short of the place Tuway meant for him to be. His shoes sank into water covered over with slimy moss. Tuway shook his head and with one hand reached down and pulled him up enough so that he could scramble onto what felt like tree trunks sunk under the water. Berl made the jump easily, and then they were off, following close behind Tuway, inching their way along in the darkness while the lantern swayed back and forth, lighting their path.

It was not until Monday evening that anyone in the Spraig household discovered he was missing. His routine was to stay the weekend with the Vances and return late Sunday night after supper. By then everyone was usually in bed.

Monday, in the late afternoon, Shell had gone out in the front yard to search down the road that led to town. If he was late, she could usually see him coming in the distance. Often she would run to tell him to hurry up. Her daddy didn't like it when John was late for supper.

She had watched the road for several minutes, sure she would see his familiar shape moving toward the house. After a time of watching, she walked around the house to the door to his room. She knew he wasn't in there. He would have heard her mother calling everyone to supper a few minutes earlier. She pushed open his door, scraping it across the floor. Late-afternoon light streamed through the opening and the cracks in the planking that served as a back wall. Dust kicked up by the moving door danced into the light streams. The room was still except for a small mouse scurrying into one of the cracks in the floor. She saw only stacks of fertilizer, his bed, and the note.

Shell tucked it in her shirt and closed the door as she left the room. She must show the note to Little Luther before anyone else could see it. She couldn't read it, but it might be something that would get John another whipping. He was always doing the wrong thing.

The Bend

Tuway couldn't remember when he had started the business of bringing people to the Bend. It was a short time after he had come back from Tuskegee, sometime right after the war was over. Colored soldiers had come back home wanting more, now that they knew more was out there. Most had left and gone north on their own. Others had gone, out of money and on the edge of starving. He had seen all of this and had not paid much attention. Working for the Judge and trying to get back to the Bend when time permitted was all he could handle. Even though he stayed in a house on the outskirts of Lower Peach Tree, it wasn't home. Once when he was talking to his cousin Obadiah, who had been a porter for years and knew all the trains that passed through Lower Peach Tree, they had figured a way to cut his travel time to the Bend by more than half. Obadiah could find out which cars on the freight trains were empty and open and he would pass the information on to Tuway. Obadiah said Tuway could hop the train and be in the Bend in thirty minutes as long as he didn't mind walking through the swamp once he got there. Tuway had said no, he didn't mind. He'd just as soon walk over a few snakes as spend a half day going the long way around to the Bend by the old hunting road.

Then came the night Obadiah's cousin got in trouble and needed a place to stay. It was the perfect hideout. White people never came to the Bend. Even the owners hadn't been out there in years. Besides, he was beholden to Obadiah.

After that came the Leroy twins and then that girl from over in Burnt Corn. Then, of course, there was the older couple, the Tagways. He couldn't refuse them. They had no place to go when their children left for up north and they couldn't keep up the farm by themselves. They had liked the swamp so much, they decided to stay on and not go on up to Chicago to join their children. Now they were still there. He had helped them build a house on stilts near the trail in the swamp, but out of the way, so that nobody would notice it.

Every time any of this happened, his reputation grew and grew, way out of proportion, he felt, to what he was really like. Colored people began to look up to him. He hadn't meant to be their leader or to save them, or maybe he had, or maybe Mama Tuway had.

Until now, he had liked the two lives he led. He had liked the way people respected him, feared him.

But lately, it had started to weigh heavy on him. Things began to creep into his thoughts—things about Ella—about how they might go off to Chicago and live, just the two of them, with little Willie—someday. He had a right, after all these years.

CHAPTER 40

AFTER what seemed like hours of John slipping and sliding off the submerged logs and Tuway reaching back with his big hand to pull him out of the stagnant water, they made it to the boat.

The first gray, before light, was on them when they reached it. John could make out the outlines of a flat-bottom boat sitting next to a big tree with roots dug into the water. Tuway motioned him to sit in the front, Berl in the middle. He picked up a big pole that had been lying in the boat and began to slide out through the water, around trees, under curtains of moss, past old stumps. Even as it got lighter, it was dark and covered with shadows where they moved through the water. High up in the trees, ospreys screeched as they flew out of their nests, hunting morning food. Fish jumped off in the distance. Turtles and water snakes slid quickly off logs and stumps into the water at the first sound of Tuway's pole digging in the black water, or pushing off a passing tree. Tuway knew the trail through the trees and underbrush so well that it was as if they were traveling down a road, with signs at every turn that only he could see. It was a maze of trees and water, a few small islands here and there and bushes that seemed to spring right up out of the water in the early-morning shadows.

"We ain't got no time to waste. It'll be light before you know it, and I don't like to be in this part of the Bend in daylight."

"I could never find my way," John said.

"You'll learn it."

"But I won't be here that long," John said. "I'm goin' to Chicago."

"Stop talkin'," Tuway said, and lifted the pole out of the water. They glided along in silence.

"We comin' to the road," he whispered. The boat front hit against a grassy shore. They had come to what looked like the track bed, but it wasn't as high and it had trees and bushes growing up its sides. It extended to their right and left as far as the bushes and trees would allow them to see. He poled the boat alongside, jumped out, and walked a few yards up the slope, then came back to them. "It's okay," he said in a normal voice. "Once in awhile, hunters think they wanta come in here. Course that ain't happened in five years, but I don't take no chances." He began to tie the bow rope to a tree. "We usually go round the other way, but we was too late to do that. Can't let nobody see us, so this here way is better."

He looked at them just sitting there. "Well, get on out. What you waitin' for? We gonna go on over the road and walk the rest of the way in."

"I'm ready," Berl volunteered. "I ain't had no sleep for three days runnin'. I'll be glad to get to a place I can lay down."

"Me, too," John said, but the thought of sleep had never entered his mind.

When they got to the top of the road, they came upon what looked like someone's garden, rows of corn, tomato plants, okra plants, all in neat rows, as if they were tended and chopped every day. John could appreciate whoever was doing the chopping.

"I thought you said this here was a place to hide out till the train come," Berl said. "Look at all this here garden business. Look like the middle of town."

"Done put a garden in this year to feed all them mouths we done ended up with."

"What's you mean, 'all them mouths'? I thought it was just me and the boy here, maybe one or two others."

"Used to be one or two." They passed the garden and headed on down the other side of the slope to a tiny path that led off in the swamp. As they walked along single file, someone called to Tuway. They looked up, to see a house built on stilts right up out of the swamp. It was made of scrap wood and pieces of tin that looked to be discards from a henhouse or some other farm building. Farther on, there was another, and then another, all half-hidden, built up out of the water. Someone in one of the houses would call out to Tuway. John and Berl would look up and see them staring, especially at John, from crude cut windows.

At the end of the trail, which was maybe a quarter of a mile long, there was a small clearing. In the center was a very old house of wood siding faded to a silver gray, its four corners resting on lumps of rock and cement. It had originally been a house with only a dogtrot in the middle, but on second thought, and years later, someone had added a porch that ran the full length of the front. Deer antlers were nailed over one of the doors. Rockers with faded flowered cushions were scattered on either side of wide steps made of rough-cut lumber that gave entrance to the outdoor living room. Along the porch railing were tin cans of various sizes, sprouting herbs and other swamp plants. In the yard, various ornaments hung from low tree branches, giving off a tinkling sound with the slightest breeze. Two hound dogs dutifully trotted out to sniff the new people.

The old woman held a rusted watering can that slowly drenched the plants and railing as she watched them approach. Eyes, yellowed around their dark centers, stared first at John and then at Tuway. A long flowered dress hung loose round a thickening middle. She looked down and moved the watering can on to the next group of plants. The morning sun caught the clench of her jaw flexing. Finally, the water was gone and she set the can in a space on the rail. By then, they had moved within a few feet of her.

She would not look at them, instead turning to Tuway, who had a foot on the bottom step. "You got good cause for this, I know. I just can't think of it."

Tuway moved slowly up the steps and to the door that he opened for her. He motioned for her to go inside. To Berl and John, he said, "Sit down right there on them steps and don't move a muscle till I come out."

They both sat down on the wood stoop. Berl pulled out a pouch of tobacco and began to roll himself a cigarette. "Done had the last of my store-bought. From now on, it's roll your own."

The morning sun summoned the first sounds of the cicadas. A light breeze brushed the Spanish moss against tree branches.

None of the houses they had just passed was visible now. Without thinking, John got up and started walking back down the trail to see if he had imagined it all. He walked a few feet, peering up into the trees, until he saw one of them, almost camouflaged by moss and tree branches. A brown face was looking out at him from a doorway high off the ground. The little boy, who was smaller than John, maybe five or six years old, watched a moment longer, then threw down a rope that was attached to the side of the house and shinnied down so fast, John blinked. He let go of the rope and stood looking at John.

John raised his hand ever so slightly.

Just then Berl called to him. "You better get on back over here, boy, if you know what's good for you. Tuway'll tan your hide."

John raced back to the front stoop and sat down. "I forgot."

"You better not go forgettin'." He took a deep drag on his cigarette and let his head droop down. "I sure wish they would get done with decidin' whatever it is they decidin'. I'm gonna fall asleep right here if I don't get a place to lay my head soon."

They could hear his voice from time to time. He must be telling her how they came to be here. "I couldn't do nothin' else," he was saying. "You 'spect I shoulda throwed him off the train? Is that what I shoulda done?" There was silence and then: "There ain't another one for two weeks. That's what he said. I can't do nothin' 'bout that." Tuway's voice was getting more and more irritated as he talked.

"Berl, who is that he's talking to?" John asked.

"I don't know for sure, but if I was to guess, I'd guess his mama. They say he raised in the swamp, and sure as hell, this here is one big swamp, and we right in the middle of it." He slapped at a mosquito. "I ain't partial at all to places like this—full of things you can't see comin' at you. Sooner I'm out of here and on my way to Chicago, the better."

"Me, too." John pretended to slap at a mosquito.

After awhile, the door opened and Tuway stood there, a disgusted look on his face. "Willie," he yelled out without looking up. The same little boy John had seen in the stilt house appeared on the trail in front of them and ran to stand at attention before Tuway. "Take this one"— he pointed to Berl—"to stay at the round house. Take this one"—he pointed to John—"to stay with you and your mama. Tell your mama I'll explain to her later. And tell her to put some of that mosquito medicine on him to get rid of as much of that white as she can." He turned to go back inside, mumbling to himself.

Berl was standing up to follow Willie. "Uh, excuse me, Tuway, I know it's early to ask, but when you think I might be gettin' out of here?"

"No tellin', Berl, no tellin'." He closed the door.

They both turned to their new guide. He had on short pants and a T-shirt, no shoes, and faint streaks of what looked like gray ash marked his body. They ran across his arms and legs and lined his face. He motioned them to follow, turned, and started back down the trail.

John gestured to Berl as they walked along, pointing his finger at his face to ask in sign language why he had that stuff on his body. Berl shrugged his shoulders. "Damned if I know. Look like some Zulu warrior, if you ask me." He brushed flies away from his face as they walked. "This place got more varmints than a fruit orchard in season."

"I am damned, too," John said, and spit out what must have been a gnat that had flown in his mouth.

They walked down the dirt path some distance past

Willie's house, until they came to another one, which was bigger and seemed to have more rooms. Willie pointed upward. "This the round house. It's where you stay."

"Up there?" Berl stared. "Why can't I stay on solid ground like that?" He pointed back to the house in the clearing.

"'Cause that's Mama Tuway's house." No other explanation seemed to be necessary.

Berl stared upward. "How you suppose I'm gonna get up there?"

Willie walked over to the side of the house, reached around back of one of the poles, and untied a thin rope. When he let it go, a rope ladder rolled down out of the floor of the house. "Usually, it stay down, but everybody off fishin' this mornin'."

Berl sighed. "They ain't got nothin' better to do than go fishin' round here. Look like I done come on me a 'resort' for rich people."

Willie looked at Berl, blank-faced. "They don't catch no fish, we don't eat no supper. When they get back, they tell you where to put your things." He turned to leave and motioned John to follow.

"Hey, wait a minute," Berl called after them. "When you think they be back?"

"After they catch enough fish."

Berl set his bag down and leaned up against a tree.

"Best mind where you lean," Willie said. "Snakes."

Berl jerked away from the tree, cussing under his breath.

John and Willie walked on toward Willie's house.

Chapter 41

Mama, Tuway say"—Willie pointed to John—"he gonna be stayin' with us."

They were standing on a small porch that was in front of Willie's front door. Willie had climbed up a few boards nailed to the back side of two stilts. After that, he had come onto a small platform that was a landing and led up three more steps to the porch. John had followed but was unsure at every step. Now Willie's mother stood looking at him. "What in the world has got into Tuway, bringin' him here to me and he know how I feel."

"Mama Tuway say for you to cover him up with fly medicine so he won't show out so much."

"What's fly medicine?" John asked, backing off.

She said nothing, just kept studying John. Then she pulled the boys aside and stepped out on the porch. "Stay right here till I get back. I ain't havin' no white boy. . . ." She turned and left by way of the steps. "We'll just see 'bout this." She let herself down to the ground with such ease, the boy thought she must have been doing it all her life. He watched her walk off down the trail, her shoulders hunched over, her eyes watching the ground. She moved with an awkward stride that said she had no idea how strikingly beautiful she was.

Willie watched John staring after her. "I know she don't look right with her hair cropped, but she lettin' it grow out. Soon as it gets longer, we gonna go on up to Chicago, but right now, Tuway say she can't travel with her hair like that. She be noticed by everybody."

John hadn't noticed her hair. He was too taken with her dark eyes, with her long legs, with milk chocolate skin pulled over high cheekbones, looks he could not compare to anything he had ever seen before but looks that he knew would be considered stunningly beautiful.

"She done got mad, just buzzed it all off right 'fore we come here," Willie said. "Then she just lay round for a long time after . . . but then we come here and Mama Tuway done got her up and goin'." He walked over and took a seat at a table that had two straight chairs. "She be all right now," he added.

John looked around at a small room with two windows and bunk beds, three beds high, next to one wall. They were made from more sawmill end pieces. He walked over to feel the feed-sack covers that made up the mattresses. Small pieces of moss showed between the seams. On another wall, wooden shelves stored a few cans on one shelf and folded clothes on the next two shelves down. The middle shelf was wider than the others and held a washbowl and pitcher. Up this high, above the ground, sunlight streamed into one of the windows; cicadas whined in the trees.

"Do y'all live here?"

"No, we just stay here temporary. Soon we be goin' to Chicago." Willie looked around the room. "We just here temporary." He swung his little legs back and forth sitting at the table. John hadn't realized how little he was. Now that he took the time to study him, he saw a boy smaller than he was, or maybe John had grown and it had escaped his notice.

"Where's the bathroom?" John said, looking for another door.

"Out there." He lifted his hand toward the window.

John came over and sat down in the other straight chair. They sat there silently. Willie looked down at the floor, still swinging his legs back and forth. "She be back directly," he said. "She usually keep plenty on hand, but she musta run out."

"What? Of fly medicine?"

"It's what I got on." He held his hand out and showed John his arm, streaked with the lines he and Berl had noticed.

"It keeps the flies and mosquitoes 'way, and if you live here, you most always need it till you get used to them or they get used to you and don't pay you no mind. Some peoples, they don't pay no mind, like my mama. Me, they pester the daylights out of me if I don't wear no fly medicine."

"It . . . it probably doesn't hurt, does it?"

"Nah, it's made mostly out of soot and some lye, but it don't hurt. Sting a little when it first go on. Mama Tuway is the one know how to make it. She know how to do everything in the swamp, she be livin' here so long and all. She learns us all how to do."

John got up and walked over to the window that overlooked the trail. At about their height across the trail, he could barely make out another house on stilts, nearly covered by leaves and moss. If he hadn't been looking, he wouldn't have noticed. "Who lives over there?"

"Them's the Tagways. They ain't goin' to Chicago. They just like livin' here and makin' a livin' fishin', and Tuway say they can stay as long as they do like he say."

"Well, what if they tell about this place? What if they bring their friends down here? I thought this place was supposed to be secret?"

"Tell? Ain't nobody gonna cross Tuway." Willie laughed at the thought. "They end up at the bottom of the river. Don't you know about Tuway and—"

"What you tellin' tales, William Tyler Delong? I done told you 'bout that." She stood in the doorway. She had come up the ladder without a sound and stood there holding a tin can. She gestured to Willie. "Get on over here, boy." He came slowly up to her. Then, without a word, he turned around and shut his eyes tight, waiting. She gave him a good swat on the backside. "Now get on outta here and don't you go tellin' tales again. Go on down and wait for . . ." she paused, turning to John. "What's your name?"

"John." He began to back up. "It's John."

"Wait for John. And don't you go takin' him no places that you ain't suppose to go. I'll tell Mama Tuway and then—" Willie was out of the house and down to the ground before she could finish.

"Get on over here, boy." John walked over slowly, turned, and shut his eyes tight, waiting for his swat. She grabbed his arm, held it out, and began rubbing a black powder over it. "I don't never want to see you leave here without this here all over you. You understand me?"

He opened his eyes. "Yes, ma'am."

She gave him a handful and told him to put it on his legs. Then she put black streaks across his cheeks and forehead. There was the hint of a smile on her face as she looked at him when she finished. She went over to the washstand and poured water in the basin to rinse her hands. She still had her back to him when she told him to go on out and play with Willie. He was not interested in playing with Willie anymore. He watched the back of her head, her legs. He was interested in everything about her. She dried her hands on a towel and turned, to see him watching her. She flipped the towel in his direction. "Go on. Get on out of here." She turned to hang the towel on a nail. "You all alike, all alike."

He backed out of the house, only to stand on the porch, high above the ground, scared to move. The house seemed to sway with the slightest breeze. He whispered down to Willie, too embarrassed to let her hear that he could not do what she seemed to do with no thought at all. "How . . . how do I get down from here?"

"Just come on down them steps and then swing your leg over to climb down the ladder. It ain't hard."

He came down the steps, then slowly began to inch his way down the ladder.

"You'll get used to it." Willie was watching, hands on his hips. Finally, John was on the ground. He turned around, pleased with himself, and ran smack into Tuway's leg.

"Where's Willie?" he said, backing away. "We . . . we were gonna play." Tuway stood there, looming above him. John instinctively took another step back. Tuway grabbed John's shirt and pulled him close. The boy closed his eyes, waiting for a slap.

"You comin' with me." Tuway dragged him across the water that was between Willie's house and the trail, walking on submerged planks. John's feet dragged through the stagnant water. When they reached the trail, Tuway dumped him on the ground and pointed toward the house.

"Get on up there." John scrambled up and ran ahead of him to the porch, where the old woman was sitting in a rocker, watching them. He stood on the steps not knowing what to do. Tuway walked past him and took a seat in a straight chair, leaning it up against the wall. He took a cigarette out of his shirt pocket and lit it. "How come you here, boy?" He blew smoke out and trained unblinking eyes on the boy.

"Well, I . . . you brought me."

"Don't give me none of your sass," he almost yelled. "You know what I mean. What you doin' followin' me last night? Old Luther gonna send the sheriff out here lookin' for you?" His voice got lower and meaner. "Am I gonna have to throw you in the river to keep him from comin' round here?" He took a deep drag on his cigarette to let it sink in. Then he said, " 'Cause I will, too. Don't you go thinkin' just 'cause I give you some of my leftover dinner up at the Judge's house, don't you go thinkin' you mean somethin' to me." He let the chair's two front legs drop on the floor as he leaned forward. "You might have the old Judge fooled, but you ain't got me fooled for nothin'."

At that moment, John wondered why he had left the dogtrot house at Uncle Luther's, only to exchange it for one in the swamp. Tuway would kill him. He had almost killed him on the train. No one would ever miss him. No one even knew where he was. "I . . . I'm goin'," he said, and began to back away down the trail. If he was fast enough, maybe he could outrun Tuway. He turned and began to sprint down the path in the direction of the old swamp road. He hadn't gotten five yards before Tuway's big hand grabbed his shirt at the neck. With the other hand, he gave him three hard swats across the fanny. Then he pulled him back to the front porch, in front of the old woman.

As she sat rocking and watching on the porch, Tuway's mouth was in John's ear. "Don't you ever try that again." His spit landed on John's face. "Sit down there and don't move a muscle till I tell you to." He threw the boy on the ground, then climbed the stairs and sat down again.

"There ain't no way you can handle him while I'm gone, even if the whole county ain't already lookin' for him." He shook his head. His mother kept rocking. "We liable to hear hounds any minute now," he said.

She stared at John impassively. "How did you know about Tuway comin' here?"

He tried to cough to clear the lump in his throat. "I didn't know about him comin' here." John took a deep breath and tried to control his shaking voice. Tears streaked the lines of black soot. "I thought he was goin' to show Berl the way to Chicago. I . . ." His voice broke and he couldn't get the next words out.

She watched him for a minute and then motioned to a water bucket on the side of the porch. "Go on over there and get yourself a drink and wash up your face. Then come back here and tell me."

He did what she said—took a drink from the tin ladle that was in the water bucket, poured some in his hands, and washed his face, using a rag hung on a nail to dry off the water and soot. He hated that he cried, that he wasn't any better than a child. Finally, his hands seemed to steady, and he walked back over to them, his face still streaked. He cleared his throat to begin again.

"The way it was, was this"—and he told them the whole story: about how he saw Tuway in the graveyard, about how he told Uncle Luther that he was going to visit friends in the town he came from, how he believed him, how he knew the Judge wouldn't believe him but that he didn't care anyway, so it didn't matter. In the end, he jacked up his courage enough to say in a halting voice, "Even if you don't help me, I'm going to Chicago some way." He looked at the old woman, who was still rocking and listening, as if it was an ordinary, even boring, story.

He paused to take a breath, not knowing what else to say. She turned to look at Tuway. Tuway shook his head. "Ain't no way the Judge is gonna believe that. He gonna think Luther is up to no good. He's gonna be callin' up them folks in Bainbridge to check and see if John got there safe for his visit."

Mama Tuway rocked for a while, thinking before she said, "The Judge won't check if you tell him you seen him gettin' on the train. He trusts you. You could tell him you seen him gettin' on the train and he looked happy to be goin'," she said.

John jumped in. "Don't tell the Judge I looked happy. I don't want you to tell him I looked happy."

"Hush your mouth up, boy. We ain't talkin' to you," Tuway snarled. He took another drag off his cigarette and studied the ground. "Might work, if they ain't already got the police out lookin' for him." He rested his elbows on his knees. "Am I willin' to lie for the likes of him?" He didn't look at John.

"He would believe you, Tuway," John said.

"Shut up, boy. You the one's makin' a liar out of me." He turned back to her. "The Judge always done right by me and me by him. Keeps givin' crop loans to everybody in the Bend, even with them bad crops we done had, and he don't even know I stay out here. And he do me right payin' me."

Mama Tuway rose from her chair. "Ain't no other way to do it. I'm just hopin' it's gonna work. We'll know soon enough. When you get back, you can see what's goin' on and send word by . . ." She paused and looked at John. "Willie," she called. He appeared out of the bushes on the trail. "Take John here and show him what he can and he can't do. You know what I told you." She looked at John. "And if you don't do exactly like Willie say, I'll throw you in the river myself. Now get."

Willie grabbed his arm and dragged John off to the side of the house. "Don't be standing there when they say for you to go. You get a whippin' for sure."

They walked around the side of the house to a trail that quickly vanished at the edge of a dark creek that meandered through the swamp. Willie said it would lead out to the big river if they were allowed to go that far, only they couldn't because Mama Tuway had said they weren't to go near the river. Willie lifted up low-lying branches to show him his boat. "This here is mine alone," he said. "Tuway done give it to me 'cause it's too little for anybody else."

They pushed the boat out into the creek. Willie lifted a pole up out of the bottom and began to push them along. The bow cut into still water filled with swamp pictures. An osprey screeched a warning as they passed under her tree. Cicada sounds swelled, then faded as they poled along. "This here land on the left"—Willie pointed—"is the best land in the Bend." Through the trees that lined the creek, off at a distance, a patch of sunlight shone on a field of corn. "Colored peoples been plantin' that land since forever." He poled on, talking away. "Now, the swamp side is where Mama Tuway stay. Course don't nobody else want it but her.

Ain't much good for crops, but Mama Tuway, she like it. She know how to live in the swamp just fine." The creek they had been on began to spread out in all directions, so that now it ran under trees and bushes that seemed to grow right out of the water. Willie stopped in front of a huge pine tree that had fallen across their path. Off at a distance, John could see sunlight again and what looked like a large body of water. "Mama Tuway say we can't never go no more than this here tree." They sat and peered out at the sunlight in the distance. "She don't never want us to go out near the river. Somebody on the other side might see you."

"What's over there on the other side?" John crouched down to get a better view through the trees.

"That's the white folks' side. Only way you can get over there is by the ferry, and it ain't runnin' no more, ain't been runnin' since before I come here. You wanta go round by road, that's nearly 'bout a all-day trip into Lower Peach Tree, the road so bad."

Willie turned the boat away from the fallen tree and back into a low area with swamp on all sides. They were out of dappled sunlight and into deep shadows. "You see that there? That's the best place to gig frogs." He pointed to an inlet filled with reeds and overhanging tree moss. "Sometimes I can get enough for everybody to have supper on."

Willie stopped to wipe the sweat off his face with his shirtsleeve. "Now if I was to let you, you think you smart enough to get the hang of polin'?" He looked at John, who was holding on to both sides of the boat. "Now I ain't sayin' it's easy."

"I could try," John said, turning his head but not letting go of his grip on the boat.

"Well, come on then. I'll show you." Willie handed

him the pole and proceeded to instruct. After a shaky start, John began to have some success pushing them through the water.

Willie sat back, trailed his fingers in the water, and let the morning breeze cool him down. "You doin' just fine." Willie smiled. "Just fine."

Shell had gone quickly to the outhouse and waited for Little Luther to come out. When he did, she pulled him around behind it. "Quick, lookie here at this. John ain't come home. Read it to me."

Little Luther was still buttoning up the front of his pants. "What's you talkin' about, Shell? Stop pullin' my arm." He finished with his pants and took the paper she shoved in his face. "What is this?"

"Found it on John's bed. I know he's done gone and done somethin' stupid."

"How do you know that? Maybe he's just late. He's always late."

"Read it." She poked a finger at the paper.

"Is it printed?" He held it at arm's length. No one had ever bothered to check Little Luther's eyes. He stretched his arms straight out and squinted. "'Dear Aunt Nelda, Uncle Luther, and Shell and Butch.'" Little Luther let his hands drop to look at Shell and smile. "He put down Butch, just like he's supposed to." He raised the paper again and squinted. "'I have gone to visit my friend in . . .'" He paused, looking at the next word. "Must be the name of the town he's from '. . . just like I told you I would. They sent me the ticket in the mail on Friday.'" Little Luther let the letter drop again and stared at Shell. "He's left. He's left us."

"But he said when he left, he'd only be gone the summer."

"He better come on back here 'fore school starts. If he ain't here, who's gonna learn me my English homework?" Little Luther said.

CHAPTER 42

THAT afternoon, like so many afternoons in the swamp, a rain came that formed right in among them. The air thickened as the day wore on. The sun, which had been bright in the morning, grew to a misty, pale ball by midafternoon, then disappeared altogether in a solid cloud cover. No thunder or lightning announced the beginning of a steady, windless, drenching downpour. The moss-hung trees became floating coral in an underwater wetland.

At first, John was certain they would become like everything in the swamp, wet and sodden, but when he and Willie were safe inside Willie's house, it was no more than a pleasant tapping on the tin roof. Exhausted by his night's passage, John climbed to his third-row bunk and fell asleep.

Late in the day, when he woke, Willie seemed to be waiting for him. He went to the corner of his bed and fumbled under its moss mattress. "I got me some cards. You wanta play?" He had a tattered set of old maid. Many of the cards were missing and in their places he had made new sets out of pieces of cardboard. "Now these here are ones that match. I took to makin' pictures," he said, showing John rectangular-shaped pieces of cardboard with sticklike figures on them. "Drawed them off with pokeberry juice."

They played cards for the rest of the day, into the early evening. Willie's mother was nowhere to be seen. "She down at Tuway's mama's house, I 'spect, fixin' supper." They sat cross-legged on the floor, cards spread before them.

Long after the sun had gone down and his stomach was making noises, John and Willie climbed down from the house on stilts and took the trail to Tuway's mother's cabin.

From a distance, they could see a fire laid in the ground beside the house. Its flames threw light up into the big water oaks that surrounded the clearing. John had not noticed this side yard before. In daylight, he had barely glanced at the open space baking in the sun. His vague impression had been that there was a black spot on the ground, a large iron kettle, a few dilapidated tables made from fence posts and two-by-fours, and, around the perimeter, four or five tall poles with crossbraces on the top, from which hung scores of gourds. "Indian birdhouses for the martins," Willie said. "Keeps the mosquitoes away."

Now, in the dark, that same space was transformed. An evening breeze, still full of humidity, sent embers rising in the night sky each time the big logs of oak and hickory settled from their burning. The fire lighted faces working around its circle and the backs of other people seated at tables scattered about the yard. Some huddled in telling a story that ended with laughter and slaps on the wood tabletops. Others shucked large piles of corn, stacking the cleaned ears in a pyramid at the table's center. The whine of a harmonica laced itself between guitar chords that were preparing for better things.

In his ignorance, John walked faster, thinking he could somehow join in. When he reached the light, all talking stopped. He felt his face reflecting out like a full moon in a clear night sky. He wondered what he was doing here. Why had he been so stupid as to get on the train in the first place? At least when he was in Lower Peach Tree, he had his own bed, even though it was the feed-sack room. At least there, most of the people he knew were his same color.

Mama Tuway was over by a big black kettle of hot grease that smelled of frying fish. She glanced up at him. "If you ain't the dot on a domino, boy." She turned to Willie and pointed to the house with her big spoon. "I told you to keep fly medicine on him. Go on in yonder and get some." She turned the spoon on John. "And I don't want to see you standin' out like no light no more, and I ain't gonna tell you again."

He ran toward the house, following Willie.

"Isn't this supposed to be a secret place?" John began to count what he thought might be fifteen or twenty people. "Did I come all the way here and this isn't even a secret place?"

"The ones that ain't with us is from the Bend. We join in together in the summer lots of times."

"All these people aren't going to Chicago, are they? I'll be the last one they let go."

"Course not, most all these peoples born here. They granddaddies walked all the way in here from far away when they was slaves. They ain't 'bout to up and leave."

"But the ones that live where we live?"

"Some of them go on up to Chicago when they can get a ride or Tuway put'm on the train. Some stay up there long enough to get a job; then they turn right round and come on back down here, stay awhile, then go on back. Mostly, though, the ones that stay here, they older people, don't want to go on off to no big city."

That night, they had fried fish of every sort: catfish, bass, sunfish, anything the river had offered up during the day. The small fish were fried whole. The catfish were nailed to a tree and pliers were used to strip off the skin. After that, they were gutted in one easy motion and handed over to one of the women at a table by the fire. She would roll the fish in cornmeal and drop it in the big vat of bubbling grease.

When all the fish were fried and laid out on paper sacks to drain, handfuls of cornmeal mixed with egg and onion were thrown into the grease, giving rise to a mound of hush puppies draining next to the fish. John, afraid to ask if he could help, took an uneasy seat on the edge of one of the tables and watched Willie shuck fresh corn that still smelled of the fields. No one asked him to help. No one talked to him.

The corn was thrown into another large pot of boiling water, held over the fire by a three-legged iron stand. Fresh-washed tomatoes were set in a wooden crate to be taken up, salted, and eaten like apples.

The boy lurked in the shadows, hoping to get something to eat, wondering if they even knew he was there. He hurried to her when Mama Tuway finally told him to come get a plate, after everyone else had been served. By then, the food was cold, but he didn't care. He had three catfish, six hush puppies, and two pieces of corn. While he ate, if he looked up at all, he watched Willie's mother. She stood by Mama Tuway in almost everything she did, coating fish or helping make up the round balls of cornmeal that would become hush puppies. Her long, graceful arms and legs operated in an awkward, clumsy way, as if she were ashamed of them. Her body relaxed only when dealing with Mama Tuway. She called her this—"Mama Tuway"—in a timid, shy voice. The two of them would laugh over some trivia, Ella receiving a pat on the shoulder for a small job well done. All others got only distant stares from Ella's cold, dark eyes. John did not recognize any shortcomings. He saw only a beautiful face in those rare moments when it wasn't clouded with uncertainty or hardened to fend off someone thinking, however innocently, to enter her world.

The smell of frying fish lingered in the heavy air and created, among all those in its circle, a sense of satisfaction—from morning getting to evening consuming—some small circle completed.

John sat outside the circle of firelight on the roots of one of the big oaks, his back leaning against its trunk, wondering what Shell and Little Luther might be doing.

The fire logs fell in on themselves a final time, sending another spray of embers into the night. The guitar chords settled into a pattern and the harmonica whined out past the perimeter of light up into the trees,

CHAPTER 43

John slept that night in the top bunk bed. He and Willie had walked back to their house alone through the swamp. Willie had carried a lantern, which made a small circle of light around them as they made their way down the trail. Ella stayed to help clean up.

Willie placed the lantern on the table. "They used to be three mens livin' here 'fore we come. That's how come we got room for you. Get on up while I turn out the light."

John climbed up to his moss mattress and lay there watching the moon through the cracks in the wall as it passed in and out of thinning clouds. His eyes would not stay open.

It must have been past midnight when he heard the scream. At first, he thought it was a sound out of the swamp. A nighthawk carrying away some baby something. The second scream was so loud and painful that he sat straight up in his bed and hit his head on one of the roof rafters. "Willie," he whispered. "What is it?" He leaned over to look down at the dark form in Willie's bunk. Willie had not moved. She screamed again, this time calling out something—he couldn't tell what—tossing in her bed. He could see a dark outline jerking and turning on the bottom bunk. Slowly, Willie turned over and let his arm hang down toward her. "It's all right, Mama. It's just a dream," he mumbled in his pillow. She jerked and seemed to wake up, breathing as if she had been running. "Willie, you there, Willie?" He wiggled his fingers, waiting for her touch.

They both fell back asleep, holding on.

CHAPTER 44

THE next morning, Willie woke John with a whisper and motioned him to come outside without waking his mother. They walked up the trail to join the other people who were sitting on Mama Tuway's porch, talking and drinking coffee. Berl was there and the Tagways, who lived on the path across from Willie's house, and Laura, a young girl who stayed with the Tagways. Two other men, who lived in the house where Berl stayed, were sitting on the porch steps, talking to Berl.

Mama Tuway came out of the house, letting the screen door slam back against its frame. She wiped her hands on the clean feed-sack apron around her waist, looking out at the sun rising over the pines. There was a breeze brought in by yesterday's rain. The morning was as crisp and clear as it ever got in the swamp—which was to say that it was hotter than it was humid—for the moment. Water left from the night before glistened on leaves and grass. The muddy path leading up to the cabin smelled of pine needles and Black Belt earth. "If we could keep the whole day like the mornin', wouldn't that be fine?" she said.

The others nodded but said nothing, except for Mrs. Tagway, who was seated in the wood swing. "Sho would." The wood-slat rocking chair sat waiting for Mama Tuway, its frame divided in half by sunlight that cut down into the shadows of the porch. Laura handed her a cup of coffee she had been holding. Mama Tuway took a sip and rocked.

"Now, let's us see here," she said. "What do the day hold?" She took another sip. "Leroy"—she looked at one of the men on the steps—"I want you to—" She began to name each person and tell him or her what to do. Some were to go fishing; others to work the garden; still others should do the wash.

The boys sat on the edge of the porch, their feet hanging off, swinging them back and forth and listening to her. She had not looked at John. He had taken care to cover his face and arms with mosquito medicine from the can in Willie's house.

"Mind when you in the garden," she instructed. "Ain't no reason for nobody to use that old road, but mind anyway."

"Where's your mamma?" Mama Tuway asked after the others had gone off to their various chores. "She suppose to help me get breakfast."

Willie watched his swinging feet. "You told me to leave her be if she start screamin' out in the night again."

Mama Tuway took another sip of coffee and rocked a bit more. "Bad?"

"Wasn't t'all bad this time. I think she gettin' shed of it—them bad dreams and all." He looked up to watch her face. "Don't you think she gettin' shed of it?"

The old woman didn't say anything. She studied the other people going about their business. "Take that brown handle hoe, Laura. Got a sharper blade." She sat there rocking in and out of the sunlight. Then she half-stood and scooted the rocker back into the shade. "Go on inside, boys, and get yourself some breakfast, then come on back out here. I got a job for you."

They got a plate of leftover hush puppies and fresh-washed tomatoes to eat back out on the edge of the porch in the sunlight as the first machine-gun sounds of the cicadas rose out of the trees. After finishing the last bites of their hush puppies, each boy took a long drink out of the tin ladle that was hooked on a nail next to the bucket of fresh well water on the porch table.

"Here's what I want you to do." Mama Tuway had lifted a sewing basket to her lap. "Y'all go on down through the swamp to the tracks and get a message off the ten o'clock train. You know how, Willie. And remember, Willie, you look hard. I'm sending white boy along with you 'cause four eyes better than two, but don't you go lettin' him out from underneath the tree cover. You, either. Stay hid. You know that, don't you?" Willie said he did. He was thrilled to be entrusted with the job, fidgeting to go the whole time she was talking to him.

"This is the way I'm gonna go when we start out to Chicago. Every time I go, I practice," he said as he led the way. The trail ended on the swamp road where the vegetable garden grew. John and Willie waved to a woman tying up pole beans. They found the boat that Tuway had used the night they came to the swamp and the boys poled along among the trees and water, until they came to the right tree and tied up the boat. "This is the best part. I know it by heart." He got out of the boat and began to walk on the water just like Tuway had the night John came—stepping just so, with no mistakes. "I done practiced lots," he called back to John as he stood suspended, hands out, showing off, John thought. "Come on, I'll show you."

He taught John how to find the marks on the trees that told where the planks were attached underwater, how to slide his foot along just right when he took a step, how to grab the tree trunk, then change directions. John began to catch on, but not until he had fallen in the murky water several times, always scrambling out immediately, fearing the sting of a snakebite on one of his ankles.

Suddenly, in their hearing, the train whistle was blowing an approach to the bridge trestle. Willie turned in panic to get to the edge of the swamp before the train passed. John followed, but he missed steps and had to get back up on the boards to begin again.

The big engines roared past as they watched from their place under the trees. They stared intently.

"What are we looking for?" John shouted, "I don't know what to look for."

Willie was looking down, trying to find an end to the train. "Seein' if the caboose light is on the end of the train," he shouted back.

When the final cars lumbered by, there it was, swinging from its hook on the back of the caboose. They watched it disappear down the tracks.

"Why do we care about that?"

"I don't know, just long as I see it and make sure it's there. We did see it, didn't we? Didn't we?"

"I saw it. If somebody wants to send a message, why don't they use the phone?"

"What you think? We got a phone? Ain't no phones in the Bend."

The boys walked the water back to the boat and headed for home. When they told Mama Tuway about the caboose light, she smiled. "It means they ain't gonna come lookin' for you—just yet.

"You run on along now," Mama Tuway said. "Get me some good eatin' frogs for supper."

Willie hesitated. "Are you gonna—"

"Yes, yes, I'm gonna see to her."

He smiled. "Then can I use the flashlight?"

"Yes, but mind you save the batteries." She went into the house and came back out with a metal flashlight, which she handed to Willie. He gave her a big grin and put it in his pants waist. Then he stood there watching her. She had picked up her sewing basket again, but put it back down. "I'm goin'," she said and grabbed the handrail, negotiating the steps and starting down the path to Willie's house.

Willie went back inside and filled a paper sack with their lunch, more hush puppies, leftover fish, and cold corn on the cob. The boys walked around the house to a shed built out against the rear wall. Willie pulled open the door that had fallen off its top hinge, and got out a long reed pole with what looked like a metal fork attached to the end. He handed it to John and then fished around until he found two empty fertilizer sacks, slapping them in the air to get rid of the dust. They were like the one John had stolen from Uncle Luther to make Shell the colored baby doll. He wondered if Uncle Luther was making Shell do extra work to make up for him being gone.

John stood there as Willie shut the door and fastened the metal latch with a wood peg whittled for that purpose.

"What is it your mama is getting shed of?"

Willie looked at him and shrugged his shoulders without answering.

"Tell me again what the note said." Judge Vance and his wife were sitting in the garden, having their morning coffee.

"Honey, I've read it to you three times already." For the fourth time, Adell Vance picked up the piece of paper that she had found on John's bed Sunday morning. "It says that he had to do some work at home for his uncle Luther." She flipped the paper over to make sure, for the fourth time, that she hadn't missed anything. "That's all it says."

"Yes, but it's two days, and we still haven't heard from him. He should be here by now. He's usually sitting on the back steps when we get up in the morning."

"Byron, you are such a caution. You complain that he's too much responsibility when he's here, and when he misses one measly day, you act like he was whisked away by Martians.

"Maybe his uncle had more things for him to do. You know some people are still planting. Have you thought of that?"

"Are you sure that's his handwriting?"

Adell laughed. "Byron Vance. You do beat all. Of course it's his handwriting, unless some other nine-year-old slipped into the house and wrote it for him."

"Just the same, Adell. I'm going to get Tuway to go out to the Spraigs' when he comes."

CHAPTER 45

THEY spent the rest of the day poling in the creek, passing back and forth between the high ground of the Bend and the swamp. Willie agreed to let John do all the poling this time. The boat glided alongside reeds that grew out to narrow the creek path. Silent as a snake, they made their way through water cypress and overhanging moss. Sometimes in the creek, they would come upon a farmer tending his fields on the Bend side and wave to him. When the sun was straight overhead, Willie took them to a place on the Bend side where a spring bubbled up out of the rocks. They drank from it as they ate their sack lunch.

In the late afternoon, Willie directed John to the place with the best frogs. The pole breaking the water surface was their only intrusion into the life of the swamp as they entered the mouth of a small pond off to the side of the creek.

At first, they didn't use the flashlight. It was still light as the frogs began to come out and call to one another across the pond. Willie was an expert, standing in the bow of the boat, spotting them on the edge of the bank, letting the pole whip out in one easy motion, gigging the frog before it could move. His arm, the spear, his body— all worked as one, with the spear hitting its target every time. There was no thought of missing, only of how many he would get.

As he sat in the boat and watched, John thought Willie gigged frogs like he—so long ago in his mother's house—had practiced the art of afternoon tea, holding his teacup just so, never making a noise or rattling the china.

At first, John was not any good at gigging. He didn't spot them in time. He was not quick enough when he did. Then when he did get one, he got sick to his stomach, seeing the frog wiggle on the pole, watching its juices begin to spill out. After many tries, he got better— not good, but better—holding the spear at the proper angle, as Willie had taught him, waiting till the boat glided to a place almost on top of the frog. As the sun went down, they began to use the flashlight. Willie would spot them with the light and John would gig them. After awhile, it became a game, killing the little things, and he got to be good at it. Not as good as Willie, but he thought he would never be as good as Willie.

Willie let him do most of the killing for the rest of the time. They filled two feed sacks full of frogs. Then Willie used the flashlight to guide their way back through the swamp as night things watched from low-hanging branches.

That evening, as they sat at a picnic table near the fire, people came by to pat Willie on the head and tell him how good the frog legs were. To Willie, it was all in a day's work. To John, it was something else altogether.

He could hardly wait for someone to compliment him. He imagined himself standing to say, You're welcome or It was my pleasure. He pictured himself telling them all about catching the frogs, about poling the boat, about using the spear, but no one ever came up to him; no one even knew he was there.

Later, he and Willie were sitting by the fire, stuffing in the last of the fried fish and frog legs, listening to the hum of voices around them, when it happened. And to make it worse, Tuway was not there to protect her.

Something set off Willie's mother. She had been standing at a table close to the fire, using a big butcher knife to gut fish and cut off frog legs. Mama Tuway had stepped away from her side and was serving somebody pole beans and tomatoes.

Ella screamed. Everyone stopped eating and stared. "You keep them hands to you fat self, nigger." She swirled and held up the knife like a spear, her eyes wide and seething. "Ain't nobody touchin' me I don't tell to." Before he could change his facial expression, she brought the knife forward and ripped his shirtsleeve. "And I ain't tellin' you." The man jumped back just in time to avoid getting cut, spilling some of the beans off his plate. He recovered and began to smile.

"Lookie here what you done to my shirt. What's got into you, gal? Wasn't nothin' but a friendly—" His voice seemed to set her off even more. She changed the position of the knife to hold it in front of her and went at him again, slicing out into the air. "Hold on there, woman." He backed up more, dodging all the while.

Still holding his plate, he began to make a game of it, dancing backward around the fire, dodging his head like a boxer. "Well, come on now, I guess I can have me some with my supper."

Her fury made her hopelessly awkward. Each time she tried to get at him with the knife, she would lunge at the spot he had just left.

He chided, "It just like they say. You crazy, girl." He lifted his plate to avoid another thrust of her knife. "Crazy Ella."

Coming to stand beside John, Mama Tuway caught the eye of two men across the fire and nodded her head toward the man who was dancing to Ella's tune. They, weary of the scene, put their plates down, got up, and made a move toward him. Immediately, he began to back off, glancing at Mama Tuway. "I didn't do nothin'. Just funnin' with her." He held up his free hand. The men sat back down. Mama Tuway walked into the circle of firelight, took Ella by the shoulders, and walked her to the house. All the while, Ella was protesting like a child but going, doing as she was told.

Everyone began eating and talking again. Willie sat next to John, staring down at his plate, his appetite gone. "We ain't never gonna get to no Chicago."

Much later, the boys sat on a log near the fire, watching it until the red-hot center had crusted over to a black heap. They waited there for Ella to finish helping the other women with cleanup. The three of them all walked back to their house together. One of Ella's hands held a kerosene lantern. The other rested on

Willie's shoulder as they took to the trail. She told John to walk out in front of them.

When they reached the house, she went up first and then let them follow. Inside, Ella lit another lantern, and after she had poured water from the pitcher into the washbowl and dropped in a bar of soap from a dish on the shelf, she told them to wash up good. Then she threw their water out the window and filled it with fresh before washing her face and hands—after that, taking a cloth and cleaning her legs and feet. Willie lay in his bunk, immediately falling asleep. John watched her as she slid the cloth up her long legs. He watched her until she looked up and saw him, and her face turned menacing. He rolled over immediately and turned his head to the wall. After a minute, the lanterns went out. He could hear her undressing in the dark, then getting into bed.

He thought it was around three or four in the morning when he heard her again. This time, he only lay there listening. Her moss mattress made a rustling noise as she tossed and turned, shifting her weight. He had no way of knowing what was happening in her world, but presently she began to call out, first only sounds, then disjointed words. "Oh no, oh no." She would be quiet for a while, then say, "Get on out of here," then another time of quiet. He had almost drifted back off to sleep, when he heard her speak in what sounded like a child's voice. "You hear me now, what I'm tellin'—it's my baby doll, not you, not you."

The hard breathing began again, just as it had on

the first night he had heard her. When she started yelling out, John leaned over the side of his bed and saw little Willie's hand drop down to save her.

After that, the night passed without comment.

Chapter 46

"F ELT low as I ever felt," Tuway said. "Tellin' him I seen the boy get on the train—said he was all smilin', had him a trunk, look like he gonna stay gone a long time."

"And what did he say?" Mama Tuway sat in her porch rocker with her mending basket. She pulled out a sock and a darning egg.

"Didn't say nothin', just sit there shufflin' papers round on his desk, like he could see what he was doin'. Say he thought Mrs. Vance gonna be mighty sad. Say she set great store by the boy. Course I know he the one gonna miss him most. We was walkin' home yesterday, everybody we pass say, 'Where your little shadow, Judge? What come of John, Judge?' By the time we get to the front steps, he say, 'I guess he be back in the fall, don't you 'spect, Tuway?'"

"I mumbled like I thought he would be." Tuway looked down the path he had just walked. "Leastways, now we got a month or so to figure out what to do with him." He sat down on a portion of the porch railing not taken up by plants in old coffee cans and pulled out a cigarette.

"Anyway, the Judge say had I heard Timrod and his people done took off last week with a crop planted in the field. Nobody ain't seen hide nor hair of him. Judge say everybody know the bank done furnished Timrod 'cause he rentin' from L.B."

Tuway paused to watch her flying fingers lacing the needle over and back with precision born of countless repetitions. Thread filled the worn spot in the sock like a sewing machine at the mill. He wondered sometimes if all the games they played as children—jump rope, slap hands—weren't just preparations for these adult assignments. Her fingers never stopped tapping out little dances on the sock as she looked at him, waiting for him to continue.

"Now L.B. in the catbird seat, sneakin' round sayin' how sad it is 'cause another one of Judge's loans done gone bad on him," he said.

There was silence as they contemplated.

"You hear anything 'bout Timrod?" he said to her.

"No," she said, and didn't look at him.

Tuway struck a match against the porch post. "I 'spect he knowed I'd get on him for leavin' with a crop in the field."

In one quick motion, she bit the thread, pulled the sock off of the darning egg, put it in her basket, and retrieved another. She rethreaded the needle, knotted the thread with thumb and forefinger, and began again.

He smiled at her quick fingers and got up to get himself a cup of coffee, then came back to sit again and change the subject.

"Friday, Luther come by the bank. He say he wanted to tell the Judge John done gone off for the summer but it sure would be nice if the Judge was to pay him John's money, like a paid vacation, and he sure would see to it John got the money." Tuway laughed. "That man beats all."

She didn't laugh. "Remember when we sent you in to get that job with the Judge right after you come back from Tuskegee? We done it so we would always know what was goin' on with them white peoples."

It had been a good idea ten years ago. She had heard that the Judge needed somebody to deliver fertilizer. It had come from the maid of the Judge's next-door neighbor. Mama Tuway realized the job was beneath Tuway's capabilities, but she also knew that the Judge, from what she had heard about him, would soon come to recognize that. Mama Tuway had spent all the cash money they both had to buy him a new suit, a real silk tie, and a pair of dress shoes. She had learned from the maid next door that the Judge always walked to work each day after dinner. They had planned a chance meeting with the Judge right there on the sidewalk, had planned what he would say, and rehearsed it. "I'm just back from Tuskegee and lookin' for work." Did the Judge have any suggestions 'bout anybody needin' work?

She knew the Judge would jump at the chance to employ Tuway, and she was right. He had started out delivering fertilizer and cottonseed, but not three weeks later, when the Judge had seen how he kept accounts, how hard he worked, he had asked Tuway to put his suit back on and come to work for him upstairs in the bank as his driver and assistant. It had been just as she had planned.

The added bonus had come when the Judge started having trouble with his eyes and so became more and more dependent on Tuway.

From Tuway, she had learned about the finances of everyone in the county. She knew which colored families were in trouble and she could warn them to go on up north or to stay another season. Mama Tuway was much more knowledgeable about the customers, both black and white, of the Planters and Merchants Bank of Lower Peach Tree than its board of directors. When Mama Tuway called someone of the colored community in to have their fortune read, they knew to take heed.

Tuway took no notice of what she said. It had skipped his mind that they had planned the whole thing in the first place. He had grown to like the Judge for what he was. He didn't think of himself anymore the way she did, as a spy.

He continued with his story about Luther, like she had not even mentioned it. "Judge say to old Luther he don't pay for no vacations when his help don't give him the time of day to tell him he goin' off.

"Old Luther have the nerve to say, right out to the Judge, how come the Judge wasn't in Biloxi, and the Judge say he didn't know he have to tell Luther his vacation plans. I almost laughed out loud."

He took a sip of his coffee and leaned back against one of the porch braces, remembering more news from town. "But that ain't the worst thing. They say L.B. gonna try and call a meetin' of the board. He think he finally got the votes to get rid of the Judge."

Mama Tuway had finished another sock and was changing thread. "Them white folks gonna end up killin' each other." She began to shuffle through the basket for a different color. "Fine with me, long as me or mine ain't in the middle."

"What makes you think you ain't gonna be in the middle?"

Mama Tuway looked up, holding black thread in one hand and a needle in the other.

"You forget about the furnishin' everybody got here at the Bend this year and last they ain't paid out yet?" he said.

"Nobody ever gonna stay at the Bend but colored. You and me gonna see to that," she said.

CHAPTER 47

FOR John, life at the Bend quickly fell into a routine that gave him some sense of security, if not belonging. Each morning, he and Willie would come to Mama Tuway's front porch along with everyone else. After she had assigned others their tasks for the day, she would turn to the boys and tell them what to do. Their two main jobs were to bring water for drinking and cooking and to keep a good supply of firewood on hand. When those two things were done, they were given other responsibilities. Some days, they would work in the garden, tying up pole beans or carrying water from the nearest creek to irrigate the vegetables during dry spells. Other times, they were sent out into the swamp to search for herbs and plants Mama Tuway needed.

"Go on out to the edge of Elroy Clancy's cotton field, the one closest by the river. Fetch me some of that new red clover in bunches, and don't come back 'less you have the baby shoots. Don't want none of them old plants. And if you see some horehound, bring me some of that, too, leaves and stems, no roots."

Willie would know where, and they would get in their boat and search until they found what they thought she wanted. When they got back to the house, if it was not exactly what she had in mind, she would send them out to start over again.

The clapboard wall on the east side of the house was thick with bunches of plants she had tied in bundles and hung up to dry in the sun. Mama Tuway would go each day to look them over and decide which were ready to be taken down and brought inside. At night, when he and Willie were sitting on the porch and there was a breeze, they could hear the noise of the dried leaves chattering up against the boards of the house. "Mama Tuway's medicine wall," Willie said. "She cure 'bout anything you got wrong with you. That's how come we here. She gonna cure Mama so she won't be so sour 'bout everything."

Sometimes in the evening, others would come to Mama Tuway's cabin for help. When this happened, everyone had to leave the house. The two boys were sent out to light candles along the trail from the Bend into the swamp. Mama Tuway would put on her big black shawl and light all the candles in her room. John and Willie would sit in the swing in the darkness of the porch, not moving a muscle while Mama Tuway greeted her visitors and took them inside. Then all they could see was the faint glow of candlelight through the curtains drawn over the window; all they could hear was the chatter of the dried leaves on the medicine wall.

Mama Tuway would come out on the porch as the visitor left. She would let the person be gone a good time before she sent Willie and John off with a flashlight to gather up the trail candles.

Once, a man from the Bend rushed into the swamp in the middle of the day and told her his wife was having trouble delivering her baby. Mama Tuway left, carrying a bag, and was gone two days.

While she was absent, Willie and John went fishing in the swamp creek or played cards on the front porch of the cabin.

When she got back, she was furious. She stood Willie and John in front of her, hands resting on her ample hips. "I don't care if I'm dead and buried, they two jobs you got to do every day, rain or shine, dead or alive, and you know what they is—cut wood and bring water—and I see you ain't been doin'm, have you?"

Willie lowered his head and put his hands behind his back in agreement with her that he was a pitiful no-account.

John, embarrassed that he was the older and had let her down, dared to speak. "But we just thought—"

"What's you sayin' to ME?" she roared, her voice echoing up under the porch rafters and out into the yard.

Willie, horrified that he was within the vicinity of one so stupid, stepped away from John so as not to be struck by the thunderbolt that would surely obliterate him any second. John was so frightened, he, too, backed away from her, falling backward off the porch steps into the dust of the front yard.

That day, he cut wood until it was too dark to see, until she finally called him to come get his supper, after everyone else had eaten.

Sometimes she would send them to help out a farmer over in the Bend who was behind with his crop. It was dubious as to whether she was sending them for their skills as laborers or if she was more interested in getting them out of her hair for a time, but they went with all serious intent.

The first person they were called to help was a young farmer, Claude Ingram. Claude's wife had just had the baby Mama Tuway delivered. His land bordered the river and was considered some of the richest soil in the Bend.

While Claude used a pair of mules to plow between the rows of cotton, John and Willie hoed by hand. Now John felt at ease with his hoe. He would go to the work as if he had done it all his life, clearing weeds from around cotton plants, making sure he had his hat on and that he drank plenty of water.

At noon, they would stop to have dinner and water the mules. The boys followed along as Claude unhitched his mules and walked them back up to the house and the watering trough next to the well. "Y'all go on and water these here and I'll tell Lucile we ready to eat."

The mules stood in heavy harness, heads lowered over the watering trough, waiting. John was not sure what he was supposed to do, having never been associated with mules before, but Willie was right at home. He walked up to the well and began lowering a large wooden bucket on a chain down into its depths. The chain on the bucket was attached to a mechanism made of two pine-tree trunks. One, planted in the ground, resembled a telephone pole with a V shape in the top; the other pole sat perpendicular across its top, wedged in the V. The bucket chain was attached to one end of this pole and a rusty old plowshare was attached to the other as a counterbalance. Every time the bucket went down to retrieve water, it was hauled up again by the opposite weight of the plowshare.

Willie stood on a wooden box beside the well, not so much pulling as guiding the bucketful of water up to the surface. He then directed John to pour the water in the wood trough that ran from the top of the well down to the watering box for the mules. "Mr. Claude famous for his water. This here well got the best water in all the Bend." Willie and John took deep drinks out of the bucket after they had provided for the mules.

The federal government, during the time when Roosevelt was president, had built Claude's house. Solid wood floors and electricity were conveniences that not every Bender was lucky enough to have. Claude made a noticeable show of turning on the electric light that hung down over the kitchen table on a single wire.

After the blessing, they feasted on huge portions of collards, cornbread, and beans that had been cooked over Lucile's woodstove and laid out on a table covered with a bright blue-and-white oilcloth.

"Course this ain't the first house we had with 'lectricity," Claude said as he passed cornbread to Willie. "First one we had, it was over on Ball Road. 'Member that one, Lucile? They run wires to that house, and me and Lucile would stand outside at night lookin' at the light comin' from out ever crack and cranny in them logs."

"Look like venetian blinds." Lucile smiled.

"Lord, if that ain't the truth." Claude's rough fingers reached over and touched the face of his baby girl, who was sleeping in her mother's arms.

For dessert, there were strawberries out of Lucile's garden.

After dinner, he and Willie would lie under the shade

of a front yard tree, resting before going back to the fields.

John's head was cradled in his outstretched hands. He had taken off his shoes, which were rapidly getting too small, to cool his feet in the grass. They would look up at the passing clouds and tell what they saw. John always saw things he had read about in books, knights and cowboys and Indians. Willie always saw things his mother had told him about, things from Chicago, tall buildings, and "peoples, armies of peoples marchin' along."

"So what are you gonna do when you get to Chicago?" John asked.

"We gonna have a 'partment. Mama gonna get a job in one of them big hotels cleanin' rooms. On Friday night, we gonna go on out dancin', just me and Mama. We ain't gonna have no mens round." He would take a stick and draw in the dirt exactly how their apartment would look. "We ain't gonna have no room together. I'm gonna have a room and she gonna have a room and we gonna have a separate room for livin' and eatin' in."

John turned on his side, propped his head in his hand, and studied Willie's drawing in the dirt, afraid to ask if he might come along.

They worked at Claude's farm every day for two weeks and then every afternoon went home to chop wood and bring fresh drinking water to the front porch bucket and cooking water to the kettle. They would haul buckets of water from the pump in the backyard around to the side yard to fill the kettle for the night's cooking. John was barely passable at this chore, sloshing water on his shoes and pants legs, the weight of the bucket keeping him off balance from the pump to the kettle. By the time he was ready to pour out his water, about half of it remained.

Willie seemed to know just the right amount to put in his bucket in the first place. He would lift it with two hands and in one quick barefooted motion glide across the yard, arms swinging back just as he was about to reach the kettle. One hand would leave the handle and lift the bottom of the bucket at the precise moment he reached the kettle. Making an arc with his walking, he would hurriedly start back toward the pump, knowing he wasn't finished until water reached to the midpoint of the kettle. Sometimes he would pass John in their trips back and forth. The boy felt embarrassed to be the older and yet the less skilled, but the more he tried to hurry, the more water he spilled out of his bucket. He had settled for a slower pace and wetter shoes.

Days after they had finished working for Claude, Mama Tuway had rewarded them by letting them go frog gigging again. He and Willie had gone to search the shed for sacks and gigging sticks. "You see these old sacks?" John shook out one of the old fertilizer sacks they used to put their frogs in. "If you wash them up real good, there's a doll pattern on the outside you can put together." He held it up for Willie to see. "You wanta do that?"

"I don't want no doll. That's girl's stuff. Why would I want that?"

"For your mama. I thought we could make it and give it to your mama. I've seen it done before. You know she's always talking about baby dolls when she . . . well, when she's in her sleep. We could make it for her to put on her bed, like a throw pillow."

"A what?" Willie had not shown much interest. He was still searching for the gigging stick. When he finally found it, he pushed the toolshed door closed.

"It might make her sleep better, you know. She's been, uh, talking every night now."

Willie came over to examine the dirty sack. "You think?"

"Maybe."

Willie took the sack and held it to the light, trying to make out the faded drawing of the little brown baby doll, one hand in her mouth, the other holding her bonnet. "I was wonderin'," Willie said, his eyes still on the sack. "What come of your mama?"

John stared at him and then turned quickly to look at the sack. No one had ever asked him that before, not outright. Everyone had always known. He had never had to say it before, out loud. He could feel his throat closing up and his eyes beginning to water, as in times past when he had thought of her. There was such a long silence, Willie finally turned to look up at him.

John cleared his throat. "She's dead." A feeling of release washed over him. He had said it and it had sounded clear, without any sign of his voice cracking. "She died a long time ago," he repeated almost to himself. His whole body seemed somehow to relax. "Yes, she died a long time ago," he said.

Willie began to fold the sack and stuff it in the back waist of his pants. "I been thinkin'." He didn't look at John. He was looking out at the tops of the trees. "You ain't goin' on off to Chicago before me?"

John looked at the big trusting eyes and the missing front tooth, which showed when he smiled. He had never really thought about it before, but Willie was a kid, like he used to be. He put his arm on Willie's shoulder as they turned to walk to the boat. "I been thinkin' we'd go on off to Chicago together."

Willie reached his hand up to John's back. "That's what I been thinkin'. You and me together, we could take care of Mama."

CHAPTER 48

THE Fourth Day was approaching, to mark the mid-point of summer. Most of the farmers had their cotton crops laid by and work would slack off until cotton picking commenced. The Fourth Day was a time everyone in the Bend and in the surrounding counties celebrated.

When he thought about it, John was astounded at how much time had passed since he had come to south Alabama. This Fourth of July would mark over a year that he had been in the Black Belt. He could barely remember the train ride from Bainbridge with Aunt Nelda, the sunburn that turned his skin raw, the bare feet that were so tender, he could hardly walk through the cotton fields with Shell. Now he ran without shoes half the time. He had outgrown the ones he came to the swamp in. His skin was so dark, even the fly medicine didn't mark him with that much notice anymore. Every day, he was up early, carrying water, hoeing in the garden, sawing wood for the woodpile, working so hard that by the time night came, he ate enormous amounts of food and then fell dead asleep. And—he had to pause when he thought of this—he was getting better at his chores and—this amazed him most of all—he liked it. The thought crossed his mind one day on the way to get a bushel of corn in the garden: What would he be doing now if he could somehow go back to Bainbridge and live with his mother in their house again? That had been the one thing he had once longed for with all his heart when he was sitting on the train leaving Bainbridge—to have all his toys again, to be safe in the basement where he spent most of his summers, to be the most important person in his mother's life.

The thought somehow made his heart race just the way it had that night on the cattle car when Tuway had held him out the door of the speeding train, ready to drop him into a black void. Now his old life seemed just that, old, and far away in time.

He thought of another place when he crawled in his bed at night and stared out at the stars for the few minutes before sleep came. He thought of the smell of his pipe, of sitting on the sunporch and reading the Sunday paper, of their family dinners together. But now he thought of it not as something owed to him, something he deserved, as he had with his mother, but as a memory, something he longed for but something he could live without seeing or doing ever again if he had to.

Later that day, he and Willie were cutting wood out near the edge of the yard, where the swamp began. They had set up a sawhorse next to a tree Tuway had felled for them when he was home last. After they stripped the small branches off the old hickory and cut a length of branch long enough to lift on the sawhorse, they would cut it into small pieces. Then they carried this green wood over to the woodpile behind the house. This stack of fresh-cut wood was separate from the wood that had been cut and aged since last winter. After they had made a stack several feet high, he and Willie sat down to rest on the old stack of wood. He remembered turning to say something to Willie and seeing Willie's face frozen in fear.

John had seen many snakes in the swamp, at a distance, but this one was not six inches from Willie's head. They had taken a seat almost on top of a three-foot-long cottonmouth moccasin napping in the shade. It had been beautifully camouflaged in among the aging kindling, and when disturbed, it immediately coiled, ready to strike. They both sat frozen for a moment. John's right hand was resting on a short piece of wood, which his fingers now grasped. He decided, without thinking it through, that the best thing to do was to push Willie down off the woodpile with his left hand and kill the snake with the piece of wood in his right hand. He had seen Mama Tuway kill one once with a garden hoe and it had looked easy.

He pushed Willie forward off the pile and brought the wood around much too slowly. The snake had all the time in his world to sink his fangs into John's left arm, which was coming back from pushing Willie. The open white mouth, as if a released spring, darted upward, fixing itself to the underside of John's arm. He stood up, amazed that the huge snake still clung to him. He could hear Willie shouting and running to the house. John grabbed the snake with his other hand and tried to pull it off. This only drove the fangs deeper into the fleshy underside of his upper arm. They stood there, snake and boy, wrestling with each other as Willie ran toward him with a hoe.

That was all he really remembered. There was much confusion around him after that, and he began to feel dizzy and sick. He remembered looking at his arm where the snake fangs had entered, after Willie had flung it off him with the hoe and chopped its head off. He remembered seeing his arm begin to swell and feeling it burn, as if someone was holding a match to the skin. He remembered Ella and Mama Tuway leading him to the house. It was the first time he had been inside one of its rooms. They put him on top of a bright quilt that covered what he thought must be Mama Tuway's bed. He remembered looking around and seeing one wall lined with shelves that contained all manner of jars and bottles. Mama Tuway was taking a small glass vial off one of the shelves and, at the same time, Ella was tying a piece of cloth around his upper arm. "Just give me time to mix up some iodine with this here. That's the best I know of for moccasin." They wrapped another cloth, which felt cool and wet around his wound, then gave him something to drink that tasted sweet and made him sick to his stomach. After that, he seemed to drift away into blackness.

Intermittently, for what must have been days, he woke and could hear people moving about him. Once he thought he saw Tuway come to his bed and sit beside him, the big black-and-white hand reaching up to touch his forehead. "You better make it, boy. The Judge gonna need you when I go off to Chicago." He knew the snake poison was confusing everything in his brain. He, John, was going to Chicago, not Tuway.

Another time, he thought he remembered Willie saying he would save the snake's skin for him, and once he thought he could hear Berl laughing out on the porch. He remembered feeling a terrible throbbing in his arm whenever he woke.

Mostly, he dreamed wild dreams. Uncle Luther, Shell, the Judge—all floated in and out of nonsensical stories about picking cotton and swimming in a river of snakes. Once, he was on the train with Tuway, and this time Tuway dropped him from the boxcar out into an endless black night. He must have yelled out, because he thought he remembered Ella coming to his bedside and holding his hand and kissing his cheek. He knew it must be an Ella he had dreamed up, one he had never seen before and would never see again.

When he finally woke long enough to see and hear what was going on in the real world, he was tired and sore and hungry. Mama Tuway would let him eat only small amounts of food. He looked down at his arm, swollen to twice its size and turning purple and black around the skin the fangs had held to.

While he lay there on Mama Tuway's quilt, Willie was outside, telling the story of how they had killed the snake. He had told everyone of how John had wrestled the snake while he, Willie, had gone to get the hoe and chopped its head off. Willie had sat on the porch that first night and told everybody the story as they came in from working. The more Willie talked, the better it got.

"John just take that snake and he wrestle him to the ground, all the time fightin' with him." When the listener seemed at all skeptical, Willie would refer them to Mama Tuway, who could truthfully say, "When I got to the side yard, John had holt of that snake with both hands 'fore Willie flung it off him with the hoe."

"And then, I"—Willie smiled—"I kilt it."

Gradually, John seemed to get better in the rest of

his body, but the place on his upper arm where the fangs had dug into the skin was still hot with infection and draining pus and blood. He didn't like looking at it and turned away when Mama Tuway changed the bandage.

The first night he was allowed to join the others, on the porch swing in the evening after supper, Willie pointed with pride to the snakeskin he had tacked to the wall to dry. Mama Tuway had put John's bad arm in a sling, but he walked over and touched the skin with his right hand and felt weak in the knees, remembering.

He had not seen the significance of any of this until his first night back around the supper fire. John was usually the last one to be served, and he waited for Mama Tuway to tell him and Willie to come get their plates, but this night she called them to be first. "Come on over here, snake men. You get first tonight." All the talking stopped as they walked across the yard to get their plates. She had stacked them high with everything they liked. The boys walked back to their table, John holding his plate with his good arm. No one moved toward the dinner line until they had taken their seats.

John lowered his head, pretending to concentrate on his food but knowing the tightness in his throat had taken away his appetite. He glanced over to a smiling Willie and tried to smile back, but he knew he couldn't control the muscles in his face. They might have him crying, when all the while he felt absolute joy.

Aunt Nelda had come to Little Luther's room before sunup. The kerosene lamp she carried filled the center of the room with light. The corners stayed in dark shadows. She put the lantern on top of the chest near the wall and came to sit down at the foot of Little Luther's bed. "Wake up, Little Luther." She rested her elbow on the end of the old iron bed frame and cradled her head in her hand. She didn't bother to look at him. She was too tired. "He didn't come home again last night. That's three days we ain't seen hide nor hair of him."

"I know, Ma." He rolled over, still half-asleep, and pulled the cover over his head to block the light. "What's you wakin' me up to tell me that? I coulda got more sleep."

"This is the third time this summer he done this."

"I know, Ma."

"I know where he's at."

"Me, too—Arlo's, or him and Arlo done gone off on some toot over at Demopolis."

Her head still rested in her hand, but she turned it to look at him. "Demopolis? How do you know that?"

He pulled the cover off his head and lay there with his eyes closed. "Lou Ann, Arlo's girl. She says soon as her daddy and my daddy get any money, they go over there and drink it all up in store-bought."

"Money? He don't have two cents since he stopped gettin' money from the Judge, since John left. Where's he gettin' any money?"

"Lou Ann says he had some left over from a long time ago when he done sold John's mama's stuff. Says Arlo keeps it for him." Little Luther kept his eyes shut as he spoke. "Says he had to use most of it to pay back Arlo for all the drinkin' he done over the years, but he had some little left."

She was too tired to be incensed. "I want you to go right over there and get that money back," she said in a monotone.

He didn't say anything. She thought he had gone back to sleep.

"Did you hear me?" She took her free hand and shook one of Little Luther's legs. "Did you hear me?"

"Ma, you know I can't do that. He'd beat the livin' shit out of me, and then you wouldn't have nobody to work in the fields with you." He rolled over and went back to sleep.

She lay back on the foot of Little Luther's bed to get a few more minutes of sleep before the day began. "I guess," she said.

CHAPTER 49

By the time John was up and about, the preparations for the Fourth Day were under way and Berl was in charge. He had seemed to take to life in the swamp and at the Bend, entering into everything that went on, getting to know and be known by everyone. Absent the burden of his farm, Berl found that the Bend took on all those things he had been going to Chicago to find. When he had first come, he had asked every few days when the train to Chicago was coming. Lately, he had not.

Berl had even volunteered to dig the pit for the Fourth Day barbecue. He and the Reverend and Claude Ingram, the farmer, had gathered on Thursday—the Fourth Day being the next Saturday—to commence with the digging. The Fourth Day celebration was to be at the church because everyone would attend. The whole Bend was celebrating the end of the long hours of labor it took to get a cotton crop up and growing in the fields.

Large mounds of dirt soon circled the pit, which needed to be redug every year to accommodate cooking the barbecue. Several men stood around watching Berl, Claude, and the Reverend taking turns with the two shovels the space would allow. When it was finished, Berl and a few others stayed to sit on the mounds of dirt, admiring their handiwork and passing around a jar of homemade.

Friday, fresh-cut logs of hickory were put in the pit and lighted to begin the burn down to coals that would be perfect for cooking the pig one of the farmers at the Bend had given up to the celebration.

John was not allowed to go to the Bend to see these preparations. He was still too weak from the snakebite. Willie, who was given permission to follow Berl, would come back and tell John what was going on.

For days, the boys begged to let John go on the Fourth Day, and Mama Tuway had finally relented, but Ella, Ella had wanted no part of the Fourth Day.

She repeated this over and over each time the subject was brought up. "Too many people over there I don't know, and I don't care 'bout gettin' in no big crowds, and don't nobody try to talk me into it."

Mama Tuway had not argued with her—not then.

"All night and two quarts of whiskey," Berl had said when Willie and John had asked him how long it would take to cook a pig so large as that one. They stood looking down at the pit in the early morning of the Fourth Day. Smoke rose out from under the large piece of tin that covered the meat. John and Willie could smell it cooking as soon as they pulled their boat on shore, even before they had

walked over to the church grounds. The sun was still behind the pine trees; a light mist was still rising off the
river. "That's how long it takes for a good pig, and this
here is gonna be gooood pig."

Willie had been there the night before to watch two
men bring the big iron grate, which would serve as a
grill, out from under the church foundation, where it
was stored. When the grill was hot from the coals, the
pig, which had been split down the middle, was laid on
and a large piece of tin placed on top of it. On one side
of the pit was extra fire in reserve, to be tucked under
the grill at intervals during the night and as the next day
wore on.

In Mama Tuway's cabin, Ella was muttering to herself for
all the world to hear—which at that moment consisted
of Mama Tuway. "Ain't nobody gonna get me out of this
house."

Mama Tuway said nothing as she stood at the kitchen
table stirring mayonnaise into a big bowl of potato salad,
which would be her contribution to the Fourth Day.

Ella sat at the table, thumbing through one of the
magazines Tuway said he had brought for his mother. "I
'spect if you leave me some of that salad, I'll put it together with a bit of bread to have me my dinner while
y'all gone." She watched the pages of the magazine flip
by.

There was no answer. Mama Tuway reached for a dish
towel to cover the potato salad bowl. Then she went over
to the sink and pumped water to wash her hands. She
pulled down the cup towel hanging from a peg beside
the sink and dried her hands, slowly watching the water

from her fingers sink into the coarse weave of the cloth. Then she leveled her eyes on Ella.

"Now you listen here, and I ain't gonna say this but one time. You 'spect you gonna stay in my house, on my land, then you gonna have to go by my rules." She turned to hang the towel back on its wooden peg, then came to sit at the table, directly across from Ella. "I don't wanta hear no more talk 'bout you ain't doin' this and you ain't doin' that. You can come with me or you can come on directly, but if you ain't over there mighty soon, I'm gonna have to make other 'rangements around here." She pulled her hands back to the table's edge and pushed herself up out of the chair. "Now look here, child, I ain't havin' nobody stay at my house can't sooner or later walk out of it."

"But I—"

"Don't wanta hear nothin' 'bout it. You ain't gonna have somethin' white peoples done to you ruin your life forever."

"But you don't know 'bout—"

"No, I don't know 'bout nothin' 'cause you ain't seen fit to tell me nothin', and that's all right. I know all I needs to know. The time comes when you got to move on. No matter how much you love or how much you hate, you got to move on. That's what life is—movin' on through all that mess."

"I can't—"

"Yes you can. Go on and get ready. Put on that pretty blue blouse I sewed up for you. You like that one." Mama Tuway stood watching, but there was no movement from Ella. She sat with her head down, staring at the open magazine.

Finally, the old woman turned and left the room. Minutes later, she came back into the kitchen, carrying her sun hat. The magazine lay on the table. The only sound was a bee that had found its way into the house and had set up a constant buzz, trying to escape, banging again and again against the window above the sink.

Mama Tuway picked up the potato salad and walked out.

CHAPTER 50

J UST across the creek that separated the lowland swamp from the Bend, smoke was rising in the afternoon sun. People from all over were gathering in the side yard of the Bright Lily CME Church, the only church in the Bend. Men milled around the barbecue pit, giving unwanted advice to Berl and the other self-appointed cooks.

"You know so much, where was you when we was up all last night keepin' the fire goin'?"

Off to the south, a little distance from the pit, a large iron pot, bubbling with Brunswick stew, was being sampled by anyone who might have an opinion. Next to the stew, and in among a grove of pine trees, a homemade wooden table, supported by braces nailed directly to tree trunks, made up a good thirty feet of flat surface that would soon be covered over with food. Women arrived, putting their offerings on one by one, until it was filled to overflowing with large mounds of fried chicken, a skillet of meat loaf, pots of green beans, bowls of coleslaw, collard greens. Most brought a dessert to go along with their other dish. These were placed in the middle of the table: fried pies, buttermilk pies, peach cobbler, and pecan pies, foods of no rhyme or reason, but specialties of the maker. Big wood bowls filled with loaves of white bread anchored each end of the spread. Smaller children had been assigned to keep the flies away. They walked up and down the table, fanning the food with dish towels.

On a smaller table off to the side, bright tin tubs filled with lemonade sat next to two more washtubs that contained large blocks of ice, which were being chipped into slivers as older children took turns with the ice picks.

Spread out at random on the grass to the front and the side of the church were brightly colored homemade quilts brought by each family to mark its sitting place.

Mama Tuway, wearing her best flowered dress and a straw hat with a cloth red rose on the brim, stood off to herself, watching Tuway, who had just arrived. He drifted through the crowd, saying hello to this one and that, but all the while glancing around to see if he could find Ella.

He was coming toward Mama Tuway now, with something approaching a smile on his face. She knew the first thing he would ask, and she didn't want to hear it. "No, I ain't seen her," she said before he could speak. "Tuway, ain't nothin' you can do 'bout that girl. Just leave her be."

Tuway tried to laugh. "I ain't messin' with her. You know don't nobody mess with Ella 'cept if she take a mind."

Frustration welled up. "You know my meanin', Tuway. . . ."

"Yes'm," he said absentmindedly as his eyes surveyed the tops of heads.

"You know where she is," she said, spitting it out. "Sittin' over there, scared of her own shadow.

"Tuway." She tried to get him to look at her. "Tuway," she said again, raising her voice.

He smiled vaguely, then looked toward the swamp. She noticed he had on a new shirt.

She was determined to make him listen to what she had to say, but he still acted as if they were talking about nothing more than the crops in the fields or the price of cotton. She grabbed his hands. "Look here, Tuway, I couldn't even get her to come away from over yonder, and she minds me. What's you 'spect you gonna do 'bout it?"

"Well, I guess I'll just—"

In a final attempt, she said the only thing left to her. "Listen here, Tuway. The fact is, you got a face with two colors. Don't you see that, boy? Peoples think that strange." She held his hands in front of him. "Look, look at you if you can't see your face. Two colors. She ain't gonna get to know a face like that."

He knew what she was doing; even so, he stared down at his hands and felt a stabbing in his stomach. She had never said it out loud, had never tried to use it against him before.

"That girl don't care nothin' 'bout nothin' 'cept what stirrin' round inside her head. Don't you see that?" Tears were in her eyes as she threw his hands down and turned to go.

He called after her. "It's all right, Mama. That's what make it okay. She strange, too, Mama."

Her back was to him, but he could see her shaking her head over and over as she walked on off.

Tuway went to the swamp, looking for her. He searched the main house, then walked down the trail to her place.

She sat on her bed, both hands gripping the side of the mattress, staring down at the blouse she had finally chosen to put on. The room was quiet and dark. Sunlight spotted the walls now and then when a breeze shifted leaves outside the window. Her few clothes lay about the room, on the bed and floor, considered and reconsidered, then discarded. He could imagine her trying on one and then the other, miserable with the outcome. There was not a mirror for her to see. It would only have made things worse.

"Ella?" He said it softly so as not to scare her. It only made him sound strange.

She didn't look up, knowing his coming was inevitable. He stood in the doorway, watching her as he had often watched some startled something he might come upon in the swamp—a beautiful ten-point buck or a red-tail fox sitting stark still, ready to bolt at the slightest hint—and he, not moving, afraid it might run away if he breathed, and wanting to take it in, all of it, before it was gone.

He had never been alone with her before, but he had thought of what he might say if it ever happened. What he might say should be said after the beginning, when she would look at his face and see him, who he really was, not now. How to begin and not scare it away? "They gonna be some good eatin' over at the church."

She had been thinking what she would say to explain to him, to anyone, why she didn't want to go, why she couldn't go. Now she got the words all wrong, but still they tumbled out. "I hated where I was before." She had crossed her arms and was holding herself, almost a stranglehold. "What I did before—but I stayed on." She looked up at him as if he could understand the whole story of her life with that one sentence. As if he could, in some way, look inside her mind to see the images that flashed there now. The night she was sitting in the barbecue joint in Selma and the white boy from over in Lower Peach Tree came in and couldn't take his eyes off her, and she was out of work and had a baby to support. "He said he was gonna do for Willie," she said.

Tuway held his breath. She was speaking to him for the first time—of her own accord. He must not lose the moment, but he mustn't frighten her. "Berl say this is the best barbecue he done ever made." He shifted his position slightly in the door frame and nervously picked a splinter out of the wood to examine it. "Course, you know Berl."

She realized he had said something back to her, but her fear would not let her hear what it was. The images were coming to her mind in great waves now. She could see the house he had rented for her, on a road just out of Selma. She could see a few happy times, followed by more and more misery. In exchange for the house, for the food, for a place to keep Willie . . . Now the worst part—she braced for the flashes of pictures that were coming, images of those terrible nights.

She blinked to try to hear what Tuway was saying. The tone of his voice had sounded caring, but she had missed the words. She let loose the grip on her arms and began to rub the tops of her legs. She knew she must try to explain the next part, but how could she when she didn't know herself? "Why did I stay?" The skirt she had on was being pulled up and down her legs by her rubbing hands. "Why did I stay?" She looked at him. She must tell him a reason he would understand. Her eyes were wide and wild now. "'Cause I couldn't get out, that's why. 'Cause I couldn't get out. He locked the door." She continued the rubbing motion on her legs. He had not believed her and she saw it. Her head dropped and her voice lowered to a whisper. "Course I could get out. Course I could get out." She sat there, seeing things from the past.

Like with the buck on a path in the swamp, he knew it was nonsensical to try to communicate, but he persisted, not because he didn't know the buck's language but because he thought the sight of it and the sense of it must, somewhere along the line, connect. Of course, the problem was that the sight of her blinded him to the sense of it.

"The choir be singin' later on this afternoon. You ain't never heard them sing. . . . " And midway through this, some part of what she had said came to him, and he ended by saying, "And whoever locked you up, I would kill'm."

She looked up at him for one moment and seemed about to smile, but then she dropped her head. There was silence as tears fell on her blouse. "I wanted so bad to get out, and now I'm out and I can't get out of where I am when I'm free." She began to cry, not an angry cry, but sad, like a child who is too tired to go on. She looked at him, pleading. "What's the matter with me? What's the matter?"

He had not imagined it would be like this—the first time he had been able to look through a crack into her jellied soul. He was overwhelmed with wanting to touch her and, at the same time, a terrible sadness overcame him. He felt a stinging in his throat, which he tried to clear by swallowing, but then his eyes began to water as he pushed back the truth. "Nothin's the matter with you I see. Ain't nothin'." He stepped toward her. She flinched and he stepped back immediately. "Don't you know you . . . you beautiful?"

Her shoulders slumped forward, a turtle pulling back in its shell. He was like the others.

But he, he was so proud of himself for having said it. It gave him courage to continue. "Come on now. Let's us go on over there, you and me. I won't let nobody touch you, and you can count on that." He knew he sounded like a boy and not a man, but he didn't care.

Tuway turned and left the house to wait for her on the ground. "You know we need to go, so come on now," he called up to her quietly.

Presently, he could hear water splashing out of the pitcher into the washbowl. She took a long time, washing away the tears, but finally she came out, slowly descending the steps to follow him along the trail to the Fourth Day celebration, still sealed in the cave of her thoughts.

And he, he walked ahead, hearing her footsteps follow. He could not ever remember being happier, because he imagined there was hope.

Lower Peach Tree

Tuway, where have you been?" Adell Vance looked up from the stove. She always cooked to calm her nerves. This day, several weeks after the Fourth of July, there were three pots of something boiling on the top burners. She lifted a spoon from one pot and began stirring another. "I sent Cal to fetch you. We waited for you, but you never came." She took a lid that was too big and banged it down on one of the pots. "Finally, I walked him down there myself."

Tuway had rushed in the back door, out of breath. "Didn't know there was no meetin' this afternoon. Cal come for me. I was, uh, visitin' a cousin over in . . . He said for me to get on over here quick. What happened?"

"It was a special call meeting." She knocked her wooden spoon on the side of a pot to clear it of what looked like grits. "Of course we all know whose doin' it really was." She walked over to the percolator on the counter to the left of the sink, poured coffee into a carafe, and then placed it on a wooden tray.

Tuway turned to rush out the back door.

She raised her hand to stop him. "No mind, it's too late now. That no-account L.B. . . ." She looked at Tuway, her eyes glazed over with tears. "Here." She shoved the tray at him. "You take it to him. I can't bear to."

"What happened? Where is he?"

"There." She pointed toward the library. "He'll tell you." She picked up a dish towel and began to dry silverware stacked on the sink drain, slinging it, one noisy piece at a time, into the utensils drawer.

The Judge sat with the curtains drawn and the French doors to the sunporch closed. The room felt still and old. Smells of yesterday's cooking and last night's pipe still hung in the air.

He gave halfhearted notice to Tuway's coming. "Do I hear the footfall of my man Tuway?"

Tuway put the tray on its usual table next to the Judge's armchair. He poured coffee into the cup and handed it to him; then he walked over to open the curtains.

"Did you tell me they was havin' a board meetin' today, Judge?"

"I am not quite in the mood for light and fresh air, Tuway."

Tuway paid no attention and unlatched the sill lock. The counterweights of the old window rattled in the walls as Tuway pulled it fully open. Air, fresher and hotter, stood outside and did not come in. "If you did tell me 'bout a meetin', it plumb slipped my mind."

The Judge was hunched over, as if he were studying the cup in his hand. A slight jerk in his shoulders meant that he was finding that humorous. "In all the years I've known you, Tuway, nothing has ever slipped your mind." He tried but didn't succeed in sounding like W. C. Fields. "Don't be condescending, my good man."

Tuway finished opening windows. Now, instead of dark and musty, the room seemed bright and musty. Dust danced into the streams of sun that lighted squares on the floor. Tuway was undeterred and moved on to open the French doors. "Well now, Judge, I guess I didn't miss much, seein' how you're back so soon. Wasn't one of them long meetings that lasted till after dark."

"It doesn't take long to swing an ax, Tuway."

In a final effort, Tuway turned on the floor fan, then went to take a seat opposite the Judge. "Did somethin' happen, Judge? Somethin' I needs to know 'bout?"

The Judge sighed and rubbed his forehead with his free hand. "I can see Adell has left the dirty work to me, as usual."

He looked up and spoke in Tuway's direction. "Yes, something happened, Tuway. People I busted my butt for, people that I was responsible for getting on the board, people that I thought had more common sense . . ." He lifted his coffee cup without having taken a drink and placed it on the tray he knew was there. "Oh, what the hell, Tuway. I got fired, plain and simple." He took a deep breath. "Which means you got fired, and probably Miss Maroon, although I'm not so sure about that. He may not want to keep her, but I don't think at this point he can run the place without her. She said she might quit anyway, but that was only in the heat of the moment. Her family needs her income too much." He considered for a moment. "No, on second thought, she'll probably stay."

Tuway was trying to conjure up a mental image of L.B. sitting in the Judge's chair at the bank. The picture would not come. "I know we always was funnin' 'bout him tryin' to take over, but . . . He don't know nothin' 'bout bankin'. He's just a boy." Tuway reconsidered this, knowing that he and L.B. were almost the same age. "Well, he seem like just a boy."

"Whether he does or he doesn't know banking makes no difference now. He has the majority of the stock and he's runnin' the show." The Judge sat back in his chair, his shoulders slumping. "It's not so much L.B. I always knew he was a little sycophant, trying to work his adolescent schemes. You know, he's like so many other Black Belt boys with too much land and too much time—ruined from the get-go." He retrieved his coffee cup back off the tray, took an absentminded drink, and winced. "The others are the ones. Why in the world can't they see through that bullshit?" He put the cup back on the tray. " 'Cause it's easier for them not to. That's why. People just take the goddamn easy way out, Tuway. People come to a meeting; they swallow hard, vote for something they know isn't right, but it's too much trouble to take exception. . . . Besides, they got dinner plans for the evening and they're thinking to themselves, How much harm can the kid do? Running a bank isn't rocket science."

Tuway was not listening. His mind was whirling. What would he do? Where would he go? Obadiah might be able to get him a job on the train. Obadiah had helped him with the trains all these years, telling him what cars were empty and when. Maybe now . . . He was looking at the Judge, but his mind was racing. A train job would take him away from her. . . . That wouldn't do. Would he stay on with the Judge? The Judge might not be able to afford him. . . . He felt a cold chill in the back of his head as it occurred to him for the first time . . . the swamp, the people at the Bend.

Tuway focused back on the Judge, who seemed not to know what to do with his hands. First he would sip coffee; then he would put the cup back on the tray and rub his hands together. "It was not naïveté," he was saying. "It made good economic sense. If only they didn't have such blinders on."

"What?" Tuway said.

"You might as well know the whole story, since you weren't at your usual listening post. Rather ironic, the biggest meeting, and you weren't there to hear it." He picked up his cup again.

"About ten this morning, Miss Maroon said that L.B. had called and wanted to have a meeting of the board. I told her to tell him it was impossible—too much going on—but he insisted. . . . Anyway, at three this afternoon, he marches in, backed up by Debo, and the rest.

"The bank's last several loans had gone bad, he said, and now the whites and the coloreds both weren't supporting me. And although they regretted it—the nerve of him sitting there and saying that—he, they, the board, would give me two months pay and . . . The upshot of it is, he got the rest of them to go along with him. They just sat there, not one word of support.

"'How do you expect to run this place now?' I said. I turned to Debo. 'You don't expect L.B. to deal with the coloreds, do you, Debo?' I outright asked him. Debo just sat there like he hadn't known me for years.

"'Well now, Byron, you have been a little naïve in your bankin' practices.' I looked at Red. 'Me naïve?'

"Red said, 'Now Byron, it don't mean things can't go on like they always have. We'll still meet every Saturday at the gin and shoot the bull. You know that. It'll be like you retired. Hell, man, I wish I could retire.'

"That's what he said, Tuway, right to my face. Like the highlight of my life was meeting at that broken-down old gin every Saturday.

"More coffee, Tuway." He held out his cup, then pulled it back. "Oh, to hell with them. Let'm run the thing into the ground. What do I care?"

Tuway tried to sound casual. "What about all them people got loans out?"

The Judge said, "What about the rest of the people at the bank? What about the businesses in this town that are in enough trouble already? Hell, I don't know.

"Tuway, why don't you get us something out of the desk drawer. If ever there was a time . . ."

"You bet." Tuway got up and took a bottle out of the bottom drawer of the old rolltop desk on the opposite side of the room.

"They'll have to deal with him." He held out his coffee cup and Tuway poured, then added a little to a glass he had taken from the drawer.

"They'll just have to deal with him." The Judge took his finger and stirred his cup, then began to sip his coffee in silence.

Tuway returned to his seat with his glass. Late-afternoon heat had finally made its way into the room. The turning face of the fan blew it first on Tuway and then on the Judge. There was only the sound of the fan and the distant noises from the kitchen as Adell Vance cooked out her disgust.

Tuway cleared his throat. "Judge, what 'bout places like people down at the Bend, places like that? You been furnishin' them for years, and the last few crops ain't been so good."

"They'll have a good year next year and pay it back—do it all the time. You know all that land is Miss Lucile's." The Judge was irritated at what he thought was Tuway's forgetfulness. "You know that. L.B. can't mess with that land."

"What's you been usin' for backup?"

"Why are you asking me that? You know, chattel loans." The Judge sat there staring into space. Then he freed himself of the thought. "Even L.B. wouldn't waste his time. He probably doesn't even know how to get out there. Hell, you and I haven't been there in years. It's so far away . . . there's nothing there to take that I know of—a few cows and chickens, maybe an old tractor or two.

"Besides, that's like money in the bank. Even L.B. isn't that stupid." The Judge took a last drink of his coffee. "Well, there isn't anything out there worth fighting over, is there?"

"Nothin' I know of, but, like you say, we ain't been to the Bend in years."

The Bend

IT had been early morning when a few of the children from the Bend came across to the swamp in their boats. They threw their poles on the ground and rushed to the old woman's house. "My daddy say come look. The sheriff or somebody gettin' ready to come cross the river at the old ferry landin'."

She sat in her rocker on the porch, shucking corn. "Nobody used that ferry in ten years. If he comin', he most likely ain't gettin' here that way."

"My daddy say come look" was all the children would say, smiling and holding out their hands, gesturing for her to come. She finished her shucking and called to Ella. "Go on and get that old green boat out from under the tree. We'll have us a look-see."

After a halfhearted attempt to beg off going, Ella had gone to the tree where the boat was tied and readied it for Mama Tuway.

Willie and John, unnoticed by the others in the rush, had immediately gone to their boat and out into the water. They poled to the end of the creek, which led out to the river, and tied up, making sure to stay out of sight of the opposite shore.

Many of the Bend people had stopped work as news of what was happening spread. The Reverend had ridden his mule from the church. Claude and his wife could see the ferry from their front porch, so others had walked over to sit with them or sit along the riverbank, watching the other side.

There was something approaching a lighthearted mood. Glad for the break in a hot working day, people sat by the bank, talking and watching what was going on across the river. Claude's wife went inside her house to make a big pitcher of lemonade, which she began offering new arrivals. The best seat on the porch was, of course, reserved for Mama Tuway's coming.

"Look like they some white peoples tryin' to pay us a visit," Mama Tuway said as she took her seat and the large glass of lemonade she was offered. Ella shook her head no to lemonade and took up a position behind Mama Tuway's rocker, her back ridged up against the clapboard porch wall.

Mama Tuway settled in and began to take a good look at what was happening on the other side of the river. It was a bright, sunny morning and millions of sun stars danced on the light ripples in the water. She had to shield her eyes from the glare to see the figures across the way and then to look up at the three turkey vultures that glided high in the air, almost out of sight, passing back and forth across the sun. Off in the distance to her right, almost a mile away, was the old train trestle over the river.

On seeing Mama Tuway's arrival, Benders who had come to take a look at what was happening and then head back to work changed their minds. Her presence made this a formal event, as if they were about to witness something important. They began to gather closer to the porch or to sit down in the grass, laughing, talking, and reminiscing.

" 'Member when President Roosevelt sent them peoples down back in '34, or there 'bout? Brought in all them workers right across on the ferry to build a community center, and what we gonna do with a community center?" Mama Tuway said.

"Well, I'm much obliged to old Roosevelt. It sho do make a fine church," the Reverend said, and everybody laughed.

"I ain't complainin' 'bout Roosevelt." Claude came through the screen door and let it slam, as his hands were full of more glasses and another pitcher of warm lemonade. "I'd still be havin' a dirt floor to walk on, wasn't for old Roosevelt. No, I ain't complainin' t'all." He gave the Reverend an empty glass and poured him some lemonade. "Wouldn't have none of these here houses all over the Bend, wasn't for him."

"You ain't forgettin' when they come over here to get peoples to go off to the war, are you?" Mama Tuway said. All eyes turned back to watch the opposite shore more intently.

Lined up in a row were four gin wagons pulled by two-mule teams. Each wagon had three colored men sitting or standing patiently waiting, as they often did, to unload at the gin, but there was no cotton, no gin, only a sheriff's car and two or three men down by the river's edge, looking at the old ferry motor that had in times past pushed the ferry from one side of the river to the other, attached to a steel cable strung across the water.

Off to the side, parked in the grass, was a Desoto convertible. The top was down and a man with blond hair sat in the driver's seat, sunning himself.

"I remember them war days," said one of the older men sitting on the front steps. "Come over here with them uniforms on, took near 'bout everybody old enough to plow a straight line."

"And half of them didn't come back," the Reverend Kay said.

Just then, Berl walked up from the path that led down to the swamp. He tried to affect a casual air, but everyone could see he was hot and breathing hard from running.

"What I been missin'? This some kind of a party goin' on here?"

"Look here now," Claude said to everybody on the porch and in the yard. "I know what it is. They done found out Berl stayin' over here and they comin' after him." There was a moment of silence as everyone looked at Berl, and he jerked his head around to follow fingers pointing to the other side.

After a second or two, Berl began to laugh. "Don't y'all go funnin' me like that. They ain't comin' for me. See that?" He gestured to the other side. "Telco County Sheriff's car. I ain't from Telco." Berl looked to Mama Tuway for assurance. "They ain't comin' for me, are they?"

Mama Tuway shook her head. "Don't take four gin wagons and, near as I can make out, twelve helpers to catch you, Berl. You ain't worth all that trouble they goin' to."

With Mama Tuway's blessing, Berl breathed easier. "All right. How 'bout some of that lemonade you famous for, Miss Lucile?" He walked over to get a glass.

People on the Bend side began to talk among themselves. Berl walked out in the yard toward the river's shore to get a better look. "Besides, they ain't gonna get that thing started for nothin'. Thing been sittin' over there for years. White folks ain't got the sense they was born with."

People on the Bend side looked at one another and smiled. Berl was right.

"They ain't never gonna get that old thing started," one said.

"Thing been sittin' over there for years in that same place," another said.

"Ain't been used since the worlds war."

The Lower Peach Tree Side

WHY didn't you tell me?" He had said this five or six times. It made no matter. Tuway wasn't listening anyway. His hands gripped the steering wheel, trying to keep the careening car—headed straight for the river—on the road. They had gone to the car the minute Tuway had told him his mother was at the Bend. It had been an automatic response, to head straight there. What they would do, how they would cross the river had not yet occurred to them. They were still in the throes of explanation.

"My God, Tuway, if you had told me, I would have . . ." His voice trailed off, for he didn't know what he would have done. Told Tuway to tell his mother to move? No, in the entire county, it was the best place for a colored person to be. Would he not have given the farmers loans if he had known she was there? Of course not. They were among the best, most reliable of farmers in all the Black Belt.

Was it his fault? Was it the economy? Was it the bad

weather they had had for the last two seasons? Was it L.B.? He pulled the pipe out of his coat pocket and twisted it in his hands. What makes one person grow into an L.B. and another with just as much to overcome grow into someone like, well, like he had hoped John was growing into before the boy gave up and sneaked out of town.

"Damn it, man. Do you want to get us killed before we get there?" The car had hit a rut in the road and the Judge bounced up, hitting his head on the roof lining. Tuway slowed to breakneck speed.

"And another thing, Judge, I ain't told you and you gonna know soon enough."

"Nothing else would surprise me, Tuway. I had no idea your mother was still living. You talked about your cousins but never—"

"The thing is, Judge." Tuway cleared his throat. "The thing is, John is out at the Bend, too. Done been out there all summer. Wasn't my fault."

"What? What John?"

"I'm tellin' you it wasn't my fault. It was all his doin'. The boy done finally gone and got hisself some backbone."

"John McMillan? That John?"

"John, your John. He done followed me one night, out to the Bend."

"You told me you saw him get on the train. You told me he was visiting friends in—"

The car hit another bump in the road. The Judge grabbed ahold of the open windowsill. Then there was silence between them. Dust rolled in huge swirls up into the air as the car dropped from the potholed paved road onto a dirt road that led to the river. Hot wind and dust blew in their faces from the open side-window vents.

The pipe turned over and over in his free hand. "In all our years together, I can't think of any other circumstance in which you lied to me, Tuway."

Tuway didn't say anything, gripped the wheel, and kept his eyes on the road.

Finally, he said, "I always told you the truth . . . much as the circumstances would let me."

The Bend Side

T HE people of the Bend had settled in now, viewing the show. Some of the children were at the water's edge, poking sticks in the mud. Others sat in their mothers' laps on the grassy space between the river and the road that ran in front of Claude's house. John and little Willie had found a place on the lower branches of a big oak in the front yard and were watching all that was going on. So far, Mama Tuway had not noticed them.

"What they doin' now?" someone said. The sounds of an engine trying to start could be heard from across the river.

"Look to me like they still tryin' to get that old ferry-boat motor started. That thing nothin' but a heap of junk."

They watched as one of the men the sheriff had brought along seemed to be pouring something directly onto the engine. There was a whining sound; then flames shot up into the air as the men jumped back to take cover.

There were roars of laughter on the Bend side. Little children held their hands over their mouths and squealed at such a sight. Old men slapped their pants legs and shook their heads, laughing. "Them white folks gonna kill they fool selves on somethin' they don't know nothin' 'bout."

Mama Tuway rocked and sipped her lemonade but said nothing.

Ella stood behind her, hands flat up against the white-washed wall of Claude's house. "Don't like this."

Mama Tuway turned to glance at Ella. "Now Ella, child. They almost a mile away. Can't do you no harm."

"I wanta go back."

"You need to get used to other peoples again." She reached back and patted Ella's hand; then she turned around to watch the opposite shore.

"What you suppose they wanta fix up that old ferry-boat for? Ain't nothin' for'm even if they do get over here," Joe Ben Kay said. He had wandered up to the porch to talk. Joe Ben and his family farmed the land up the road from Claude. His wife and children had settled down in the grass across the road. Like everybody in the Bend, they were cousins to Claude and Lucile and Mama Tuway. Joe Ben had pretended that his remark was for everyone assembled on the porch, but what he really wanted to know was what Mama Tuway thought.

She rocked a moment longer. "Don't nobody go to the trouble to bring no four empty wagons 'less they mean to fill'm up," she said. She took a last sip of her lemonade and looked straight at Joe Ben. "Joe Ben, you ain't old as me, but you old enough to remember the last time anybody come 'cross that river with empty wagons."

Joe Ben stared at her in a moment of recognition and then turned to look across the water. The same thing had happened once before, back in the 1930s, during the Great Depression. At that time, the farmers of the Bend had been furnished by a local merchant who had scotched them for two years while the weather was bad. The problem was that before there was a good crop, he had died and his wife had sent the sheriff to collect the debt. They had been left with nothing and almost starved to death. All of their pigs and cattle had been taken; even the corn out of the cribs was loaded in wagons and carried off. That winter, they had survived off of nuts and berries from the woods and a few Red Cross packages.

Joe Ben left the porch and walked to where his wife was sitting in the grass. It looked as if he was trying to convince her to take the children and go home. She shook her head no. Of course she had no idea of missing out on what was going on.

There was a whirring noise and the engine caught, roared to life, and died just as quickly. People on the Bend side stood up from their positions on the bank and began looking hard across the water. Some began backing away from the water a few steps. "I think they gonna do it," somebody said.

"Nah, they ain't gonna do it," Berl said. He had taken a seat on the front steps. "Them pistons might fire a time or two, but that block probably busted down the middle."

Now they all watched as a man on the Lower Peach Tree side walked back up the hill and got something out of his truck.

"I don't know," the Reverend said. "That's Ed's truck from over at the Texaco they got workin' on it. You take Ed and a can of Marvel Mystery oil and you can fix near 'bout anything."

On the eighth try, the old pistons freed themselves from years of neglect and began to churn up and down. The engine quickly died, but it screamed to life the next time, drinking in the excess gasoline that had been poured directly into its innards. The muffler, long rusted away, gave free rein to a grating, caterwauling sound that echoed down the river. Ospreys flapped up and out of their nests at treetop. A puff of black smoke rose up off the ferry engine.

People on the Bend side began to move back away from the shoreline and up toward the house. Children stopped playing in the water and came to hold their mothers' hands. The chance that the people on the Lower Peach Tree side could not come had faded into the probability that they would.

10:00 A.M.—Lower Peach Tree Side

TUWAY had driven to the bank in the Judge's car earlier that morning. The Judge had instructed him to clear out everything in his office and load it in the trunk. They would sort out fourteen years of banking business later, at home, when they had time.

Tuway had walked in the bank to mass confusion. Miss Maroon was in tears. She was leaving; she didn't care that she didn't have another job. L.B. had gone too far. He had been stewing for a whole week about what he could do to "turn things around," as he kept calling it. He was looking for something he could do to make an impression on the older men, to show them that this was a new day for the Planters and Merchants Bank of Lower Peach Tree and that he was their new leader. He spent his days sitting at the Judge's old desk, studying the paper-clip chain he made and "thinkin' about the situation," as he said to Miss Maroon.

By way of trying to keep him busy and out of her hair, she had given him all the files on loans that the bank had outstanding. She had never meant to put the Bend loans in with all the others. After all, they had been dealing with the Bend for years. Nobody ever did anything about those loans. They would make good when they could. Everybody knew that, everybody but L.B. He had immediately seized on them, like some starving dog.

Did she know they were almost two years in arrears? What in the world was the Judge thinking about? She had tried to explain to him that these were some of the best loans the bank made. They always paid off in the end. These were people who had been here forever. They were not about to up and leave and go to Chicago. He hadn't listened. He had called up the sheriff here in Perry County and told him he wanted him to serve papers on the Bend farmers. The sheriff had said that was crazy. What were they gonna get, a few cows, the contents of a corncrib, some mules, maybe a broken-down tractor or two? He wouldn't do it. Too damn much trouble. L.B. insisted. Hell no, he wasn't, the sheriff countered. Besides, the Bend wasn't in his county. L.B. would have to get Bart Simms, sheriff over in Telco, to get it done. Being just across the river, that was Telco County.

Miss Maroon wrung her hands. "Now L.B.'s gone on out there with the Telco sheriff to take everything he can get his hands on."

The Bend Side

As soon as the sheriff of Telco County had sent a wagon with a team of mules across, he decided to go himself, convinced now that the old cable stretched across the river would hold the decrepit ferry.

He had planned to get off work early that day and run his dogs to keep them in shape for hunting season. Then this young fellow from over in Perry County showed up, acting like he was God's gift to the Black Belt, insisting that the sheriff serve papers today, and way out here in East Jesus. He knew it was impractical to try to come into the Bend by the old hunting road. Nobody had used that for years. It would take all day. His other choice was to get Ed over at the Texaco to fix the old ferry. He had hoped Ed wouldn't be able to get the motor started; then he would have had a perfectly valid excuse to say he couldn't do it. Now the fucking motor had to start, and what was he gonna get anyway? Nothing but niggers over there. Just his luck his two deputies had to be off. He could have sent one of them. He felt for his gun and waited for the ferry to slide into shore.

The sheriff stepped off the ferry and stopped to let the wagon driver coax his team onto dry land. A group of people had gathered around the first wagon that had come to a halt in front of a white clapboard house. He walked toward them, and as he walked, he took papers out of his back pocket and consulted them.

"I'm looking for a Claude J. Ingram," he said to the assembled crowd.

The Benders stared at him as if they had never heard the name.

The sheriff smirked and put the papers back in his pocket. "What the hell, I don't need'm anyway." Then he turned to the group of people standing there.

"Now listen here. I've come to serve y'all with papers that say you gotta give up what it is you own in order to pay back the . . . the"—he took the papers out of his pocket again—"the Planters and Merchants Bank of Lower Peach Tree." He folded the papers and turned to look at the three men who were on the first wagon. There was quiet, all except for the mules, which were making nervous pawing motions with their feet.

"What you want us to do, boss?" one of the wagon men said.

The sheriff shrugged his shoulders. "It says we're suppose to take everything that ain't nailed down, so go to it."

They sat there staring at him, still not knowing what to do, what he meant. "What you mean, 'everything'?"

"Everything, that's what it says, everything—furniture, cows—now get busy."

They still sat there.

"We'll do this place first, then head on to the next farm down the road there." Then he yelled to get some action. "I said *everything;* now get started. We ain't got all day."

The men from the wagon looked at one another and then began to climb slowly down to the ground. The driver pulled up the wagon brake, wrapped the reins around the brake handle, and started to dismount.

There was silence as everyone on the porch began to back away, everyone but Mama Tuway, who sat firmly in her chair, staring out at the river.

Lucile rushed inside to get her sleeping baby. Claude followed her. The Reverend Kay stood up out of the swing and jumped off the side of the porch. Ella was nowhere to be seen. Berl backed up into the yard.

The men hesitated and then picked up two straight chairs, walked down the steps, and pitched them in the wagon. The chairs made a hollow, rattling sound, landing in the bottom of the empty gin wagon.

They turned and looked at the sheriff, still not knowing if this was what he meant.

The sheriff shook his head. "That's it. That's what you're supposed to do. Take everything."

The wagon men walked wearily back up the steps. One reached down and picked up empty lemonade glasses and the pitcher. He walked down the steps and threw them in the wagon, then heard breaking glass as they hit the bottom. One of the children in the crowd began to cry.

The third man, the driver, grabbed some baling wire off a fence post, rounded up two or three chickens that were roaming free in the yard, tied their feet together, and flung them, squawking, into the wagon. The mules, still uneasy from their trip across the river in the noisy ferry, shifted back and forth in their traces, raising clouds of dust in the dry black ground.

The Lower Peach Tree Side

I¹'s not much farther, is it?" the Judge said. "I know this road. It's not much farther. We can look across and see what's going on when we get there. Perhaps we can get a boat and go across. Maybe the sheriff isn't there yet. It takes a long time to come all the way around on the old swamp road."

Tuway kept his eyes on the road. "I ain't worried about Mama. Mama can take care of herself. They ain't gonna mess with Mama. Truth is, it's Ella. She liable to get funny-actin' with white people round."

"He's been there all summer? All summer and I, Mrs. Vance, we, we never knew?" He held his head straight-forward, as if he were seeing the road. "She's been re-membering him in her prayers every night, you know. Talked about him almost as if he were dead, and he was right here under our noses all along. Do you see anything, Tuway?" He could feel the car crest a rise and start downhill as the ground eased its way to river level. The Judge gripped the open window frame and turned his head away from Tuway. "The truth is, we . . . I, from the first time I saw him, I—" The words blew past him and out into the hot afternoon air.

Tuway strained to see through the swirling dust. "Fact is, she ain't liable to; she bound to. That's how come she out at the Bend in the first place. Couldn't take white peoples no more."

"What are you talking about?" The Judge turned to face Tuway.

"Thought if she got used to John, it might do some good."

"What do you see out there, Tuway? That's what I want to know."

Tuway looked over at the Judge, as if he was hearing him for the first time, then back at the road. "I see gin wagons lined up down by the old ferry crossin'. Look like they done got the ferry workin'. They fordin' the wagons 'cross. I can see one now in the middle of the river." He rolled down the window all the way to get a better view. "Didn't think they could do that."

"What in the hell are they doing? That ferry can't support all that weight. It hasn't operated for years."

"Won't hold a truck's weight, but guess it will wagons."

The Bend

THE sheriff shuffled the papers in his hand and kept his head down. The ferry had started back across the river to get the last wagon. As the sheriff glanced up, he saw L.B. step on shore with the third wagon.

By now, the people of the Bend had had a chance to recover from their first shock and come to some understanding of what was happening. The sheriff of Telco County intended to go from house to house, taking whatever he could get his hands on, everything they owned.

The older people of the Bend watched with weary eyes, remembering. The younger ones, like Claude, looked through a different lens. They had been away from the Bend to fight a war. From time to time, they were visited by cousins who now lived in Chicago, Detroit; and, most important, all of them, young and old, had stood mesmerized, watching the television set in the window of McKinna's Hardware store, its screen glowing with fuzzy black-and-white pictures from another world.

Lucile muffled a cry as she saw her porch swing being heaved into the wagon. Claude turned from stunned silence and walked back to the barn to pick up a hoe that was leaning up against the inside wall. Berl followed him and found a rake. They rushed back toward the house and the wagon men, who were pitching anything they could find—furniture, pots and pans, kitchen utensils—into their wagon, if only to fill it and get out. Another wagon was directly behind. It would be next.

Claude jumped up on his porch steps and stood in front of one of the drivers to block his way back into the house. The driver knocked shoulders with Claude as he passed. "Don't you go messin' with me, nigger," the driver said. "I'm gettin' paid twenty dollars to do this here job, and I can use me the money. Ain't none of my doin'."

Claude let him pass, but he muttered, "We see 'bout that," and hit the driver in the back of the knees with his hoe. The driver's legs buckled. He dropped what he was carrying and fell to the ground. When he got up, he lunged for Claude. They rolled over and over in the dirt as the crowd of men and women from the Bend edged closer and closer to the fight.

The sheriff drew his gun and fired in the air. "All right now, back on off here, boys. Let's us get this here done and get on out of here."

L.B. had been standing to one side, watching. "I think you have things in hand, Sheriff. I'll go on back to the bank. I have work to—"

"You ain't goin' nowhere," the sheriff said. "You come in here from out of my county and want me to do your dirty work. You was the one wanted this. You can stay put." He turned to L.B., his gun still in hand.

"If you really need me," L.B. said, stepping away a few paces and taking the comb out of his pocket to give his hair a nervous swipe.

"Besides, you got to lead these wagons to where you want to put all this here stuff when we finished."

L.B. watched the wagon being loaded. It was the first time it had occurred to him that he would have to find a place to put everything they were gathering up. He wondered what the bank usually did with stuff like this.

The wagon driver got up, brushed off his clothes, and started back up the stairs, with everyone looking on.

He and his two helpers now began taking everything they could see—a small handmade baby bed, a picture of Claude and Lucile on their wedding day, knives and forks off the kitchen table.

At length, they came out to the porch for a final look around before going to the barn. One of the men stopped in front of Mama Tuway's chair. She looked up at him and threw what remained of her lemonade in his face. "You a disgrace."

He then made the terrible mistake of asking her to get up and give him her chair.

Lower Peach Tree

Tuway stopped the car and got out as the last wagon driver was leading his team of mules onto the ferry. The Judge followed, holding to the front fender, moving toward the sounds, remembering the last time he had spoken to the boy. He had lectured him about staying out too late and wandering all over the town when he was supposed to get on home

The two drivers slapped reins and called out to mules, which were unsure of their footing as they stepped from solid ground onto the decaying wooden floorboards of the old ferry. The steady cadence of the ferry's four-cylinder motor was interrupted by a backfire. The mules shied and backed in their traces, pushing wagon and drivers backward, where they had come from. The main driver flipped the reins and began coaxing again. The other two men got down off the wagon and went around to hold the front reins and pull the mules forward.

Tuway kept his eyes trained on the far shore, searching for her. He turned to the Judge, who was standing a few feet away, listening. "I'm goin' 'cross with this last wagon team, Judge. You best stay here. Ain't safe, as I see it. That old cable barely holdin' as it is."

"Don't be ridiculous, man. Of course I'm coming, too." The Judge had walked to Tuway's voice and taken firm hold of his coat sleeve.

The Bend

IN their minds, it was unthinkable for this outside wagon driver to speak directly to Mama Tuway. Claude and Berl rushed up the stairs and grabbed at the man, pulling him away from her rocker. They pushed him down the stairs and ran after him.

From where he had been standing by the oak tree, John heard himself yelling as he ran toward them. "Don't you touch her, you son of a bitch." The wagon man had hit Claude in the stomach and Claude had wrestled him to the ground, as he had done minutes before, but this time it was different. People were closing in with hoes and pieces of wood grabbed off the woodpile in Claude's side yard. Dogs were barking. Dust was swirling. John grabbed the wagon man's arm and bit it until the blood came. Willie was there, kicking at the man's head while Claude beat him unmercifully. When another wagon man came to help, he was jumped by Joe Ben and Berl.

Joe Ben's wife and the Reverend Kay used their hats

to wave at the mules of the first wagon, causing them to back and shy.

The driver of the second wagon made a clicking sound to the mules and began trying to move around the first wagon to get his mules out of the fray. The Reverend and Joe Ben's wife caught the animals' bridles to stop them. The mules pulled their heads up, uncertain of what they were supposed to do. One began to kick out in frustration. The team on the first wagon sensed their nervousness and snorted and pawed at the dust. Two more of the Benders stepped forward, took off their hats, and waved them at the animals.

The mules kicked, the brake came loose, and the first wagon rolled off the road. Its rear wheel stuck in a gully and the wagon turned on its side. The contents spilled out into the dirt. Chairs and tables, knives and forks—all tumbled into a heap in the dust, and the Benders closed in. Some grabbed at the men on their wagon-seat perches. Others rushed to unload what was left in the back of the first wagon.

This time, there was nothing the sheriff could do. The black men on the wagons were being dragged down off their high seats, thrown to the ground, and pummeled by the black men and women of the Bend.

Nobody was touching the sheriff, but he knew it was only because he had his gun in hand, and he kept it there, backing away out of the brawl.

L.B. was watching what was going on, not so much afraid as curious that something like this would happen. The possibility had never entered his mind. Suddenly, in all the dust and shouting, he caught sight of a familiar face and he called to him.

"Is that you, Willie?" The boy looked up from his frantic efforts at kicking the man Claude had grounded.

"What the hell you doin' over here, boy?" L.B. stepped in his direction. Willie turned to run, but L.B. sprinted after him, dodging in and out of fighting people and others trying to gather up Claude's possessions, which were scattered everywhere. "Hey, don't you hear me? Stop when I'm talkin' to you." He grabbed Willie by the arm and turned him around.

Ella appeared out of nowhere, catching hold of Willie's other arm. She had been picking up knives and forks off the ground until she heard L.B.'s voice. Now she stood facing him, still holding a kitchen knife in one hand.

"We ain't gonna go back to Mr. L.B.," Willie said to his mother. " 'Member, we said we wasn't never gonna go back to Mr. L.B. Ain't that right, Mama?"

Ella pulled Willie to her and then pushed him past her. "Git," she said.

"Not 'less you promise me," he said.

"I promise," she said, not looking at him.

He ran for the trees.

In the distance, the ferry was landing its last wagon. Tuway had jumped off into the shallow water before the bow hit shore, and now he was running up the hill toward her.

There was a flash of pleasure in L.B.'s narrowed eyes as he looked at Ella. "Why, lookie here, if it ain't my little old baby doll." He took a step closer, automatically reaching for the comb in his shirt pocket. "I thought you might be someplace around here when I saw little Willie." He ran the comb through his hair, put it back in his shirt pocket, and reached out to grab her arm, as he had done so many times on so many nights in Selma. "What's you doin' out here?"

His touch seemed to take her back to another place. In her mind, she might still have been in Selma at the barbecue joint down in colored town where they first met or in the house he had rented for her. She stared down at his hand gripping her arm.

"So this is where you ran off to." His free hand came to clutch her throat and pull her close to him. "What you mean leavin' without tellin' me?" he said in a whisper, oblivious now to all of the chaos around him.

She tried to pull away, and when his grip held firm, she looked into his eyes and calmly pushed the knife into his stomach just below the ribs. The expression on her face never changed. She could have been standing by the fire, gutting one of the catfish in the side yard of Mama Tuway's house.

L.B. backed away. "You always was a feisty little bitch . . ." His eyes widened, his knees buckled, and he fell, kneeling in the dirt.

She never hesitated. She dropped down over him and began to drive the knife into his back. And he—so completely unaware that he had been, and now most certainly was, a dying breed—still tried to cajole her. "Ella," he gasped, trying to rise up again, "you better cut that out if you know what's—" When she hit bone, she would wrench the knife free and begin again.

All the while, Tuway was running toward her. With each forward motion, he could feel his legs stumbling, deserting him in the race. The reality of where he was, of what was about to happen would not sink in.

Instead, as he ran, other pictures flashed through his mind—things he had only vaguely dreamed of before: the two of them, in their own apartment in Chicago, sitting in the living room, listening to the radio as they heard the overhead train rumbling past, the walls vibrating. They were smiling at each other. The noise was of no consequence to them.

He dimly heard his mother shouting at him to stay away. He never heard the bullet from the sheriff's gun tear a hole in Ella's blue blouse just as he dove between her and the sheriff. He knew he had saved her, because, of course, one bullet wasn't enough to stop her. Like some windup toy, she raised the knife again and again, plunging it in L.B.'s shoulder, his arm, his back.

He saw this happen, but all the while, he was in Chicago, standing with his arms around her. They were looking out of their apartment window, watching the sun go down through a haze of smoke and grime that covered their part of the city. Somehow, he knew that later that night they would go dancing.

And now the sheriff, disgusted because his first bullet had not stopped her, emptied his remaining four bullets in her direction, not particularly concerned about any other black bodies he might hit.

As he reached up to shield her, one of the sheriff's wayward bullets buried itself in Tuway's arm, near the shoulder. Others found their intended mark and struck Ella in the chest, making her dance as if some amateur puppeteer were pulling her strings, arms flailing in the air, head jerking from side to side, dancing as she had danced so many times for so many men, but this time, strings finally cut, she slumped forward, resting peacefully in the dust at long last.

In Chicago, he had gotten a job in the stockyards and was making good money, more than he had ever made in his life. He could buy her anything she wanted, a million periwinkle blue blouses if she wanted.

To the Benders, gunshots only meant that the sheriff was trying to quiet them again, and they were long past quiet. All around, there was yelling and shouting, pushing and shoving as they beat out their frustration on anything that moved. The mules on the first two wagons were let loose from their harnesses and slapped on the rump and yelled away. They trotted off down the road and left the wooden wagons stranded. Those Benders who weren't fighting with drivers or picking up fallen household goods began to tear the two gin wagons apart, pulling the long wooden side slats until they broke and then using them to pound the other parts of the wagon.

Tuway crawled to her crumpled body, all the while looking around, daring someone to come near. He was some wild animal protecting his young, eyes scanning the scene with menacing glances. She was hurt, yes, maybe hurt badly, but she wasn't gone. He knew she couldn't be.

After they had been in Chicago no more than a year, she had had his first baby. It was a little girl, perfect and beautiful, with skin . . . He strained to see as he strained to lift her up off the ground. Was it skin that was a beautiful brown color or skin like his? The picture faded. In the swirl of dust, in the center of the beginnings of cataclysmic change, he was standing, holding her now. It was the first time he had touched her and his whole body was on fire, as he had known it would be.

Mama Tuway was there, saying something to him, trying to reach up and touch Ella. He twisted and swung Ella's body away from her. "No," he yelled at her, and it echoed in his head.

"Didn't I tell you?" she was shouting at him. "Didn't I tell you?"

This only infuriated him. He stepped away from her and a low snarl came from somewhere in his body. She had had her chance with Ella and never took it, all the time trying to turn him against her.

"Tuway, she's—"

"*NO,*" he yelled, so loudly that this time everybody seemed to stop what they were doing and look at him.

Willie had run up, and John behind him. Willie reached up and tried to take his mother's hand. Again Tuway twisted around violently, flinging Ella's limp legs out, hitting the boy so hard that he fell backward. At the same time, he could hear the Judge calling to him.

"Tuway, what's going on, my man? Where are you?"

None of this was Tuway, these people constantly fighting, constantly wanting him to do things that were impossible for him to do. All the while telling him about what life was going to be like in Chicago, all the time talking about it and never once having a thought that he might want to go, might want the same things they wanted. The Judge pulling one way, Mama Tuway pulling the other. It was time to leave them all.

He staggered away, back down toward the river, holding her close. He knew the way better than any of them. Who did they think had taught them all they knew and then acted like it was theirs alone to share? He turned around and headed for the mouth of the creek. He knew the way. He would ford the creek, head around through the swamp, and wait for the train. Others had done it hundreds of times, and he would do it now.

He turned around one last time and saw John and little Willie dogging him, calling after him. He took a few steps toward them. Then he kicked out as hard as he could, catching little Willie a glancing blow on his shoulder. It sent the boy backward into John, and both of them went sprawling in the mud.

"Git," he yelled, and turned back around to walk into the water, holding Ella high away from the wet.

"Tuwaaay," John called out one last time. The sound was loud enough to scare a flock of crows out of their nesting in a big water oak, but not loud enough for Tuway to take any notice.

He watched the water turn red as he forded the stream up to his waist, but it was his blood, not hers. He knew that. He could feel the sharp pain in his arm where the bullet had gone in. He was the one who was bleeding, and he still had plenty of strength—so she would be all right, if he could just get her to . . .

Mama Tuway had come to little Willie and was tending the gash on his shoulder. "Don't you worry none. He's plumb out of his head. He come to his senses and bring her back directly." They watched him reach the other side and disappear into the thick undergrowth.

The Bend

THE sheriff of Telco County had had enough. What had begun as an ordinary day had somehow turned into a horrible mess. Two of the four gin wagons that he was responsible for were almost in ruins and the mules had run off. His hired coloreds would have to get paid, and they hadn't done what they were supposed to do, and, for that matter, neither had he. He had been a fool not to bring deputies with him. On top of that, he had what was probably a dying white man on his hands. He would have to be able to explain this. And to top that off, the crazy black-and-white-looking nigger had run off with the colored girl like some ape in the goddamn jungle. After all these years, there was still no explaining niggers. What did he think he was gonna do, bury her out there in the swamp? She was dead as a doornail. He had seen to that. Well, if he was, it was fine with him. All he had been trying to do was to protect the smart-ass banker, and it had ended up like this. That's what happens when you go to dealing with coloreds. They didn't seem at all concerned about the white man. Just like them, not caring about civilized people. The kid banker probably had a mama somewhere that the sheriff was going to have to answer to.

Somebody had even led the old blind Judge over to where the kids were on the ground, and he was kneeling over them in the mud, getting his clothes all dirty, for Christ's sake.

The next time anybody from outside his county came in and wanted to stir up trouble, and on his day off, he would tell'm to go screw themselves.

"Put that one in that wagon." He gestured with his empty gun to the last wagon down near the ferry. "And be careful—I think he's still alive." He had kept his gun drawn because the men he had hired had stopped fighting after giving a half-ass account of themselves, and the people of the Bend were edging closer and closer.

"You heard me." He gestured again with his gun and backed up a few steps closer to the wagon.

"We're leaving now, but we'll be back," he said, having no idea of returning if he could possibly help it.

The wagon driver coaxed his team up the hill enough to turn around and head back down to the ferry. People were yelling things at him and his niggers as they got back on the ferry. He thought they were cussing him, but you couldn't make out what they said sometimes. Surely to hell they had more sense than to cuss him. If they were, he should have done something about that— gone after them and beat the living shit out of them— except that a big crowd of coloreds was following him down to the water's edge and he needed to get the white man back to the other side. Probably it was useless, but he thought he had seen his chest rising once or twice.

Besides, he might be somebody important, and he needed to make the effort, no matter that the whole thing was the stupid half-ass banker's damn fault in the first place.

Tuway had skirted the river, then gone inland to walk the water boards to the bottom of the train embankment and wait. He had laid Ella on the ground and straightened out her skirt and blouse, brushed his hand through her hair, and tried not to look at her wound, except that he knew he had seen her chest move slightly when she would breathe. She would be fine as soon as they got to . . . He had ripped off the sleeves of his shirt and bound up his wound. Blood kept soaking through.

He heard a train whistle off in the distance. In the haze that was clouding over his mind, he vaguely remembered that it was still daylight and that this one seemed to be coming from the north and going south, but no matter. He would figure it all out once he got them on board. He remembered that you had to change trains in Memphis, and once they got to Memphis, he would know what to do. He would figure something out. Just get on the train.

He heard the whistle coming closer and stooped down and waited for the engine to pass before he began staggering up the hill with her in his arms.

When the last mule team and wagon were halfway across the river, the sheriff noticed some of the Benders had come to the river's edge with a sledgehammer and were taking turns swinging away at the pole that held the ferry cable. Each time there was a blow to the cable, the ferry momentarily stopped in the water as the vibrations ran along the cable line. Moments after it reached the other side, the cable pole and line gave way and collapsed into the brown depths of the Alabama River.

The two o'clock to Mobile was visible to all of the Benders as it entered the bridge trestle that spanned the river maybe three-quarters of a mile from where they stood. They all looked up to watch it cross, an easy place to rest their eyes after a day of so many terrible sights.

Tuway had managed to run alongside the train enough to catch up with one of the cattle cars. He had done this millions of times. Pull open the door and fling yourself in. He had done it that night when John had surprised him. He had watched dozens, maybe hundreds of others do it—fathers and sons, whole families, women and children. He knew it was easy if you knew what you were doing. He managed to get a foothold and grab the side of the car with one hand while with the other he held Ella like a sack over his shoulder. But somehow the door wouldn't slide open.

The Benders were milling around on the shore, talking and preparing a boat so that Berl and John could row the Judge back across the river to his car. From where they stood, off at that distance, it had looked like nothing more than a large fertilizer sack that had slipped out of one of the freight cars and banged against

Lower Peach Tree

THEY had come into the kitchen, the Judge's grip firm on the boy's shoulder. He had even been reluctant to give him up to Adell Vance's hugs and kisses. Now the two of them were seated side by side at the kitchen table. As they told her what happened, they would touch each other's arms or finish each other's sentences, especially when Tuway entered the telling. The Judge would fumble with his pipe and John would continue with the story.

Adell Vance sat across from them, a handkerchief over her mouth, tears streaming down her face, doing their crying for them.

After a time, both the Judge and John were talked out and Adell Vance was cried out and an easy silence fell over the kitchen table. The overhead fan swirled steam that rose from a pot cooking on top of the stove. A breeze drifted in through the door that was open to the back porch.

"The funeral will be next weekend. We'll need to start early in the morning to come into the Bend by the road," the Judge said, glimpsing the empty rocker on the back porch. "I don't think we can take another trip back across the river in one of those rickety old boats, although I certainly appreciated Berl rowing us."

John sat staring at the beads of sweat trickling down the outside of his ice tea glass.

Mrs. Vance finally pulled up out of her chair, put the handkerchief back in her apron pocket, and began clearing the table of the tea and sandwiches and cookies she had hastily put together when they had come home.

"As soon as I finish this, I'm gonna go get your room ready, John honey."

John was silent.

She looked at the Judge and then at John. "You will be stayin' on with us, won't you?"

"Yes, ma'am," he said, but he didn't look up at her.

He took up his teaspoon and swirled the ice cubes around in the glass. "This is the first time I've had ice since Willie brought me a glass of lemonade on the Fourth Day—on the Fourth of July, I mean."

Mrs. Vance finished putting dishes in the sink. "I'm gonna go on up there right now and get everything ready. You must be dog-tired, both of you. Y'all might want to take a little nap before supper." She disappeared into the hall. They could hear her footsteps on the stairs.

"She's right. I'm bushed," the Judge said, "but it's too late for a nap. What say we go in the den? I could use a pipe right now. I even have some fresh tobacco that Tuway—that I got a couple of weeks ago." He got up. "You coming?"

"Yes, sir." John drank down the rest of his tea and slowly got up to follow.

The Bend

IT was late afternoon now—6:00, maybe 6:30—from the length of the pine-tree shadows pasted on the ground in front of the cabin. The old woman sat looking down into the tea leaves in the bottom of the china cup she always used. She had brought little Willie back home with her, and after awhile she had brewed them a cup of tea, "to take the chill off," she said, but it was still blistering hot so late in the day.

Soon they would bring Tuway and put him in the main room of the cabin. They hadn't been able to find the girl, and Mama Tuway thought it good riddance. She hoped she washed all the way down to Mobile Bay. If it hadn't been for her . . . so tainted by the whites.

In awhile, the cabin would fill up with people and stay that way until the weekend, when they would have the biggest funeral the Bright Lily CME Church had ever seen. She would see to that. They would never forget him.

She studied the leaves. This was really why she had made the tea, to see what they would say.

The same thing they always said: Someone was coming—some black Jesus was coming to lead them to better times.

It was just like her mother and her grandmother had told her—"Don't trust the tea leaves for yourself, only for other people." She, Mama Tuway, had given them their leader, and now he was gone, killed by the white man's girl. Why did she think the tea leaves would know that? She got up, went to the edge of the porch, and threw the contents of the cup out in the dust.

Now she took a seat in her rocker and watched the line between the sky and the pine trees turn to a silhouette.

It was almost dark, so she got up and went to the wall and got a lantern off its hook and lighted it and placed it on the table beside her. Small things began to dance in and out of its glow. Night sounds came from up out of the swamp, like they had every night of her memory.

"Willie," she called as she commenced slowly rocking again. He had been round back of the house, bringing small loads of firewood to stack in the kitchen. His sore shoulder would not let him carry much. He came running and stood in front of her. His eyes were almost swollen shut from crying. Tears had washed his face clean of the mosquito medicine.

She looked him up and down for a long moment. "Did I ever ask you if you knowed your numbers?"

He stared at her and slowly shook his head.

She gestured toward the screen door. "Go on in yonder and get me that book, the one on the shelf in my room, and bring it on back out here to me."

Lower Peach Tree

THEY could hear a door close upstairs. Mrs. Vance was taking fresh towels out of the linen closet. The Judge sat down in his chair in the study and took the pipe from his coat pocket. "I can fix it." John walked over to the Judge's chair.

The Judge smiled and held the pipe up. "I'd be much obliged."

While he looked around the room, John packed tobacco in the bowl like the Judge had taught him. Everything was so familiar, as if he had never left, the books on their shelves, slightly dusty, the view of the side yard out the window. All those nights in the swamp, and this was the place he had dreamed of coming back to, but now that he was here . . . "I always thought of comin' back here," he said out loud but to himself, "but when I thought of it, I thought of comin' back the way it used to be." He handed the pipe to the Judge.

"Tuway being gone is going to be a big adjustment for

all of us," the Judge said. He picked up the lighter on his side table and touched its flame to the tobacco.

John didn't say anything. He went over and turned on the floor fan and then took a seat in Tuway's old chair. There was silence except for the fan.

"What is it?" the Judge said. "It's not just Tuway, is it?"

John looked at his feet. "I was thinkin' that Shell probably hadn't had ice in a glass all summer." He was to the point of tears and didn't know why. He studied the mud that had caked on his ankles and the tops of his too-small shoes. "Is that a stupid thing to think after all this time, after wantin' to be back here?"

The Judge inhaled smoke deep into his lungs and then blew it out in a perfect smoke ring that hung in the air. He chewed on his pipe stem and sighed. "No, it's not stupid." He took the pipe out of his mouth. "It would be stupid if I thought things hadn't changed, if I pretended you hadn't changed."

Mrs. Vance appeared in the doorway, smiling. "Everything is ready, John sweetheart. I put you clean towels in the bathroom and your bed has fresh sheets."

The Judge felt around for an ashtray and deposited his pipe. "I don't think John will be staying with us tonight, Adell," he said.

"What? What are you talkin' about? Where would he stay?"

John stood up out of his chair.

"But I thought . . ." She looked at John.

"No, ma'am. I need to be gettin' on back home. . . . I need to be seein' about Shell and them."

"Those terrible Spraig people?" She looked at the

Judge. "Byron, I will not have him associating with those terrible Spraig people anymore."

The Judge got slowly out of his chair, as if he hadn't heard her.

"Byron, I am perfectly serious. All this summer, we were worried sick about him, and now we have him back and you want to send him—"

"I don't want to send him, Adell; he wants to go."

"Well, you tell him he can't go."

"Now listen here, Adell. I am not going to raise up another L.B. into this world. If the boy feels a sense of responsibility, we should be proud of it, instead of—"

"But it's dangerous out there. Luther Spraig is—"

"Is his uncle, whether we like it or not. Now go get the car, Adell. Berl left it in the front drive." He didn't hear her move. "Bring it around to the side door . . . please."

She glared at him, then turned abruptly and left the room. They could hear her slam the front door.

The Judge reached down to feel for his pipe. "Turn off the lights, son, and don't forget to turn off the fan."

The boy did as he was told and came to stand in front of the Judge, intently watching his face. "There's just one thing," he said.

"What's that?"

"Well . . ." The boy crossed his arms over his chest. "Well, what I want to know is, did you say . . . did you say you were raisin' me up?"

The Judge smiled and reached for John's shoulder and found it exactly where he knew it would be. "I did," he said. He put the pipe in his mouth and immediately took it back out again. "I most certainly did. I'm raising you up." The Judge was silent for a long moment before he could speak again. "Now, go get me a cane out of the umbrella stand in the hall."

He could hear the boy running and leaping all the way to the umbrella stand and back.

John stopped short when he came in the door and saw the Judge framed by the light from the window and smiling at what he had heard.

He took the Judge's hand to give him the cane. "I couldn't help it, 'cause it's just like you said."

"What did I say?"

"You know, about words." John turned and tried to jump up and touch the top of the doorsill as he started back down the hall to the car.

"I don't remember. What did I say about words?" the Judge called after him.

John swirled around in the hall and stuck his head back in the door frame.

"You know," he whispered, embarrassed to say it out loud, "about how sometimes they're like pieces of gold."

Very late in the afternoon, they drove out Highway 80 and turned left onto the dirt road. The car stopped where the rise in the land gave the first view of Aunt Nelda's house. The three of them sat there for a while, watching the sun ease down into the cotton fields.

Before John left them to walk the rest of the way home, he reached over from the backseat and, with arms browned and muscled and rapidly changing into the man he would become, he hugged the Judge for a long moment. Then he got out of the car to stand in the same place he had stood once long ago. From here, he had watched Uncle Luther scatter his toys, his books, everything he owned, everything he thought he was—scattered in the dirt. Now he couldn't remember why he had been so upset by it, but that had been years ago, when he was a child.

Author's Note

There is a place, deep in south Alabama—Gee's Bend—much like the Kay's Bend in this story. The tea leaves were predicting a far greater leader for Gee's Bend than Mama Tuway might ever have imagined. In 1965, Martin Luther King, Jr., visited Gee's Bend, and after that, things were never the same.

In 1968, when Dr. King was assassinated, the mules that pulled his casket through the streets of Atlanta were from Gee's Bend, Alabama.

INVICTUS

William Ernest Henley

Out of the night that covers me,
Black as the Pit from pole to pole,
I thank whatever gods may be
For my unconquerable soul.

In the fell clutch of circumstance,
I have not winced nor cried aloud:
Under the bludgeonings of chance
My head is bloody, but unbowed.

Beyond this place of wrath and tears
Looms but the horror of the shade,
And yet the menace of the years
Finds, and shall find me, unafraid.

It matters not how strait the gate,
How charged with punishments the scroll,
I am the master of my fate;
I am the captain of my soul.

Acknowledgments

I think putting the words down is the easy part. It is the mechanism whereby they are heard that tells the tale. My thanks to my Warner Books bosses, especially Maureen Egen, who, with such a fine hand, keeps me pointed in the right direction. To Frances Jalet-Miller; my manuscripts are just pages of words until Frances works her magic. Thanks to Jackie Joiner for her hard work on my behalf and her natural-born kindness as a way of doing business. To Harvey-Jane Kowal for making sure I know what I'm talking about, to Carol Edwards for her meticulous eye and to Chris Dao for keeping the book and me in the right place at the right time.

A special thanks to my agent, Molly Friedrich, and to Paul Cirone and all the folks at the Aaron Priest Literary Agency.

Blessings on my fantastic sister Joanne Walker, always the first to have the manuscript dumped in her lap. To her mother-in-law, Mrs. Milton Walker, for her wonderful stories of the Alabama Black Belt. She is as clear-eyed in her ninety-third year as she was when she first moved to the Black Belt in 1945. And to her son, Bill Walker, for imparting so many of his childhood memories of Uniontown, Alabama. To Jackie and Frances Woodfin for our good walks in the Uniontown cemetery. To Gail Black of Uniontown, who makes the best banana pudding in Perry County. To Polly Bennett of Gee's Bend and Alberta, Alabama, for her beautiful quilts and her stories of the Freedom Quilting Bee. To Laura Seabron of Atlanta for her tales of church homecomings. To Dr. Richard Detleff for information about various skin disorders. To my uncle Weakley Cunningham for providing the background material on cotton farming. To Jack Corley for remembering his days in the fields. To Anne Knight and Jim Baggett of the Birmingham Public Library for letting me wade through the great wealth of information on Gee's Bend, and to the Alabama Department of History and Archives for letting me do the same. A special thanks to Kathryn Tucker Windham, an Alabama treasure.

Most of all, to my father, who made sure that I understood, from a very early age, the highs and the lows of the southern farming landscape.